MW01113954

A NOVEL BY

K.D. Wentworth

HAWK PUBLISHING : TULSA

Published in the United States by HAWK Publishing Group.

HAWK and colophon are trademarks belonging to the
HAWK Publishing Group.

Printed in the United States of America.

LIBRARY OF CONGRESS CATALOGING IN PUBLICATION DATA
   Wentworth, K.D.
      This Fair Land/K.D. Wentworth—HAWK Publishing ed.
      p. cm.
      ISBN 1-930709-29-3 (Hardcover)
      ISBN 1-930709-30-7 (Trade paperback)
      1.Fiction—Science Fiction
      2.Fiction-Oklahoma
      I. Title
      [PS3563.I42145R4 2000]
813'.54   80-52413
CIP

HAWK Publishing web address: www.hawkpub.com

H987654321

For Sammie and Kita,
who first brought this book to mind,
and for Bear,
who keeps it alive

From the log of the Blessed St. Christobal, martyred in the year of our Lord, 1492

Friday, 12 October 1492

At dawn, we saw naked people on the beach, and I went ashore in the ship's boat, armed, accompanied by the captains of the Pinta and the Niña. I unfurled the royal banner and had the captains bring out the flags. I produced glass beads and other worthless trinkets and gave them away. Once the natives develop a friendly attitude toward us, we shall convert them to our Holy Faith. Afterwards, I was attentive and tried hard to learn if there is any gold here.

Monday, 15 October 1492

These people are unskilled in arms and I thought at first they could be conquered with little force, but shortly thereafter I discovered they possess magic of the vilest sort, which the Holy Mother Church has purged from our own continent.

One of my men, long absent from his wife, desired the company of a young girl, who went about, as do they all, quite naked. When he drew her into the decent cover of trees, one of her fellows objected and was fired upon by another of my crew. Instead of fleeing in terror, as I expected, the savages retreated only as far as their primitive huts, then commenced to dance and sing and drum. We watched with curiosity, little suspecting what would come next.

A cloud of blue light formed on the beach before our very eyes and took the shape of a great beast which then killed two of my crew. We escaped immediately thereafter to our three ships and sailed south, much sobered. This fair land, so beguiling to look upon, is possessed by the Devil.

chapter one

Father Declan Connolly leaned against the rail and watched the green-brown river fight the boat's progress up-stream. The unruly river, so different from the rushing clear waters of Ireland, was a constant reminder of how far he had come from home in the two months since he had graduated from the seminary at Maynooth. It was 1763 and his entire twenty-three years had been lived completely within a twenty-mile radius of Dublin. He remembered no other ambition during all that time, but to go out among people whose lives were dark and bitter and make a difference, to serve God and shape the world into a better place.

He tingled with excitement as, on either side, the river bank passed in a slow undulation of tangled emerald and olive foliage and boggy flats. Strange birds of every possible hue shrieked from the trees or waded on stilt-legs through the shallows. The muggy air was redolent of sun-heated mud, stagnant side pools, and the exotic perfumes of a dozen unrecognizable flowers.

A flag of trade flew from the boat's mast, no more than a green square of cloth, but Father Fitzwilliam, who had traveled amongst the savage Tsalagi for the last two years, said the natives would know what it meant and allow them to pass unmolested. The older priest joined him at the rail, tilting his head back in the breeze, his white hair standing out like a wreath. Above, the mast creaked as the sail shifted.

The father's eyes were an odd pale gray, the color faded as though, down through his many years of service to the Lord, his outer shell had gradually worn thin so that the brilliance of his spirit shone through. Declan had only known him since mid-winter, when they had met at the seminary, and he often wondered what the old man had been like as a youth.

He tugged at his high black collar, sweltering in the fierce southern sun. "What river is this?"

"The British have named it Savannah, after their town, but they only rule the first thirty miles," Father Fitzwilliam said. "The Tsalagi have some unpronounce-able name which I can never remember, no matter how many times I hear it, but they usually just refer to it as `Long Person' or `Long Man.'"

Declan's lips tightened at the mention of the natives inhabiting this region. Would they be anything like the luckless, copper-brown Catawbas, who had once controlled the coastal lands? When the passenger ship had landed, the natives had portered their luggage into the sprawling town at the mouth of this immense placid river. Their faces had been dark and sullen, and he had been shocked to see they went about almost naked, unless forced by their English masters to wear more civilized clothing. Their only ornaments were ovals of white shell inserted into the knife-slit lobes of their ears, making them look deformed. Their apparel of preference was nothing more than a few brief strips of badly cured hide to shield their loins. Their brown eyes were as flat as a mad dog about to spring. How such mindless primitives had kept the white man out of this land for over two hundred years after St. Christobal's neglected discovery was beyond his understanding, but now, he thought with relief, *now*, finally, things were chang-ing. The Lord's work would be done on this lonely and deprived continent.

"Shall we practice the Tsalagi tongue for a bit, lad?" Father Fitzwilliam said. "It's important for you to be able to converse with them easily."

Declan switched to Tsalagi. "As you wish, Father." He caught a glimpse of tawny fur through a stand of hickory trees ahead and shaded his eyes against the fierce afternoon sun. "What's that?"

Father Fitzwilliam squinted. "Bless me! I think it's a dog scout. We must have come farther already than I had thought."

As large as a sturdy Irish pony, the tawny-gold creature bounded into a clear-ing and paused, its immense head cocked, pointed ears pricked forward, resem-bling an ordinary canine no more than a lady's pampered lap-dog resembled a wolfhound. Declan leaned over the rail, straining to make out the details. "It's magnificent!"

A lean bronze-skinned man sat astride the dog's back, a beaded quiver strung across his shoulders, his hands buried in the thick golden fur. A ring had been shaved around his crown and the remaining tuft of thick black hair sprang wild-ly from a shell ornament. His feral black gaze watched the boat sail past.

Declan set his jaw, remembering the terrible things he had heard of these sav-ages—how they burned captives alive, relishing their cries and suffering, how they considered vengeance to be a holy quest, traveling a thousand miles to avenge a wrong, however slight, and how their shamen conjured black magic as foul as any European witch had ever conceived. They were obviously more in need of the grace of God than any other people on the face of this earth.

"In all the times I've been back in this country, this is one of the few really good looks I've had of those dogs. They are raised by the Dog Clan for hunting and scouting and war. Few of them spend much time inside the village, once they are grown." Father Fitzwilliam's gnarled fingers drummed on the rail. "Each village is composed of seven clans, three of which keep the animals for which they are named. The Deer Clan tames a few deer, the Bird Clan a few hawks, but the Dog Clan is responsible for the safety and well-being of the entire village. If our soldiers were mounted on such magnificent creatures, events might have had a very different outcome all those years ago." His pale eyes studied the motionless man astride the huge dog until the receding vine-draped trees slowly hid them from sight.

The river murmured against the boat's hull as the two crew members tacked against the current. The sails billowed as they filled with air. Declan bowed his head and clasped his fingers in silent prayer.

Smoke sat in rigid silence until the white-topped boat skimmed around the river's bend. "What do you think?" He slid off the dog's back and looped an arm around his clan-mate's furred neck. Sunrunner gravely snuffled his ear, licked it, then lay down in the grass.

Two Hearts, the holy man he had fetched from Kitasi, emerged from the cover of a blackberry thicket. His weather-beaten face was etched with wrinkles, but his limbs were still as strong and straight as those of a much younger man. He knelt, then cupped his divining crystal in both hands, staring deeply into its core. "You were right to seek guidance. The vessel carries blackrobes, not the red-clothed warriors, but there is more present than the eye can make out. I sense some form of medicine power."

Smoke's mouth tightened. "Disease?" He remembered the fate of the coastal people, how the relentless strangers from across the waters had finally, one cold season day, had the wit to slaughter the Catawba shamen. Not long after, the virulent spotted sickness had come again. Since no one had the skill to drive it out, the disease had killed three of every four of the people by the sea. Now they were only a wretched few and subsisted no better than crows, scavenging the white man's leavings, living on their former lands at his suffrage. Their vast sandy flats and marshes were overrun by white-skinned, mostly blue-eyed strangers who cut down the towering trees to construct strange tall lodges, and who as often slaughtered turkey and deer for sport as for food, leaving the carcasses to rot in the forest, a shocking sacrilege.

Two Hearts held the clear quartz up to the sunlight, chanting under his breath. The unsettling blankness of the older man's expression warned that he was listening to the spirit realm. Smoke had no talent for such matters, but he knew better than to touch a shaman in that heightened state. He hunched down and leaned against Sunrunner's thick sun-warmed fur. The dog's ears pricked, but the black muzzle remained propped on his paws.

Finally Two Hearts rubbed his eyes and lowered the crystal. "They do not bring disease, but I cannot tell what form this power takes, or if it can be used against us."

"If we return to Kitasi for help, we can kill these white demons after they beach their big canoe tonight." Smoke stood, and Sunrunner's liquid brown eyes watched his clan-mate. "It will not be hard to find them; their camps are as noisy as mating bobcats."

"They show the cloth of trade, so if you kill them without seeking council, Lone Bear will be furious." The older man grunted as he heaved to his feet. "He's looking forward to trading for a steel knife to replace the one he broke at the last festival." He brushed his knees off. "He is a fool, of course. What use will fine knives be if the spotted sickness comes?"

Smoke signalled Sunrunner. The dog rose slowly, stretching until his back cracked. His pink tongue lolled sideways as he looked at the man inquiringly.

"There is another way." Two Hearts sighed and dropped the sacred crystal on its leather thong back underneath his deerskin shirt. "I can test this power tonight before it reaches Kitasi. I will send dreams and see what lies hidden within their hearts."

Smoke sprang onto Sunrunner's broad back, then reached down for the shaman. "Then we will follow until they make camp."

After a miserable dinner of salt pork and underdone beans, Declan knelt in the grass at the edge of the clearing and prayed at Father Fitzwilliam's side. This close to the river, the air was still hot and muggy. Insects whined around his unprotected ears and face, biting with an unprecedented ferocity. He fingered his rosary and tried to concentrate on the familiar litany as the two sailors laughed over a coarse joke.

At last, Father Fitzwilliam sighed and raised his head. His pale eyes seemed to glow in the dimness. "Best we get what sleep we can, lad." He indicated the blanket rolls.

Declan nodded, then unrolled the coarse blanket and pulled it over his black cassock, grateful for the protection against the vicious insects even though it made the soggy heat worse. He lay on his back, blinking up at the same brittle stars which had shone down on our Lord, who had suffered far worse than he, Declan, was ever likely to encounter on this earth, and the Son of God had been sinless, at that. What did it matter if Declan was uncomfortable and worried? Nothing in this world was of any value except the state of his immortal soul. His eyelids sagged and he drifted into an uneasy, light sleep.

✳ ◇ ✳

It seemed he walked beside a river distended by flood. He saw Father Fitzwilliam riding in a wooden rowboat, gesturing to him from the center of the current. He wore a brilliant white cassock, instead of the usual black, and seemed to be afraid.

Declan waved his arms over his head. "Father, row the boat over here!"

"It's no good, lad!" Father Fitzwilliam motioned him back. "I'm lost! You must save yourself!"

Declan's breast heaved. "No, you can't give up! It's a sin to throw your life away! Row!" Then he saw the boat's oarlocks were empty. Father Fitzwilliam spread his useless hands and shrugged.

The younger priest threw himself into the rushing river. The blood-warm water soaked quickly through his cassock, pulling him down. The little boat turned in the current, then swirled around the bend. He slogged after it, lost his footing in the mud and floundered, windmilling his arms. The river closed over his head with a gurgle and rays of light refracted down from above, green as an emerald. The river's pulse pounded in his ears and his lungs ached.

The cold certainty rushed through him that he would die here in this Godless land, washed up somewhere on the shore as a bloated, fish-eaten corpse, never to lie in sanctified ground or receive the last rites that would cleanse the sins that stained his soul, never to bring others before the glory of God, a failure in every way, as he had always feared.

As he descended, though, he realized he was not alone in the increasingly dark depths. Something watched as he fought not to breathe in the water, something long and sinuous, glitter-eyed. It glided forward, a sleek diamond-backed body longer than a man was tall and without limbs of any sort. *Serpent!* his mind cried, and he recoiled. He had read of such creatures in the Bible, but he had never seen one. Long ago, in the beginning of the Christian age, the blessed St. Patrick had cast such abominations out of Ireland.

A brightness blossomed behind his eyes, then tingled through his entire body, radiating from his fingertips as blue-white light. He curved his hands and watched the light pool into a shimmering blue-white ball. The serpent paused, staring past him with impassive, flat black eyes. Declan turned and saw another man floating a few feet away, an older native with a dark head-tuft shot through with gray and a long tunic that fell past his knees. Treading water, the man met his gaze, and then Declan felt his alarm that Declan was here, dreaming this wild dream of snakes and water. Somehow the man had caused this to happen; he meant him to die!

Frightened, Declan flung the pooled ball of light at the dark-eyed Tsalagi. It spread into a sheet of coruscating brilliance that enveloped him. The man jerked back, shuddered, dissolved into a cloud of white sparks that quickly faded. The serpent's eyes glittered with what seemed to be approval. A dry, whispery voice surfaced inside his head. *Well done, grandson.*

Declan's feet touched the river's muddy bottom. Terrified, he jackknifed his body and shot up toward the mirrored surface. His lungs were bursting, demanding air, spasming. Just as his mouth opened, he broke through the water, flailing. His fingers, still outlined in a shimmering blue-white light, grazed the edge of Father Fitzwilliam's boat—

—he woke gasping for breath, his body shuddering. He bolted up convulsively and stared around the silent campsite. Father Fitzwilliam was only a dark muttering lump on his right, rolled in his blanket. The two morose sailors had curled up on the other side of the fire, now burned down to a few sullen red coals. The darkness lay heavy and thick, oversweet as though something dead were decomposing nearby. He huddled over his hands, shivering even though the muggy night air was oppressively hot. Then he saw the last vestiges of incandescent blue-white light fading from his fingers.

Two Hearts' eyes flew open and he cried out. Smoke was at his side, although he had more sense than to touch one deep in the grip of medicine energies. Pain lanced through the shaman's head and he pressed his hands to his temples. "Such—power," he managed finally through gritted teeth. "I did not think any of that breed could wield it. They have never given any sign that they knew the spirit world or the medicine ways."

Smoke poked the fire until the sparks flew, then added more wood. His eyes were concerned. "Are you hurt?"

"No." Two Hearts focused on the growing flames, willing his spirit to return to peace and balance. He leaned his head back, narrowing his eyes to slits, seeking the center of his being where he could comfortably walk the narrow overlap between the worlds of flesh and spirit. He drew in a deep, steadying breath, then let it out again in a controlled hiss. "I sent a dream of death, which each man shaped according to his own fears." The pain began to seep out of his skull and his neck muscles relaxed. "Three of the outlanders dreamed of ordinary dangers, falling off a cliff, dying in a battle, being trampled by one of their big awkward elk-dogs. None of them showed any ability to shape medicine power."

Smoke's lean face watched him through the shifting flames. "And the fourth?"

"His dream shaped a river, a manifestation of the sacred power of Water, from which the world itself was born, and then he—drew me into the dream, and there was another presence there, aiding him, Rattlesnake, one of the principal spirits of Fire." He sat up and leaned toward the flames, his face haggard. "*Both* Fire and Water, which are opposing energies. In a single dream, he wielded two out of the four sacred medicine ways, and it is rare for any man or woman, even a Fireheart, to be gifted with more than one. Rattlesnake turned against me. I would have died, had this stranger possessed any skill, which fortunately he does not."

Smoke's enigmatic expression sharpened into worry. "What can we do?"

"Other than killing him in his sleep, I don't know." Two Hearts stretched out on his side. The encounter had cost far more energy than he'd expected; he had to rest now, then upon awakening, eat well to replenish his strength. He sighed. "He wields the strength of both Water and Fire, two of the great embodiments of life-giving medicine power, and beyond that, I sensed even greater depths of untrained talent. No one with that much potential has been born among us within my memory. He is undoubtedly dangerous, but we dare not kill the source of so much raw power without consulting the elders."

He heard the scrape of Smoke's moccasin as the other man settled outside the firelight to keep watch. He was tiredly glad this solid young scout had come to him when he discovered the strangers on the river. Smoke had a noble spirit which glimmered in true reds and pure whites whenever Two Hearts looked at him without eyes. He might have been one of the Thunder's robust sons living in the West. A man like that could be trusted—anywhere, anytime. The fire crackled and the night birds called softly to each other. Two Hearts fell into a troubled sleep.

The morning dawned gray as an eel and just as wet. Father Fitzwilliam slowly became aware of the soaked blanket clinging to his back. He rolled over as a warm, fat raindrop struck his forehead. "Saints preserve us!" He sat up and wiped his face.

A few feet away, Declan lay with an arm thrown over his eyes, breathing shallowly. Though a faint beard shadowed his cheeks, he still looked so much like a boy that it was hard for Fitzwilliam to think of him in any other way.

When the British had first come to the Irish Catholic Church, demanding aid in their quest to conquer the New World, he had been adamantly against any involvement. After all, what had the English done for the Church's followers down through the bloodied years except persecute, disenfranchise, and enslave them? Why should the Holy Mother Church lend England her aid?

But wiser heads than his had prevailed. The Pope himself had been applied to, and subsequently sent both approval and instructions back to Ireland. In particular, he had pointed out the unwiseness of provoking the King. The Penal Laws still existed, although they were rarely invoked these days. Irishmen practiced their religion, but it was technically against the law. Catholics were not even permitted to own land or vote. Would it not be better, the Pope asked, to use the English even as they sought to use the Holy Mother Church? The savages of the New World were lost to Christ in their present state of Godlessness. Regardless of its source, here was an opportunity to bring these poor creatures to a state of grace.

And so, in the end, Fitzwilliam had understood how God's purpose might be accomplished, even at the hands of the traitorous, Protestant English. He was selected to go to the New World, one of forty priests, and subsequently made numerous trading forays into the back country before he finally requested a young assistant, reasoning that since youth was so much more flexible and resilient, a young man would be of greater help.

The diocese had considered a number of possible appointees, then assigned newly ordained Declan Connolly to do a man's work among the heathen. A decent-spoken lad, he had the soul of a saint, his teachers said, an exceptional purity of spirit. He would be a splendid example to the savages. If this assignment cut his life short, the Lord would receive him into heaven just that much sooner. Bringing these savages to Christ was so important, Fitzwilliam could conceive of no higher calling.

He was not surprised Protestants had no stomach for this work. They were a thin-blooded lot, living as they did by the word and law of such a watered-down version of Christianity. No wonder the Portuguese to the south had done so much better at defeating heathen magic and establishing working colonies. *Their* missions were absolute wonders at conversion, and the flow of gold from New Portugal into Portuguese coffers was the envy of every country in Europe, rivaled only by the Dutch who had made slight inroads in the north. Much of that gold was funding Portuguese ships bristling with cannon and Portuguese armament. Unless England could feed her coffers too, she might find her children obliged to learn Portuguese one of these days.

So, if the British required information in return for funding his mission, it was a fair exchange. They expected him to map the location of Tsalagi villages, and to develop a relationship that involved not only the establishment of Catholic missions, but trade. When it was time for the soldiers to exterminate their foul shamen, it would be his work and that of his brother priests up and down the length of this vast continent which made it possible. He bowed his head, grateful, as he was upon every awakening, that the British, Protestant though they were to a man, had seen fit to bring the word of God to this heathen continent.

Over by the sturdy boat, the two scruffy sailors, Jenkins and Scott, were squinting up at the clouds and conversing in low mutters. They were crude heathens themselves, far worse than the natives, because the Tsalagi, poor creatures, had never had a choice in their Godlessness, but these shiftless English sailors certainly had.

"Hey, friar!" Jenkins, the shorter of the two called. "Roust out the slugabed and let's get on our way before the river rises." He had a thin face with sallow pock-marked skin and was missing both front teeth.

Scott, the other sailor, cross-eyed and massive shouldered, muttered something under his breath. They laughed and nodded their shaggy heads.

Fitzwilliam grasped Declan's shoulder. "Declan, lad, it's time you were up."

He jerked awake, his bloodshot eyes staring, his arms flailing.

Fitzwilliam shook him gently. "No, it's all right. You're safe."

The younger priest passed a shaking hand across his face. "Yes, of course, Father," he said hoarsely. "I'm sorry."

Fitzwilliam regarded his flushed cheeks critically. "Have you taken ill?"

"No, no." Declan rolled to his knees and pushed off the wet blanket which now smelled strongly of rain-soaked wool. "I—just slept poorly, that's all. I'm fine."

"Those two misbegotten wretches want to get started." Fitzwilliam jerked his chin toward the boat. "And, regardless of the state of their immortal souls, I agree. The rain may have been heavier in the hills ahead and cause the river to rise."

Declan raked his fingers back through his wet hair. The damp black curls clung to his hands. He heaved to his feet and folded the blanket carefully and neatly, just as he did everything. Fitzwilliam sighed. Declan's poor mother had obviously raised him well, before she fell ill and begged the seminary to take him several years early. He was a good lad, but too delicate for this harsh country. He ought to have been sent to Rome and educated; he had a fine mind. Well, the Lord obviously thought otherwise and would make of him what He could. It was Declan's part only to be a ready vessel for His purpose.

He rolled his blanket up, then trudged through the wet grass to the moored boat. He heard Declan's footsteps follow, then a muffled exclamation.

"What's wrong, lad?" He turned around.

The boy was staring down at the ground. "It—moved," he said hesitantly. "I swear I felt it move beneath my boots.

"Did you step on a wee snake perhaps?" Fitzwilliam bent down and parted the trampled grass, but saw not even a groove in the muddy earth to mark a snake's passing. "Well, it doesn't matter." He patted Declan's trembling shoulder. "It's gone now."

The younger man nodded convulsively, then hung the blanket over his arm. Fitzwilliam used a gnarled tree root rising out of the mud as a step up to the boat. Declan followed, gripping a slender birch limb for support, then cried out, staring at his hand.

Fitzwilliam reached for his hand and spread the fingers wide to examine his palm. "Did you cut yourself?"

The skin was unmarked. Declan's nostrils flared as he withdrew his hand and touched the gray bark again with wondering fingertips. "The tree is *breathing*, Father."

chapter two

The tangled trees slipped by as the boat tacked back and forth up the river. Declan hunched against the crates stacked in the center, hands tucked under his arms, shivering as though in the grip of a fever, but his skin remained cool to the touch, even clammy. The outrageously colored birds took on personalities as they strutted and shrieked in the trees. They seemed to be tiny people now instead of beasts; a red bird with ebony wings was a wise grandmother chiding the rest against their folly. A white bird striped with black warbled a wrenching song about loss of kith and kin.

And the river . . . He covered his ears. He must be going mad. The river was a grizzled old man, bearing the boat on his back, telling an ancient story of rain and flood that repeated over and over again.

Father Fitzwilliam's hand gripped his shoulder. "Come on, lad, why don't you eat a bite? It might settle your stomach."

Declan shook his head, afraid to speak.

"Do you hurt somewhere?" the older priest persisted. "You must tell me, so I can treat your ills."

"No, I'm all right!" he forced out between clenched jaws.

Father Fitzwilliam sighed. "Why don't you pray a bit then? Perhaps the Lord can ease your mind."

Declan pulled out his wooden rosary with shaking fingers and gripped the cross so tightly that it cut into his palm. "I believe in God, the Father Almighty," he intoned under his breath.

Long long ago, said the river in a deep bass voice, *when the mountains were still cooling . . .*

Declan pressed his eyelids shut until he saw waves of shimmering red. "God, the Father Almighty," he repeated, "Creator of heaven and earth . . ."

First Rain fell on the hot rock and then danced across the sky vault as joyous, billowing steam.

Blood pounded in Declan's temples. "And in Jesus Christ, His only Son, our Lord . . ."

Sun, having been made before all others, was willing that it be so, but . . .

"Our—our—" But Declan could not recall the familiar words now. River's smooth voice was in his head, insinuating its liquid words into his thoughts until there was no room for anything else. "Get out!" he whispered fiercely. "Leave me alone!"

A deep bass chuckle rippled through his mind, then the river was still. Declan hunched over the rosary, rocking himself. The demons that ruled this heathen land were trying to steal his soul. He must be stronger, more vigilant. He straightened and untangled the rosary. The little wooden crucifix lay in his reddened palm. He closed his fingers over it again. "I believe in God . . ."

✳   ◇   ✳

The bumping of the boat against the shore awakened Declan. He raised his head and saw a long low sweep of sandy bank where the river curved, and a palisade of sharpened logs beyond. A multitude of copper-brown people streamed out of the narrow overlapped opening, laughing and talking, gesturing toward the boat. The women wore belted and fringed deerskin dresses that left their dusky arms bare. The men were clad in fringed buckskin leggings and brief breechcloths. They were mostly bare-chested, as well as beardless, and tended to be wiry in stature, rather than tall or stocky.

A dozen or so flat-bottomed log canoes rested on the bank, half out of the water. The boat had come to ground just short of them. Father Fitzwilliam turned back from the rail and smiled down at him. "A little sleep seems to have done you good, lad. You look better. Come and meet the Tsalagi of Kitasi."

He did feel rather improved. Declan stretched, then realized he still held the rosary. He opened his hand and saw the imprint of the cross impressed into his flesh. The beads clicked as he slipped them into his pocket and joined Father Fitzwilliam.

The natives' voices rose in an excited tide. Declan concentrated, trying to single out a thread of meaning, but in spite of his exhaustive studies, it all blended together and he comprehended not more than one word in twenty.

A gruff older man slipped through the curious onlookers to stand in front. The colorful beading on his belt was richly ornamental and gray threaded the tuft of hair springing from the top of his head. His black eyes appraised the boat, the sailors, the two priests. "I am Lone Bear, Uko of Kitasi," he said finally in the melodious Tsalagi tongue. "Have you come to trade?"

"Yes, we have much trade goods," Father Fitzwilliam said haltingly in the same language. "We want stay, work among your people, know you."

A disapproving murmur rippled through the crowd. Lone Wolf's full mouth tightened. "You have come among us many times before, and always you ask the same question. You may trade with those who are willing, but you may not stay more than two nights. White men kill the land and drive out its spirit. I myself have travelled to edge of that which was the abode of our brothers, the Catawbas, and felt it for myself. Their land is now merely dirt and rock, lifeless, unspeaking and unfeeling. No Real Person could ever live there."

Father Fitzwilliam turned his head aside to Declan and said in a low whisper, "We'll agree for now, and see if we can change their minds. Say and do nothing the least bit threatening."

He turned back to Lone Bear. "Is there a guest house where we might stay?"

"You have no clan." The native's black eyes narrowed. "So there is nowhere for you but your big canoe."

"No." A shorter man, also clad in a richly beaded hide shirt and leggings, but with an air of power implicit in the carriage of his head and muscular shoulders, approached from downriver, the same direction from which they had come. He had a broad, sun-seamed face with sharp cheekbones and a nose like the blade of a knife.

At the edge of the clearing, Declan saw another man, younger and fit, standing beside a huge golden dog with a black muzzle, either the same one they had seen the day before, or very like it.

The speaker stopped before the two priests, his dark eyes glittering. He studied first Father Fitzwilliam, then Declan. The younger priest backed away as the man's gaze caught and held his own. He seemed to see shapes in the black pupils ...a great eagle swooping out of the sky...a naked woman with sweeping green hair weaving something on a frame...

He shuddered and looked away. A finger touched his forehead, and then all the voices came back, the bass rumble of River murmuring its eternal story, the screechy old-woman voices of the birds in the surrounding trees, and even the sibilant voices of fish in the water behind him. He swayed, overcome with the rush of sensation.

A callused hand grasped his wrist. "I will take this one."

Declan's eyes flew back open and he tried to pull away from the steel fingers, but the man held him without effort and he could not think with so many voices crowding his head. They built into a roar and the whole scene was overlaid by a buzzing white mist. Every nerve in his body was laced with fire.

Father Fitzwilliam laid a gentle hand on the newcomer's arm. "I come with him? I want know Tsalagi."

Declan realized he was close to passing out, and knew he must not make himself ridiculous in front of these savages. Father Fitzwilliam had stressed that the only thing the Tsalagi respected was strength. They would never accept God's message if His messenger betrayed himself to be a weakling. Again he tried to pull away from the insistent man, but the rough fingers only cut deeper into his flesh.

"Father," he forced his numb tongue to say in English, "I'm sorry, but—" His knees buckled. Father Fitzwilliam grasped his other arm. "Friend sick," he said quietly. "Need lie down."

The native jerked his chin back toward the village and pulled Declan with him, his black eyes as hard as obsidian. The crowd opened to let them pass, then closed behind them again like a restless copper tide. And all the while, Declan could not shut out the cacophony of voices, each insisting on its own tale.

✳   ◇   ✳

Berry was astonished to see Two Hearts, her uncle, appear in the doorway of their house with a pair of white men smothered in long billowing black robes. The entire village of Kitasi trailed after them, crowding and murmuring.

"Make a pallet on the floor!" her uncle directed. His arm supported the waist of the smaller of the two strangers, a young man by his smooth cheeks. His cropped black hair curled in damp ringlets above his ears and his head lolled back against her uncle's shoulder. A shock ran through her as she peered into the pale, sweating face; he had sky-eyes, blue as the sky vault on the clearest of days. Those eyes had haunted her for two full seasons now in her dreams.

Hastily, she dashed into the sleeping area and pulled furs from the beds. She heaped them before the doorway where the light was better. The other white man supported the younger one's head as Two Hearts eased him to the dirt floor. The ill one mumbled, pressing his hands over his ears, writhing and squeezing his eyes shut as though in great pain.

"What is wrong with him?" she asked as the older white man knelt beside him and felt his forehead.

Her uncle reached for his medicine pouch. "I think he hears the spirits for the first time." Frowning, he sifted through the contents until he found what he wanted and shook a dusting of fine brown powder into a carved wooden cup. "Fill this to here—he indicated a level—with hot water and make him drink it all."

Hurriedly, she fetched a cooking pot, filled it with fresh water, then used sticks to fish two hot rounded stones from the family fire-pit outside. She slipped them into the basket, then sat back on her heels and watched the water heat, wondering at what her uncle had said. The seeds of the sacred power of Earth medicine ran strong in her line. Her mother had possessed great skill working with the plant people to heal the sick, as had her mother before her.

At sixteen, Berry had been working all of her life, learning to listen to the plants that filled the forest, to follow their advice and use their gifts respectfully. Such sensitivity to the world of spirits was usually present from birth. She, herself, could not remember the first time the plants had spoken to her. They had always been there, whispering at the edges of her awareness, telling her this leaf was safe to eat and that was good for fevers. How then could this stranger only now be coming into his inheritance? And why had she dreamed of him, over and over until she knew his face like a bit of beloved country long wandered?

When the water steamed from the transferred heat of the stones, she filled the wooden cup as instructed and stirred it with her finger. The young stranger was shivering, although the day was hot, and he muttered in a low guttural language she had never heard before. While her uncle watched impatiently, she knelt beside the sick man and held out the cup in both hands. "You must drink this."

His odd blue eyes roamed the room; he did not see her. The older white man looked distressed and spoke to his friend softly in the same guttural tongue, pulling his hands away from his ears. The young one shuddered and covered them again. Two Hearts frowned, then went outside to the cooking pot and plunged his hands into the hot water until they reddened with heat. Quickly, he ducked back inside, then leaned down and took the man's tossing face between his hands, soothing him with the warmth.

"The voices you hear are a sign of medicine power," he said slowly, as though speaking to a frightened child. "There is no reason to be afraid." He released him, then took the cup from Berry. "Drink this and you will feel stronger."

Still shivering, the young man reached for the cup, but could not fit his trembling hands around it. Two Hearts guided his fingers, then supported his head as he sipped the hot drink. The young man swallowed, then sputtered and coughed. Her uncle nodded grimly. "It tastes bitter, but you must drink it all."

Resignedly, the stranger choked the rest down, then sagged back on the furs, his eyes closed, his skin almost transparent with strain and shock. Berry took the cup from her uncle, then settled by the wall where she would not be in the way. She had seen that look before in people who had been badly hurt or were terribly sick, when their spirits were trying to decide whether they should fight to stay here in the Middle World, or travel on to the Night Country.

A fly buzzed through the open door as they all watched his face, but no one paid it any heed. Who was this pale youth, Berry wondered, that her uncle should care if he survived? Two Hearts was a great holy man and the white intruders who had enslaved the Catawbas and ruined the coastal lands were less than dust beneath his feet.

Well, whoever he was, it had been intended by the Above Beings that *she* should care. In her dreams, she had walked with him, touched his face with wondering fingers, shared both joy and pain. There was a connection between them which ran beyond this world, and he was important in some way, necessary to the scheme of things.

At length, the young man's contorted face smoothed and his chest rose more slowly and evenly. The older stranger sat back on his heels with a sigh of relief and looked up at Two Hearts. Berry saw his eyes clearly for the first time; they were an unsettling light gray, like fog that rose over the river in early morning.

He cleared his throat. "What wrong with him?"

"The voice of the land overwhelmed him." Two Hearts brushed off his knees and stood up. "He is old for this; it usually comes to the very young who are more flexible. He lost the thread of his thoughts and could not find the beat of his own heart amongst so much noise. He will have to learn to listen only to the voices he needs to hear, and those but one at a time."

The older man looked baffled, then doubtful. The openness in his eyes faded. "Look better. I grateful."

A face appeared at the door, peering into the dimly lit room. It was Lone Bear. "So," he said gruffly to the white-haired stranger, "did you bring any knives to trade?"

"Yes, the stranger said, "in canoe." He glanced down, but his companion lay still and peaceful on the mound of soft furs, black hair plastered damply across his pale forehead. "Come. We find one fit you hand." He heaved slowly to his feet and ducked outside into the bright afternoon light.

"Why have you taken this man in?" Berry asked after they had gone.

"Because he hears the spirit world as few among us ever will." Her uncle's black brows knotted fiercely over his prominent nose as he stared down at the young man. "I have already seen him wield the sacred power of both Water and Fire, and, although it frightened him, his connection with Fire was so strong that he may potentially be a Fireheart."

Berry studied the familiar dream-face, now at peace. Born with more access to Fire medicine than other shamen, Firehearts were people out of legend and exceedingly rare; some said the talent was too great for ordinary flesh to bear, and indeed many such died young in the process of learning to control their own gift. Great power lay in being so open to the strongest of the four medicines, along with great peril.

"Whatever his beginnings," her uncle said, "the Above Beings do not make mistakes. There must be something within him worth saving."

Declan woke to a soft, dry, rhythmic rattle that seemed oddly comforting. His cheek was pillowed on something deliciously silky and he felt rested for the first time in weeks. He turned over and pried his reluctant eyes open.

He was lying on the earthen floor of a cramped room, lit dimly by a low fire outside just beyond the open doorway. The night smelled of pine and damp earth. A shadowed figure sat on a stool beside him, shaking a gourd rattle. Declan blinked at him bewilderedly. Where was he? Where was Father Fitzwilliam?

He hitched up on one elbow and gazed around the room. The stern-faced man, dressed only in a hide shirt and breechcloth, gazed down at him, his dark eyes mirroring the flames from outside. The rhythm of the rattle never varied.

Declan started to sit up, then remembered the terrible roar of voices and put one hand to his ear.

"They still speak." The man stopped shaking the rattle and suddenly he heard voices again, but different this time.

A low-pitched voice was saying, "—took the stars from my basket and cast them into their places, one by one, and I—"

A harsh garbled one was saying, "—snap snap this is my place fishes cannot hide from—"

And there were many more, most too soft or distant to make out. Declan stared wildly out the door into the blue-black darkness, his heart pounding, waiting for the voices to inundate him as they had before.

"Concentrate on one." The man laid aside his rattle and leaned closer. He smelled of wood smoke and herbs. "That pleasant low voice is the North Wind, talking about scattering stars in the sky each night in their proper order and then spinning them with his breath so that their journey is always just finished by morning."

I must be dreaming, Declan thought, but he caught at the tale Wind was telling, felt how the words rose and fell with the cool evening breeze coming through the door. "*—spin them just so, each one, so that they sparkle and shine and drift in their proper pattern. I took the stars from my basket—*"

"He repeats himself when he does not have much to say." The man's tone was dry. "Some nights, he is more informative. For instance, three nights ago, he told me that four strangers were riding up Long Man's back."

"*—and cast them into their places one by one,*" Wind continued, "*and I—*"

"Now . . ." The man stepped forward and pressed Declan's head between his hands. "Listen to me, only me. I know what it is like to be open to so many voices. Shut the rest out or they will drive all reason from your head."

With a shudder, Declan let North Wind's voice go, and then, all the rest too, the soft, sibilant, harsh, demanding voices chattering out in the darkness.

The man sighed. "It is good. Now, perhaps, you have a chance to live."

Declan sagged. He heard only the ordinary night sounds, insects whining, crickets singing, the pop of the fire. He lowered his head into his hands, unutterably weary. "Where Father Fitzwilliam?"

The native stared at him blankly.

"The other man," Declan persisted. "Where he?"

"The blackrobe has gone back to the river to trade knives."

"I go him." Declan struggled to rise, but the ground seemed to tilt beneath his feet. He slumped back against the heap of furs, sweating.

"He is part of your old life, along with the dead world." The man crossed his arms and leaned back against the wall. "All that passed away the moment you opened your heart to the spirits. You can never go back, so you must forget him and all his kind's ways. Now and forever, you belong to the Tsalagi."

Lone Bear ran his finger along the fine silvery blade that the stranger was offering for trade. There were handfuls more lying there on the soft blanket, but this one was a good weight and fit his palm, almost as though it knew him. It would skin a deer almost without direction, or rip the heart from an enemy's chest. It would do.

He studied the stranger's fish-belly-white face in the shifting shadows thrown by the meager fire built of driftwood on the sand. There were some among the seven clans who maintained that all strangers coming out of the dead lands should be killed immediately, that it was dangerous to have any sort of contact with them. They pointed out the sobering fact that the Catawbas had thought it safe to trade also, and had in the end paid with their lives, their homes, and the future of their children. The Tsalagi must be ever vigilant.

But few whites ventured this far inland, and those who did flew the green flag and had interesting items to trade, mostly metal, which the Tsalagi lacked the knowledge to make for themselves. Lone Bear liked new things and new ideas around which to wrap his mind. As long as the strangers were few and did not menace the shamen who summoned the power to keep Tsalagi land alive, he saw no harm in brief visits.

He held the gleaming wooden-hafted knife out to the stranger. "How much?" The man's odd gray eyes blinked back at him. "Please take as gift, Lone Bear."

A gift? Lone Bear's jaw tightened. A gift implied obligations and relationships, a whole range of problems. A gift was far too expensive to accept. He pretended not to understand the other's atrociously accented Tsalagi. "I will trade you two fine mountain lion skins and three doeskins, already worked by my woman, who is very skilled."

The breeze ruffled the man's sparse white hair. He bowed his head in thought. "You honor me, but I wish *give* knife, is not right word? I ask nothing, but stay in Kitasi, learn ways."

Lone Bear placed the knife next to its mates on the blanket, then rose abruptly. This cunning stranger's price was too high, and the clans would never let him pay it. He stalked stiffly back to the gap in the palisade, feeling the other's astonished eyes on his back.

chapter three

Thready voices whispered just out of hearing. Declan groaned and opened his eyelids, tensing for the pain and disorientation that had hammered him before, but the voices remained almost inaudible, humming at the edge of his awareness. The air in the Tsalagi dwelling was still cool from the night, scented from a mixture of dried herbs hanging in bunches on the wall. The furniture was crude, but solid—several broad beds raised off the floor on planks, wooden chests, a low stool and a long bench along the opposite wall. The bed in which he lay was heaped with soft furs.

A doe-eyed native girl of about fifteen or sixteen, her black hair wet and shining, peered through the doorway into the room where he lay. She was not handsome by white standards, with a broad, round face and prominent cheekbones, dressed in a simple shirt and skirt of tanned deer-hide, but he felt drawn to her somehow, as though they had known each other a lifetime.

His cheeks warmed and he dropped his gaze. He had no business looking at a woman like that, *any* woman, no matter how innocent the circumstances. Down that road lay perdition. His older brother, Patrick, had trained to be a priest too, in the very same seminary at Maynooth, seven years ahead of Declan, then fallen prey to a woman's wiles in his first year as a full-fledged priest. Their mother had been heartbroken and Patrick had afterward fled to England where hopefully no one knew of his grievous fall from grace. He had employment as a bricklayer, as well as the encumbrance of a wife and an infant son, the last Declan had heard of him. His name had never crossed his mother's lips again, not even on her deathbed.

The girl's eyes widened as she realized he was awake. She ducked back outside and spoke softly to someone.

Declan sat up and combed his fingers through his tangled hair, feeling washed out, but much improved over the previous day. He seemed to remember strange voices called River and Wind, and the off-hand observations of fish and birds, and he had the impression someone had sat at his side last night, trying to help. Most of it was confusing and vague. He must have been feverish.

He heaved to his feet, then caught himself against a bench as his head spun. Groping along the wall, he followed the girl outside and found her conversing in low tones with the middle-aged man who come to him at the river. He was a native of medium height, strong featured, with somber lines that turned down at the corners of his mouth as though he rarely found anything amusing. His coarse black brows knit together as he concentrated on the girl's words. Declan remembered suddenly how this same man's touch had made the mysterious voices resurge inside his head.

"You slept a long time." The Tsalagi met his eyes and something unsettling smoldered within their depths. "That is good. You need strength for what is to come."

"I thank for sleep in you lodge," Declan said awkwardly. He sat on a log before the fire pit, but then had to retreat when the flames leaned hungrily toward him. He edged around the hearth, thinking to avoid the wind, but the flames followed as though they had a mind of their own, reaching for him, no matter what side he tried. Finally, he settled a good arm's length away.

The Tsalagi's dark eyes narrowed and emotion flashed across his face, recognition, perhaps, or surprise. Declan cleared his throat. "Where Father Fitzwilliam?"

"The blackrobe has gone to the river with the other strangers," the man said offhandedly, as though he were discussing the fate of a discarded rock. "I am Two Hearts, shaman of the Tsalagi."

"My name Declan Connolly—"

"No." Two Hearts' mouth tightened. "English names have no connection to the spirits, no power. You must have a Tsalagi name that befits your new status." He paused, narrowing his dark eyes. "Perhaps we will call you...Acorn. Although you are not much now, something great may come of you. I suspect you have something special to do, or the Above Beings would not reach out to you so strongly."

Declan sagged onto a log bench against the house, baffled. He understood most of the individual words, but his Tsalagi was still slow and the meanings didn't mesh.

The tang of wood smoke and the aroma of cooking food from other hearths threaded through the village, and the morning breeze was soft as a whisper against his face. The girl shaped patties from a dampened mixture of grains with slim, expert fingers, then laid the resulting reddish-brown cakes on a flat stone at the edge of the hearth and covered them with hot coals. She sat back on her bare heels, humming under her breath, occasionally glancing up at Declan with shy, deep-brown eyes. He had a flash of another image superimposed over hers, a fall of long, dark-green hair that trailed to the ground, upturned eyes green as moss, an oval, more serious face.

The girl held out a steaming cake in one hand and looked at him questioningly. He had a sudden impulse to touch her. Horrified, he pressed his hands over his eyes and tried to slow the racing of his heart.

She calmly pulled his hand down and transferred the cake to his palm. The thin grainy cake was still hot enough to make him flinch. He blew on it, then sampled the edge. It was cornmeal, mixed with another vegetable that accounted for the red-brown color, and quite tasty. He ate it, then licked his fingers clean. She offered him another, which he warily accepted, making certain their hands did not touch.

"Declan, lad!" Father Fitzwilliam cried in a relieved voice as he rounded the big tree towering beside the house. "How do you feel?"

Declan jerked to his feet. "Better, thank you, Father. I must have taken a fever, but I feel much improved."

Father Fitzwilliam's eyes were pale as quicksilver, his cheeks hollowed with weariness. "Well, I must say he is eager to oblige you." He rubbed his bloodshot eyes with one hand. "Two Hearts, here, insisted you bide in his house where he could keep watch over you. In all the times I have visited this village, these people have never allowed me to stay a single night inside the palisade." He noticed the steaming cake in Declan's hand. "But, sit back and eat your breakfast."

Declan resumed his seat on the bench, leaving room for the older priest to join him. Two Hearts leaned against the sun-shade's post, his arms crossed, and watched them with unreadable brown eyes. His bearing was proud, haughty even, fit for the richest nobleman back in Declan's homeland.

The girl fixed two more cakes, one for Two Hearts and the other for Father Fitzwilliam. They all ate together in companionable silence as the village quickened with activity. Naked, sun-browned children of two and three dashed through the trees, laughing and squealing, drawing affectionate and forbearing glances from the adults. Chattering women drifted toward the river, carrying water jars, then returned with wet hair and pleasant smiles. The odors of cooking corn and sizzling fat wafted through the air.

"Father," Declan asked in English, "what shall we do this morning? Do you want to unload our supplies from the boat, or shall we begin to spread God's word?"

"In a fortnight or so, perhaps, lad." Father Fitzwilliam clapped him on the shoulder. "We must do what we can to earn their trust first." He turned to Two Hearts and struggled with the liquid Tsalagi syllables. "I thank for care my young friend. You healing powers much great. Please come river. Take small gift."

Declan rose, but the native shaman stepped between him and Father Fitzwilliam, barring the way with a sun-bronzed arm. He scowled over his shoulder at Declan. "I have told you—your old life is finished!"

Father Fitzwilliam's forehead furrowed. "I not understand."

Two Hearts gripped Declan's wrist in his strong, callused hand. His touch kindled a blazing heat that shot through Declan's body. He cried out and fell to his knees, gazing at the blue-white light emanating from his hands.

"In the name of God!" Father Fitzwilliam said in English. "What have you done to him?"

Two Hearts released Declan, then took up a staff decorated with a single blue-and-white feather and many long tufts of straight black hair. "This one has been touched by the spirits," he answered as though he had understood the question. "In each generation, a few are born who can hear the spirits, even fewer who can see them. Least in number are those who can actually walk both this world and the next. This one—" He planted the staff before Declan. "—is a Fireheart, with great openness to Fire medicine, and perhaps even a Spiritwalker. He has been selected for some high purpose and must prepare himself, or power of such magnitude will burn him to ashes."

Declan hunched over his shining hands, sweating, more afraid than he had ever been in his whole life. This was soul-damning magic. He clasped his traitorous hands together and tried to pray, but the glow only brightened and his lips could not shape the words.

"Get away from him!" Father Fitzwilliam cried and pushed the Tsalagi priest aside.

"*Listen!*" a redbird cried from the branches of a hickory tree. "*You'll die if—*"

"*First Rain—*" said the River.

"*Fool!*" whispered the leaves in a wispy chorus.

"*Fool!*" echoed the stones at his feet.

People gathered, dark eyes wide in their broad copper faces, as every stick and pebble and insect chastised him for being an idiot until he could hear nothing else. He turned to Father Fitzwilliam, his heart racing, even the blood in his veins singing its own wild song. "We must go back to the boat!"

The other man nodded. Declan saw his lips move, but heard only the blaring cacophony inside his head. Father Fitzwilliam shouldered roughly into the press of villagers, heading for the palisade. Declan stumbled after him and the staring natives fell back before his upraised, shining hands.

They closed in behind and followed as the two men hurried to the river. On the boat, Declan could see the startled sailors sitting beside the mast. He was drenched in sweat as Father Fitzwilliam turned and reached to help him onto the boat. His fingers met the older priest's hand and he felt a tremendous shock as though lightning had discharged though his body. Father Fitzwilliam fell back, his face contorted with pain, then slumped to the deck, pasty-skinned and unconscious.

Declan struggled onto the boat, his head seething with voices, and stared helplessly down at the injured priest. He didn't dare touch him again, but knelt at his side and watched for the rise and fall of his chest. Father Fitzwilliam still breathed, although shallowly.

The sailors were frozen as they watched his glowing hands with gap-toothed alarm. On the shore, the entire population of Kitasi spilled out of the palisade and milled, pointing at them. "Put the sail up!" Declan shouted at the crew. Blood thundered in his ears. "We must cast off!"

Blue-white flames danced at the edges of his vision, filled with shifting, ephemeral shapes . . . to the right, an eagle hovered in the sky, its wings spread . . . on the left, he saw a shimmering man mirroring his own face . . . then a great snake with interlaced diamonds running down its back. He whirled on the sailors. "Put the sail up now, or I'll throw you both overboard and do it myself!"

Scowling, they waved him back and set to the task of unshipping the sail. Minutes later, they hauled the sail aloft, then hopped down into the sand and waded out in the river to shove the boat into the swift green-brown current. Declan huddled beside the fallen priest, clutching the beads of his rosary and repeating "Hail, Mary" over and over, although he could hear nothing, but the disapproving supernatural voices.

As the boat slipped into the center of the river, Declan saw Two Hearts standing stiff-necked by the palisade, his face stern, his feathered staff clutched high above his head as though invoking something. Declan buried his face in his shimmering, possessed hands and wept.

✳ ◇ ✳

Summoned by the noise, Lone Bear left the Council House and fought his way through the astonished crowd to Two Hearts' side. He stared as the big white-topped canoe heeled to the right and glided around the river's bend, out of sight. "What happened?"

Two Hearts lowered his staff. "The younger one, who names himself `Declan,' has been called to be a shaman." His eyes glittered with anger. "The spirit world has gifted him with the potentiality of more power than anyone born among us for generations."

How was such a thing possible? Lone Bear mulled it over as the people dispersed back into the village and the fields beyond the sheltering palisade. Shamen were dedicated at birth and carefully nurtured through boyhood until they knew which medicine way they were destined to wield, taught every nuance of fasting, purification, divination, and all the other essential mysteries. This white man had no background, no preparation. He scowled, well aware, that even though he himself was Uku of Kitasi, the highest of the priests who ruled in peacetime, his actual ability was much less than that of Two Hearts, who did not care for high position, and this stranger was supposed to possess even more. "Then why is he leaving?"

"He is afraid." Two Hearts turned and glanced through the scattering men and women, his eyes bleak. "He has never experienced this before. Medicine power would not manifest itself in the dead lands."

Lone Bear considered the danger an Englishman who could summon such power might represent. He liked fine knives and axes as much as the next man, but if the English learned to channel energies of the spirit world, would the Tsalagi be able to keep them from overrunning their lands? And what of the terrible diseases that so often followed the white man? Would the Tsalagi contract the spotted sickness and die like the Catawbas? "Should we not kill him then?"

Two Hearts drew the rawhide thong around his neck out of his shirt, then uncovered his divining crystal. Holding it up to the sunlight, he studied the splintered image within its facets without blinking. Finally, he slipped it under his shirt again with a sigh. "That won't be necessary." The corners of his mouth tightened. "He will die if he leaves the living land."

chapter four

Scott and Jenkins piloted the boat down the twisting course of the river with more care and energy than Declan had seen them muster since the slovenly pair had been hired back in Savannah. They watched him with shifty, feral eyes and kept their distance. He huddled against the mission's crates of vestments and trade goods and Bibles, his glowing hands tucked under his arms where he did not have to look at them. Sleep buzzed around his mind like a hungry mosquito and his head kept nodding, but he clung to consciousness with all his remaining strength. If he slept, even for a second, he did not doubt that one of the shaggy, black-hearted sailors would crack his skull and kick him into the boat's swirling wake. Killed by the Godless savages, they would say when Father Fitzwilliam awoke, if indeed, he ever did, and no one would be able to prove any different.

As the sultry afternoon wore on, gradually the supernatural tree and bird and river voices faded into a ragged murmur. He sagged his aching head back against the crates, watching willow fronds trail from the bank into the green water as the boat slid past, listening to the river gurgle around driftwood snags, a comfortingly natural sound with no sense in it at all. The boat rode the current easily, tacking only for the occasional rock or shallow bend. A rich, green, warm-mud smell permeated the air, leavened from time to time by the heady perfume of the flowering vines twined through the thick brush.

In the middle of the deck, Father Fitzwilliam finally stirred, his papery eyelids fluttering, but Declan resisted the urge to touch him. Instead, he turned to Jenkins, the shorter of the two sailors. "Fetch him water."

The stubby man scowled, but brought the dazed priest a dipper from the water cask. Father Fitzwilliam sipped, then coughed.

Declan drew a shaky breath. "Father, are you all right?"

"Yes . . ." The priest's voice cracked. He sat up, leaned over his bent knees. "What—what happened?" He squinted across the deck at Declan, shading his eyes from the mid-afternoon sun with a trembling hand.

"I cannot say for certain." Declan dropped his gaze. "My—hands gave off a kind of—light, and when you took my arm to help me aboard, you tumbled to the deck, bereft of your senses."

"I . . . remember little of the incident." Father Fitzwilliam glanced at the

sailors hunched on the other side of boat, studiously watching the sail and nib-
bling hard biscuits. "Why have we left the village?"

"Two Hearts wanted me to learn his heathen magic." He closed his eyes
against the memory. "I had to flee."

The priest sighed. "And right you were too, but it's a terrible thing for our
mission to fail right off like that. I cannot think what Father Abernathy will say
about this matter, not to mention General Carleton."

Declan nodded numbly. The British Army had funded this mission, and
would no doubt expect a proper return on their investment.

Father Fitzwilliam lurched to his feet and tottered over to him. The ropes in
the rigging creaked as the boat heeled to avoid a tiny island. "Show me your
hands."

Declan held them out and was relieved to see only normal skin and bone with
no heathenish glow to them. The other priest compressed his mouth thoughtfully, then reached out a trembling forefinger and touched the back of Declan's
hand. Declan jerked, but there was just the warmth of ordinary flesh meeting
flesh.

"Praise be to God!" Father Fitzwilliam clasped Declan's hand between his
two gnarled ones. "The Devil's taint has left your body." His thin white hair ruffled in the breeze as he bowed his head. "Let us give thanks."

Declan exhaled slowly and the terrible knot of fear within him began to ease.
Perhaps he had been cleansed. He closed his eyes to pray, reaching for the peace
that prayer always bought.

"Oh, Lord," Father Fitzwilliam began, "we thank thee for the delivery of your
servant, Declan, out of the hands of Darkness—

A field of blue-white sprang up behind Declan's closed eyes, drawing him into
a bracing warmth that surged along his nerves until his entire being floated in its
light.

"—and grant us safe passage—"

Something moved within the light, shapes of blue-white . . . a coiled snake . . .
a maiden, lithe as a willow wand with unbound tresses that swept to her feet . . . a
plunging eagle with outstretched talons . . . a shining man bearing his own face.

Shaking, Declan stumbled to his feet. Light flickered at the tips of his fingers—white—blue-white—blue. He swallowed hard, willing it away, *pushing*
somehow with all his might. The light flickered, then died.

"—Amen." Father Fitzgerald opened his eyes.

Something shiny caught Declan's gaze. He knelt to pick up a single eagle feather at his feet, bright gold as a newly milled Portuguese coin.

* ◊ *

Two Hearts entered the vast silence of the darkened, seven-sided Council House alone and knelt on the hard-packed dirt before the ashes in the central fire pit. The air was cooler inside, and a bit musty. He cleared the ashes with a clean-smelling pine bough, then heaped cedar branches in their place before resting his open hands on his knees and stilling his mind. The spirit realm was as close as his own breath and yet infinitely far away. Strength of purpose was required to reach it, as well as purity of mind.

His primary talent lay in Earth medicine, but like most who dealt with the spirit world, he could call upon Fire medicine enough for divining purposes. When he was ready, balanced in heart and spirit and mind, he sang a low melodious chant, offering himself as a channel for the sacred fire. After the first repetition, his fingers tingled as though they had been cramped and circulation was returning. With the second, they warmed as though the spring sun had just broken through the clouds of winter.

Upon his third completion, his hands heated with the fierceness of boiling water, and then with the fourth, they blazed as though he had thrust them into the roaring heart of the sun. Denying the pain, he stretched his fingers toward the pile of twigs, pouring forth *fire* until the wood blazed and he could see the golden flames with his eyes closed, feel them in the pounding of his blood, taste them on the back of his throat.

He opened his eyes and poured sacred tobacco, grown and harvested in the most ancient of ways, into his open palm and then exhaled over the dark-brown powder, imbuing it with the essence of his own body to increase its power. For two seasons now, his dreams had foretold dangerous times when events would alter the future of the Tsalagi in any of several directions, but he had never been able to understand what the Above Beings wanted of him.

He tamped the tobacco into his carved pipe, held it to the golden flames, then puffed. Fragrant smoke swirled through the dim room, which was large enough to hold every member of the seven clans who abided in Kitasi. With one hand, he wafted it over his head, then in each of the four sacred directions. Closing his eyes, he framed his problem: Because of Two Hearts' actions, the young white stranger who called himself Declan had been awakened to his gift for wielding medicine power. Not only had he demonstrated his potential for the sacred power of Water, but Two Hearts had noted how the flames gravitated to him earlier this morning, as well as the aid of the Fire spirit Rattlesnake in his dream, both potent signs of a Fireheart, highly gifted in the most powerful of the four medicines. If he possessed even the slightest affinity for the other two remaining medicine ways, Air and Earth, he might become a Spiritwalker, one who could bodily walk the spirit world without harm, as few shamen ever could.

If Two Hearts had not challenged him in a dream, he might never have tapped into the raw power of the spirit realm. And now that power, unleashed, was like an unhafted knife sharpened on both sides. Without training, the stranger had no way to direct it or control the bleed-over from the spirit realm that so confused the senses. He was a danger to himself and everyone else in that open state. Once sensitized, it took only the touch of someone like himself, in constant contact with the spirit realm, or the invocation of medicine power against him, or even a moment of stress, and this man called Declan would be wide open, a channel for power he had no way to control.

Two Hearts leaned forward, balancing the pipe on two fingers, drawing the pungent tobacco smoke deep into his lungs. What should he do? How could he finish what he had inadvertently set in motion? The Above Beings did not allot such power without a reason; what must he do to conclude this situation responsibly?

Go, a voice whispered in his mind. *This gift must not be wasted.* The wavering form of a heavy-shouldered stag formed out of the gray smoke above his head.

Go where? he asked it.

The stag cocked its head. *To the edge of the dead lands to bring him back, before it is too late.*

Two Hearts' hands trembled as he held the smoking pipe over his head. But there is no time! he protested. Traveling downriver, it is less than two days to the edge of our land, and the big canoe has already been gone most of a day. I will never catch up.

The smoke wavered and the stag's form swirled. *Go now.* Then the image faded.

Head bowed, he considered his options. He could take one of the village canoes, but they required ten men to paddle them, and still that would not be enough to catch the strangers. Well, he would make preparations, then ask if one of the dogs would consent to carry him.

✳ ◇ ✳

At dusk, the taller sailor, Scott, insisted on tying up beneath a willow, where the trailing fronds provided a bit of cover. Father Fitzwilliam felt weak, but clear-headed, as though he had come through a terrible illness. He remembered nothing of the instant in which he had touched his young assistant, but though he had apparently been unconscious for hours, the time afterward had been dream-like, filling his mind with intimations of sweet-voiced heavenly choirs and the peal of golden bells. In some curious way, he felt refreshed, even at peace with himself and the world.

Declan, however, looked as though he had been to the gates of Hell and back. His eyes were feverish in his ashen face and he jerked at the slightest sound. The two sullen sailors studied him at every opportunity with over-curious eyes, much as a prowling cat watches a canary, and Fitzwilliam began to fear for the younger man's safety.

They off-loaded supplies for the evening to the grassy bank, where the grumbling, cross-eyed Scott laid a small fire and stirred up a pot of rank-smelling beans. Declan braced his back against the willow, his exhausted face half-obscured by lacy willow fronds drifting in the breeze. His hands lay on the ground beside him, twitching as though they had a life of their own.

Fitzwilliam accepted two bowls of beans from the sailor's grimy paw, then ducked under the trailing willow canopy. "Declan, lad, say grace with me over our evening meal, poor as it is."

The younger priest's haunted eyes blinked. "Grace?"

"Yes, and then you must eat a bit." Fitzwilliam held out the steaming bowl. "I know you feel poorly, but we'll reach Savannah tomorrow and then I will have a proper doctor examine you at the fort."

Declan flinched as the fire popped. His face, ghost-pale in the gathering darkness, floated above his limp black collar. "I can't—pray."

"Do you wish to be confessed?" Fitzwilliam set the bowls aside in the grass and squatted beside him.

"And I—cannot go before God." Declan squeezed his eyes shut. "I'm afraid."

"Afraid of what?" Fitzwilliam asked, his voice gentle.

"Afraid of the—" Declan hunched over his arms as though in pain. "Afraid of the *light*." His voice was choked. "It comes back—every time I pray—and it is not of this earth!"

Fitzwilliam reached for his hand, but the younger priest jerked back. "Don't touch me!"

Over by the campfire, he heard the low murmur of the sailors' voices, rising and falling in some sort of argument. On the opposite bank, frogs sang in a creaky chorus, and somewhere out in the dark current, a fish leaped after a flying insect. The air was thick with the rich scent of mud and crushed grass and the oversweetness of a bank of red flowers. Fitzwilliam sighed. "It's just your fever come back. Such maladies often worsen at night. Why don't you lie down?" He picked up his own bowl and returned to the flickering firelight to doggedly eat the beans, spoonful by tasteless spoonful, wondering what ailed the boy. Of course, a new land was bound to hold many fevers.

He took Declan a blanket, then rolled up in one himself, trying to ignore the biting mosquitoes and compose his mind for sleep. "Not my will, but thine," he whispered to the blue-black endless night sky and felt comforted.

✳ ◇ ✳

Something splashed, then a muffled curse rang out through the darkness. Fitzwilliam jerked awake, staring in bewilderment up at the bright scattering of stars overhead. On his left, the fire had died down into sullen red coals. He sat up, rubbing his stubble-covered chin.

The black shape of the boat shifted, then the ropes that hauled up the sail creaked. Fitzwilliam stumbled to his feet, his heart hammering. "Stop! You can't leave us here!"

A dark figure grunted, barely discernible against the outline of the boat, then leaped onto the almost invisible deck. "Good-by, friar!" one of the sailors shouted, then they both laughed raucously.

Fitzwilliam followed them helplessly to the bank. His chest heaved with anger; enough moonlight glimmered down from the cloudless sky to silver the metal rings and fittings and reveal the boat was already out of reach.

Declan emerged from under the willow. "What are they doing?"

"Stealing our goods and abandoning us to die!" Fitzwilliam ground the words out. "May their heathen souls burn in Hell!"

"No!" Declan turned to him, his face half-illuminated by moonlight. "The mission's supplies—they have no right!"

"There's no one to stop them, lad." Fitzwilliam slumped as the fight drained out of his tired old body. "Unless we make it back to the jurisdiction of English law, the scoundrels can do whatever they like, then concoct lies to cover their tracks."

The younger priest flung himself into the dark water and waded after them. The sailors hooted at his efforts as they heeled the boat about to catch the current.

"Come back, lad!" Fitzwilliam called. "It's no use!"

Declan was struggling through water up to his waist. The night had fallen silent, the frogs and insects suddenly voiceless. Fitzwilliam saw his moon-limned figure raise dripping arms from the water, saw his hands gleaming with eerie blue-white light not born of this world. Light rippled over the younger man's body, radiating from every pore until he was outlined in a shimmering brilliance which hurt the eyes.

The water took up the light, and then the slim, darting fish beneath the surface, the turtles and the long-legged frogs, even the bits of driftwood and other flotsam. The light burst downstream, accompanied by a shrill, building hum which worked its way into Fitzwilliam's bones and set his teeth on edge. He pressed his hands over his protesting ears as the light intensified, reaching for the boat which had almost cleared the bend.

It crawled over the hull as fire consumes a log, converting the craft to a ghost ship. The river and its banks, every living creature suspended in its depths, the boat, all blazed with a terrible unearthly light. Fitzwilliam sank to his knees, his heart squeezed until he couldn't breathe. "Lord God Almighty," he forced past his trembling lips, "deliver us from evil."

The two sailors cried out as they stared down at their shimmering hands, then one of them snatched a pistol from his belt and sighted back up the river at the incandescent man of light. The hum transmuted into a roar as the shining river bulged beneath the boat, then rose in the shape of a giant man.

The river-man wore Declan's face. The familiar features contorted in silent laughter, then, gripping the boat between his immense, gnarled hands, the spectre cracked it like a rotted stick. The sound reverberated through the trees like a shot. He raised the pieces above his head, then dashed them back into the water. The sailors screamed as they fell. Fitzwilliam saw the shattered halves of the boat drift against the far bank and turn slowly in the grip of the current. The river-man glanced back at him, his face an unholy blue-white, and melted back into the river with a faint gurgle. The brilliant light that permeated the landscape faded into a glow, then a faint luminescence, then disappeared.

Declan, in the water, was solid black against shifting charcoal-gray now. Fitzwilliam's light-dazzled eyes could barely make him out. He moistened his lips. "Declan?" he called, his voice shaking.

The dark figure turned, but remained silent. The current whispered around his torso.

"It's—over," Fitzwilliam said. "You can come out now."

Declan took one step back towards the bank, then hesitated as though he were lost.

Fitzwilliam struggled to his feet, feeling every one of his sixty-two years. His heart pounded and terror rushed through him when he thought of touching the thing in the river that had been his assistant.

The dark figure raised an arm, then slumped and slid below the moon-silvered surface with only a ripple. "Saints preserve us!" Fitzwilliam hobbled into the river, so afraid he could not breathe, groping beneath the strangely warm water for Declan's body. His hands met only the liquid rush of the current and he surged forward, using his whole body to search.

His arms ached and the breath wheezed in his lungs. The current was strong, forcing him downstream, out into the middle of the river where the water was far over his head. He bobbed and spluttered, fighting for his own life, and just when he thought he could struggle no more, a limp hand grazed his side.

He jerked the arm upward with the last of his strength and saw the wet curls of black hair floating around the dead-white face. Shivering from shock and exertion, he flipped Declan's water-logged body over on his back, then swam, angling for the shore as the river swirled them downstream. They fetched up finally against tangled tree roots protruding from the eroded bank. Gasping for air, Fitzwilliam looped one arm around the wiry root while he clutched Declan's limp body to his chest and waited for daylight.

chapter five

Declan felt a wrenching of energies. Stars turned inside out; trees reached to anchor their roots in the sky. He tasted fiery hot reds on the back of his tongue and the cool peppermint of blue-greens, the lemon-tartness of yellows. Wind skittered the dry scent of cedar across his face, and then the clean pungence of pine resin. He stirred, realized he lay upon naked stone, then struggled to open leaden eyelids, surprised to find himself on dry ground. Hadn't he just been slogging towards shore, waist-deep in a river?

"So, grandson, you have come at last." The contralto voice had a reverberate quality to it, as though it were somehow bigger than the body that contained it. He felt the fierce warmth of the sun itself in it, and the strength of a roaring river in full flood.

He tried harder and finally peeled his reluctant eyes open.

An arm's length away, a shriveled old native woman sat on folded knees, watching him with overbright emerald eyes. She wore a dazzling white deerskin dress with a belt of white beads, and the braids of her darker green hair were tufted with eagle feathers. White lightning streaks were emblazoned on her cheeks.

A black dog, as large as a full grown bear, sat at her side, tail wrapped neatly around its feet. The white star on its forehead seemed to glow at him through the dimness. A spotted owl, no bigger than his fist, gripped the woman's shoulder and appraised Declan with eyes like golden plates. He sat up, then gazed over the edge of the rock in baffled amazement; they were perched on the crest of a soaring mountain. Down below, the world spread in every direction in a misty carpet, earth-brown and leaf-green, shimmering blue where it was divided by winding rivers and dotted with lakes.

"The Above Beings sent you to me." Although sun-lines had seamed her copper face into a maze of wrinkles, the old woman's voice was full and steady. *"They say you have something to do."*

"I—I not Tsalagi," he said haltingly in her tongue. "I not believe Above Beings, believe only—" He broke off, unable to recall the words in Tsalagi which he and Father Fitzwilliam had chosen to explain God the Father and his divine Son to the savages.

"I give you a gift now," she said, *"full command of the Tsalagi tongue to better understand what it is you must accomplish in the Middle World below."* Leaning for-

ward, she bracketed his head with her hands. A tingling warmth exploded through his body, traveling every nerve, every nook and crevice of his being until he was alive with it.

The huge dog rose to its feet and whined low in its throat, straining toward him. The old woman released Declan's head and her wrinkled lips parted in a smile. She laid a restraining hand on the dog's shoulder. *"He will come to you in time, Nightshadow."*

Declan started violently at the sound of that name. It called visions into his head of wild rides through stygian darkness, and excitement pumping through his veins instead of blood. He tasted power on the back of his throat like a heady potion, the promise of joy. Shaken, he turned back to the old woman. "Who are you?"

"Names are powerful. Never surrender them without careful consideration." She cocked her head. *"Actually, I have many names, as do you."*

His eyes strayed back to the jewel-like view below. This spectacular mountain seemed to be single, not part of a range, rising up like a sentinel in the exact center of the world. He felt the life brimming below it, a great tapestry of interwoven beauty in which he somehow had a part. "I'm dreaming," he blurted in English, and staggered to his feet. "None of this is real!"

"Everything is real." She rose in one liquid movement, belying her appearance, as if she were somehow both ancient and young at the same time. She touched his cheek.

His hands warmed and he stared down in horror as blue-white light erupted from his fingertips.

"Child from beyond the sea, you have the gift of all four medicine ways, Fire, Water, Earth, and Air, which is rarely bestowed, and never without great solemnness of purpose," she said. *"Your strongest gift is Fire, both the most potent and dangerous to wield. Power is ever a two-edged knife, able to create great good in the world, or much evil. You must learn to use it wisely."*

"But I have no wish for such power!" He shuddered and thrust his shining hands behind his back. "Take it away!"

Her aged face was serene. *"Power is a responsibility, given to restore the earth to balance when the crucial time comes. If you hide from it, or deny it in any way, all your relations will suffer—whites, Tsalagi, furred people and feathered people, tree people, finned and shelled."*

The light from his hands enveloped him with a fiery warmth which was seductive, binding him to the mountain and the woman and the dog and everything below, a warmth for which he had hungered without understanding. For a second, he basked in it, savored it, desired never to be without it, then he stared at her in horror. She must be a demon, sent to tempt him into heresy.

She waved a hand as though dismissing his fears. *"You have been called across the sea to do a job, and although it will be difficult, you must find the strength to carry it out."*

"No!" He turned and fled down the towering mountain, dodging tumbled boulders. His foot slipped on loose scree and he fell, flailing at the low scrubby brush. The immense black dog followed him to the edge and stared at him with luminous, anxious eyes as he fought to lever himself back up, the blood pounding in his ears. The star on its forehead expanded until it was a vast white moon, a beacon somehow urging him back.

The old woman appeared beside the dog, the wide-eyed owl still clinging to her shoulder, and chanted a low, repetitive song. The rhythm beat through him as she sang, compelled him to hear, to be quiet and consider what she had said. He struggled against its thrall. "No! Stay away!" He could not listen, or he would lose his soul. Better to die now and reside in Heaven with God. Shuddering, he loosened his hands and let himself fall backwards toward the distant earth.

The wind screamed in his ears as he plunged, and its fierce, unforgiving chill ate into his bones, seeped through his blood until he was made of ice. His freezing thoughts slowed until it was ... impossible ... to ...

✳ ◇ ✳

"Declan! Declan, lad, you must wake up!" Fingers gripped his face. "I can't hold on much longer."

Chill water lapped at his chin, sloshed over his mouth and trickled up his nose. He coughed, choked, forced his eyes open. A gray half-light reflected from the pewter surface of the murmuring river. The air was filled with the dankness of cold mud and the brisk current dragged at his icy, water-logged cassock.

"God be praised!" Father Fitzwilliam's ashen face floated into view, then the weary priest urged Declan's hands onto the wet roots dangling from the steep bank. "Now, try to pull yourself out of the water. I cannot manage both your weight and mine."

Declan concentrated, but his hands were numb with shock and the river's chill. He seemed to remember the water being warm last night, and there had been a brilliant blue-white radiance—

Shivering, he thrust that memory away and fought to close his hands around the slick, wiry roots where the bank had washed away. They were too thin though, and he could not get a proper grip. Finally, he let the current carry him along the bank until he reached a low spot where sand and silt had accumulated in the river's bend.

Hand over hand, he crawled onto the grassy overhang, then sprawled on his back, his feet still in the water, feeling battered in every part of his body. The older priest sloshed after him, muttering, then stopped abruptly. Declan raised his weary head in alarm.

Father Fitzwilliam was kneeling in the shallows, staring down at something large which bobbed like a cork against the sand bar. His shaking hand sketched the sign of the cross over his breast.

It was the drowned body of the sailor, Scott, fish-belly white, bloated almost beyond recognition.

Berry awoke just before dawn with the bitter taste of terror in her mouth. She had dreamed first of the young stranger with his brilliant sky-eyes, his skin gleaming palely, coming to her though the singing darkness. He enfolded her in his arms, held her so tightly they seemed to be made of a single flesh. Then he faded and she found herself part of a terrible, cold journey in which the Real People were forced to walk to a far rocky land burned brown by the relentless sun, where the grass was not aware of their feet and the sky no longer recognized them, where they were squeezed into tiny gray lodges and forgot how to speak to the four-legged and the winged and the plant-people, where they lost even their true names.

She rubbed trembling hands over her goosefleshed arms, frightened. The dream had that electric tingle which always signalled truth. The Above Beings were warning her; a time approached when vital matters would be decided, and the Real People would be called upon to give all they had. She had something important to do, a task to prevent these terrible things from coming to pass, and the stranger was somehow part of it. She must do her best to understand her role before that critical moment arrived.

On the other side of the darkened room, her uncle shifted on his heap of furs. She slipped from her own bed and went outside into the cool grayness to stir up the fire. Two Hearts had returned last night in the company of two Kitasi dogs and the noted scout, Smoke, saying he must leave at first light to find the stranger. The huge dogs, one gold as ripened corn, the other black marked with white, had gazed at her with dark, knowing eyes and through them she had felt the urgency of this trip. It involved somehow the future of not just Kitasi, but all Tsalagi.

Her dream must be connected with her uncle's journey, she reasoned, adding twigs to the banked embers. She had some part to play in that too. Her face warmed as she remembered the gentleness of the young stranger's hands on her bare shoulders in her dream, the beat of his heart pressed against hers, then she thought of the people's hopeless faces, their listlessness, their empty hands and hearts. An ache built within her chest, a rising need to act.

She closed her eyes and tipped her head back, letting the cool morning breeze bathe her face. Her hands lay on her thighs, still and relaxed. The air brought the scent of pine and dew-moistened earth from the southern edge of the village. She formed her question, inviting that other, unnamed presence which came to her from time to time: Should she go with her uncle?

A tingle began in the top of her head, spread to her cheeks, her mouth. *"Yes,"* a resonant voice said with her lips, vibrant with green life. *"All the medicines must now unite for the time when either a terrible ending, or a new beginning will be made."*

A breath later, she heard Two Hearts in the doorway behind her. Suppressing a sigh, she opened her eyes and bent over the fire. "I prepared traveling food for you last night, and laid out fresh clothing."

He squatted beside her, silent, as was his way. She had learned volumes from his silences down through the seasons, the way children of other lineages learned the signs of deer in the forest, or read the next day's weather in the clouds. This particular silence had nuances of posture and facial expression which said he had much on his mind; he was not sure what to do.

She glanced at him out of the corner of her eye. "I dreamed last night of the young stranger, then of losing our land and our homes, even our names."

He turned his head sharply, his brows knotting over his proud hawk-nose.

She plopped two heated stones, rounded by the river, into a pot to make an herbal tea. "I think I should go with you."

His jaw tightened. "No."

She turned to him, her face warming. "I *feel* it." She touched her chest where the need to act burned. "I am involved, and I cannot stay here and tend the fields when there is trouble coming."

His dark eyes smoldered at her. "*I* have not seen that a woman is needed, and—" He broke off and stared over her shoulder. His expression was bleak. "We will follow this man all the way out to the dead lands, if we must, a place I fear to go myself." He closed his eyes. "Your gift is with the plant-people and there is little you could do on this trip. I will not risk more than those whose names I have already been given."

She scrambled to her feet, the dream making her speak words she normally would have choked back. Her cheeks burned. "And what about what *I* have been given?"

"You must seek your own answers while I am gone, sister's daughter." His big-knuckled hands twitched. "We will speak more once I have returned."

If you return, she thought as she snatched up the water jug, but she had the wit to stay her tongue.

The two-legs' pack, scattered across the hollow inside the dead-tree-place in many small above-ground dens, roused and shook itself slowly. At the edge of the enclosure, Sunrunner lay with his nose propped on his paws, watching for many blinks of the eye, many sniffings of the deliciously scented morning air.

The enticing rankness of badger stirred outside the two-leggeds' tall circle of dead trees, and he smelled squirrel, *many* squirrels, and the hot, sweet scent of rabbit, feeding in the early light of dawn. Saliva pooled on his tongue. Rabbit was easy to run down, when he was rested. The pack should be careening through the thickets and trees, digging their nails into the moist earth with each bound, giving chase to their brother four-leggeds in that ancient, much beloved dance of predator and prey.

But two-leggeds were ever obstinate and events would flow in the same agonizing slow *slow* pattern until the dogs could coax their clan-mates from this boring place-of-dead-trees. This Sunrunner knew, for it was always so.

The black-she, Nightshadow, curled at his side, warmth against furred warmth. He felt her quiver with the desire to run. She smelled of hunger and boredom. The white on her forehead shone in the thin gray morning light like the bright relative above in the day sky. She snuffled her repressed excitement and Sunrunner flicked an ear at her. *Soon.*

His two-legged clan-mate, Smoke, walked up the path to the four-leggeds' den where he spoke the windy two-legged mouth noises that meant *come, we have places to go, work to do.*

Sunrunner sprang to his feet, wriggling with excitement, and sniffed his clan-mate thoroughly from top to toes. Smoke smelled of unease, as well other two-leggeds, several of them immature and Dog Clan as was he, and then one older two-legs, whom he had met in the last dark time, who was not-clan. The dog disregarded all not-clan scent as uninteresting. Four-leggeds tolerated every two-legged who dwelled in this made-place, even though many of them were one variety or another of not-clan. Clan however was as close as pack. Clan was *self.*

Nightshadow rose too and sniffed Smoke's extended palm, but more reservedly. Her two-legged had gone to the Night Country several seasons ago in a fight at the edge of the living land. One of the pale, bad-smelling strangers had pointed a stick and made a terrible thunder that hurt the ears, then Nightshadow hunted ever after alone. Each time the two-leggeds presented prospective clan-mates to the unmatched, Nightshadow came forward and sniffed, but the scent was never right, and she returned to the forest, forlorn and single.

Today, though, she was full of snuffling excitement and nose-nudges. *Come,* her dancing ears cried, they had something to do, much hunting and much much running, out in the cool shadows beneath the trees and across sun-filled meadows and through streams. Last night she had found herself in that strange other place where Those-beyond-sight had instructed her to bear a particular not-clan two-legged. Together they would seek another of that breed out, one who was not-clan now, but would become Clan.

That puzzled Sunrunner until his ears drooped. Two-leggeds were either born Clan or not. No one *became* Clan.

He and Nightshadow followed his clan-mate, Smoke, to a dead-tree-den where another two-legged not-clan stood, a male, trading mouth noises with a two-legged she. The two dogs waited, tails quivering, tongues lolling with excitement. Smoke spoke to the not-clan, who nodded, then raised his flattened palm to Nightshadow. The black-she sniffed it deeply. Sunrunner took his scent too and all it revealed . . . this one was worried and tired . . . still wet from the river, as were all the two-leggeds in the morning . . . older than Smoke.

The two-legged spoke mouth-noises to Nightshadow, then climbed clumsily onto her back and anchored his hands in the thick ruff of her neck. Sunrunner glanced back over his shoulder as Smoke leaped astride in one smooth jump, then he trotted toward the gap in the surrounding dead trees, eagerness pricking his ears, puffing out his chest. The two-leggeds, young and old, large and small, all parted as he and Nightshadow padded out into the living forest.

＊   ◇   ＊

Declan helped Father Fitzwilliam scrape a shallow grave on the river bank with sharp-edged rocks, then drag the sailor's body into it and cross the limp arms over the bloated chest. They tried repeatedly to shut the staring eyes, but Scott seemed determined to watch them cover his fish-nibbled corpse with dirt and rocks. Father Fitzwilliam placed a crude cross of wood bound with grass at the head of the grave. "Eternal rest grant unto them, Oh, Lord, and let perpetual light shine upon them."

Declan mouthed the familiar words at his side, but felt none of the serenity they usually brought. He shivered as he remembered leaping into the river last night, and soul-searing light everywhere.

"Oh, hear my prayer," Father Fitzwilliam continued, reciting from memory. "Unto Thee shall all flesh come."

Blue-white fire danced behind Declan's eyes. He lurched to his feet, his fists clenched.

"You must fight it, lad." Father Fitzwilliam turned sober gray eyes up to him. "'Tis the taint of Satan upon your soul, which we came to cast out of this benighted land."

"I—don't know how." Declan glanced wildly around at the river, the lush trees festooned with vines, the fluttering leaves. "Every time I try to pray, it comes back, like a banked fire smoldering inside my heart."

The older priest crossed himself, then climbed laboriously to his feet. The drying cassock clung to his wiry body like a loose black skin. He gripped Declan's shoulders in his gnarled fingers. "You can do nothing by yourself. Open your heart and ask God to cleanse your soul."

Declan started to comply, but just the thought of prayer brought blue-white flames behind his eyes. He shuddered as the river found its voice again, speaking in a bass rumble of some ridiculous tale about First Snow. A flock of crows took up the chorus. Grass whispered beneath his feet; rocks chuckled. The color drained from his face and he covered his ears.

Father Fitzwilliam pulled his hands away. "Repent!"

"Forgive me, Father, for I have sinned," he whispered. And he must have, but how? "I have in many ways offended—" As if he had opened a gate, blue-white fire roared through him, illuminating his hands and face, his whole body.

Father Fitzwilliam cried out, then released Declan and stared at his own blistered palms. "Turn it away! Deny Satan's power over your soul!"

The blue-white fire blended with the river and the earth and the air, and then with the living creatures who inhabited them. The boundaries of his soul dissolved. He and the world were one and the same; everything down to the smallest rock was alive, related intimately to him and inseparable. "It's no use!" he cried. "I am lost!" He turned and fled into the trees, crashing through thickets and vines, slogging across boggy pockets of sand and mud.

Father Fitzwilliam followed, calling his name until Declan felt he would go mad from the sound of it, but eventually, he was alone in the vast green silence, but for the frenzied pounding of his heart.

chapter six

Two Hearts had ridden the great dogs occasionally, but always in tandem with the dog's clan-mate, never alone. Now, as the two dogs surged out of the Kitasi palisade, he realized his former mounts had been severely limited by the double weight. Unimpeded, the immense black dog, Nightshadow, bounded forward, running with her nose low to the damp earth, her muscles working, confident of her direction. She twisted through closely set trees, leaped without effort across streams, scrambled up rock falls with a terrifying abandon that would have signalled death-wish in a man. And the only sound was the faint rush of the dogs' steady breathing and the occasional click of claws on stone.

Was this wild ride what those of the Dog Clan experienced every time they rode scout or led the hunt? If so, Two Hearts was glad to have been born to the Deer Clan. He set his jaw and pressed his face to the warm black neck, clutching fistfuls of fur, fighting with all his strength not to fall off as the dog wove through the forest's dappled emerald shade. Sunrunner followed close at her heels, running effortlessly, evidently content that his companion take the lead.

The trees passed in a dark jumble of trunks and limbs, interspersed with yellow-bright patches of brilliant sunlight. Nightshadow never flagged or hesitated, just dug her nails into the yielding carpet of leaf mold and pine needles, grass and moist red earth, reveling in the one thing given to her kind to do best.

A massive fallen log loomed ahead, as big in diameter as a Tsalagi lodge, covered with the stubs of broken branches. Two Hearts thought she must go around it, but Nightshadow gathered her strength and leaped, claws scrambling for purchase. Thrown back by the upward motion, Two Hearts lost his grip and tumbled off into a pile of dead limbs.

Caught in the deadfall, he struggled to free himself without shredding the flesh from his bones. A hand parted the spiny branches and reached for him. He clasped it and eased out into the cool shade of a towering white oak. Nightshadow sat on her haunches, dark eyes reproachful, while Sunrunner danced at Smoke's side, tongue lolling in silent dog laughter. Even Two Hearts, son of the Deer Clan, could understand that much.

The corners of the scout's mouth twitched. "Are you hurt?"

Two Hearts shook his head, but made no move to remount. His arms ached, not to mention his back, and his scratches oozed blood in a double handful of places.

The black dog stood, stretched until her joints popped, then advanced upon Two Hearts, crowding him back into the deadfall until he couldn't move. On either side of her muzzle, her jet-black eyes swelled to obsidian moons rising in a blazing black sky. Two Hearts gazed into them helplessly, lost in their vast, rich blackness. Figures emerged; a craggy-featured Tsalagi man riding a younger leggy black dog, their two bodies twisting in perfect synchronization, two halves of the same person rather than two separate beings, as the pack tracked a party of strangers who had entered Tsalagi territory from the dead lands. One of the strangers pointed a long stick at Nightshadow's clan-mate; there was a loud crack and a terrible nose-burning smell, and he tumbled from her back into the leaves. The other scouts fell upon the invaders and killed them, while the black dog threw back her head and howled her pain to the Above Beings and the rest of the universe. He felt the piercing dark echo of that loss and shivered at so much pain, made to understand for the first time the smallest part of what the dog had lost that day.

Smoke gripped his shoulder and the image faded. Two Hearts rubbed his eyes, shaken by the depth of the black dog's grief.

"Now," said the scout, "Nightshadow has opened her soul so that the two of you may run more as one."

Two Hearts put aside awareness of his hurts and gripped Nightshadow's thick black ruff. The dog stood steady beneath his hands and Two Hearts managed to throw his leg over her tall back.

"Close your eyes," the scout advised. "Empty your mind and let Nightshadow find the way. She *feels* where to find this man."

Two Hearts leaned over the dog's strong neck again, heart thudding, felt her muscles bunch between his knees. Nightshadow loped off through the whispering bushes and across a shallow stream. He opened his heart to the spirit world and felt the land give beneath the dog's paws, welcoming her mission, felt the breeze cool his hot face, and the leaves impart directions. A savage joy filtered through him, *her* joy of companionship after such a long time, joy of speed and strong legs and fierce teeth, joy of a thing which needed doing and the strength to get it done.

The dog's pulse evened out into a steady beat, and the man felt his quicken until the two rhythms were one.

✳ ◇ ✳

Father Fitzwilliam at length returned to the river, reasoning that once Declan calmed down, he would follow it downstream back to civilization. His blistered hands still throbbed and he was afraid of the heathenish black magic that had possessed the younger man—yet was not the Lord God stronger than any spell? Once Declan returned, no matter how afraid Fitzwilliam was, he would cast out the demon and salvage the young priest's soul.

Declan Connolly had such purity within, such innocent conviction and purpose, he could not be abandoned to the Devil. Fitzwilliam had never seen a youngster so selfless, so committed to the glory of serving God. He was meant for greater things and Fitzwilliam must find him before it was too late.

He tipped his head back and gazed up. Overhead, the sun beat down from a sky so piercingly blue and without blemish, the eye got lost in it. This land had a startling beauty, even in its savagery. He closed his eyes and recalled the softer greens of County Kerry on the western shore of Ireland where he had been born, as wild and rough in its own way as this land, with mountains that swept down to a rocky coast and poor thin-soiled fields that grew bracken and heather more readily than grass and supported only a few straggling wild-eyed sheep per acre. He remembered the constant buffet of the wind and the ache of his shoulder muscles when he hacked out black rectangles of peat for his mother's hearth. He could smell the sweet smoke of a peat fire on a chill morning when the rain misted down so fine that it wet his face, but he could not see it.

He eased under the trailing willow fronds to wait and rested his burned hands palms-up on his thighs. It was pointless to look back. His parents were long dead and most likely he would never see the land of his birth again. God had called him to this vast wilderness where he was needed desperately, and here he would stay until it pleased God to send him to his final rest.

Sweat rolled down his neck and soaked his high black collar, and he heard mosquitoes buzzing. He fanned himself with one hand and tried to compose his mind for prayer, but the hot humid air was stifling and the words hovered in a formless lump in the back of his mind, refusing to come to his lips. Weariness clouded his mind; the few hours of restless slumber before the terrifying river incident last night were all the sleep he'd had before spending the remaining hours of darkness in the river.

His eyelids drooped and he drifted into a light reverie, picturing this fine land as it would be someday when it was properly civilized and settled, how sheep and fine fat cattle would wander its lush pastures and lumber from forests would build strong towns, how the rock would make stone walls and farmers would till fields they actually owned, as few ever could in faraway Ireland.

The breeze shifted, whispered, fluttered through the slim, overhanging leaves. A feeling of uneasiness washed over him, as though someone angry were watching. The mossy ground warmed, then writhed like the spine of a bucking horse. He tumbled backwards, had the sudden dazed impression of trees and bushes flying past in a swirl of distorted greens and browns as he bumped along, spinning head over heels, faster than the swiftest horse could run. Each time he hit the ground, it flung him forward again, until he was sick and disoriented and despaired of ever stopping. And still the wild passage went on and on, his terror and pain building and—

He came to rest with a final thump and a terrified cry. His trembling, outflung hands struck prickly branches instead of the green lace of leaves. Where, before, he had been surrounded by a rustling willow canopy, he was now sprawled within a thicket.

His heart raced. He lurched to his feet, the reek of his own terrified sweat strong in his nostrils. The brambles raked his unprotected face and hands as he struggled to free himself. More magic, foul and black! He fought harder as the breath rasped in his straining lungs.

He burst through the last briar and fell full-length on the ground, staring. The winding river had moved far to his left, and the willow grove was nowhere in sight. A dense oak and hickory forest flanked him, then the ground sloped down toward the horizon where the restless sea, capped with blue-white breakers, glittered under the afternoon sun—and there in the distance, close to the shore, he made out a flash of red, blue, and white, the British flag flying above the fort.

Declan huddled at the edge of a creek, arms locked across his chest, afraid to look at his hands. He longed to simply stop existing, to die, but suicide was a mortal sin. In the space of a few days, he had lost everything which made his life worth living. Instead of bringing the natives to God, *he* was now sundered from the light and comfort of God's divine presence. He had to deny the damning magic which tainted him and find his way back to God. Resolutely, he clasped his hands and bowed his head. "Oh God, come to my assistance." A hum of voices sprang up. "Oh Lord, make haste to help me. Let them be confounded and ashamed that seek my soul."

"*Welcome, brother,*" a wispy girl's voice said.

He glanced up convulsively. A pubescent girl, her long hair as green as the grass back in his beloved Ireland, peered shyly at him from behind the dappled trunk of a birch. She wore a long fringed doeskin dress, but her slim brown arms and legs were bare. She slid farther around the tree, her expression sober. His heart stuttered as he saw the pale-gray birch bark outlined clearly through her body. He groped for his rosary and held the cross up before him. "Go—away!" he said in Tsalagi.

She cocked her head questioningly and reached for the little wooden cross. As her translucent fingers grazed his trembling hand, the hum of voices sharpened.

"*This is my territory, mine!*" the mockingbird cried above his head and ruffled its gray wings.

Declan clasped both hands to his ears as if he could shut the damning voices out. A rust-colored squirrel poked its muzzle through the fluttering leaves. "*Afraid!*" it chittered harshly. "*You can't stay here, here, not here!*"

He lowered his head and splashed across the cool stream. He would not listen, could not! Branches tore at his face, snagged his arms and ripped holes in his cassock. He fumbled over deadfalls and snags, crashed through bushes until every inch of his body stung and ached, and still the voices followed. Finally, when he could run no more, he collapsed to his knees, gasping for breath.

"*Blood,*" said a tiny buzz-voice next to his ear, "*is the foundation of life, but there is never enough.*" A stilt-legged mosquito landed on his hand and gazed up at him quizzically with many-faceted eyes.

Concentrate on one, someone had told him. *Shut the rest out, or they will drive all reason from your head.*

Swallowing convulsively, Declan shook the mosquito off his hand and glanced around at the endless green-swathed trees and vines and scrubby bushes. The swell of voices rolled over him like a giant wave and he curled against a gnarled willow. "*First,*" the tree said in a slow, careful voice full of creaks. "*Sister sun . . . streams down through my leaves . . . a glorious hot, golden river of light . . .*"

At least it wasn't a vicious, predatory voice like the mosquito, Declan thought, or mean and argumentative like the mockingbird or the squirrel. The willow's voice was strong and gentle, kind.

"*The leaves . . . transform the light to nectar,*" continued the willow in its stolid, woody tone, "*and send it . . . to the patient trunk . . . and then to the questing roots.*"

Declan pressed his cheek to the willow's rough bark and concentrated on the words, each one slow and careful, as though its selection were the most important thing in the world.

"*The roots . . .*" said the willow."

Yes, the roots, thought Declan, a man was nothing without roots. The other voices faded as he learned what it was like to thread thirsty white roothairs deep into the loving red earth and reach for the sky with a thousand thousand leaves, each one made to an ancient and exacting pattern, and what it felt like to suckle the sweet gold of the sun. His arms stole around the willow's solid trunk, and they were one.

✳   ◇   ✳

Fitzwilliam, washed, shaved, and freshly arrayed in one of his brother priest's cassocks, felt strangely removed from the ordeal he had just undergone. Deep inside, his head still spun with the wild tumbling that had thrown him at least thirty miles straight toward the sea, but his hands barely twitched. Bruises covered his entire body, and scratches as well, and he could do little to hide that. Ushered into General Sir Guy Carleton's office in Fort Pembroke, he folded his hands loosely to avoid irritating his blistered palms while he listened to the tick of an expensive clock, smelled the heady blend of the general's fine tobacco, imported from Portuguese plantations to the south. On the other side of the room, the general shuffled through a sheaf of requisitions.

Carleton was a relatively young man for the position he held, no more than five and forty. Though dressed casually in his shirt sleeves, his white wig was well powdered, his carriage was crisp, his blue eyes sharp. His brow wrinkled as he read the last few lines, then signed his name with a double flourish and reached for a walnut pipe carved in the shape of a leaping stag. He looked up as though realizing Fitzwilliam's presence for the first time. "Yes—?

Fitzwilliam stepped forward. "Father Fitzwilliam, Sir Guy."

Carleton nodded as he opened his violet-sprigged ceramic tobacco jar. "Father Fitzwilliam, what seems to be the problem?"

"The two brigands obtained by your staff to sail my supplies up the river cast off in the night," he said quietly, "stealing our goods and leaving us stranded in

Tsalagi territory. The next day, Father Connolly and I became separated in the woods. I need supplies and men to help me search for him."

"The lad has gone missing, has he?" Sir Guy raised an eyebrow. "Are you sure he didn't spy a likely looking native wench when your head was turned and go off with her?"

Fitzwilliam's face warmed. "He was—ill, quite disoriented, a fever of some sort. He'd fallen in the river the night before, trying to save our supplies, and I was unable to get him to dry land until daylight. He very nearly drowned."

"I see." The general opened a drawer in the immense pine desk dominating his office and rummaged through the contents before pulling out a single letter with a golden seal. He ran a manicured finger down the page, then looked up, his blue eyes chill as the Irish Sea in December. "The exact wording of this document directs me to assist your mission in any reasonable fashion."

He settled in a wing-backed chair before the window and tamped tobacco thoughtfully into his pipe with long patrician fingers. "It is, regretfully, not reasonable for me to send a rescue party of men into Tsalagi territory at the moment. Men involved in such expeditions have a distressing tendency to perish—of rather strange and horrible causes."

Fitzwilliam put a hand out to steady himself against the desk, unutterably weary. "But—"

"But—nothing!" Sir Guy plucked a coal from a brazier with tongs and thrust it into the bowl of his pipe. "You did not get those burns by peaceful trading, to say nothing of those bruises. It's obvious that some sort of devilment was worked against you."

Fitzwilliam glanced down at his burned palms.

"It's not safe to send my troops into those woods, not yet at any rate." Sir Guy exhaled a cloud of white smoke. "That was to be your job, was it not, converting these savages from their devilish practice of magic into God-fearing Christians so they can be dealt with in a timely fashion?"

Fitzwilliam's lips tightened.

"I have word that several of your fellow priests farther north, especially Father O'Neil at Fort Hampton, have had splendid success with their assignments, while down here at Fort Pembroke, we have nothing to show for the King's indulgence and considerable investment except lame excuses and an unending series of *requests*."

Fitzwilliam set his jaw. "Father Connolly is not responsible for *my* shortcomings, Sir Guy," he managed to say evenly. "He is quite young, only three and twenty, and newly graduated from seminary, and yet he has attempted to do everything required of him on this dangerous mission."

"I shall note that in my report." Sir Guy puffed on the pipe, his eyes glacial. "I am afraid you must consider him a casualty of war, like any other, mourned but unretrieveable. We shall, of course, return his remains to his family, should they be discovered at some later date." He leaned back in his chair and stared up at the lazily wafting pipe smoke. "If you desire another assistant, I will see what can be done, although I warn you—time is growing short. If you cannot produce results here on the field of battle, we shall ask your church for someone who can." He closed his eyes.

"I—see," Fitzwilliam heard his own voice say distantly. "Thank you for your time, Sir Guy." He fumbled at the doorknob with his burned hands.

chapter seven

Declan drifted through the mellow afternoon, caught in the sonorous sway of the tree's voice as it told of warm spring rains which thawed the frozen soil and birds who filled its lonely branches with bustling life in the proper seasons. After a time, it seemed a soft cheek lay against his, and he drew in the scent of green wood. Warm, full-bodied curves pressed sensuously against his back, but he could not summon the energy to open his eyes.

With the advent of dusk, the pleasant tree voice slowed and finally faded. Declan began to find room for his own thoughts again. He pried open heavy eyelids, and stared, heart stuttering, into the smooth brown face of a naked girl curled against him. A mane of emerald-green hair draped most of her body and as well as his. He scrambled away, dazed and afraid. "Who—who are you?"

"*A relative*," she said, although he could not have named the language in which she spoke. She sat on her bare heels and studied him. Her breasts were like pale moons and her dark-green eyes reflected what little light remained. She wore innocence about her slim body like cloak.

He averted his gaze with a shudder. "I swear to almighty God that I've never seen you before!"

"*We are all relatives,*" she said in a soft, husky voice. Her shadowed face seemed sad as she rose and embraced the gnarled trunk like a lover until her body faded from sight.

A violent fit of shaking overwhelmed him. The world had transformed itself beyond all reason and nothing made sense. Perhaps he *had* died back there on the river and this was Hell.

The everpresent voices still hummed in the background, but didn't separate into discernible conversations and inundate him as before. Then, above them, he heard something else in the brush, not loud, yet clearly making its way closer. Father Fitzwilliam? If so, he must go deeper into the forest. He endangered everyone decent now.

An indeterminate dark shape rounded a gnarled cottonwood tree and loomed in the growing darkness. He held his breath as two black eyes gleamed down at him from a height that promised immense size. Too big for a wolf. A bear?

The animal hesitated, then surged forward. Declan fled, stumbling over rocks and roots invisible in the near darkness. The beast gave chase and shouldered him into a patch of grass. He sprawled there on his stomach, gasping for breath. Why run? his mind whispered as the beast turned back for the kill. Better to have his throat torn out here than to return to civilization and burn at the stake. He squeezed his eyes shut and waited.

Warm breath feathered over his face. A cool, wet nose bumped his temple, chin, throat; a warm raspy tongue licked his right ear. The animal whined, then lay beside him and propped its muzzle on his back.

Declan stirred, trembling, but it made no move to attack, just sighed heavily. He eased out from under its muzzle and studied the beast by the faint light of the stars. It was as long as a midsized pony, and black as the sky at midnight. He could make out two pointed ears standing erect on its head, but its profile was too finely drawn to be that of a bear.

It cocked its head as though appraising him too. A white spot on its forehead shone through the darkness like a star, reminiscent of something he had seen not long ago ... somewhere. He eased to his feet. The beast watched for a second, then rose in one graceful motion and shook itself until its ears flapped. Standing, its withers were chest-high to him. The black eyes gazed into his; it seemed to want something, almost as though it knew him.

Then he remembered the dream, the old woman on top of a mountain in the center of the world and the immense black dog with a white star on its forehead sitting by her side. He reached out a tentative hand and touched the soft furred neck. The creature leaned closer and rubbed its cheek against his face.

The brush crackled again as something else approached. Declan edged back, his heart racing, but the large dog cut him off, pressing against him in a way which seemed companionable, rather than threatening.

"So, Nightshadow, you found him," a man's voice said in Tsalagi out of the gloom.

The black dog yipped and sat at Declan's side, tongue lolling. A dark figure took his arm and pulled him closer. The forest's voices sharpened and Declan tried to draw away. "No, listen only to me," the man said, and Declan thought he recognized the voice. "Save the rest for when you need them."

Need them? Declan could not imagine ever needing to hear benighted trees and stones talk. Another man approached through the darkness, and a second beast as well. "What—do you want?" he asked as the stranger drew him into a small clearing under the stars.

The man stopped and studied him as though he could see perfectly well in the darkness. "To save you from the dead lands, of course."

*   ◇   *

After Two Hearts kindled the fire and it was crackling merrily, the scout, Smoke, returned from the darkness with a brace of squirrels on his belt. A cricket burst into song close-by as Two Hearts eyed the small carcasses doubtfully. "Will that be enough for two dogs?"

The golden dog, Sunrunner, flattened his ears, then sneezed and turned away disdainfully. Smoke untied the squirrels and hunkered down to clean them on a broad rock close to the fire. "They prefer to hunt for themselves, and then only every few days."

The stranger sat on the other side of the fire, the great black dog huddled against his back. As before, the flames reached hungrily for him, no matter where he sat. His face was haggard with lines of strain etched around his mouth. Dark shadows lay like bruises beneath his eyes. His hands were clenched as though he held onto something with all his remaining strength and feared to let go.

Two Hearts accepted a skinned and gutted squirrel carcass from the scout and spitted it on a stick to roast. "You should not have left Kitasi," he said over his shoulder to the stranger. "In your condition, you might have died, even before you reached the dead lands."

Wind gusted, stirring the leaves. The startling blue eyes jerked up and met his. They held so much pain, Two Hearts had to look away. "I *want* to die." He looked dully into the darkness. "I cannot live like—like this!"

Interesting, Two Hearts thought. The stranger's terrible accent was gone. He now spoke Tsalagi as though he had been born to it. Two Hearts swung the spitted squirrel over the fire. His brows knotted as he tried to unravel the stranger's meaning. "You do not wish to live in the forest?"

"No!" The younger man lurched to his feet and the black dog cocked her head, watching him closely, ready to intervene if he tried to escape again. His chest heaved as though he had run all the way from the mountains to the sea. "I do not want to hear—things, voices of things which cannot possibly talk, like birds and trees." He pressed his hands over his eyes. "I have lost my..." His voice choked. "My hands shine and I cannot get away from these voices that are wrong for me to hear. My people will kill me because I am filled with badness!"

Greasy squirrel fat drizzled into the fire and the scent of roasting meat filled the air. Two Hearts turned the stick to brown the carcass evenly. "Your people think it is bad that our brothers the birds speak to you? How then will they learn the wisdom of Air? They have no feathers to fly themselves."

"Birds cannot—should not talk!"

Smoke grunted as he finished skinning the second carcass and laid the bloody hide aside. "It has not been given to me, or to most of the Real People, to understand the language of birds or other creatures, but I would welcome such a gift from the Above Beings. It is a good thing, this ability, not a badness, a sacred responsibility."

Two Hearts' lips compressed. "It comes from the Above Beings."

"There is only one Above Being," the stranger said. "We call him God. There is no other."

"Blackrobes always speak of a single Above Being who was killed by his own people and then returned from the Night Country." Two Hearts shook his head. "Our Above Beings still live, still watch and guide us. No wonder your people can live on dead, unfeeling land, and say, not to mention, do, such strange things. You have lost all touch with the spirit world."

"There is only one Above Being!" The stranger stared at him with crazed eyes. "To say anything else is to be—lost forever!"

Smoke grimaced. "That is foolish. How can a person be lost forever? Even in the heart of the forest, you have only to wait until the sun comes up, and then you will know where you are."

Two Hearts reached into his waist pouch with his free hand and withdrew one of his niece's cold corncakes wrapped in leaves. He held it out to the stranger. "You are so tired and hungry that you are not making sense. Sit down and eat."

The stranger looked at the corncake as though he feared it, then faced the wall of darkness that surrounded them.

Two Hearts tested the roasting squirrel with a forefinger. "This gift you have been given is difficult to bear. I understand that, having walked with it all of my days, though in lesser measure. There is so much life in the world and it all crowds into your head unless you learn control." He tore off a small haunch and laid it aside on a rock to cool. "Such ability is given for a purpose. I believe you must be the reason I was gifted with two medicine ways, rather than one, as is most common. I am meant to train you to do what you must."

"I cannot live like this." The stranger did not turn around.

"The path to such knowledge is often dark and difficult, even for a Real Person." Two Hearts nodded to the dancing flames and they seemed to nod back with sizzling flamelet heads as they strained toward the stranger. "You may yet find yourself on the trail to the Night Country."

Sir Guy Carleton checked the row of figures again, then thrust aside the requisition and rubbed the persistent ache between his eyes. Blast that idiot priest for failing yet again! Success at establishing missions varied up and down the coast, but Fort Pembroke had the worst record of all. Only thirty converts in the ten months Father Fitzwilliam had roamed Tsalagi territory last year, and most of them were Catawba refugees. Even Harrison down at Fort Bligh had done better than that!

Of course, Fort Bligh was within three days' walking distance of the nearest Portuguese mission, San Christobal. Perhaps word had spread among the natives and made them more amenable to the priest who worked that area. All Sir Guy knew for sure was that, on the whole, the Catholics the King had acquired from Ireland were much more effective than any of the English Anglican missionaries sent on earlier efforts. Most of the Anglicans had disappeared in the first few months of their assignment, never to be seen again, and those who had survived won few converts.

He reached for the tea left by his manservant earlier and poured a cup. It was tepid, but he tossed it down anyway, wondering if he should call for something stronger. He had too much on his mind to find sleep easily tonight, or on any night in the near future, for that matter. He had to show better results soon, or the King would recall him, and there were plenty of officers with solid family connections waiting for the chance to make their mark in this Godless country. According to reports, Portugal was amassing a huge armada, financed by gold from its more successful colonies to the south. They were already waylaying His Majesty's ships at every opportunity. The King needed similar riches from the lands his explorers had claimed to build up England's defenses, and even if there was not so much gold in this portion of the continent, at the very least his officers should be able to send back timber and furs and slaves.

But native spells were still preventing them from entering the richer inland territories. Sir Guy had noted the priest's burned hands earlier. That fellow had been seared by magic, he had no doubts about that. The wretch was fortunate to have escaped with his life.

Perhaps it was too late for conversion in this area. Sir Guy stared moodily into the dregs in his cup, wondering what a fortune-teller would make of the pattern. Maybe he should order a full force of crack troops up-river with the priest and have them shoot as many of the damned Tsalagi shamen as they could find before they were killed themselves. He disliked wasting trained men, but this was war, and in war one had to allow for casualties. Three shipfuls of reinforcements were arriving in the next two weeks, God willing. If the way had been properly prepared, British troops might finally prevail, giving him a glorious victory to lay before the King.

As for the potential loss of Fitzwilliam, a few less Papist priests in the world would only be a blessing, when all was said and done. He had five others working this area besides Fitzwilliam, and he could always have more imported, if he lost these. His mouth tightened. There was clearly no shortage of priests in Ireland.

He reached for a quill and a clean sheet of paper, then tapped the pen against his chin, composing the orders in his head before he wrote. Let the fool priest think they were searching for his lost assistant. It would keep him in line a little longer.

*   ◊   *

Declan woke in velvet darkness, his heart pounding. He gazed wildly about, at the red-embered fire, at the huge golden dog sleeping just beyond it and the sturdy Tsalagi warrior who slept with one arm across the creature's neck. The black dog lay a few feet away, her dark eyes watching him soberly. Frogs sang somewhere in the night, but their voices remained only noise, as they should be. All was peaceful. He did not know what had broken his sleep.

He turned his head and saw Two Hearts sitting cross-legged just outside the circle of firelight. He was smoking a pipe shaped into a seated man. The smoke curled, gray against the starry darkness. He exhaled a stream of smoke. "I was asking the Above Beings why they wish me, of all who might have been sent, to watch over you, a weak and ignorant man, no good at all as a student."

Declan bunched his filthy cassock in one hand and scrambled to his feet. "Then let me go!"

Two Hearts drew another draft on the pipe, then released the smoke in a thin stream through his nose. The stern lines around his mouth deepened. "I have no desire to teach you, but the Above Beings insist a time is coming when change, like a maddened bear, will trample everything in the world that is good, if left unopposed. My gifts are not nearly as great as yours, but I must do what I can."

Declan flushed as he thought of the red-uniformed troops back in Fort Pembroke, drilling endlessly for the day they would advance into the wilderness and make it safe for English settlers. In his mind, he saw the dull eyes of the defeated Catawbas as they loaded the great ships docked at Savannah, their loved ones dead and their copper faces cratered with smallpox scars. "Change is coming," he said slowly, "but it does not have to be bad. The English have metal knifes and axes and pots and fine blankets to trade, and we will bring the word of God to your people so that you will all live forever."

Two Hearts regarded him steadily. "Take off your moccasins and let your feet feel the ground."

Declan hesitated, thinking perhaps he should run and try to lose himself in the night.

"Do it!"

The black dog sprang to her feet and snarled, her body planted squarely between him and the sheltering darkness. Declan knew he could never escape her. He sat down and fumbled at his boots.

The native shaman held the smoking pipe above his head and chanted softly underneath his breath, swaying back and forth. Declan wrenched the first boot off, then started on the second.

"Now, do you feel the life in your mother the Earth?" Two Hearts rose and stood over Declan as he pulled the second boot off. He touched the younger man's shoulder.

Declan's bare feet tingled against the cool wiry grass and red clay soil that nourished its roots. The ground seemed to expand, then contract under his soles as though it were breathing. He staggered backwards.

"You say your Above Being will make us live forever." Two Hearts paced a slow circle around him, holding the smoking pipe aloft. "Has not this spirit person told you that everything is already alive—all the time and forever, the rocks and the stars and the mountains?"

A blue-white light glimmered beneath Declan's bare feet where they touched the earth. He sucked in a shocked breath. "Stop it!"

"I can neither give this gift, nor turn it away." Two Hearts opened his arms to the sky. "It is medicine power, bestowed by the spirit world upon those who have need of it. Whether I approve or not, you have it in full measure, the power of Fire and Water, and perhaps the other two as well. You must learn to wield it with reverence and proper preparation, or it will burn you to ashes faster than a winter leaf that strays into the cooking fire."

The light shot up into Declan's ankles and built into a rapidly increasing warmth. He clenched his fists, willing it away.

"Decide!" Two Hearts grasped Declan's wrists; his touch burned. "There is too much to be done and I can waste no more time chasing after you!"

It was as though a great river of flame surged up from the earth through his legs and body and on through his arms into Two Hearts, then back into the ground again in a continuous, agonizing circuit. Shapes appeared out of the darkness, a great golden eagle, a woman with green hair that flowed down to her heels, an immense snake with lightning eyes, a shimmering man. They watched as the heathenish light surged ruthlessly up into his legs and torso, then through his spread fingers, illuminating the darkness as though it were mid-day. The trees gleamed a stark, ghostly blue, and each blade of grass, even the tiniest pebble shone molten white as though made of stars. He stared bleakly, aware this display of magic damned him more thoroughly than any blasphemy his tongue could have uttered. In his pain and fear, he closed his eyes against the terrible soul-destroying magic and begged God with all his heart for forgiveness and salvation, to be admitted once again into His blessed presence, seeking the comfort he had always experienced at the peak of Mass with his fellow priests—and found its presence in the brilliant light that surrounded him.

chapter eight

Two Hearts sensed spirit-people gathering as the stranger channelled more and more medicine power, opening a rift too large to close on its own. He set his jaw—if he or Declan strayed too near, the potent energies would burn their bodies to cinders before either had time to draw breath. Only a true Spiritwalker could enter the spirit realm bodily and live.

The air hummed as though alive with millions of bees, and the wraithlike outlines of beings who could not be seen with mere eyes hovered just beyond the light. He made out an old woman with trailing willow-frond hair, a golden eagle, a shimmering man, and an immense snake, Earth, Air, Water, and Fire respectively, all four of the medicine ways. Who was this man to draw so much attention from the spirit world?

Two Hearts shuddered as the fierce energies seared through him; human flesh was not meant for such power, but this was the moment in which the future would be made. If he could not turn Declan's will to acceptance of his path, it would matter little if either of them lived another day. His vision flashed blue/white/blue. The air swelled with the nebulous shapes of strange birds not of this world, their long necks intertwining to form graceful signs. The fearsome power threatened to boil his brain, but he hung onto the stranger's wrists, making of the two of them, one flesh, united in both pain and power.

Just when he thought neither of them could take any more, the stranger's resistance shattered like a logjam before a spring flood. He felt the other's heart open to the spirit world, and then the medicine-energy flowed through the two of them more easily, an even blue-white current rather than an angry, raging torrent. Declan's knees buckled and Two Hearts eased his limp body to the ground with the last of his strength.

The black dog crouched at their feet, watching warily as he propped the unconscious man against one of the packs. Declan's breathing was shallow, but steady. Two Hearts sat back on his heels and chanted in a low voice, welcoming the spirits who had come to bless this moment.

The way is difficult, grandson, said the green-haired woman, *but nothing worth having is easily obtained.* The eagle took wing and soared in a circle over the fire, then disappeared into the darkness. The shimmering man melted into the ground. The woman stepped out of the light and the huge snake glided after her, leaving the three men and two dogs alone in the clearing. The blood pounded in Two Hearts' head as he chanted to close the rift between the Middle World and the Above World.

The energies knit back together slowly, smoothly. When he had finished, he returned to the fire, now burned down to a bed of smoldering coals. The stranger's face was as pale as newly fallen snow, his skin clammy. The brilliant light suffusing his body faded as Nightshadow lay beside him.

Smoke raised an inquiring eyebrow. Two Hearts shook his head. "I will keep watch."

The scout sighed and stretched out against Sunrunner's furred side.

Nightshadow nosed the stranger's colorless cheek. He looked like an ailing child; his skin was translucent and the shadows beneath his eyes were like bruises. Raw red flesh circled each wrist where Two Hearts had held him. The shaman glanced at his own palms, but they were unblemished. Though his potential was not nearly so great as the stranger's, he had trained since birth, performed all the important rituals, purified himself regularly and prepared for difficult workings. Unfortunately, the stranger's already punished body would now have to pay the price of dealing with medicine energies without preparation.

He added wood to the fire, then sat back and watched the red-gold sparks swirl up into the blackness. His body felt hollowed out, as unfamiliar as the clothing of a stranger, but that was common after a working of so much power. His hands trembled from weariness as he retrieved the pipe from the grass where he had dropped it and emptied the powerful remade tobacco into the yellow flames, giving thanks to the spirits with each pop and hiss. There was so much to be done, so terribly much, and very little time in which to do it, and they had barely made a beginning.

Sighing, he began to remove the stranger's dusty robes.

Declan leaned over the silken neck of an immense black dog as it carried him up the side of a towering mountain. The chill wind sang into his face and he inhaled the sweet tang of pine along with the pungent scent of cedar as star after scintillating star flashed past, near enough to touch. The dog gave a last, great heave over the edge of a looming escarpment to the pinnacle of the mountain. Her tongue lolled as she looked over her shoulder at him. Declan slid off her back, then peered over the ledge at the clouds swirling far below.

"Why have you come to this sacred mountain?" a soft voice asked.

Declan turned. A girl of about sixteen regarded him solemnly. Her waist-length hair, black as a raven's wing, hung in loose waves and shadowed her eyes. She wore a fringed deerskin dress, belted at the waist. He remembered seeing her in the village before, in her uncle's house. Her name had been ... He cudgeled his memory ... She was called Berry.

"I—" He swallowed hard. She was more beautiful than he remembered, so much so that she terrified him. He could not let himself be tempted from his vows by the forbidden pleasures of the flesh. Palms sweating, he tore his gaze away from the curve of her brown cheek, the sheen of her skin. "I seek God."

"Then what you seek is everywhere and in everything," she said simply.

"You know God?" he said. "Even here, in this heathen place?"

"I know the spirit world, as do you." She gestured at the misty patchwork land far below. "Open your heart. There are many paths to that which you seek. Walk this one for now."

"Many paths?" he echoed numbly. "To God?"

"There is little time left." The wind ruffled her hair back from her solemn face so that her clear brown eyes shone like the sun. The air trembled and she seemed to have another, different face, a new richness about her, a subtle assurance which said she understood everything. Her hair gleamed with green highlights. He felt himself drawn to her as a tender seedling seeks the light and was even more afraid. "Time left for what?" he asked, and then saw he was alone with the black dog at the top of the world.

The morning dawned gray and sticky over Fort Pembroke. Fitzwilliam break-fasted with Father Dermot O'Neil in the cramped priests' dormitory reserved for their use when they were not working in the wilderness. O'Neil was a bluff, broad-shouldered man, a few years younger than Fitzwilliam. He was city-bred, hailing from the bustling town of Cork, not so far in miles from Fitzwilliam's own County Kerry, but very different in temperament.

Fitzwilliam wrapped a handkerchief around his burned palm and then cut up his overcooked egg with a fork. "So, Dermot, how goes your mission in the south?"

O'Neil scowled and reached for the teapot. "The same as the last five times you asked, you black-hearted scoundrel. The bloody Creeks have no interest in

God or praying or the like. If I so much as carry a Bible in my pocket, I won't see one of those red devils for days, but if I pack in trade goods, they will walk for miles to trade for a fine blade or pretty glass beads for their women. They care for little enough else." He leaned closer. "What happened to your face, man?"

Fitzwilliam flushed. "I had a—bad fall, yesterday, on my return to the fort."

"I see." O'Neil splashed steaming tea into his cup and stared down at it moodily. "That's what we all say, up until the moment we're killed. How many of us do you suppose now lie somewhere out there in the heathen forest, bones scattered by wolves and bears across unhallowed ground? Ten? Twenty? The British will never say."

The slatternly serving wench came in with a plate of toast. Her mousy hair strayed down the nape of her neck and her brown eyes had a disdainful look as she handed the plate to Fitzwilliam. He accepted it and quietly thanked her. She raised an eyebrow as she swept back out the door, but said nothing. He sighed. She was English, of course, and the English had no use for Catholics as a whole, and Irish Catholics in particular.

He wished sometimes he had never accepted this assignment. No matter what King Robert II promised, Fitzwilliam had trouble believing Catholics would be allowed to practice their religion freely in the New World once it was settled. He thought of the ruined abbeys that dotted Ireland, Scotland, Wales, and England, their naves open to the wind and the pounding rain, their windows, formerly splendid with the finest stained glass, staring like empty eye sockets. How many good men had been driven from their avocation, with no one to take up their burden amongst the poor, all so that Henry the VIII could bed yet another in a long succession of wives? In the end, he feared this new world would only be Ireland all over again.

"And what of you?" the other priest asked between hearty bites of toast. "I hear you are to go right back out."

Fitzwilliam nodded. "My assistant has gone missing. General Carleton has assigned a troop to search for him."

"Missing?" O'Neil paused in the act of sopping up his egg with a piece of brown bread, his expression thoughtful. "What sort of character does he possess? This would not involve the black arts, would it?"

Fitzwilliam paled as he fought to butter his toast without trembling. It was a sin to lie, he told himself, yet to tell what he had seen would doom young Declan, and he had hopes yet the youngster might be cleansed of the terrible evil which threatened his soul.

O'Neil was studying his face with shrewd blue eyes. "Never mind. I have walked those Godless woods even longer than you, and I have seen it all—trees which pull their roots right out of the ground and dance, animals that speak your name, witches who conjure fire in the palm of their hands." He broke off, gazing out the window into the dusty exercise yard. "Sometimes I'm so afraid I think I cannot bear it for another day, but then I know I must."

"I'm—sorry." Fitzwilliam closed his eyes. "It's just that I'm so worried. Declan is quite young for the position he has undertaken, and it is entirely possible we will be too late to save his life, even if we do find him."

The priest gripped his shoulder. "Think on the future when this land has become neatly plowed farms all the way to the horizon, when the natives live clean and wholesome, decently attired and freed from the Devil's taint, when a Christian can walk from shore to shore without fear. What we're doing here is God's work. There is far more at stake than the life of any one man."

Fitzwilliam nodded. "You're right, of course, Dermot." He pushed back his chair. "If you will excuse me now, I have to find Captain Jones and see if there are any final preparations to be made before we leave."

Declan was awakened by the singing of the trees. He groaned and rolled over, his head splitting. The voices of the nearby beeches were liquid silver, underlaid by the deeper chorusing of oaks, solid and rich with maturity.

A cold, wet nose prodded the back of his neck insistently, then his ear. He pushed it away.

"You must eat," a man's voice said above him. "Your body is depleted from its labors last night."

Declan sat up and peeled open his gummy eyes. He stared about in shock. He still saw the soaring mountain top from his dream, and no sign of another man or a dog or even trees. Billowing clouds blew across a vein of exposed gray-green granite a good two miles down—and he was alone. He flinched as someone pushed a leaf-wrapped cake into his hands. He fingered its crumbly texture, lowered his head and smelled corn mixed with meat, but saw—nothing. He dropped it with an inarticulate cry.

An invisible hand turned his face from side to side, peeled back an eyelid. "Is it your eyes?"

Declan swallowed hard. "I see the—the mountain from my dream, and clouds gathered below."

Two Hearts grunted, then fell silent, as if considering. "You summoned too much medicine energy last night without training or preparation. Your mind has been burned, and part of you is still caught among the spirits." Strong hands pushed him back against something yielding, and then fingers touched his eyelids, urging them shut. "Rest."

The mountain top danced behind his closed eyes, seared into his brain. And her face—he thought of the girl whom he had met there last night, Berry, how her eyes had shone. 'What you seek is everywhere and in everything,' she had said, so very strange. Could that really be true? It hurt his head to think about it.

He pushed the images away, reaching for the refuge of darkness ... for peace, but then remembered the red-coated soldiers drilling in the forts up and down the coast, the stockpiles of muskets and rifles and bayonets. There was no peace anywhere this side of Heaven, not in England or Ireland or this untouched wilderness, only poverty and misery and death.

The song of the trees altered as he lay there, hands pressed to his aching head. Magnolias added their wispy treble, then were joined by the cheerful lilt of a hickory stand. The music was compelling and beautiful and frightening. He would never understand why he heard such terrible things ...

The application of a steaming compress across his eyes woke him. He started, but hands steadied his shoulders. "Rest," the voice told him. He lay back as the warmth eased the ache in his head, soothed his eyes.

"You said we had little time," a different voice said.

"That is true, but we win nothing if he dies."

Declan breathed in the sharpness of crushed herbs and drifted back to sleep.

The mountain—the mountain—Berry thrashed in her bed, then sat bolt upright, suddenly awake. Her lungs worked as though she had been running all night. Her long hair clung to her cheeks in damp tendrils. She pushed it back from her face, straining to remember her dream. There had been a mountain, full of bare rocky crags, soaring high up into the sky vault, beyond where the eagles flew, higher than even the ice-bright stars. She had stood on the pinnacle, breathing in the chill air, looking back down at the hazy world below. And he had been there with her, the stranger.

He was seeking the Above Beings, who were everywhere and in everything, as close as the beat of your own heart. Even the youngest child of the Real People knew that much. It saddened her to see him so bereft. What he sought was at his fingertips. Why hadn't her uncle allowed her to come? It would have been so much easier to help if she had been with them.

Cheerful, teasing voices outside her house caught her attention. She shrugged into her skirt and blouse, then was shocked to find the sun halfway up in the sky. She had slept well past the time she should have risen. She should be in her cornfield by now. The golden ears were almost ripe and very restless. If she didn't keep a close eye on them, they would wander off in the forest before the harvest. Then she and her uncle would not only go hungry this winter, but have no seed for the following spring. And everyone would know how careless she was, a terrible prospect for a wife.

She threw her hair back over her shoulders and hurried toward the river for her morning purification.

Captain Evan Jones was a massive Welshman with the haunted look of one who had once worked in the mines. His nose was crooked, no doubt smashed at a very early age, Fitzwilliam thought. His face was etched with frown-lines, as though he had known decades of privation, though he could hardly be more than five and thirty. Fitzwilliam watched the big man casually knee the excess air out of a chestnut gelding in order to tighten its cinch. The horse grunted and flattened its ears.

"Did the bloody natives make off with Father Connolly?" Jones turned to him. "What kind of magic did they use?"

A few feet away, a half-naked Catawba glanced up from where he stood, holding the headstall of a sway-backed roan nag, his glittering black eyes full of hate.

Fitzwilliam wondered if the native was to be a member of the search party. "My assistant was feverish and wandered off into the forest." He eyed the hammer-headed gray mare brought forth for him, uneasy. He had never been a strong rider. "I searched for him as best I could, but I was afraid to get too far from the river, lest I lose my way too."

"You thought right, friar." Jones ran several fingers inside the gray's cinch, then repeated the kneeing ritual. The gray's tail switched angrily and Fitzwilliam dreaded mounting a horse so provoked.

"Now—" Jones passed him the reins, then studied him with icy gray eyes. "Don't feed me this swill about a so-called `fever.' Anyone can see those walloping bruises, not to mention the burns on your palms. I want to know what kind of magic they used as I have no intention of riding into a bloody trap!"

Fitzwilliam looped the reins over the gray's head and stared at the worn saddle. "He wandered into the forest," he repeated stubbornly, "but I did experience some difficulty." He hesitated, trying to think how to explain what he himself did not understand. "I . . . sat under a tree to see if Father Connolly would come back of his own accord, and I was drowsing off when, suddenly, I was flying through the air, head over heels, spinning like a child's top." His heart pounded as he remembered. "When I finally came to rest, I was within sight of the fort."

"I've heard of that happening to a few blokes before. It's only a little spell, not too dangerous, and it never works unless you're alone." Jones steadied the stirrup and motioned impatiently for Fitzwilliam to mount. "I suppose you was thinking about farming or some such other fool thing—the trees hate that. He glanced at the silent Catawba. "You get all of that, One Eye?"

The sullen native ducked his head, but not before Fitzwilliam caught sight of dreadful smallpox scars and a gaping eye socket. The gray feather knotted in his greasy black hair dipped. "I get."

"Then keep watch for spell sign and such," Jones said harshly. "It'll be your hide if we're caught unawares."

The native grunted, then vaulted onto the roan in one smooth motion. Fitzwilliam inserted his foot into the stirrup, grasped the pommel, and pulled himself up. Heart pounding, he gathered the mare's reins and managed to get her started after the others.

It took five hours of hard riding to reach the grassy spot on the river bank where he had last seen Declan. A silent hawk glided on the hot air thermals above the whispering river, but there was no other life in evidence. An indentation marked the bank where the boat had been beached, but there was no sign that Declan had returned after Fitzwilliam's unceremonious departure.

Jones swung down from his chestnut and hunkered on his heels to examine the rut left by the prow of the boat. "What happened to your transport?"

Fitzwilliam shifted his aching hips out of contact with the saddle. "The two crewmen abandoned us in the night and stole our supplies."

Jones rubbed his chin. "Sounds like them. Those river rats are a bunch of low-life thieves. Anyone with a smidgen of sense never turns his back on scum like that." He straightened and dragged a hand across his sweating brow. "It hasn't rained yet so there should be some sign left."

The copper-brown guide swung out of the patched saddle and looped the reins over his arm. He scanned the bank, quartering back and forth across the ground like a hound. Fitzwilliam knotted his hands over the pommel as he watched.

At length, One Eye pointed at scuff marks on the ground, almost hidden by the long grass. Jones passed his reins to another soldier and knelt beside the native. "A fight of some sort here, two men it looks like, both of them booted." He looked up accusingly.

Fitzwilliam's face heated. "Father Connolly—was out of his head, because of the fever. He was not responsible for his actions. I tried, but I couldn't stop him."

"I see." Jones strode angrily over to Fitzwilliam's gray mare and wrenched her head aside so he could stare into the priest's anxious eyes. "And what else did you forget to mention, friar?" His fingers wadded the reins. "Exactly what kind of magic sent this young fellow over the edge?"

chapter nine

When Declan woke again, later in the morning, he heard the breeze sighing through trees. The air smelled of sun-baked stone and earth and the leather that pillowed his head and shoulders. He stirred, feeling vastly more rested, then fumbled at the covering on his eyes.

"Wait," a voice commanded, then fingers eased the cooled compress from his face. "What do you see?"

Hesitantly, Declan pried open his eyes and blinked. Everything looked watery, but he made out the green-black shade of an immense chestnut tree spreading above. He focused on the dim figure looking down on him. "I see—you, Two Hearts," he said in relief, "and the trees."

The Tsalagi grunted and sat back on his heels. For a second, there was something else in his usually stern face, a sense of relief, almost of . . . good will. "You must not summon so much power again without proper training and preparation."

Declan sat up and rubbed his temples, light-headed. The air was sensuously warm against his skin and he suddenly realized he was clad only in a native-style breechcloth; his cassock, boots, and undergarments were all missing. "Where are my clothes?"

"They were torn, and thick with the stink of the dead lands." The other man's lip curled as he glanced at the fire. "I burned them. Now you must eat and regain your strength." He handed Declan a corncake. "Then we will return to Kitasi."

Burned his clothes? Why didn't they just kill him and be done with it? According to Father Fitzwilliam, that was the fate of Tsalagi prisoners, usually after days of torture. Why were they dragging this out with talk of medicine power and destiny?

With a scowl, Two Hearts pushed the crumbly cake into his hand and turned away. Shaking, Declan surprised himself by wolfing it down. The cornmeal had been mixed with honey and then fried. Even though it was cold, it tasted better than anything he'd eaten within recent memory.

"Nightshadow and Sunrunner are hunting with Smoke." Two Hearts squinted up through the whispering canopy of leaves. "When they return, we will leave." He handed him a cold haunch of roast squirrel from the night before. "Eat as much as your stomach will hold."

Declan shook his head. "I'm not going with you."

Two Hearts' dark eyes shifted, became flint. "You will die if you leave this land."

"Then God will take me." Declan lurched to his feet and supported himself against the corrugated bark of the tree. "I am more than ready!"

Two Hearts' weathered brown hand shot out to pin his wrist against the tree, and, as always, the ordinary sounds around him sharpened into a flood of words. Declan tensed as bird voices and tree voices and rock voices swept over him, all clamoring for his attention, seemingly upset about something, or someone. *"Danger!"* they shrilled at the edge of his awareness, then somehow—somehow —he concentrated and shunted them aside into mindless whispers which didn't quite make sense. He sagged back against the trunk, limp with relief.

The Tsalagi priest grunted and released him, his dark eyes thoughtful. "You are learning."

The wind gusted, and then Declan heard something in the underbrush. He thought at first it must be the two dogs, but then recognized the distinct four-beat clumping of hoofbeats. A whip-thin man burst into the small clearing. He was a native also, wearing the usual breechcloth, but his greasy black hair was separated into two plaits, very unlike the wild tuft of hair worn by the Tsalagi. His dark, pock-marked face tightened as his gaze met Declan's, then he melted back into the brush.

Two Hearts threw an arm around Declan's neck and dragged him backwards into the maze of trees. Startled, Declan dug in his heels and flailed at the older man's choke-hold, but was forced over protruding roots down into a shallow ravine where Two Hearts knelt behind him, still pinning his neck in the crook of his arm. "Be silent," the Tsalagi breathed hotly into his ear.

Above and to the right, a horse snorted and Declan heard voices call in English. "Here!" he answered, struggling to free himself, but Two Hearts tightened his grip, cutting off both Declan's air and circulation.

He wrenched at Two Hearts' arm as the blood pounded wildly in his ears and his vision constricted, but Two Hearts held on grimly until darkness swooped over his mind like the wing of a great raven. His body slumped and he saw only pinpricks of light. The voices were closer now. As though in a dream, he heard horses champing at bits, the creak of harness. His body sagged helplessly against Two Hearts' sweaty chest as he struggled for breath.

A twig cracked on the other side of the immediate trees. Two Hearts rolled Declan's unresponsive body into the grass and then eased away into the whispering green shade. Declan's fingers bit into the damp earth as he drew in shuddering lungfuls of air in an effort to clear his head. Shouts erupted as something crashed through the brush and he heard horses pound away from him. He struggled onto his hands and knees. His head throbbed, but sight began to return. He made out the grass ... the bushes around him ... the eroded red clay of the ravine ... and a pair of filthy, split-seamed moccasins.

Fingers seized his hair, jerked his head up and back. A knife pricked his exposed throat. "So, English!" The words were only a low hiss. "You belong One Eye!" The native, stinking worse than a garbage midden on a hot summer day, kneed him in the back. "Get up!"

He stumbled to his feet, careful of the knife at his throat. A warm line of blood trickled down his neck and chest. The shorter native released his hair to wrench his right arm behind his back and propel him toward the source of the noise. They broke through a thicket and he was hurled to the ground, scratched and gasping.

"Declan!" Father Fitzwilliam dismounted and knelt at his side. "Are you all right?" He touched the blood on his throat.

Declan nodded weakly, still winded.

"This is your assistant, then?" an English voice asked. "The one who wandered into the forest?"

"Yes." Father Fitzwilliam helped Declan sit up. "I need some water and bandages."

"And was he dressed in this fashion when last you saw him?" There was a hint of amusement in the steely voice.

Father Fitzwilliam stiffened. "Of course not."

A red-coated officer with tall black boots and a black-handled whip in one hand swung down from his horse. "Then perhaps he won't mind telling us what he's been about since yesterday." The whip lifted Declan's chin. "Will you, lad?"

Declan fumbled the whip handle away. "I was lost," he said slowly, "and the Tsalagi found me. They—burned my clothes."

"Did they now?"

Father Fitzwilliam stood. "Captain Jones," he said evenly, "surely such questions can wait until we get him back to the fort. It's obvious that he needs medical attention and rest."

"But do we dare take him to the fort?" The English captain smiled thinly. "Aye, that's the real question." He motioned to several other soldiers who dismounted. "The General won't thank us if we bring a viper amongst his troops, now, will he?"

Father Fitzwilliam paled. "I do not take your meaning."

The two soldiers seized Declan's arms. "What—?" he began as they tied his hands behind a pine.

The captain stood over him. "Now, start at the beginning, after you separated from the good friar here, yesterday, and tell us what you've been about." He tapped the butt of the whip against his free hand. "And leave nothing out."

Declan leaned his aching head back against the tree. None of this seemed real. Perhaps he was still on the mountain top, the clouds boiling below. He could almost feel the cold wind against his face—

The whip slashed Declan's bare chest, drawing a muffled exclamation of pain from his lips. "Get on with it!"

"No!" Father Fitzwilliam cried. "You have no right! He's done nothing wrong!" He wrenched at the captain's arm.

"Except a bit of magic." The captain shrugged him off and leaned over Declan. He smelled of sweat and boiled cabbage. "Tell us how the friar here burned his hands."

They *knew*, Declan thought bleakly. Father Fitzwilliam had clearly told them nothing, but they somehow knew he was tainted and no longer fit to live among God-fearing people.

"He—touched me," he said. An owl called through the whispering shade. Another answered softly. He wondered what were they saying to one another, and almost reached to understand.

The butt of the whip jabbed his throat. "Go on."

A low growl rumbled through the undergrowth. The horses threw up their heads and snorted, eyes rolling. Declan wrenched vainly at his bound hands.

"Damnation!" The captain whirled. "Look sharp, over there on the right!"

A musket fired. "Savages!" a soldier shouted as he plunged into the brush, bayonet fixed. Two snarling dogs, almost as tall as the horses, burst into the clearing, one golden as the sun, the other black as midnight. The golden one leaped at the tethered mounts, slashing, while the darker beast turned on the startled men afoot. The horses screamed and reared, fighting their reins. Another musket fired. The golden dog yelped as the smell of burned powder filled the grove, then leaped upon the soldier who disappeared beneath a savage whirl of golden fur.

Father Fitzwilliam fumbled at the knots binding Declan's hands. An arrow whizzed past his head and buried itself in the heart of the nearest soldier. Smoke appeared, thrust the old priest aside and slashed the ropes.

"Come!" The scout's fingers bit into his arm.

Declan stumbled up as several horses tore their reins free and fled into the forest. Suddenly the immense black dog was at his side, eyes flashing, hackles raised. A terrible growl rumbled in her chest.

"Ride!" Smoke shoved him at Nightshadow.

Declan gripped the dog's black ruff, but hesitated. If he went with the Tsalagi, there would be no going back, not to the fort, or Ireland, or the Holy Mother Church. He would lose everything.

The whole scene was chaos, those horses still tied or mounted plunging in fear against their reins, soldiers struggling to reload their muskets, Father Fitzwilliam staring at him open-mouthed and unbelieving. Sunrunner darted in and out, snapping at the horses, maddening them so that their riders had no control. A trickle of red blood matted his golden fur, but he did not seem to be seriously wounded.

The old priest put out a hand. "Declan—"

The English captain scrambled up from the ground and trained a pistol on the older priest. "Tell them to go, or I'll shoot the old bastard!"

Father Fitzwilliam sank to his knees, his uplifted face strained.

"Please, God, no!" Declan bolted between them. "He is blameless!"

"And what about you, bucko?" The captain sighted his pistol. "Are you blameless too?"

Declan tensed for the bullet, then intense blue-white light erupted from his hands, shot through his body, streamed from every pore until he felt himself in the center of an immense whirlwind of light so intense that all shadows disappeared. The English captain stumbled back, the planes of his face harshly delineated by the shimmering brilliance.

"Declan, no!" Father Fitzwilliam pleaded from behind.

More light awoke on the other side of the tree. Sunrunner lowered his head and moved aside as Two Hearts approached, his body outlined in rose-colored light. The Tsalagi spread his hands and the light flowed outward, seeking a shape, shifting toward something which looked like a giant...stag.

As though in answer, Declan's blue-white aura flared to meet the rose. The stag-shape disappeared as the two colors melded, then settled over Declan in the form of a huge blue-white snake, twice the height of a man, with gleaming eyes and a strange rattling tail. A pattern of gleaming blue diamonds ran down its back. It coiled around Declan, then wove its flat head back and forth, regarding the soldiers with a terrifying calm. Its forked tongue flickered like lightning.

Caught inside the apparition, Declan longed to scream, to turn away, even to close his eyes, but could do nothing.

Musket fire shattered the silence. The snake's head darted at the unfortunate marksman, seized him like a rat and swallowed him whole. An inhuman scream burst from the English captain's throat. He stumbled back, then fled, followed by the rest of his men.

The Tsalagi scout edged around the snake/Declan and darted in to free two fear-maddened horses who had not yet torn loose their reins. Turf flew as they pounded away into the forest, their ears flattened, foam flying from their mouths.

Two Hearts swayed, sagged to his knees, and his head drooped. The rosy light emanating from his body pulsed, faded. The snake reared above Declan, looking down, its bright eyes seeming to recognize him, then it dissolved into a shower of sparks and disappeared. Declan stared dumbly down at his hands as the light ebbed.

His head throbbed as though it would split. He sucked in a terrified breath, afraid to move or even think. It was just like his dream, only worse. He fell to his knees, too dizzy to stand.

"D-Declan?" Father Fitzwilliam's voice quavered.

Two Hearts raised his head. His dark face was hard as granite. "There is no person named Declan, only this man, who has just proved himself to be a child of this land and no other."

A massive fit of trembling seized Declan as Father Fitzwilliam circled into his field of vision. "Lad, beg Almighty God's forgiveness, now, before it's too late! Ask the Lord to save your immortal soul!"

"I—have!" Declan's voice came out in a strangled whisper and he had to set his jaw against the fierce pain behind his eyes. "And all I ever receive in answer is the light—and the accursed voices of *things* that have no right to speak." He squeezed his eyes shut. Grief swelled within him, so large, he thought he would burst, warring with the terrible pain in his head. He had lost his soul, and with it, any chance to serve God. "I will go mad from this. I—can't bear it another second!"

"Then come back with me!" Father Fitzwilliam's feet shuffled closer through the carpet of leaves and grass.

Nightshadow thrust her massive black body between him and the priest, growling low in her throat.

"He cannot go," Two Hearts said, although they had been speaking in English. "The spirits speak to him and through him. They have given him a task to do, and where his path leads, no man can say for now. He must stay with us." He pointed back to the east. "And you must leave, while you still can."

Father Fitzwilliam bowed his head and made the sign of the cross over Declan. His shoulders shook as he turned to make his way back through the forest toward the fort.

*　◇　*

Two Hearts forced the dazed stranger deeper into the heart of the forest, although there was little chance the English would return. But they had left behind three dead bodies, one killed by arrows and two more with their throats torn out by the dogs, and the English, who seemed to understand nothing of the sacredness of revenge or the principal rules of warfare, had been known to do foolishnesses like put themselves in great danger to return for their uncaring dead.

His mind kept coming back to the spirit who had answered their calling. Rattlesnake was a creature of Fire, akin to his sky brother, Lightning. Two Hearts' own strengths lay in the medicine ways of Earth and Air, a balanced pair of opposites, and the source of much power. Still, he could never have called such a creature unaided. As he had seen over and over, beginning with that dream encounter on the river, the stranger was gifted, though untutored, in the medicines of Fire and Water, the other powerful pair of opposites. The two pairs together comprised all four of the medicine ways, and four was one of the most sacred of numbers, second only to seven. The snake spirit they had summoned between them had been a massive working, impossible for one man alone, no matter how experienced.

Back in the village, he had thought to call this man "Acorn," until he had shown himself worthy of another, more impressive name, but now it was plain that Acorn would not do. The stranger had already proved himself deserving of a more powerful name. Two Hearts would have to give it careful thought.

Before he had Nightshadow move the stranger, he told Smoke to take Sunrunner and trail the strangers to the brink of the dead lands. "If any remain, we must know of it." He rubbed his forehead with the heel of his hand. "When you are sure they have gone, return to the village and warn them of what has happened here."

Sunrunner's golden ears pricked as Smoke gestured to him. He had taken a wound from the red-coats' firesticks, but fortunately it was little more than a scratch. Smoke vaulted onto his clan-mate's furred back, and together they sped away into the endless trees, silent as ghosts, unlike the elk-dogs of the English, great, clumsy, clumping creatures that anyone could hear long before they were close enough to see. They frightened easily too, and were difficult to control, and fled at the sight of danger, unlike a Tsalagi dog, who was as much protection to his clan-mate as a mount. Two Hearts wondered why the English had never thought to bring their dogs to this land. It was fortunate they had not.

The stranger lay propped against a knobby maple root. His eyelids were shut and his chest rose and fell as though he had been running. Sweat beaded his forehead. A fine covering of beard stubble covered his cheeks and chin. Sometimes one of the Real People had hair on the face like that, but it was rare.

Two Hearts hunkered down beside the exhausted stranger and went back to the matter of a name. Names gave shape to a man's or woman's character. They had to fit just so, and help the individual progress in the direction they needed to travel.

Nightshadow padded out of the underbrush and dropped a limp fawn at his feet. Her black eyes danced, saying she had done well, hunting alone, and she knew it. She lay down beside the stranger with her muzzle propped on her forelegs, and watched him breathe as though it were the most important thing in her world.

Two Hearts pulled out his knife and set to work skinning the fawn. He did not know how long it would take Smoke and Sunrunner to trail the intruders back the edge of the dead lands, but this young stranger needed rest and food after such a great effort, as did Two Hearts himself. Such deeds were not accomplished without cost. It was fortunate they had Nightshadow's help.

The stranger stirred, his eyes darting beneath his closed eyelids, dreaming. He turned over, then bolted up with a shout and stared at the place under the tree where the great snake had been called into existence. His blue eyes were haunted.

"It was a great working, although you put yourself at risk again." Two Hearts cut the fawn's hide from the tender flesh. "I could not have done it alone."

"What I did," Declan said, "was wrong." He passed a trembling hand over his colorless face. "I have taken wrongness into my heart and now I shall die for it."

"Your old life is dead." Two Hearts flipped the fawn carcass over. "But you are young and will make a new life here among the Tsalagi where you are needed. We shall give you a fitting name." He thought back to the first time he had seen Declan riding on Long Man's back, and then of the dream they had shared. He had called a snake then too, so that spirit obviously had special significance in his life.

He narrowed his eyes. "Your name," he said, "shall be Snake."

chapter ten

Insisting that Declan ride the black dog, the shaman took him so deep into the forest that he could no longer make out the sun, just layer upon layer of interwoven tree limbs imprisoning him beneath in cool shade. Vines twined the trunks of trees and hung like fat serpents from overhanging branches. Gray, lichen-covered rocks lay tumbled about, and the glen where they finally stopped had a feeling of great antiquity. What little light filtered through the trees was just a another hue of green, barely discernible beneath the fluttering leaves.

"Those who are given power spend their life in service to the Above Beings," Two Hearts said. Although he was only of average height, he seemed taller somehow in the heart of the vast forest and his brown eyes burned fever-bright. "Rattlesnake is sacred to us, and he has come to you twice now. He represents balanced pairs of opposites, death and rebirth, male and female, sickness and healing—"

Declan remembered the look of betrayal on Father Fitzwilliam's face when the serpent apparition had been called into being. Declan Connolly had died in that instant. He must be Snake now, as Two Hearts had named him, because Declan would never do what *he* had done, never open his heart to the Devil and cast his immortal soul aside like so much refuse. But Snake had done that, had he not, and so very much more.

"—call the sacred fire," Two Hearts was saying. "Watch and see how it is done." He bowed his head and chanted in a low, melodious voice.

The shaman's words rolled over Declan like a river rushing inexorably downstream, carrying him toward some vast, dark sea. He looked away, wishing he could stop thinking, stop breathing, stop caring altogether what happened to him.

Two Hearts' chant droned on as the older man rested his hands palm-down on his thighs. His stern face relaxed as he sat swaying before a pile of gathered wood. The feather in the hair tuft on top of his head nodded in time with his words and his eyes closed to mere slits.

Declan felt an alteration in the air, a subtle building of energies. He saw the Tsalagi raise his hands toward the twigs. The hair on the back of Declan's arms stirred and then shimmering red-gold-orange fire streamed from Two Hearts' hands in a joyous outpouring that touched Declan inside somehow. He flinched, both drawn and frightened.

The flames danced over the piled wood without consuming it, composed of independent figures intertwined in some preordained fashion. The smoke generated was as sweet and soothing as any balsam Declan had ever burned before a church altar.

Two Hearts leaned forward. "What do you see?"

He was afraid to look, but the gyrating figures caught his eyes and would not let him go. He moistened his lips. "An eagle . . . dancing with its wings held up like arms . . . " The flames expanded until they were the whole world, and he was within the fire, rather than without. He shuddered, imprisoned within walls of naked yellow flame. ". . . and a snake with eyes like diamonds . . . a man with a shimmering face that keeps changing . . . and a . . ." He squinted. ". . . a woman with hair that touches the ground." The fiery figures danced and spun, each in harmony with the other three, forming a pattern that tugged at his heart and made it difficult to breathe.

Two Hearts stepped through the wall of flame and stood before him. His eyes grew into fierce black stars and Declan fought to break away from their stare. "Has Eagle ever come to you before?"

Declan started to say no, but his lips would not form the word.

"When?" Two Hearts demanded.

Declan trembled. "I—do not know."

Two Hearts seized Declan's head between his hands. His dark eyes bored into the younger man's helpless gaze. "Remember."

A dizziness rushed over him as though he were falling. He was there, suddenly, on the boat with Father Fitzwilliam after leaving the village and trying again, futilely, to pray. Blue-white light simmered behind his eyelids, filled with unfamiliar shapes, these same figures. "On the . . . boat."

"And what did he say?"

"No-nothing," Declan faltered, but there had been something, some sort of sign, the back of his mind insisted.

"What?" Two Hearts' fingers bit into his temples. "Think back."

"He left me a golden feather," Declan heard himself say, then the flame-figures drew him out of his body to join their wild, spinning dance. He slumped to the ground and knew no more.

*　◇　*

One Eye huddled against the bark of a lightning-split oak, arms crossed over his scarred chest, fighting the pain that wracked him from toes to ears. He hurt, oh yes, he hurt more every time he scouted for the detested English on Tsalagi land. With the first step and each one thereafter, *life* tingled up through his feet and into his lungs, shimmered behind his eyes until he could hardly see, as painful to his entire being as the return of sensation to a limb whose circulation has been cut off.

But this was Tsalagi life, not Catawba, only a cruel echo of the connection to the land his people had known. With the coming of the English, the proud trees had been felled to construct their stinking lodges, the soil had been ripped apart by plows, even the very water fouled with their wastes. Each additional indignity leeched the lifeforce from the Catawbas' land until, with the death of three out of every four of his people from the invaders' foul diseases, the spirit of the land had been extinguished forever.

Even if the English left tomorrow, the Catawba shamen had all died at the hands of the red-coated soldiers and none were left who knew the ceremonies for paying proper respect to the spirits and calling life back into the desecrated land. The Catawba women who had survived the ravages of the spotted sickness now warmed the beds of white men and the children they bore were pale, weak creatures who often died as well without the proper rites to welcome them into the world. Soon, there would be no Catawbas left on the face of this earth, but at least then their pain would be over.

With an effort, he straightened his emaciated frame. As long as he did not think about the enormity of his people's loss, walking this land was more bearable, but the potent medicine power called up between the Tsalagi shaman and the runaway English stranger had shattered his indifference and forced him to remember his previous life. Remembering made him hurt, and hurting made him angry, filled him with the galling blackness of hate until he was overflowing.

He heard crashing in the underbrush, heading toward the nearby river, one of the foolish English, no doubt, on foot without one of their stupid, empty-headed elk-dogs to bear him on its back. No Tsalagi, man or dog, no matter how badly hurt, would ever make such a clumsy commotion. Gritting his teeth against the pain, he set off after the source, holding his hate before him like a shield.

He would locate those English who had survived and guide them back to the fort because it was only through their kind that he would ever find surcease. When all the land lay under English control and was finally, safely dead, then at last he would be able to forget what it was like to be alive.

It was not much, but it was all he could hope for.

*   ◊   *

Ears down, Nightshadow settled in the black shadows of a gully between the exposed roots of an ancient maple, and watched the two-legs call that strange fire which was more-than-fire. Now it burned, half here, where she could smell it, and half in that place-beyond-sight which she sometimes visited when her eyes were closed and her body stretched out in sleep. She had encountered such half-things as this before, and always they perplexed her.

More than once, when her eyes were thus closed, she had seen the other two-legs, the new one, in that other place, smelled the exciting rightness of his essence, the blandness of not-clan laced with the familiar spicy essence of Clan. When she carried him on her back earlier, his hands had shaken, and he smelled sad and despondent, as far beyond mere weariness as death was beyond sleep. Somehow, he was both Clan and not, two opposite things at the same time, equally compelling and puzzling. She whined. It hurt her head to think about that.

Since her beloved clan-mate had gone to the Night Country, she had hunted alone for many bright, steamy days and then many more cold ones, the wind keening in her ears like an abandoned pup and always a fierce, hollow ache behind her ribs as though she hungered for something she could not name. More than once, she had lain down, intending to go to that other land-beyond-eyes, where she might find the one she had lost, but each time, those-beyond-sight, who lived on a great windswept mountain, turned her back, saying she had rabbits yet to hunt, forests to run, a man for whom to fight.

Now that *he* had finally come, she would guard his back as they explored the forest and climbed the soaring rock-crested hills together, two creatures with but one fierce mind between them, and the wind in their nostrils would always be sweet.

She shifted uneasily as she watched the two-leggeds make mouth noises at each other and wave their spindly forelegs. Beyond the surrounding tangle of vine and bush and tree, she smelled the itchy musk of deer and the enticing hot scent of foolish, overbold turkey, but stilled her eagerness. Not yet.

Her new two-legs cried out, then slumped to the ground, hurt in some way she could not understand. She leaped to her feet, the fur bristling across her shoulders.

The other man, the not-clan, waved her back. She evaluated the set of his head, the line of his spine and legs. They spoke "worry" and "dissatisfaction," and then "strong need," but nothing of intention to harm. Reassured, she curled up between the gnarled roots again to wait for the running times which surely would come when her new, much cherished two-legs woke. He would throw back his head and howl his love of the hunt, and together they would share the hot excitement of the kill.

✳ ◇ ✳

Two Hearts sat back on his heels and contemplated the sacred fire. What now? Snake had seen Eagle, who was an Air spirit, and Rattlesnake, who was made of Fire, a shimmering person, who had to be Long Man, a Water spirit— and a woman. It could have been Willow Woman or Old Corn Woman, who were both of Earth medicine, or even some other spirit. Perhaps he should have allowed his sister's daughter to accompany him on this journey. Although Berry was young, she had trained in the ways of the plant-people and her perceptions were often enlightening.

Snake lay in a hollow lined with fallen leaves, limp as a new-born, breathing with a shallowness that told of exhaustion. His face gleamed palely in the dimness and his eyes moved beneath closed lids. With no preparation or chance for understanding, he had already seen more of the spirits in the last few days than most shamen experienced in a lifetime. Nightshadow stretched out a few lengths away, her alert black gaze trained, as always, upon the stranger.

No, not "the stranger," he corrected himself, *Snake*, who was to be one of them now in spirit, if not in body. The Above Beings knew what they were doing, although often their intent was difficult to interpret. They always had a reason for what they did; it was up to him to puzzle it out.

They had sent Snake to him, untrained and afraid, reluctant to bare his spirit, so that must be Two Hearts' first goal, to reconcile him to his new status. He would teach him to purify himself and to meditate, to be quiet and learn from the spirit-voices that presently terrified him. Medicine power was an awesome responsibility, but it was also full of wonder and joy when approached properly. It was his function to make Snake experience that wonder.

Snake groaned and opened his eyes.

Two Hearts hunkered down beside him. "How do you feel?"

The younger man threw an arm over his eyes and turned away, his shoulders hunched.

Two Hearts pulled his arm aside. "I ask this for a reason—how do you feel?"

"It does not matter."

"Everything matters." Two Hearts swept his arm to indicate the space under the spreading tree. "Everything is connected. How you feel is part of how stars glide through the sky and how deer feed in the evening, how the river rises after rain—"

Snake cried out something unintelligible and buried his face in his arms, shivering, even though the air was steamy. Next to the tree trunk, the dog's ears pricked and she crept forward to prop her muzzle on his knee, her dark eyes anxious.

Two Hearts settled on a fallen log on the other side of the fire, chin in hand, pondering. Snake had come late to the abilities which now transformed his life. He had reached manhood on the other side of the big salt water among people with vastly different ideas about life, who, as far as he had been able to tell, knew nothing of the spirit world.

If he had been born Tsalagi, preparations for his future would have begun at birth, for the portents would have predicted a child of potential and a shaman would have been on hand when first he drew breath. He would have been trained to avoid unclean people and foods, monitored carefully by parents and relatives, taught to fast and purify himself, and eventually assigned to the care of a shaman, such as himself. He would have spent his entire childhood in preparation for what Snake was now experiencing.

A new name was only the beginning. Snake needed to unlearn the erroneous concepts and values his foreign upbringing had taught him, so he might absorb what he needed to know now. As it was, the contradictions and fear were killing him. Two Hearts reached into his medicine pouch and withdrew a pinch of sacred tobacco, remade in the most exacting of ceremonies to endow it with more power. He sprinkled it over the fire, and then, closing his eyes, chanted to the Above Beings, asking for guidance. After the fourth repetition of the chant, he felt his spirit drift into the overlap between the worlds.

He saw an old woman with green hair shot through with silver threads the shade of the full moon. She stood before him, bent as an elderly willow and yet as beautiful as the loveliest maiden he had ever seen. Her eyes shone like stars and he could not look away.

"What would you ask of me, grandson?" The corners of her eyes crinkled and the goodness she wore about her like a cloak warmed his heart.

"The stranger you have given into my hands is sorely troubled," he said. "I cannot find the words to ease his mind."

"There are no words for him as he is now." The wind blew her long hair back behind her shoulders until it filled the sky and the stars became her ornaments. *"His mind has been bound into the most rigid of patterns and he hears nothing you say."* She gazed sadly at sleeping man. *"Like the tobacco, he must be remade so he may come into his full power."*

Two Hearts bowed his head. "I—do not understand."

"Build a sweatlodge," she said, *"and once you have taken him within, cast sacred tobacco that has been remade with lightning onto the coals . . ."*

Her voice faded, although Two Hearts waited until every muscle in his body ached in the hope she might continue, there was nothing more. Finally, he opened his eyes and stretched. Snake slept, curled up on his side, his breath stirring the blades of grass. The sacred fire had lapsed into ordinary flames and then burned down into glowing embers. Above the trees, the afternoon had faded into the soft dusk of early evening, but beneath the dense canopy of leaves, it might as well have been the deepest part of the night.

A sweatlodge . . . He glanced around, already planning, but it was too dark to find saplings of the proper thickness. Tomorrow, then, he would start.

Declan found himself in the nave of a huge cathedral whose ceiling was lost in a haze of golden light. The pillars were not the usual polished marble columns, but the trunks of massive, gray-brown trees. Jays scolded him from the branches and he heard the scritch of claws as squirrels leaped amidst the leaves. The floor, which should have been marble, was soft springy moss and grass, and fallen leaves strewn over dark-red soil. Honeysuckle and pine and the faint musk of deer scented the air.

He had toured St. Patrick's in Dublin, as well as Christchurch, both mighty cathedrals of stone, originally built by the Catholic Church, although the King of England had long ago appropriated them for his own watered-down denomination. Declan remembered the breathless, echoing silence which filled the shadowy aisles and how he had walked, enthralled, studying the exquisite work produced by devout artisans over generations. This place had the same sort of immense importance, a feeling of both great weight and freedom.

He wandered toward the altar, barely visible at the end of the long double aisle of trees. Slender-necked does peeked through the trees, watching him with luminous brown eyes. He edged past a fat black bear scratching its back against a stump, then a brown one, digging under a fallen log with great curving claws. They stopped and snuffled at him, their dark gaze mysteriously wise. Overhead, a mockingbird burst into song.

Each animal fell in behind as he passed, deer and bears and birds and wolves. Ahead, where transept and nave intersected, stood a huge altar of rough gray stone. A tall woman waited beside it, her eyes sober. She had the broad face and high cheekbones of a native. Her long green hair was bound with strips of brown fur and she wore a hide dress decorated with elaborate green and blue beading, trimmed with rows of red feathers.

"What is this place?" He turned slowly, taking in the vine-draped trees, the branches stirring in the breeze, the inquisitive wolves who watched him with sharp black eyes. "I've never seen anything like it. A cathedral should be made of stone and plaster and wooden beams."

She took his hand and her touch shocked like fresh, cold water straight from the spring. "Before there were men to quarry stone and cut wood," she said softly, "before men learned to shape and paint and plaster, *this* was the first cathedral."

The wolves pressed closer until their fur brushed his legs and he could smell the oiliness of their coats. The grass floor came alive with gray-brown rabbits and bright-eyed mice and chipmunks and tiny blind moles feeling their way with minute pink noses. He could not move for fear of trampling some creature.

"Where can you give thanks, if not here, in the most sacred of places?" she asked. "Where else can you know the measure of those who made the world?"

He snatched his hand from hers. His adam's-apple bobbed as he swallowed hard. "*God* made the world, no other!"

She gazed at him serenely. "Bide here, and, these, your relatives, will tell you the secrets you most long to know." The surrounding animals studied him with eyes that plainly understood far more than he ever could.

He turned and fled.

chapter eleven

Declan awoke the next morning to the sound of blows ringing through the trees, as though someone were chopping with an ax. For a moment, he couldn't remember where he was, then despair surged back over him; he wasn't Declan anymore. He was Snake, a miscreant cast out of God's grace and living unshriven among heathens.

A pile of long, slender saplings lay beside the ashes of yesterday's fire, and the huge black dog was curled up a few feet beyond, her steady gaze trained upon his face. Two Hearts stalked back through the maze of trees, his arms filled with cut saplings. His face was set, and his already prominent nose stood out, sharp as a knife, as though something had leached away everything in his nature that was vulnerable or uncertain. He frowned when he saw Declan awake and then laid the saplings with the others he had already cut. "We must go to the stream and purify ourselves."

Declan wavered onto his feet and limped after the older man, too miserable to protest. The rocks and brush cut his already abused feet and made him even slower. The black dog rose, shook herself and followed, never allowing him to get more than a body length ahead. By the time he reached the moss-edged stream, Two Hearts had already stripped and was drenching himself from the head down with scooped handfuls of water.

Declan hesitated, but the stream was clear and inviting, and every inch of his skin itched as though it had been years since he was clean. He waded into the cool water up to his shins and followed Two Hearts' example, washing as thoroughly as he could without soap. The water's tingle penetrated, not only his skin, but bone and nerve, and oddly enough, seemed to wash something more than dirt away as it trickled back into the stream. He felt lighter somehow, energized.

After they had dried themselves with handfuls of moss, Two Hearts led him back without a word or glance. Hunkering on his heels, he picked up a sharp-edged stone and drilled holes in the rich red earth. His lined copper face was intent on his work and he seemed unaware of the younger man.

Declan settled in the cool shadows, his stomach hollow with hunger, and watched him work. The black dog turned three times in a tight circle, then curled up, nose on forepaws, and narrowed her eyes to watchful slits. He leaned his head against the trunk and let the forest sounds flow over him: the whine of insects and the creaking of frogs, the cheerful rasp of crickets, the scrape of the knife over wood.

Midday came and went without any notice from Two Hearts. He bent each sapling into an arch and seated the ends in holes he had already dug. Now he was weaving rushes through the poles, making the framework of a small rounded house. Declan watched him through slitted eyelids, but it all seemed very distant and uninvolved with himself.

The insect whine sharpened into tiny predatory voices, savage with blood-lust, and he had to concentrate to shut them out. And each time he relaxed and let his mind drift, they came back, along with the frogs' soulful mating calls and the crickets' cheerful celebration of living.

By evening, hunger was a constant torment and Declan's hand shook as he raised it to brush away an insistent fly. Nightshadow had followed him to the stream several times and allowed him to drink, but then, ears flattened, firmly herded him back. As far as he could tell, the Tsalagi had foregone both water and food the entire day.

Two Hearts finished with the reeds in late afternoon and began to coat the structure with handfuls of mud, making a shell on the outside. Declan watched him dully, fighting an increasingly difficult battle to keep the voices out of his head and wondering how long it took to die of starvation.

When the coat of mud was completed, Two Hearts crawled through the small opening and began digging a pit inside. It was quite dark when he reemerged and sat, head hanging for a moment.

Declan cleared his throat. "What—is that?"

Two Hearts raised his head. "It is a sweatlodge, a very sacred place, combining all four of the medicines."

A prickle ran down Declan's spine. Father Fitzwilliam had mentioned such structures on the long sea passage when he was educating Declan on the customs of the Tsalagi. They were used in ceremonies of some sort. Nightshadow came to lie at his side, her muzzle touching his leg. Hesitantly, he rested a hand on her soft head. She sighed and pressed closer.

Two Hearts piled twigs inside the sweatlodge, then kindled a fire with two pieces of wood, twirling the stick between his palms so quickly that Declan's eyes could not follow. Finally, a trickle of smoke wafted upwards. The Tsalagi fed bits of moss to the tiny flame, and gradually the fire grew. When it blazed, he placed several burning brands inside the sweatlodge. After a minute, smoke curled lazily from a small hole on top of the structure.

"I will keep the fire going through the night so the lodge will cure by morning." Two Hearts sat cross-legged and rested his hands on his thighs. His eyes looked past Declan, past the trees, focused on something only he could see.

* ◇ *

General Carleton studied the three mud-spattered, insect-chewed men at his study door with barely restrained anger. He raised a tumbler to his lips and sipped before he spoke, letting the brandy's smooth amber fire roll down his throat. "You lost an entire troop of men out there in the backcountry, and you have the nerve to stand here and tell me that you didn't even kill one of the shamen who attacked you?"

Evan Jones, the captain in charge, stepped forward, his big Welsh hands crushing the tattered remains of his hat. "We were all set to bring that runaway priest back, sir, as you instructed." His voice was hoarse with exhaustion and hunger. "Then they was upon us, damned Tsalagi shamen with those big devil dogs that scare the horses witless. I hit one of the blasted dogs right off, and I thought we would take the whole lot down."

His throat worked and he passed a hand over his face, struggling for control. "Then that young priest got loose and started making magic with the natives—" His voice broke and he set his jaw.

Sir Guy's voice was chill. "What kind of magic, Captain?"

"They conjured a—a big snake, sir, out of light." Jones squeezed his eyes shut. "It was twice as tall as a man and it—it—" His chest heaved.

"It what?"

"It ate Bingham, sir. After that, there wasn't anything we could do but run for our lives. Not all of us made it, although I still have One Eye out looking for stragglers."

Sir Guy swirled the amber liquid in his glass, watching it catch the glow of the lamp and fire. "And Father Fitzwilliam?"

"No sign of him yet, sir, but it's too early to give up hope."

Hope . . . Sir Guy's lips twitched at the corners. Not exactly the word he would use to describe his present emotions concerning the troublesome Irish priest. He set the glass down on his desk. "Take yourself and your men, what's *left* of them, that is, down to the surgeon and have your wounds tended. I'll expect you back here in the morning to give a fuller accounting of this inexcusable—" His eyes narrowed. "—misadventure. Do I make myself understood?"

"Yes, sir." Jones saluted wearily, and was echoed by the two dazed soldiers behind him. They turned and clumped out of the room, closing the door behind them with exaggerated care.

Sir Guy leaned back in his chair and fit his fingers together, tip to tip, staring over them at the formal portrait of his Roman-nosed wife hung on the wall. A satisfied smile shaped her lips. They had never been able to stand each other. Her father had sought the Carleton name, while his had desired the girl's considerable dowry. She would laugh if she were here, laugh in his face and flaunt her amusement.

Damn priests! Employing them in this project had not been his idea, and he had yet to see that most of them were doing much good, but working magic, now that was a new and unexpected development. If Connolly's actions were an indication of things to come and more priests took up magic against the English, the entire breed had clearly outlived its usefulness to the King's cause. He'd never trusted them as far as he could see them anyway.

Just how much of this had Fitzwilliam known when he asked for decent God-fearing English soldiers to accompany him on his search? Had he been aware that young Connolly had gone over to the other side, and how solid were his own loyalties anyway? Little love had been lost between the Irish and the English down through the centuries.

Clearly, the policy of conversion had proved ineffective. The time had come to modify their tactics. He would insist that Fitzwilliam, if he survived, and the rest of the priests under his command, stop their useless proselytizing at once. He would authorize instead a series of "trading" expeditions flying the green flag of trade, which the natives now recognized, and instruct the priests to identify all shamen immediately upon arriving in each village. His troops would receive orders to fire at that point, eliminating all chance of reprisal. Any priest who refused to comply with orders would be shot as a traitor and left to rot.

Reinforcements were due within the next two weeks. If all went well, the villages would be in a turmoil by then. With any luck, once the shamen were eliminated, smallpox and measles would follow just as they had with the Catawbas. Most of the natives would die, as they had weak constitutions, and England would control this stretch of land before any of his counterparts stationed up and down the coast managed to do the same.

He picked up his brandy again and toasted the whole concept. The King would reward him with money and lands. He would sail home a hero and never have to set foot on this benighted, magic-infested continent again.

He folded his arms behind his white wig and smiled to himself.

✳ ◇ ✳

After spending a miserable night in which his stomach tried to turn itself inside out with hunger and the stars whispered incessantly in hard bright voices of virtuous maidens and brave heroes and all the wondrous things they had supposedly done, Declan opened his eyes in the first vague light of dawn to see Two Hearts still seated beside the sweatlodge, hands resting loosely on his thighs. A wisp of gray smoke seeped from the hole on the top of the round hut.

The Tsalagi's eyes shifted as Declan sat up. "We must purify ourselves." He rose stiffly to his feet and stalked toward the stream without a backwards glance.

Declan buried his face in his hands, too weary to move, but Nightshadow nudged him with her cold nose and then licked his ear, seeming to urge him to follow. He pulled himself up using the tree trunk for support and stumbled after Two Hearts, too light-headed from lack of food to watch where he placed his feet.

Two Hearts stood in the middle of the stream, already naked and waiting. The water gleamed like quicksilver in the uncertain light filtering down through the trees. "You must wash seven times," he said gruffly.

Declan stared at him dumbly.

"To purify yourself." Two Hearts scooped up a handful of water and doused his head. "You must be ready."

"Ready for what?" Declan asked, but there was no answer. His legs trembled and the leaves were waking over his head, greeting the light with thin green joyful voices. He shuddered and splashed into the stream, still clad in the breechcloth, then fell to his knees as his vision blurred and everything seemed to tilt sideways.

Nightshadow plunged in after him and thrust her head under his arm. He clung to her neck.

Two Hearts watched him with no apparent concern. "Seven times," he repeated firmly and bent down for another handful.

Leaning against the dog's warm side, Declan lifted the clear water in his cupped hands and poured it over his head. The cobwebs in his brain lessened with the first cool rush and he breathed deeply, fighting to regain his strength.

A redbird alighted on a low hanging branch and regarded him with eyes like two black beads. *"Get on with it!"* the creature said saucily and fluttered off.

He stared after it, then with a sigh, went back to his ablutions. When he finished his seventh dousing, Nightshadow scrambled out of the stream and shook herself dry while he rubbed the water from his shivering body with his hands. Two Hearts nodded and walked purposefully back to the sweatlodge, still naked and dripping. Declan followed, clearer headed than he had been in hours, but unable to shut the murmuring voices of the trees and the creatures out of his head.

Two Hearts gestured at the hut. "Go inside."

Declan stared.

The Tsalagi took his arm and at his touch, the voices swooped back in full measure, deafening him as badly as the very first time. He swayed and covered his ears with his hands.

"Go inside."

Declan's knees bent and he found himself crawling through the small doorway into the smoky darkness where a pit of smoldering coals contained four round stones from the stream and just enough room for two men to sit. His eyes burned as he scooted as far from the smoking fire as possible.

Two Hearts crawled in after him, dragging his medicine pouch. He edged around to sit cross-legged. "The sweatlodge is a place of great power, combining the four sacred medicine ways, wood and mud and stone for Earth, steam for Water, smoke for Air, and coals containing the essence of Fire." He poured a bark cupful of water on the hot stones and chanted in a low, monotonous tone. The water danced and hissed over the stones, rising as steam. Two Hearts' unintelligible words swirled through the sweltering dimness, lulled Declan, weighted his eyelids so that it took all his will to keep them open.

Taking a pinch of something from his pouch, Two Hearts cast it onto the coals. A pungent, not unpleasant odor filled the sweatlodge. Declan squinted as the smoke took the shape of a face, an old woman with silver-streaked green hair blinking solemnly back at him.

"Grandson, you are distressed," she said in a surprisingly vibrant voice.

He glanced at Two Hearts, but the other man did not acknowledge the apparition. He shivered, wishing he did not see it either. More damning magic, he thought, more freight for his damaged soul to bear. "I beseech thee, Oh Lord," he cried in an unsteady voice, "hear my prayer!"

"I do hear you," the old woman said. *"Did you think I would not, no matter what*

shape I wore, what name?"

Declan's chest heaved. "There is but one Lord!"

"The Great Creator has many names and shapes," she said, *"but they are all one."*

He turned away, hands over his ears, squeezing his eyes shut. He would not listen to such blasphemy!

"Your path is long and burdensome, grandson, and in my name you will bear many troubles before your day is done." Her voice was gentle. *"Therefore I remake you now to both increase your power and relieve your burden for a time, so that you might better learn and be prepared for what is to come."*

A warmth blossomed in the middle of his forehead and spread in widening circles through his body, soothing away fear and distress . . . uncertainty . . . thoughts of damnation and unworthiness . . . guilt . . .

Cocooned in love and acceptance, he closed his eyes and slept.

chapter twelve

He awoke mid-morning, shaded by whispering green leaves and surrounded by the scent of grass and pine and flowering sweet-gum. Dappled light trickled down through the interwoven foliage, skipping over his forearm as a breeze stirred the trees overhead, teasing him like a lover. He watched it, bemused.

Fat sizzled, and he realized someone was cooking nearby. He rolled over and caught the scent of roasting meat. His stomach immediately cramped with hunger. He sat up, brushing twigs and a few leaves from his bare shoulders. A middle-aged man with a fierce tuft of gray-streaked black hair on the crown of his head glanced up from a small fire.

He met the man's intense dark eyes, not recognizing him, or anything else, for that matter. Uneasiness filtered through his mind as he examined the scene for something familiar and found nothing. Just behind the man stood a tiny mud-wattled hut, and beyond that sat a massive black dog, watching him with an alert expression.

The man gestured at the roasted rabbit. "Eat."

"Uh, thank you," he said in the same tongue, which sounded strange, yet somehow came easily to him. When he stood, he saw, to his consternation, that he wore only a piece of hide wrapped around his waist and groin. It didn't seem right to be dressed in such a brief fashion, and yet the unfamiliar garment was durable and cool and comfortable.

The other man tore off a browned haunch and held it out. He accepted it, juggled the hot meat from hand to hand, then laid it on a rock to cool. "I do not know your name."

The man looked away, but a tightness loosened around his eyes. "I am Two Hearts, an uko of Kitasi."

He did not know what that meant, but picked up the haunch again and nibbled cautiously. It was tender and juicy, so he took a larger bite. "Have we met before?"

"You are Snake, my apprentice." Two Hearts dug several roasted roots out of the coals with a stick and pushed one toward him.

"Snake?" He sat silently, probing his mind.

"It is an honorable name," Two Hearts said. "Rattlesnake is a powerful sign, combining many dualities, capable of both great good and evil, both deadly and life-giving like all the most potent energies." He picked up a roasted root and peeled the steaming skin back. "What do you remember?"

Snake reached into his mind, but where his memories should have been, there was only a vague sense of something missing. "Nothing—I cannot remember you or anything else!"

Two Hearts waved a greasy hand at him. "That is as it should be. For now, you have shed your memories as our brother Rattlesnake sheds his skin, so that you may grow strong and wise. You will remember when the time is right, so do not waste your strength in trying before you are ready." He wiped his hands in the grass. "For now, we will continue your training."

Snake finished the meat in silence, then ate a second serving Two Hearts pressed upon him. It was troubling, this not remembering. A breeze skittered through the trees, swaying the branches, cooling his skin. The black dog, as tall at the shoulder as a man, picked its way between roots and bushes to sit at his side. He reached out a hand and let the coal-black nose take in his scent.

"She is called Nightshadow," Two Hearts said offhandedly. "She runs with you because you are her clan-mate."

"Clan?" Snake echoed in confusion. "I do not understand."

"Dog Clan." Two Hearts picked up a steaming root and blew on it.

Nightshadow lay down and leaned against Snake's back companionably. He liked the clean, faintly musky scent of her fur. "Do you have a dog too?"

"No, the great dogs choose only from those born to, or adopted by the Dog Clan. I am of the Deer Clan." He took a bite of root.

Nightshadow rested her muzzle on his shoulder. He turned and stroked her silken forehead with its dazzling white spot. "How did she get so—" Snake hesitated. For some reason it seemed to him that dogs ought to be much smaller. "—so *big*?"

"Long long ago, dogs were no bigger than their wild brothers, the wolves." Two Hearts swallowed the last of the root. "They lived at the edge of the village and barked when strangers came. They were wise and good-hearted, but too small to be of any real help in hunting or war. Finally one day their chief, a fine dog, whiter than sunlight dancing on snow, said to the others, `For many seasons now we have wished to help the people of our village when it came to the hard work for which teeth are especially suited, such as hunting and fighting, but our small size has always prevented us.'

"The other dogs all yowled their grief that this was indeed the way of things.

"`So, from this day forward, we must do everything we can to grow bigger. We will kill only our brothers the bison and the bear and the elk and eat of their flesh, that we may share in their great size. And at the time of mating, each female shall select only the largest of males for her mate, so that she will birth larger pups, and then only one pup at a time, so each will have the best chance to grow.'

"The other dogs argued and growled, for they could see many of them would starve if they could not pull down one of the bigger animals, and most of them would no longer mate, if only the largest were permitted.

"But they watched the men of their villages fight their fiercest enemies, the Pawnees and the Creeks, and hunt without teeth, knowing they could help if they could just grow bigger, until at last all agreed to the white dog's plan. As time passed, the villages noticed how fine and large dogs were becoming, and how, when enemies attacked, dogs fought at their side with sharp teeth and claws. They realized what dogs had always known, that men and dogs have been brothers all the way back to the beginning times.

"There had always been six clans among the Tsalagi living together in each village, but now the people said, `Let us form a seventh clan, made of those among the other six who best love our brothers the dogs.'

"And the dogs sent their chief, a descendent of the white dog, a fine brindle-brown containing every color that a dog might be in his coat. The brindle said, `Let *us* select those who will be of the Dog Clan, for we know them already.'

"They prowled through each village along the winding rivers and sniffed out each man and woman who truly loved their kind. These became the first Dog Clan and their descendents have hunted and scouted and fought alongside their dog clan-mates ever since."

Two Hearts brushed his hands off and stood. "Now, we must break camp and journey to the foot of the great stone mountain."

Snake stuffed the last bit of chewy root into his mouth. "Why?"

"Because it is there we will find a place of great power with which to teach you control." Two Hearts bent to pick up a pouch and then tied it to his belt. "If you do not learn control, you will never survive what is to come."

✳ ◇ ✳

Riding double into Fort Pembroke on a skittish black gelding behind the sullen One Eye, Father Fitzwilliam could not believe he had only been gone two days. In that short length of time, the world had turned itself inside out. Not only had young Declan been contaminated with native magic, he had employed it against his own kind and *killed* a man. Fitzwilliam passed a hand across his sweating forehead, sickened at the memory.

One Eye slid off the horse, limber as an eel. Fitzwilliam attempted to follow, then half-fell to the ground. His head seemed incredibly distant from his feet and the earth had an insubstantial feel to it. He clung to the horse's tangled mane with trembling fingers. He'd had no food since before the disastrous encounter with Declan, but the enforced fast was a just penance for his sin of overwhelming hubris. He had been so foolish to think he knew more than other men and could save Declan's soul, could wash him free of the Devil's terrible stain when only God could accomplish that miracle, and then only if Declan truly repented.

The sentry stepped forward and took his arm. His lips frowned underneath his brown mustache. "Father Fitzwilliam, General Carleton left word for you to report to his office the second you arrived."

Fitzwilliam nodded, not trusting his voice. Standing at the gelding's head, One Eye watched him with a dark eye too dull to be truly alive. A black-agate eye, he thought, set into the sockets of a dead man's skull. He shuddered and released the horse's mane, managing to stand unassisted.

He watched his unsteady feet as he climbed the stairs up to the office, afraid if he lost focus even for an instant, he would fall. At the top, he brushed at his stained cassock, then knocked on Carleton's door.

Footsteps thumped across the floor. "Enter."

With great care, he grasped the porcelain doorknob with both hands and turned it. Everything had a glaze of unreality, as though he were only dreaming.

"Fitzwilliam!" Carleton's urbane face scowled beneath a well-groomed white wig. "I wish you to explain just what the hell you thought you were about when you conducted my men into an ambush!"

Fitzwilliam kept a close watch on his feet again as he walked into the office, one step—two—three. The room smelled of hot tea and freshly baked bread. He caught a glimpse of a heavily laden tray on a table in the corner, then returned his gaze to the floor. The carpet was cream-colored, with a riot of flowers in the center surrounded by dark-green borders. Expensive, he thought, and hard to clean, impractical in this wild land of red clay and frequent rain. He blinked down at it, tracing the curving vines and the nodding red-orange heads of the flowers. The pattern seemed to hold a hidden meaning—

"Father Fitzwilliam!"

He glanced bewilderedly up into the general's aristocratic face. "Yes?"

Carleton seized his arm and maneuvered him into a chair. He poured a fingerful of brandy into a glass tumbler, then forced it into the priest's trembling hands. Fitzwilliam got it to his mouth on the third try. The amber liquid slid down his throat and left a trail of fire.

"The ambush?" Carleton repeated caustically.

"Oh, yes." Fitzwilliam took another fiery sip. "I—had no idea, of course, that Father Connolly would resist being rescued. It was a terrible tragedy and I—regret the loss of your men more than I can say." Tears stung his eyes. He wiped them away with the back of his mud-encrusted, scratched hand. "I will pray for their souls."

"Will you?" Iron rang in Carleton's voice. "And will that be of sufficient comfort to their mothers and wives and children? Shall we write and tell them how very sorry we are, but that you are *praying* for them which somehow makes the whole unsavory mess better?"

Fitzwilliam squeezed his eyes closed against the flood of grief that threatened. How many men had died, he wondered. He had seen several killed by the huge dogs, and another eaten by the apparition. Had the toll been even higher?

"Yes, I rather thought not." Carleton's steps crossed the room and a chair creaked. "Pull yourself together, man. You're of no more use to me than a damned woman in this condition."

Fitzwilliam raised the glass to his lips again, holding it carefully with both hands as he drained the last of the brandy, then opened his eyes and set it aside on the general's immense desk. "I'm sorry," he said softly.

Sitting opposite him, Carleton drummed his fingers on a side table. "You will see the post surgeon, after which you will get cleaned up and eat properly. On the morrow, you will accompany a hand-picked squad of men to every village which you have contacted in the past. Before leaving, you will brief the company as to the dress and demeanor of the shamen in this area, then upon arrival at each village, you will point out all shamen known to you personally."

Fitzwilliam's throat closed with dread. "And then?"

Carleton's hard blue eyes glittered. "Marksmen will pick them off, depriving the savages of supernatural protection. Once the shamen are eliminated, my men have orders to kill as many dogs as necessary to cover their retreat, since they will likely give chase. After that, they will deal with any warriors who hinder their progress. I have reinforcements arriving within the next fortnight and I intend to prepare the way for a massive invasion. We are done waiting for this land."

Without magical protection, most of the natives would die of disease, Fitzwilliam thought, as the Catawbas had, and afterward those few who survived would be forced into slavery. But as slaves, they would have a chance for redemption, if they could be made to accept God's word. As long as they clung to their heathenish magic, they were all doomed to suffer everlasting torment in Hell. He had to try to save those whom he could, no matter what the cost. The consequences of failing were even greater.

He bowed his head in acceptance, then levered himself onto his feet. "Until tomorrow, then, Sir Guy."

It troubled Two Hearts to withhold the truth from Snake, but since the spirits had "remade" him to facilitate his training, it was not for Two Hearts to reveal the past. So, without liking it, he kept his silence. The spirits had done what they must, and so now would he.

He outfitted Snake in a deerskin shirt, full-length breeches, and moccasins from his pack so that he could better travel. As they packed what little else he had brought, Snake was like a child, fascinated by everything he picked up and wanting explanations. Freed of guilt and doubt, he possessed a clarity of spirit and perception beautiful to behold. Two Hearts realized he might have been a great holy man if he had been born to the Tsalagi and able to accept his gifts without question.

Power was both an advantage to the gifted and a danger. Some who were born with the potential to wield medicine energies never learned to cope. They were so flooded with perceptions of the spirit world that they lost their grasp on the world of men and sat around the village, vacant-eyed and distant, cared for the rest of their lives like the most helpless of children. Others, frightened by the potent forces at the edge of their awareness, hardened their hearts and turned away from the spirits, deafening themselves to that confusing, often terrifying realm. Only the hardiest and bravest, who passed every test of both body and mind, came into their own, and that passage was a matter of many seasons, not days.

But they did not have seasons. He did not even know if they had days. Each morning now, just before waking, he dreamed of a gut-wrenching wrongness descending, something soulless and gray, sowing chaos where there had been peace, and emptiness where the land had teemed with life. He saw rivers without fish and skies devoid of birds, men with dull, lifeless eyes and a land contaminated by poisons. The message beat through his brain until it governed the pulse of his blood; the time to act was almost here. But it was Snake who was being called. Two Hearts was only required to prepare the way.

Nightshadow rose and padded forward, ears pricked expectantly. Two Hearts turned to Snake. "You must ride on her back."

"Ride? Like a—a—?" Snake shook his head, looking puzzled. "I cannot remember the word, but there is another animal to ride upon, not like this one. It has—" He frowned, shaping the animal in the air with his hands. "It has long hair on its neck and hard feet, like stone."

"Yes, they have a name in a different language." Reluctant to voice the English word, lest it jog his memory, Two Hearts touched the dog's neck. "Come, we have far to travel."

Snake uncertainly placed his hands on the furred neck and flung his leg over her back. Nightshadow stood patiently, permitting his clumsy efforts to pull himself astride, then Two Hearts set off on foot before them. They could have travelled faster if he rode too, but he did not know how Smoke and the others of the Dog Clan guided their dog companions. For now, he would walk.

He had decided to conduct Snake to a huge gray mountain of stone, a place of immense power that sheered up out of the gentle green hills to the northwest. Though he had never journeyed to the top, he had felt its potential when he placed his palms against the face of the granite, tasted its electricity in the surrounding air, dreamed the most vivid and important dreams of his life at its foot—dreams of waterfalls and green-furred bears, caves and rock drawings, and another, more jagged mountain that rose up in the center of the world.

Nightshadow followed his lead silently, her paws whisper-quiet across the grass, over fallen logs, through streams, up shaded inclines. Snake sat stiffly on her back, clutching her ruff with both hands, his eyes gazing about in wonder.

Sweat trickled down Two Hearts' neck as he angled to the northwest, navigating by glimpses of the sun in the occasional clearings. The wind gradually stilled until the only sign of life was the flicker of birds from tree to tree and the overlying whine of insects.

When Nightshadow paused at a creek to quench her thirst, Snake slid off her back and stretched, humming under his breath. Two Hearts felt his skin prickle.

"Where did you learn that song?"

"It was just there—in my head." Snake's strange blue eyes stared over the older man's shoulder. "Why does the light move like that?"

Two Hearts turned. A shaft of golden light speared down through a gap in the trees, almost solid enough to touch. The hair on the nape of his neck crawled as he realized the entire glade now seethed with medicine energies. Snake's song had opened a rift into the spirit world.

The younger man cocked his head, listening. The electric feeling increased, as though lightning were about to strike, or a tree to fall. The breath caught in Two Hearts' throat and he heard another song, wild and sweet, pitched higher than any human voice could possibly sing. It wove through his head, softened his knees, made it hard to think. The molten-gold light flared until Two Hearts' eyes watered and he felt as though they were caught inside the sun herself.

Four large stags with spreading racks of antlers sprang out of the light. The coat of each gleamed a different color—pure white, blood-red, sun-yellow, the last black as the emptiness between the stars. They paused, their liquid black eyes fierce and unafraid.

The singing sharpened to an unbearable pitch. Nightshadow whined and pressed her belly to the grass, ears flattened in misery. Two Hearts stood his ground, unsure of what to do. He had seen such things in dreams and visions, but never like this, while he wore his physical body.

The four magnificent bucks came abreast and faced the men from a low rise across the stream. Snake watched them with curiosity, but no visible fear.

Two Hearts moistened his lips and turned to Snake, his blood racing. "You have breached the gap between our world and that place beyond where the spirits dwell. I dare not go any closer or the energies will flay the skin from my bones."

The red buck lowered his head, threatening them with his fierce antlers. Muscles rippled across his shoulders while his three companions pawed the grass with their cloven hooves. Two Hearts saw they were not to be allowed to merely close the rift and go on their way. "Speak to him, as one man to another. You have entered his territory. Ask his permission to pass."

Snake waded across the stream, his young face enrapt. "May we pass?"

"Why have you come here unpurified?" the deer demanded. His eyes sparked like a stirred fire.

Snake squinted through the brilliant light at the angry deer. "We did not mean to offend you."

"We are a sacred nation," said the deer, "and because we sense you possess the seeds of all four medicines, we would make you our brother, but first, to prove your worthiness, you must wrestle the strongest of us. If you can kill me, you and your companions may go on. If not, we will dispatch your spirits to the Night Country." The deer's body softened, changed, and then a young man with broad shoulders and the almond-shaped eyes of a deer stood before him, fists braced on his lean, powerful hips.

Before Snake could answer, the deer-man leaped and knocked him back into the water, then closed his hands around the Snake's throat, squeezing. Nightshadow growled, but Two Hearts urged her back as the two men floundered in the stream.

"We cannot interfere," he whispered into her pinned ears, not sure of how much she understood. "This is a trial and only by his own actions may he pass it." The dog trembled, but crouched at his side.

Slippery with water and mud, Snake broke the deer-spirit's grasp. The spirit laughed and flung himself upon Snake again, grabbing his ears and holding his head underwater until bubbles rose from his mouth and nose, then Snake flailed free, gasping and dazed.

"What is the nature of strength?" the deer-man demanded.

Snake blinked. "I do not—know."

"All strength begins with purity." The deer-spirit kneed Snake in the back and forced his face down into the now muddy water. "Only the purified are strong."

A moment later, Snake burst out of the creek again and slipped the other's grasp. He stood gasping, staring at his open hands. "The water—it makes me—stronger."

The deer-spirit sprang at him once more, but this time Snake dodged and pitched him into the water instead. Breathing hard, the deer-man climbed out of the stream onto the far bank and sagged to his knees, black hair plastered to his head.

Snake turned back to Two Hearts as though they could leave now, but the Tsalagi gave a quick jerk of his chin. "You must finish what you have begun."

"Kill him?" Snake glanced back at the proud deer-spirit. "But the water has made me stronger than he is. It would be dishonorable."

"It is the way of nature for the strong to kill the weak." Fear gripped Two Hearts, but he set his jaw, fighting not to let it show. If Snake failed this test, they would die, and his terrible dreams would become reality. "You must honor the sacrifice your deer-brother makes so you may grow and learn."

Snake stared mutely at the waiting deer-spirit, his hands clenched.

"The spirits' ways are not ours," Two Hearts said harshly, "and you will not always understand. You must put your foolish pride aside and do what is necessary!"

His blue eyes glazed, Snake stepped toward the deer-spirit who rose to meet him, clawing savagely at his face. Snake seized his shoulders and wrenched the muscular body to the ground. There was a sickening crack. The deer-man's body arched in a great convulsion, then . . . stilled. The dark-haired head lolled loosely to the left at a sickening angle.

The three remaining deer raised their slim muzzles, nostrils flaring, and advanced upon him. The bushes whispered and suddenly the forest was filled with hundreds of leaping, surging, dancing deer, their coats a seething mass of black / white / red / yellow. Their hooves struck fire from the rocks and their antlers shredded the leaves overhead so that tattered pieces drifted down like green snow.

Snake staggered, fighting to keep his feet as he was buffeted first one way, then another, and then finally fell beneath their hooves.

chapter thirteen

Hooves thundered as Snake fell and fell. He flung his arms out, bracing for an impact on the rocky forest floor, but instead tumbled through jewelled colors, soft as spider silk on his skin. His progress slowed to mere drifting, warm and easy as though he floated in some vast tropical sea that smelled of freshly cut lemons, tasted of cinnamon on the back of his throat. Within the rainbow-light, the four colors of deer wove around him, singing the same song that had mysteriously surfaced in his head.

This song, they said, *is a pathway to power for those who seek it with a pure heart. We offer it to you for use when the right moment has come.*

Use for what? he wanted to ask them, but the words would not form, and they scattered without another word, each color in a different direction.

Gradually, he became aware of a cold wetness prodding his neck—here—there, and a raspy warmth repeatedly swabbing his cheek. One of his fingers moved, and then a toe. He felt a weight on his chest, and then his entire body, bruised and aching. He pried open his eyes and saw Nightshadow, her head propped on his ribs, regarding him mournfully.

Darkness had fallen and the heat of the day had lessened, although the air still had the humid taste of damp leaf-mold and nearby running water. He heard the breeze ruffling the leaves overhead and the rasp of crickets courting under logs. The dog leaped to her feet and sniffed him enthusiastically from crown to toe, licking his face in a frenzy of joy.

"I am fine," he protested, wincing against the throbbing behind his eyes.

Just beyond the great dog, Two Hearts sat on his heels beside a small fire of glimmering gold and green and red flames. His dark-shadowed eyes were closed as he chanted under his breath. The flames jumped as Snake sat up, then strained toward him. The multitude of deer were nowhere to be seen, nor could he make out their tracks on the stream bank by the flickering light of Two Hearts' fire. He settled back against the dog's warm side, baffled, aching as though he had run all day.

"You must be more careful." Two Hearts' voice was harsh with weariness. He looked up with bleak eyes. "The spirits are not gentle with their lessons."

"Careful of what?" Snake kneaded his aching forehead. In the back of his mind he still heard the beat of hooves, the low voices of deer.

"You opened a crack between the worlds with that song, a dangerously wide one. Small rifts often close by themselves, but a shaman must always check to be sure after he summons medicine energies. The larger rifts are much more difficult." Two Hearts rose and stretched. Lines of strain creased his face. "I have been working to seal this one since the sun was still halfway above the horizon." He passed his hand over the fire and the flames changed to a more normal yellow-orange. "By opening such a rift, you could have lost yourself in that other world forever. A few steps closer and I would have merely died, the flesh torn from my bones."

Snake shuddered. "What other world?"

"There are three worlds." Two Hearts sat back down and placed his hands on his knees. "The Above World, where the Above Beings dwell, the Middle World, which was given to men and dogs and plants and all the other creatures who roam the earth, and the Night Country, where the spirits of those who are born to the Middle World abide after death." He stared into the darkness. "The energy of the Above World is in opposition to that of the Night Country. If the two ever came in contact, they would grind each other to shreds, so the Above Beings created the Middle World to exist between them and hold them apart."

Two Hearts passed his hands over the fire again; it guttered and then went out, leaving a darkness thick enough to cut. "Tomorrow, I will instruct you as we journey. I had hoped your training could wait until we reached the stone mountain, but I was wrong."

Nightshadow rose, turned three times in a tight circle and lay back down, nose to tail. Snake stretched out on the grass beside her and pillowed his aching head on his arm.

"Some spirits have no sympathy for the cause of men, and would snap up the spark of your life without a second thought," Two Hearts said in the darkness, his voice hoarse. "Monsters, such as the terrible Uk'ten, range the lower uninhabited reaches of the Night Country where sorrow flows like a river, and even the friendly spirits of the Above World are often careless of mortal flesh. You must gain more control before we reach the mountain."

The mountain . . . Behind his eyes, Snake saw a great mass of naked gray stone, rising from surrounding green forested hills like the bald pate of a wise old man, calling him somehow, knowing his name. He looped an arm around Nightshadow's soft neck and pressed his face into the clean, wild scent of her fur.

✳ ◇ ✳

At first light, One Eye rolled out of his ragged blanket on the beach and stared at the swollen red sun, hanging just above the pearl-gray sea. Waves rolled in, white-crested and angry, clawing at the sand. He drew the salt air deep into his lungs. This was the day it began, the end of the Tsalagi, who deserved to die for being stupid enough to think they could trade for the white man's metal and beads and cloth, without falling prey to his insatiable desire for land and domination. He could not bear them to live on in blissful ignorance when his own kind had perished.

One Eye rolled up his evil-smelling blanket and tied it with a worn leather thong. Washing was women's work, and he had no woman left to wash for him, and besides he liked watching the English noses wrinkle when he passed, liked how English moved aside and commented when they thought he did not understand. It was a subtle game he enjoyed playing, one of the few things left to him in which he could take pleasure.

The red-coated soldiers at the fort scowled as he stalked through the tall gates. One Eye did not even look up. The same proud soldiers had stood on these wooden heights, their coats bright as redbirds, and laughed when his people had run screaming into the sea, trying to cool the fever in their diseased bodies, laughed even harder when the survivors crawled to their doors and begged for food and water, and then turned away as orphaned Catawba babes had wailed for their dead mother's breast. If he were not dead himself, he would have slit the throats of each and every one of them, but his spirit had perished along with his soft-eyed wife and four sturdy sons, and all that was left of the man he had been before was this bitter husk who played angry games.

The gray, sway-backed elk-dog they provided for him to ride was tied to a post before the place where they kept the rest of the brainless creatures. It was a poor thing, half-dead itself, with drooping ears and a slack jaw. Here, on the coast, he could travel faster on foot, but on Tsalagi territory, he always rode so that his dead flesh avoided painful contact with living land.

Soldiers poured out of the wooden structure like an angry red tide, each one carrying a heavy pack and a long gray firestick with a knife on the end. The black-robe emerged with them, his face still pasty and creased with weariness. When One Eye had found the old priest the day before, he'd brought him back to the fort more as a joke than anything else. White-hair, who commanded these soldiers, clearly disliked blackrobes, for all that their skin was the same lifeless color as his own. One Eye savored the distaste in those watery blue eyes.

Blackrobe mounted a raw-boned bay with a stiffness that said plainly he should not be out of bed. One Eye turned his back; the blackrobe's condition was not his concern. He grasped his beast's coarse gray mane and vaulted onto the worn saddle, disdaining the dangling stirrups and sliding forward to grip with his thighs. The elk-dog snorted and shifted uneasily beneath him.

Broken-nose, whom the English called Jones, strode briskly out into the dusty yard, still chewing, his black boots shining in the early sun. His face tightened at the sight of One Eye. "We're going to the villages, all of them, starting with the closest and working our way up-river." He narrowed his chill blue eyes. "Do you understand?"

The scout grunted and gazed back impassively. It pleased him to make them think he comprehended little of their guttural tongue.

"How long until we reach Idjoku?" Broken-nose demanded.

One Eye shrugged. "Less than one sun." He wrenched the elk-dog's head around and kicked it toward the gate. A clatter of hooves told him the soldiers and the blackrobe followed.

The time had finally come, One Eye told himself with satisfaction. Another few days would see the annihilation of the Tsalagi and the easing of his pain.

Berry awoke sweating in the dim silence of her uncle's house, the dream still painfully vivid in her mind. She had seen a huge gray mountain rising before her, a place of raw, unrestrained power that attracted her as a starving man was drawn to food, or a childless woman was drawn to the touch of a new-born babe's sweet-smelling skin.

Behind, she had felt the roiling blackness of pain and fear and death, smelled the acridness of smoke, heard the crackle of approaching flames. Her heart still raced at the memory of that wrongness, the lack of balance and harmony. Something terrible was approaching and little time was left to turn it aside.

She pushed sweat-dampened hair back from her face and swung her legs over the edge of the hide-frame bed, slowing her breathing, composing herself. It was still very early, the sun's light barely graying the eastern sky. She would purify herself in the river, then go to one of the shamen and ask him to interpret her dream.

At the river, the cool water sluiced over her face and bare shoulders as she ducked beneath the surface. The current tugged at her bare legs, rinsing away the accumulated negative energies of both thought and body, preparing her for the new day. She immersed the proper seven times, then waded back to the bank and dried on a soft old skin she had brought along. The other women and girls of the village were just emerging from the palisade, yawning, chattering among themselves. They stared at her curiously, for she was not known as an early riser.

"Did you come by yourself to ask for a husband?" her age-friend Picks Corn asked with a twinkle in her dark eyes.

Berry smiled and lowered her head. Since her monthly moontimes had begun two summers ago, she could take a husband if she wished, but she was not yet so old that she must accept any man who wanted her. It was true the other girls her age were actively considering the eligible young men for mates, but she could not escape the feeling she had something else to do now and more important considerations than forming her own household. And then there was the stranger—she had seen his face and those odd blue eyes in her dreams a thousand times. The two of them were linked in some fashion she did not yet understand.

The other women and girls laughed good-naturedly as they shed dresses and skirts and then waded into the shallows. Water splashed as they began the daily ritual she had already completed.

She found the Head Uko, Lone Bear, at his lodge with two of his grown sons. Their lean dark faces appraised her from the doorway, for both of them were unmarried and, through their maternal line, of a different clan than she, thereby eligible suitors. The older man sat on a log bench with his arms crossed and waited for her to speak. Bowing her head, she knelt just beyond his thatched porch. "Uncle, a troubling dream came to me in the night."

"Speak, child," he said, for he was born of the Deer Clan, as was she, and thereby her relative.

"I saw a great rounded mountain of stone with no greenery at all, rising northwest of Kitasi."

"There is such a mountain," he said. "I have traveled there myself."

"It—calls me." She hesitated, trying to remember the details clearly. "But in my dream, even as I went, behind me followed a sea of death and disease and fire." She bit her lip and tried to stop trembling. "Something terrible is coming. We should all travel to this place and seek shelter."

Lone Bear's mouth tightened. "I will look into my crystal and see if you have dreamed truly."

She looked up. "But—"

"Not everyone has the gift of dreaming," he said. "Sometimes a dream is only a dream. We cannot abandon our village and our crops and lodges just because one frightened girl thinks we are in danger. This requires prayer and consideration."

Berry's throat constricted. "But there is more; every night now I dream of a time when we are no longer Tsalagi, when the land will not know our name and we will be lost forever!"

"And you said nothing?"

"I told my uncle," she said softly, "but he left with Smoke and I do not know when he will return."

"Two Hearts is gifted in the art of dream interpretation." Lone Bear rose as his wife and three daughters returned, wet and beaming, from the river. "If he was not concerned over your dreams, then they must be false."

Berry stared at her clasped hands, watching the knuckles whiten. Her stomach twisted as she remembered the darkness from her dream, the dry, aching loss, the wrenching pain. She could still feel the flames on her face, smell the bitter smoke. "Something terrible is coming. We are *all* going to die if we stay here!"

"Not as long as we keep our festivals in the proper fashion," he said impatiently. "Now, go tend your fields before your corn slips away into the forest and your lodge goes hungry this winter." He turned away. "Come back tonight and I will have an answer for you then."

She jerked to her feet, heart pounding, cheeks burning. By sending her this message, the spirits had entrusted her with the future of her people. If even one person died because she could not find the words to make them listen, the shame and dishonor would be on her head. She had to convince them before it was too late.

✳   ◇   ✳

Snake woke from a troubled sleep in which he saw rows of smooth stone columns in a great building filled with light of many colors, amazing oranges and blues and yellows and greens. Voices rose in song and echoed from a ceiling so high above his head that it blurred when he tried to gaze up at it. He had worn a flowing black garment and stood amidst others similarly garbed. They had turned to him reproachfully, as though he had done something terribly, irrevocably wrong.

But now trees whispered above him and he smelled running water and the clean scent of wet leaves and mud. Life brimmed around him, joyous, graceful, alert. He sat up and rubbed the sweat from his face. From behind, Nightshadow licked his ear reassuringly. He looped an arm around her neck to pull her close. Although he could not remember his previous life, he could not imagine being without her.

Two Hearts rolled over and sat up, his weathered brown face still pinched with weariness. He gazed up through the trees, assessing the sun's position in the sky. "We must purify ourselves and go on."

Snake stretched. His muscles were still sore from yesterday, but improved. He grimaced at the few remaining twinges as he followed Two Hearts to the stream just beyond the trees. They both peeled out of buckskin shirts and leggings and plunged into the chill water. It felt electric against his skin, wildly invigorating. He stood with his head back, his eyes half-closed, letting the current sheer around his planted legs.

Two Hearts' expression softened. "Water is the first of the four medicine ways. Its power is the same something-in-movement which underlies all life. It runs in our blood and the tide, pours down with the rain from the great sky-vault. Without it, no life is possible."

Snake felt himself enter the stream, flow down the silver-blue-green artery and merge with other larger streams again and again until he reached Long Man, the river, who stood with his head in the mountains and his feet in the sea. He raced the sunbeams with Long Man, played with curious silvery-green fish, cascaded down waterfalls and exploded in wild spray against the rocks below, only to come together again, unhurt. He left part of himself in each quiet pool, each deceptively still lake, each creek, each puddle, for always there was movement, downstream, to lower ground, into the air to rejoin the clouds. He was a miraculous single entity existing in an infinite number of changeable forms, rushing toward the deep, restless, briny fellowship of the sea.

"When I first encountered you, I knew you had great affinity for Water." Two Hearts' voice reached him in the gravelly bottomed creek, in the wispy clouds, in the relentless undertow of the tide. "In the morning, when you purify yourself, take from Water its strength, its ability to adapt to any shape, its inevitable forward motion."

The sense of being in a thousand different places and forms faded. Snake came back to himself, standing naked in the stream, sunlight trickling down the interwoven branches onto his upturned face. The wind surged, whispering against the leaves, carrying the scent of moist earth and leaf-mold.

Two Hearts turned away as though nothing had happened. "We must leave."

Snake squatted down and ducked beneath the flowing water the requisite seven times. With each dousing, he felt lighter, somehow more ready for the day. He thought of the deer-spirit's words: "Strength begins with purity." He understood better now exactly what kind of strength that was.

The older man submerged a final time, then stood dripping in the middle of the stream, blinking up into the canopy of trees. "You must walk all four of the medicine ways in turn, because you have much ahead of you to do."

"At the stone mountain?"

Two Hearts waded to the bank. "Yes."

"If I have to go there, why do I not remember it?" Snake splashed out of water after him. "Why have I forgotten everything?"

"I have already explained—these days are a time of grace, so that you might learn without the burden of the past." Two Hearts regarded him bleakly. "You must make the most of it." He donned his clothes with savage jerks and stalked back through the underbrush without another glance.

Snake pushed the water off his pale body with his hands, puzzled that his skin was so much lighter than Two Hearts' rich bronze. The amazing energy of Water still tingled like liquid sunlight in his veins. How could this knowledge be anything but wonderful? He wondered how his past had been a hindrance and what would happen when he did remember. Would he be pleased with all he had done and learned at this strange man's side, or sorrowful, or angry?

Would he ever understand?

nake spent the morning walking beside the great dog, rather than riding, one arm across her shoulders, carrying his moccasins in order to savor the vitality of the land against his bare feet. The shade was so thick in this part of the forest that little undergrowth had survived and the combined carpet of pine needles and leafmold was soft against his soles.

Overhead, the trees were alive with a variety of birds, nesting, feeding, quarreling, courting. Two Hearts bade him concentrate first on the voice of one species and then another. In this way, he learned that birds were part of Air medicine, a powerful discipline which included wind and sound and flying insects and all other creatures who rode the skies. Snake took in the uncomplicated wisdom of sparrows, admired the caustic wit of the fiery woodpecker, absorbed the pragmatism of robin and thrush.

The three travelers emerged on the crest of a gray limestone cliff which looked out over a still blue lake, shaped like a double teardrop, and a lush valley dotted with meadowlands. Above the valley floor, the air sparkled, invisible to the eye and yet tangible.

"The strength of Air," Two Hearts said gravely, "is two-fold, arising in both its invisibility and universality. Unseen, it is forever with us; out of reach, yet always touching."

Snake let the breeze stream through his splayed fingers and wondered how a substance so tenuous as air could also possess strength. A flicker of movement caught the sun below the cliff, then he retreated as the air filled with tiny, shimmering green birds, each no bigger than his smallest finger. Their delicate wings beat so rapidly that they seemed but a blur.

Drawn to the jewel-like creatures as they darted out over the valley floor, something within him broke free and followed, merging with the air and an almost inaudible hum of which he had not been aware before. A fierce joy ran through that hum, joy of freedom and health, joy of the balanced dualities of light and dark, of all things both seen and unseen that moved through existence.

He expanded until he covered the face of the world, reaching for something he could not begin to understand, gathering, concentrating, sweeping along until he was a mighty current that uprooted trees and leveled mountains, changed the course of rivers, and he was alive with power and movement and music. The whole of creation lay beneath his vastness, listening as he sang, and nothing could withstand the force of his presence if he so desired. Light did not shine, except through him, nor darkness fall without his cooperation, and he knew the hiding place of every living creature. He was above everything, yet part of it all, essential, but separate. Violent and forceful, invisible and weak and—above all—sacred. He stretched, reaching, striving, wanting it *all*!

Two Hearts' hands steadied his shoulders and his awareness snapped back into his body.

"Air is breath," Two Hearts said into his ear, "the essence of life. Respect its strength and seek its counsel."

With a shudder, Snake realized he stood balanced on the rocks at the edge of the cliff, his arms thrown wide. The tiny emerald-green birds swarmed around his face, regarding him with knowing black eyes. *"The gift of Air is joy,"* they said. *"Walk with it until it as familiar as your own heartbeat, and then, in the coming days, when the world lies in peril, remember what it is to taste joy."* Then they dispersed in a hundred different directions.

Snake sagged to his knees, trembling, unable to bear being confined in the cramped space that was all a man's body occupied. Breath shuddered through his lungs as he longed for the wild, sweet freedom of the skies. Nightshadow came forward to lick his face and neck over and over, as if she understood his distress. When his shaking eased enough for him to stand, Two Hearts helped him mount the dog and bid him ride the rest of the afternoon, his hands buried in the warm black fur of the dog's ruff so he would not fall.

Father Fitzwilliam sat rigidly on his bay gelding as the party of soldiers followed the river, riding in and out of the sporadic shade at a steady pace. The sun-heated smell of mud this close to the water was strong, combined with rotting vegetation and his own sweat. He ran a finger under his high collar and wondered if he could take the sweltering heat much longer.

He tried instead to concentrate on the four-beat rhythm of his horse's hooves, but as always, his mind went back to the cries of the dead and dying in Idjoku, the small village they had raided the day before. They had ridden up to the palisade under a green flag of trade, a duplicity which still made his skin crawl. The smiling natives had crowded around the horses, their upturned copper faces eager to see the goods the English had brought, inquiring about blankets and beads and fine knives. He had sat his horse, his throat tight as he quietly pointed out to Captain Jones the telltale long woven shirts of the three shamen present in the crowd.

Earlier, the soldiers had been instructed to kill the shamen, then afterward eliminate only those dogs or warriors who interfered with their retreat. They were not to fully engage any one village, but go on to the next settlement and repeat the pattern, thus preparing the way for the new troops, due any day now to effect the final submission of this area. But, as soon as the shooting began, the soldiers fired at anything which moved, even the smallest of the children, mere infants too young to wear clothes in this savage culture. Horror-stricken, Fitzwilliam had dismounted in order to trace the sign of the cross over one beautiful little girl, sprawled in a thick scarlet pool of her own blood.

Several of the soldiers had died as well when a fourth shaman emerged from a lodge to cast some sort of spell. A wave of purple-green fire had roared over the two foremost soldiers before they could retreat and their blackened bodies shattered into cinders as they struck the ground. Fitzwilliam, caught on his knees clasping the dead child, had stared, witless and afraid, until Captain Jones had seized him by the collar and dragged him behind the cover of a tree.

Then a marksman had picked off the remaining shaman and the magical fire dissipated. The villagers had rallied, shooting arrows, firing poisoned darts, rushing them with knives and hand-axes. Three more British soldiers fell, two before the great slavering dogs, before they could pull back into the forest.

Fitzwilliam had feared the natives would follow and later slaughter them in the night, but so far there had been no sign of reprisal. Captain Jones had insisted they continue on to the next village, Kitasi, and pursue their orders to kill all the shamen on Tsalagi land. It was a fool's errand, thought Fitzwilliam, crazy and impossible.

And wrong? he asked himself as his horse stumbled and threw him forward against the saddle. Thou shalt not kill, the Bible said, and yet these savages had allied themselves with the Devil. By working their hellish magic they had already forfeited their immortal souls and damned the rest of their kind down to the youngest babe-in-arms along with them. The Bible also said, If thy right eye offend thee, pluck it out, and cast it from thee. And so it must be.

"To every thing there is a season," he whispered, "and a time to every purpose under the heaven." He straightened his weary back and sat taller in the saddle.

God's work was often difficult, but it would not do for him to lose faith now, not when the real work of saving souls was finally at hand.

*   ◊   *

That night Snake lay on his back and studied the stars through a gap in the overhanging trees while Two Hearts related how the First Man had spoken to Fire, and then First Woman to Water, creating two of four medicines which ruled the universe. Their children, First Boy and First Girl, spoke to Earth and Air. Most shamen walked only one of the four medicine ways; a talented few had the ability to learn two. Usually, a man of Fire learned Water medicine, or a man with talent for Earth medicine learned the way of Air—Two Hearts himself was versed in the lore of both Earth and Air. Only a true Spiritwalker was born to all four medicine ways, and there had not been such a man or woman in the last five generations, until now.

"Place your hands on your mother the earth," the older man said quietly.

Snake turned over and spread his fingers over the ground, feeling a slow steady pulse emanating from deep within the earth.

Two Hearts nodded at him across the waning fire. "The strength of Earth lies in patience. It combines the steadfastness of the stone-people, the fertility of the plant-people, and the wisdom of the animal-people, all of whom are our brothers."

The rhythm surged through him, over-ruling his pulse and commanding the beat of his heart, the rate of his breathing, the blink of his eyes. Nightshadow lay asleep an arm's length away and did not stir as a massive cinnamon-brown creature shambled into the firelight. Snake sat up slowly and stared into the bottomless black eyes of a female bear. She met his gaze, then turned to a second bear, larger and darker brown in color, and then two more, both small, nimble, and black. The bears danced in time with the heartbeat of the earth, their luminous eyes full of timeless secrets, and Snake found himself dancing with them beneath moon-silvered trees.

The rhythm was slow, but irresistible, each beat like distant thunder, full of meaning and strength. He felt the trees swaying with them, the squirrels' chittering keeping the powerful rhythm in their sleep, the stones within the earth push against each other, trying strength against strength for the time of trial that would surely come.

The brown bear lumbered forward and gazed deep into Snake's eyes. Her pupils were alive with black fire and in that fire he saw a flying creature, monstrously huge against the sky, breathing flame over the living forest. *I give you strength for the coming battle,* she said without words, and then breathed warmly into his face. He smelled the dryness of cedar and the rich moistness of fresh earth.

The second bear, the dark-brown of seasoned pine, reared up on her hind legs and placed her wickedly curved claws on his shoulders. Her eyes expanded to the size of plates and within he saw an army of soldiers advancing into the forest, taking aim with their muskets at the very heart of the world. *I give you wisdom to know the way,* she said, and her fur held the pungence of pine needles and the sharpness of newly cut wood.

The two black bears ambled to his side and danced with him the slow, careful pattern that was becoming as familiar as his own pulse. *In nature all creatures are created in twos,* they said in unison. *In twos you will find the sacred balance.* They wove a circle of black fur around him, and in their dark eyes he saw a man and a woman making love, cleaving to each other as a single flesh, unashamed.

When it is time, they said, *remember.*

He danced and the bears danced until the trees were a blur and the stars descended to weave in a great circle around them, until he could not tell where his flesh ended and the earth began, until he found himself a part of every twig and pebble and deer, until his head swam with weariness and he knew nothing more.

✳   ◇   ✳

The following day, Nightshadow took it in turns to carry the two of them over the ridges, through the dells, across the unexpected deer pastures that separated arms of the forest. Snake mulled over the lessons of Water, Air, and Earth, wondering what each meant and how he would be expected to make use of them. A time was coming when something would be asked of him; he could feel that much, but he had no idea of the task's nature and Two Hearts would tell him nothing. It was an unsettling feeling.

That night Two Hearts sat him before a pile of gathered wood and bid him reach within for balance.

Snake was confused. "Balance?"

"To find balance, you must acknowledge all facets of life." Two Hearts laid his hands on his knees and let his eyelids descend. "Good and bad, easy and hard, fast and slow, all opposites have their balancing point in the heart of your being, and so it is with the four medicines." His voice drifted through the darkness. "Fire balances Water, Earth balances Air. We each have all four energies within us. Find that center within yourself, and then reach for Fire."

Snake closed his eyes, feeling foolish, without the slightest idea as to what the older man was talking about. He had experienced the beauty and power of Water, Earth, and Air medicines, but to find the balance between them, what did that mean?

He settled his hands on his knees, as had Two Hearts, and let his mind drift. His breathing settled into the slow, steady rhythm of the earth, like the dancing of bears, water dripping over rocks, the soft, insistent flow of the wind through the trees. Though on the surface very different, at their heart, they were the same. He felt one with them all, at peace.

"Yes," Two Hearts said softly. "Now open your mind to the realm of our fearsome brother Fire, where stars derive their energy and Lightning his crooked, bright dance, the realm from which at the end of the day, each family calls a fragment of our sister the sun to warm their lodge and cook their food and push back the darkness."

Power . . . somewhere beyond the night, on the other side of the blackness, it reigned. Snake felt the seething richness that fed the stars and the sun and lightning and every fire kindled in the Middle World, whether by accident or design. Fire medicine was at the center of creation, and without it, nothing else would exist.

"Rattlesnake is a powerful spirit of fire, as is his cousin, Lightning, and Lightning's numerous nephews, the stars," Two Hearts said. "Fire is at the heart of everything, and so an essential part of the sacred balance."

Snake saw Fire in the velvet blackness behind his eyes, felt its power, how it fueled the something-in-motion of Water, the touching-and-yet-not-touched quality of Air, the wondrous heartbeat of Earth; it was all connected, unified in a way he could only begin to comprehend.

"Reach for Fire," Two Hearts said, "and call it here."

Snake reached and felt power stream from the spirit world through him into the gathered wood. His hands warmed, then his whole body. He felt as though he were flame, feeding the world with his substance in a brief flare of glory, then the summoned flames poured through him out into the ready pile of wood and roared up until they grazed the trees that overhung their camp.

Two Hearts lurched to his feet and moved back. Snake watched as the sacred fire burned green and gold and white and red, a multitude of shapes within its heart. It seemed a living being, responsive to his moods. The tiny shapes flowed together, separated in a joyous dance ever familiar and yet never twice the same, drawing him within to join their wild exuberant dance, where he learned the strength of Fire was transformation, for everything it touched became something else. He found himself twinkling high overhead with the myriad stars, riding the sun's rays toward the waiting earth, flashing across the skies with Lightning, blazing in every hearth across the living land. He was everywhere, but only in brief bursts, for fire was a temporal medicine, more powerful than the other three, but finite.

"You are a Fireheart, with great affinity for Fire medicine," Two Hearts said, sitting on his heels a safe distance from the roaring flames. "It is your greatest strength, but you must take care, for being the strongest, it has the potential to burn you to ashes, if you have not properly prepared. Respect its power or you will be consumed."

With a shudder, Snake found himself back in his own body, but then at his core, he saw the sacred flames, feeding his soul.

＊　◇　＊

On the third day, they rose and purified themselves in the nearest stream, as usual. Snake hummed unselfconsciously as he dried with a handful of moss, then a redbird lighted on a low-hanging branch and studied him with bright black eyes. "You journey to the stone mountain?" it asked in a tiny chirp-voice.

"Yes," he said cautiously.

It fluttered to the ground at his feet and pecked at the grass with sharp, jerky movements. "What will you do there?"

Snake pulled on his shirt which then stuck to his damp back. "Two Hearts refuses to tell me until we arrive, and we have yet some distance to travel."

"But," said the bird, "the stone mountain lies just over there." It hopped to his shoulder, looking behind him, and he turned around. A huge round gray mountain of striated granite rose above the trees, dominating the early morning sky. Snake's heart pounded; surely it had not been there before. The dome of granite crawled with colors as though clothed in a rainbow. He found himself pushing through thickly spaced saplings.

"Snake!" Two Hearts called.

He wanted to answer, but his eyes were caught by the dazzling play of color and light over the naked stone. The mountain seemed to be covered with faces now, great knowing eyes that looked down from the heights, full of mystery and promise. *Come to us,* they seemed to say, *learn all there is to know.*

He was running now, bouncing off trunks and scraping his arms on the rough bark, filled with a wild urgency. He heard the dog panting up behind him, then her teeth snagged the back of his shirt. He tripped, fell hard to his knees, and blood trickled down his abraded arms.

"Snake!" Two Hearts was closer now. "Go no closer!"

The mountain shimmered green and gold and purple. He could feel how he was needed there, no, not just needed—*commanded.* "The mountain!" Snake fought the dog's hold. "I see it—through those trees!"

Two Hearts caught up and took his arm with both hands. "We cannot go that way."

"But it is so close!"

"You have opened another rift into the Above World, and distances are different there." Two Hearts glanced back over his shoulder at the looming mountain. "It would cost my life to set foot there, and you have not acquired enough knowledge to pass that way alone." He motioned to Nightshadow and she released Snake, her muzzle wrinkled, her dark eyes worried.

Snake rose, his arm still in Two Hearts' grasp, watching the colors dance over the granite face of the mountain. A keening rose inside his head, slicing through blood and nerve and will. They both stiffened as the trees shimmered an unearthly green-purple and the air thrummed with hidden energies. The stone mountain expanded until it filled the sky, a universe unto itself, and he could see nothing else. Everything around him, the air, the ground, the leaves, whispered in a rising chorus, *"Come!"* His hands began to glow with a strange blue-white light that should have frightened him, but somehow did not.

He tore his arm from Two Hearts' grasp and dashed to the foot of the shimmering stone mountain.

nake reached out and spread his fingers across the massive gray flank of the stone mountain. At his touch, the cool granite took up first the blue-white glow of his hands, then the heat of his flesh, softening beneath his touch. The formerly gentle breeze whipped into a fierce, roaring wind filled with leaves and twigs and he sank up to his wrists in stone which now had the consistency of melted butter.

"No!" Two Hearts shouted above the wind. His voice had a distorted quality, as though heard from a great distance.

Snake glanced back over his shoulder. Both the man and dog stood behind a barrier of purple-green fire, staring after him, fear uppermost in their eyes. His conscience pricked him, and he hesitated, his hands still within the softened stone, but a voice inside his head said, *Too little time remains. You must come now.*

A violent electricity surged up through his arms and then, knowing suddenly what he must do, he walked into the warm gray stone. It frothed past his face, electric to the touch and yet almost as fluid as water. A distant light beckoned him through the misty grayness. He followed it, emerging finally into a realm of cool blue-white fire that shimmered from every surface of a vast cavern.

"Welcome, grandson." The words echoed until it seemed a hundred voices had spoken.

Half-deafened, he turned and saw a man garbed from head to toe in white deerskin. The stranger studied him with appraising blue eyes and a mild expression, and features, topped with black curly hair, which seemed somehow familiar. Snake looked closer and realized with a start that this stranger bore *his* face, as he had seen it just that morning in the stream.

He backed away, his throat dry, the blood racing through his head like a river in full flood. "You look like me!"

"You are surprised?" the other said, and his eyes crinkled merrily at the corners. "Long Man always reflects those who gaze into him." He waved a hand at the walls and the scintillating blue-white light danced as if in answer.

"I don't understand." For a second, Snake felt foolish, but then other, darker feelings surfaced, shame at being so easily used, and smoldering anger, bitter as green almonds. Since he had woken in the forest with no memory of the past, everyone seemed intent on shaping him to their purpose, not his own. Who was this man and exactly what did he want? Why had he gone to the trouble of luring Snake away from his only friends?

"If you had been born to this land, you would have had many seasons to come to terms with your gift," the man said. "As it is, you have over-much to learn and time is very short, even here where time can be compressed, bent, or stretched to some degree."

"Just what do I have to learn?" Snake turned and gazed angrily up at the walls of light. "And if it's so important, why can't I remember?"

"You lived another, very different life before this one," the man said, "in a land severed from almost all contact with the world of spirits eons before you were born. Although you have great potential for wielding medicine power, that life prevented you from learning what you need to know, so it has been stripped from you, for a time."

Another life . . . Snake reached back into the frustrating blankness in his mind, searching for some sense of who he had been and what he had once wanted, but there was nothing. Surely he'd had parents, friends, a place to call home, a purpose of some sort, but now all of that was simply gone. He clenched his hands. "You had no right!" The blue-white radiance flared into a blinding blaze and he threw his arms over his eyes.

The man spread his hands and the light calmed. "How can your temporary loss be measured against the coming destruction? You are but one drop in an entire sea of living beings."

Snake lowered his hands, trying to blink away the spots in his vision from the intense glare. He realized they were afraid he wouldn't do as they wished, if he remembered his past, and suspicion sharpened his voice. "I have to remember!"

"Then you will, but first, you must climb," the man said. His face wore a confident tranquility that Snake was suddenly sure he himself had never possessed. "Follow the path upward. If you survive, you will remember everything by the time you reach the top."

"What do you mean—if I survive?" Snake demanded, but the man burst into a shower of fiery white drops that merged with the blue-white fire limning the walls and floor and then Snake was alone. His heart pounded, and he had a bitter taste in his mouth. He should have listened to Two Hearts, should have been patient and taken the long way. Now he was truly lost with no prospect of help.

He turned, examining the glimmering walls. The man had said to climb and then he would remember. If that's what it took, then climb he would. Setting his jaw, he searched each crevice and cranny until at last he found a path hacked into the living rock. He began to climb.

When Berry arrived at her cornfield, the far southern corner was bare, where it should have been dotted with the rustling green stalks of nearly ripened corn. She set her wide-mouthed jar of river water down on the red earth and sighed. This was her fault; she had not watered the hills of tasseled cornstalks for two days and now a double-handful had wandered away into the forest. What must Old Corn Woman, the spirit who came in the night to place the true corn inside the green ears, think of such carelessness in a person of her age?

She tipped the jar into the furrow between the first two hills and watched the water stain the soil a rich dark-red. Each night, she slept badly, haunted by the same terrible dreams, and then spent her days seeking some way to avoid the approaching, seemingly inevitable dark times. But that was no excuse to neglect her field. Corn was the center of life, both food and a spiritual blessing, and its care was a woman's sacred responsibility. As shaken as she had been by her dreams, she must not add failure in her duties to the list of her faults.

Once she had watered every remaining hill of corn to her satisfaction, she filled the jar again, then knelt in the missing section where a few stragglers remained, turned her face up to the sun. Her braided hair clung damply to her neck and shoulders as her eyelids descended. "Where have they gone?" she whispered and then *listened*. The wind played over her cheeks, tugging tendrils of hair loose from her braids. She felt the sun beating down on her forehead, sweat pooling between her breasts, breathed in the cool tang of pine needles . . .

Into the forest, she heard one of the stalks say finally in a wispy, dry tassel-voice, *to the stream*.

She straightened and opened her eyes. Now, she must persuade the plants to return to the field where she would take *much* better care of them. Chanting a Green Corn song under her breath, she plunged into the cool dappled shade with the water jar in her arms and angled along the game trail toward the nearest stream.

Before she had gone more than a few steps, sunlight flashed on gold between the trees up on the next ridge. She drew back into the shadows and pressed up against a leaning hickory tree, her heart pounding. "What is it?" she asked the tree.

A four-legged, it answered in its solid woody voice. *It has run far and long.*

She heard labored panting, claws scrabbling over earth and fallen logs.

It wearies, the hickory added stolidly.

Berry stepped into view, shading her eyes. A golden dog with a black muzzle, carrying a man on its back, loped through alternate patches of shade and shadow, its tongue lolling from the side of its mouth—Sunrunner and Smoke.

She waved her arm. "Over here!"

Sunrunner's ears raised, then he swerved toward her. She set the water jar down before the spent dog as he trotted to a stop. Smoke slid off the golden back, his face creased with weariness.

The dog glanced from the jar of water to the man.

"Drink, my brother," Smoke said, one arm across the furred neck.

"Where is my uncle?" Berry asked as the dog lowered his head and lapped water noisily from the jar.

Smoke dragged an arm back over his sweat-sheened forehead. "After we drove the English away from the stranger, Two Hearts sent us to trail them back to the dead lands and then kept watch to see what they would do."

She touched the dog's golden head. He stopped drinking to snuffle her hand, his muzzle dripping, then went back to the water. "And my uncle?"

"We left Two Hearts in the forest." Smoke raked his fingers back through his topknot. "He and the stranger have not returned?"

"No." She worried at the edge of her lip with her teeth. "I thought they were still with you."

Sunrunner finished the water and raised his head, still panting. Smoke smoothed his hand along the sturdy back, then slid back into his accustomed place behind the massive shoulders. "The English rode into Idjoku yesterday with a green cloth as though they had come to trade. Then, when the people came out of their lodges to greet them, the English killed the shamen with their firesticks."

Fear settled like a cold stone in the pit of Berry's stomach.

"They killed many others too, even elders and women and children, but they came for the shamen." Smoke's brown eyes were bleak. "A blackrobe pointed them out, along with a Catawba. They killed every holy man there."

"We must go to them and help!" Idjoku was the closest village. Berry's mind whirled, thinking of the dried healing herbs she had stored back in her uncle's house, the many things she must take with her.

"No!" Smoke reached down and grasped her arm. "The English now ride toward Kitasi, but they are some distance behind us yet. Their elk-dogs are not so agile as our great dogs." He levered her up behind him on Sunrunner's back. "Kitasi must be ready for them when they come."

The dog lowered his head and loped toward the edge of the woods and her cornfield. Berry clutched Smoke's sweat-sheened back to keep from falling off and thought of her lost corn plants; they were probably safer scattered amongst the trees. Even though Lone Bear had not believed her, the terrible fabric of her dream seemed almost upon them.

✳ ◇ ✳

Two Hearts stared at the place where the vision of the stone mountain had filled the sky. There were only maple and hickory trees now, interspersed with the occasional pine, and a grassy meadow beyond where a doe and two fawns grazed cautiously. The rift between the worlds had sealed of its own accord this time, leaving him on this side and Snake on the other. He had failed in his guardianship.

Nightshadow's cold wet nose nudged his hand. He turned to the great dog. "He has gone where we cannot follow."

She pricked her ears and whined low in her throat, gazing intently in the direction they had been traveling, plainly wishing to continue their journey.

He laid his hand on her silken back. "He is gone, so there is no point in going to the stone mountain now."

Nightshadow danced away from his touch, then back again, head up, ears high, insisting.

Two Hearts considered. Snake had crossed over to the stone mountain in the spirit world. If he survived and found the strength to bridge the gap between the two worlds again, it was possible he would emerge, not here in the forest, but at the real stone mountain, still several days' travel away. He turned to the huge black dog. "Perhaps you are right."

Wagging her tail, she allowed him to mount, then sped into the forest, running with joyful purpose.

✳ ◇ ✳

The rising path Snake followed inside the mountain became a tunnel weaving through solid rock, illuminated by the same blue-white light. The floor rose steeply, littered with loose stones that bruised his feet. The air was close and hot, and, after a time, his stomach cramped with hunger. His tongue stuck to the roof of his cotton-dry mouth, but there was neither food nor drink in this inhospitable place, nor even a place to rest. He could only walk on and on until finally, after what seemed like days, he came to a cavelike opening in the wall.

Inside, a woman sat before a blue-white fire, her long green hair tumbled in a great pile across the floor. She bent over a wooden frame, working on something he could not make out, humming a low song that seemed vaguely familiar. He hesitated outside, wondering if he should speak.

She looked up with eyes the same clear green of the first spring leaf and he caught a glint of coppery breast and thigh beneath the long flowing hair. He turned his eyes away, embarrassed.

"I am Willow Woman," she said. "Come in, grandson."

He hesitated. "Did I know you before—in my other life?"

"I comforted you one lonely afternoon," she said, "but when you looked upon my face, you were frightened and knew me not. Sit here. Your time is short and there is much I must tell you."

The fire flared at his approach, as though it recognized him. He smelled the aromatic tang of cedar as he sat opposite her and tried not to look at her nakedness.

She bent her head back over the frame so that her hair obscured both her face and body. "Do you know where you are?"

Snake examined the small cave. "Somewhere inside the stone mountain."

"You are in the spirit realm." She turned her green-eyed gaze upon him.

He saw leaves, suddenly, a thousand different shades of green on branches questing up into the boundless sky, each bearing acorns, or apples, or flowers, or some other bounty, all filled with a verdant slow-growing strength as irresistible as the cycle of the seasons. His breath caught in his throat and he could not break away from her gaze.

"This world is formed of energy. Close your eyes and feel how it flows all around you."

"I don't under—"

"Do it," she said softly and his eyelids descended against his will.

He felt a humming against his cheeks and forehead and chest, a vibration as though he were inside some vast musical instrument in the midst of an ongoing song.

"You were born with a sensitivity to this realm and its energy is available to you when you walk the living land," she said. "Are you hungry?"

"Yes," he said stiffly, unable to open his eyes.

"And thirsty?"

"Yes."

"That is good."

He heard her bare feet whisper against the stone, then smelled the subtle spice of her body as fingers pressed against his temples. Misty images moved through his mind...an eagle...a great tree...the flash of lightning...a roaring river. "If you would use this energy for healing or protection or to prophesy, you must first purify yourself through the sacred power of Water."

He saw himself and Two Hearts standing in the forest stream, immersing a full seven times.

Her supple hands slipped down to his shoulders and his muscles quivered at the warmth that spread from her touch. "After that, you must make proper preparation. Spirit energy is not of your world, and calling it into an unprepared body can cause weakness, severe pain, unconsciousness, and even death. You should fast to clear your mind before attempting a great working."

Then hunger and thirst are tools, he thought, not just deprivations.

Her hands slipped down and rested over his belly, as though seeking something within. Her cool breasts pressed against his back. He stiffened as a sensual fire burned through him, building until he ached to take her in his arms, fit his lips to hers and drink of her pliant body.

She sighed against his ear. "How unusual—despite your obvious maturity, you have never lain with a woman. Used properly, this condition can be a source of immense power."

Dismay flooded through him, though he did not remember whether he had ever lain with a woman or not. He flushed and would have pulled away, but she held him close, her flesh cool, her voice serious and low. "Always remember that those who would work a massive calling must abstain from coupling. The energy generated when a man and a woman take pleasure of one another interferes with the channelling of medicine power."

She moved away. "When you have need of power, you must sing the song you have been given, open your heart to this world and ask for guidance."

"My—song?" he asked.

"Do you not remember?" Her hands slid up to lie across his eyes and forehead.

He saw the four colors of deer weaving about him, heard low deer-voices singing. *This is your song,* they had said.

"You have come here, fasting, abstaining, your mind clear and ready. There may come a time when you need the strength of all that draws its life from the earth. In that moment, call and I shall come to you."

Her hands fell away and he found he could now open his eyes. She stepped back from him. "Sing your song."

He opened his mouth and sang the simple chant, feeling the power of it wind through the cavern. The blue-white fire that glimmered on every surface flickered with the rise and fall of his voice.

She stood before him and swayed in time with his song, her long green hair shifting like the fronds of a willow tree in the wind. "Now open your heart and ask for what you need."

Still singing, he tried to think what he should ask for. Everyone he had encountered since waking up without his memory seemed to think he had some important task to do and momentous things to learn, but all he really wanted at this particular moment was to understand what was going on, and to do that, he had to *remember*.

She sighed, and her breath hissed like the wind through an entire forest of leaves. "Then remember." She braced his head between her hands and blue-white light exploded through his mind.

He saw broad emerald-green fields fenced by heaped gray stone and watered by frequent rain, agile black-and-white dogs herding sheep, narrow twisting tracks up the sides of rounded, green mountains, a horde of bustling, pink-cheeked men and women, chattering in a lilting tongue, a vast building of gray stone with a smaller pointed structure on its roof and a multitude of rainbow-colored windows, an older man in a long black robe who gazed at him with shocked and saddened pale-gray eyes.

All of this he remembered, and so much more, but none of it meant anything. They might as well have been the memories of a stranger. He staggered to his feet, about to protest he had not received what he wanted—but he was alone.

chapter sixteen

Snake left the cavern, filled with empty memories. Names drifted through his mind as he resumed his trek through the torturous tunnel . . . Father Fitzwilliam . . . Dublin . . . Maynooth . . . Declan . . . He knew they should have meant something to him, but they were little more than sounds.

Hunger settled inside his belly like a banked fire, simmering and painful, but at the same time empowering, as though enduring the discomfort made him master of something more important. Although the air was sultry, the walls and floor of the tunnel were cool to his touch and still gleamed a radiant blue-white. He stared at his hand on the stone, suddenly recalling how he had once been frightened at the sight of his skin shining with the same eerie light. When had that happened—and why?

The shrill cry of an eagle shattered the silence. The tunnel melted and he found himself instead on a shallow ledge amidst tumbled boulders, exposed to a fierce wind. He looked down and saw that he was perched on the side of a vast mountain towering above a forest that spread like a carpet of dark-green to the horizon. The sun had already set, leaving just a smudge of pink above the trees to the west. He backed up hard against the rocks, struggling to catch his breath.

A huge golden eagle, longer than a man was tall, soared past him in the twilight, wheeled and returned, landing talons first on the ledge with a flick of its immense wings. It cocked its head and studied him with one fierce molten-gold eye. "You asked my sister the willow to help you remember. Do your memories give you comfort?"

"No." The wind buffeted him and Snake pressed his spine to the chill stone, afraid he would slip over the edge of the mountain. Cold sweat trickled down his back. "I remember faces and names and places now, but none of it means anything."

"Life can be deceptive that way." The eagle's fierce beak preened at one wing. "On the surface, everything that makes up the world seems to be very different. No one would mistake a stone for the sky, or a man's flesh for the bark of a tree, yet underneath, at its core, all life is the same."

Snake's foot slipped and dislodged a fist-sized rock. It tumbled over the edge and careened down the side of the mountain. The crack of rock striking rock echoed up to him. Trembling, he tried to move back but there was nowhere to go.

"Close your eyes," said the eagle, "and tell me what you see."

Snake was afraid he would fall. "I—"

The eagle's fiercely hooked beak stabbed forward and slashed his cheek. "What do you see!"

His face throbbed, but somehow he kept from crying out and instead shut his eyes. Behind his eyelids, he saw the same blue-white radiance that had illuminated the tunnel. "I see—light."

"Where?"

Snake swallowed around the knot in his throat. "Everywhere."

"Now look with your eyes."

The brilliant light was still there, streaming out of the sky, flooding up from the rocks at his feet and back, radiating from his body, pouring from the eagle's eyes, uniting the whole of creation in one vast electric fire. Blood pounded in his ears and he was afraid his knees would give way. "What is—it?".

"Life," the eagle said. "You are part of the whole and the whole is part of you. Everything in this world is alive, and, as such, all things are your relatives. Respect the spirits of the least of these as you respect the Above Beings themselves, for in the end, all spirits are one."

Snake felt his edges dissolve until he was only one mote of consciousness in the field of blue-white light binding him to the stars and the soil and the sparrows and the rounded pebbles on the bottom of a rushing stream. He was one with the eagle and the earthworm and the sun. What happened to them, happened also to him, and everything he suffered became their sorrow.

A feather grazed his cheek and he was suddenly only himself again. He opened his eyes convulsively, feeling shriveled and small, painfully alone.

"The medicine power in this realm is the energy of all of creation." The eagle threw back its golden head and uttered a scream that echoed down the mountain. "There is great strength here, but you are only a hole through which this power is channelled."

"But what is it for?" Snake asked. "What am I supposed to do with it?"

"Climb—" The eagle passed its wing over Snake's head, bringing a chill, aromatic darkness scented with cedar. "—and remember."

Snake blinked and found himself alone on the side of the mountain, the stars glimmering in the blue-black expanse of the sky. Emotions flooded through him, shame and fear, disgust and terror, love, but he had no idea where they came from. They danced side by side in his head with the images of places and people, and none of it made any sense. He might as well have been seeing portraits of strangers, hearing bits and pieces of someone else's life.

He dabbed at the blood from his slashed cheek with the back of his hand, then turned to the narrow path that led ever upwards.

*　◇　*

Tired. Oh so very tired. Sunrunner's black muzzle drooped to the dust after he delivered his clan-mate, Smoke, and the not-clan she inside the wall-of-dead-trees. They slipped off his back and he sat down in the shade of one of the dens, head hanging, panting. His legs shook with weariness. The village smelled of cooked venison and parched corn and many many two-leggeds, a few Clan, but mostly not-clan, which made sense. Four-leggeds and their clan-mates should be out in the forest, scouting for enemies, hunting for food. Only females still suckling their young and those of the pack too old to run would remain in the place-of-dead-trees on such a fine day.

The two-leggeds gathered around the three of them, mostly not-clan by their scent, making so much mouthnoise all at the same time that Sunrunner flattened his ears, longing for the comforting babble of a mountain stream.

The young-she, whom he had carried, stood aside and let Smoke speak in low earnest tones, pointing back in the direction they had come. Sunrunner's ears flattened as he remembered the wrongness behind them, the slow, sweating four-leggeds carrying two-leggeds with thundering sticks that *bit*, leaving behind dead bodies in sticky pools of blood. The ruff rose along his shoulders and a growl rumbled in his throat.

Smoke looked down at him, then spoke more calmly to a young not-clan, who scampered away, then returned a few breaths later to set a jar of cool river water before him. Sunrunner lowered his head and lapped gratefully. His labored breathing eased and he began to watch the others with more interest.

The discussion continued with waving of arms and shouting. Sunrunner could tell Smoke was both frightened and angry, along with the young-she they had found in the forest, but the others, both Clan and not-clan finally walked away, leaving the three of them alone with Smoke's mate and their two young.

The young-she from the forest turned a wetness-streaked face to Smoke and asked something of him. His clan-mate seemed reluctant, but at the sound of her voice, a rightness tingled behind Sunrunner's eyes. He knew that feeling; it came from the place-beyond-sight. Whatever she asked was meant-to-be. He rose and shook himself, feeling somewhat rested, then licked her ear, signifying his willingness.

Smoke looped an arm around Sunrunner's neck and spoke to his mate who argued, clutching her young close to her breast. He spoke again, gesturing at the ring of dead trees, his voice emphatic. Finally, she lowered her nut-brown eyes and hurried away, one of her bewildered young tucked beneath each arm.

Smoke turned to the young-she and nodded. The two of them remounted Sunrunner's broad back and Smoke leaned low over his neck as he padded back out into the green depths of the forest.

When the tall palisade of Kitasi was in sight, One Eye dropped his mount back and glanced surreptitiously at the tight-lipped blackrobe as he rode. The foreigner had gone pale as new snow and his hands gripped the reins so tightly that his knuckles stood out bone-white through the skin. Amusement simmered in the back of One Eye's mind. The blackrobe clearly had no stomach for what was to come and yet, if he had not known how it would go before Idjoku, he surely understood now. Since he still rode with the raiding party, he would bear full responsibility for the deaths to come. One Eye saw how this knowledge was burning the other man's heart into a hollow husk. He smiled, then kicked his fidgety beast and surged back up to the front of the war party.

The red-coats halted just within the cover of the trees where they could not be detected from the palisade, then summoned the blackrobe forward to carry the green flag of trade. Ashen-faced, he hung back, mumbling and shaking his head. Broken-nose, the captain, reined his mount about sharply and cantered back to him. One Eye watched with interest.

Broken-nose spoke in a low, angry voice. The blackrobe stared down at his knotted hands on the pommel of his saddle, refusing to accept the flag until Broken-nose thrust the stick into his clenched fist. Then Broken-nose spurred his elk-dog deeper into the forest to wait for the gunfire that would signal them to join their fellows at the slaughter.

The remaining red-coats followed him, leaving only the blackrobe, the four best shots dressed as civilian traders, and One Eye. He kicked his mount toward the palisade. The soldiers surged after him and swept the blackrobe's mount along with them, talking and laughing as though this were the most innocent of trading expeditions and they expected a warm welcome.

A sturdy woman carrying a small child under each arm emerged from the palisade. Her dark eyes widened at the sight of the six elk-dogs and their riders, then she darted into the greenery at the edge of the forest, fighting through a tangle of bushes where there was clearly no path. The children wailed as they were raked by branches. The blackrobe stared after them, his face twisted with grief.

As the elk-dogs plodded through the gap in the fence, Tsalagi women looked up from weaving baskets, or wooden frames they were using to work hides, suspicion written on their faces instead of the usual curiosity. One Eye's jaw tightened; it was possible they had heard of yesterday's attack.

A stocky priest with threads of silver in his head-tuft strode forward. His eyes glittered at the sight of the strangers. He barked an order over his shoulder, then gripped the medicine bag around his neck. The women dropped whatever work was in their hands and disappeared into the shady maze of lodges and trees. An instant later, a large brown-and-white dog trotted around one corner, hackles raised and ears flattened, trailed by a pup.

The shaman closed his eyes, chanting. The air thickened around him, then sparkled like a swarm of golden bees. His skin crawling, One Eye reached for his bow, then caught the gaze of the nearest soldier and jerked his chin at the conjuring shaman.

The soldier nodded, took careful aim and fired. A neat red hole appeared between the shaman's eyes. He sagged to the ground as the snarling dog launched herself at the invaders. One Eye loosed an arrow and pierced her neck, staining the white fur with scarlet. She collapsed, kicking and snapping at the arrow. Her pup hesitated, crying out sharply in fear and confusion.

With a war-cry, One Eye picked another target, this time a silver-haired grandfather who was running, spear in hand, to join the battle. He fell in the dust while the women of Kitasi scooped up their crying children and hurried them toward the palisade's rear entrance to the fields. A rifle shot cracked from that direction; some of the soldiers had circled around to cover the back of the village. They were fairly clever, these English, he thought as he reined his nervous elk-dog in an arc, looking for more shamen.

Another dog appeared, this one a gray-muzzled liver-brown and almost as big as a bear, running on only three legs, but snarling and savage-eyed. One Eye swung his bow up as it leaped for his mount's throat. His elk-dog lurched backwards, spoiling his aim, and his arrow twanged into the dust. He lost his balance and then a million red-hot needles surged up through his body as he sprawled across the living earth, reminding him painfully what it was to be alive.

Gritting his teeth, he floundered for the reins trailing away from him, but the lame dog was tearing out his mount's throat. It screamed, thrashed, tumbled over backwards. One Eye scrambled out of its way as it fell heavily on its side, but every step seared as though he waded through fire. Images raced through his mind, the curve of his wife's smooth brown back lying before him as he traced it with one finger, his oldest son's crooked smile as he brought down his first squirrel with a blowgun, his newborn's tiny grasping fingers as they curled around his offered thumb.

He tried to push the memories away, refusing to acknowledge the mockery of Tsalagi life pulsing beneath his feet. The past was dead and only the present existed. The Catawbas' time would not come again and he would never be able to forget the agony of his loss until all land lay dull and lifeless as his own.

Breathing hard, he jerked the polished steel knife from the sheath at his waist. The great brown dog raised its blood-stained muzzle from the elk-dog's ravaged throat. It was a male, he saw, grizzled and lame, yet still alert, a credit to its pack. One Eye backed away as the old dog oriented on his knife, ears flattened, teeth bared in bristling snarl.

Red-coats streamed into the compound now, muskets firing, acrid gun smoke curling through the sweltering mid-afternoon air. A scattering of blue light shimmered back amidst the lodges, no doubt more Tsalagi medicine. Wary, he circled closer and the brown male limped after him, teeth bared. The smell of the soldiers' burned powder filled the air. He coughed, then coughed harder as smoke drifted through the village, obscuring the lodges.

In the midst of the fighting, the blackrobe still sat astride his fidgeting elk-dog, his face a mask, his staring eyes gray holes. One Eye maneuvered the priest between himself and the dog, hoping the beast would attack him. Behind them, the blueness grew brighter and he heard chanting. Something huge was forming before the trees and he caught the sweet scent of burning tobacco, powerful medicine. Fear rose in his throat like bile.

The dog lunged forward and hamstrung the blackrobe's elk-dog. Its back legs collapsed and the priest was pitched into the dirt. One Eye darted toward the trees while the screaming mount floundered and the dazed blackrobe rolled to his hands and knees. The dog ignored him, however, and followed One Eye on its three good legs.

Three elders stood on the other side of the translucent blueness, their eyes closed in concentration, their arms held aloft. The middle one raised a smoking pipe to the sky, and above them, a shimmering hook-beaked eagle coalesced out of the blue light. It cocked its fierce head, studying the battling English and Tsalagi with a bright-blue eye, then lightning-quick, seized a red-coat in its beak, cracked his back and tossed him aside like the discarded hull of a nut.

The land burned One Eye's feet and he let the pain fuel his anger, making him faster and stronger, less afraid. Killing these shamen would help stop the pain, he told himself as he slipped forward. It would hasten the day when he could stop remembering what had been and devote himself solely to the business of being dead.

The immense eagle shrieked a challenge, then snatched up another hapless soldier and bit him nearly in two. Behind One Eye, gunfire surged in a furious volley, then faded as the soldiers reloaded. The eagle cast the savaged body aside and dove at yet another. One Eye flinched as the immense head flashed down to tear the struggling soldier in its talons in half.

Women carrying children dashed toward the back entrance to the fields and forest beyond. One Eye grimaced and dodged the eagle's monstrous foot as it selected another victim.

He raised his arm to plunge his knife in the first shaman's breast, then came up short as the lame dog seized his leg, wringing a startled cry of pain from him. The air whooshed from his lungs as he fell heavily, and his suddenly nerveless hand dropped the knife. The dog shook him, grinding the bones in his leg. Screaming, he beat at its muzzle with his bare hands, and then heard a sharp crack. The dog stiffened, then melted to the ground, One Eye's leg still in its mouth. Breathing hard, One Eye pried the massive jaws apart. The blackrobe stood just beyond the unearthly eagle, one of the soldier's muskets in one bloody hand while the other traced a pattern across his breast.

One Eye staggered to his feet, blood streaming down his leg, and fumbled through the dust for his knife. The eagle turned and focused on him, its eyes bright with rage. Panicked, he threw himself at the closest shaman, a thin-shanked elder whose eyes were closed in concentration. The knife sank into the older man's breast and he wilted without a sound.

The eagle screeled and its body became transparent. One Eye yanked the knife out and plunged it into the second shaman's chest. The old man's eyes cracked open, and in their fading mirror he saw the reflection of a terrifying face distorted by pain and hate—his face. The upraised pipe slipped from the shaman's hands and he crumpled at One Eye's feet.

The eagle's body grew indistinct, and when its fierce beak slashed at the Catawba, it passed harmlessly through his body. The last shaman, stout and balding, gazed resignedly at One Eye. "Our land would have welcomed you. You could have taken a Tsalagi wife, known children at your hearth again, lived as one of us." He extended his arms to One Eye. "Have you forgotten we are all children of one mother, this earth, and one father, who dwells in the spirit world? There is not a hairsbreadth of difference between us."

The ground beneath One Eye's feet trembled; he felt its energy and vitality, the exuberant strength of its spirit. Could he find life again here, and turn away from the lingering death that was all that remained to him?

The outline of the eagle, almost invisible now, stared down at him, bright eyes peering through skin and bone, past the surface to the light that should shine within his heart. But he no longer had a heart, had not possessed even the shadow of one since he'd laid his wife and sons on the funeral pyre he'd built within sight of the sea. They were dead and he had died with them. There was nothing left of the man he had once been.

He raised the knife and slit the shaman's unprotected throat. Hot blood spurted over his face and shoulders. The eagle shimmered into tiny spheres of light and faded.

chapter seventeen

A chill wind battered Snake as he tried to make out the faint track that led up the side of the mountain. The moon had not yet risen and he could see almost nothing. His hands trembled as he fumbled at the shadowy ledges and his feet slipped again and again. His mind seethed with shame and disgust and fear, and above all, swirling, mind-numbing guilt, but it was all without meaning, as though the emotions belonged to some stranger. If these were his emotions, what terrible things must he have done? He both needed and yet feared to know.

The stars glittered down like crystalline eyes, watching, judging, finding him lacking in every respect. He stopped to catch his breath and found himself shivering under their critical gaze. His heart pounded and he almost turned away, but then remembered the great eagle's words—"Everything in this world is alive, and as such all things are your relatives."

He tilted back his head and whispered, "We are one, you and I, along with all the stones on the earth and the birds of the sky and even the smallest creatures that crawl." The stars wavered, as though considering, then settled into a steady glow that, although still very distant, warmed him in some way and made it easier to see.

As he climbed on, sometimes, above the cry of the wind, he heard a dry rustle as though something slid across the rock, but when he stopped to listen, there was only the relentless buffet of the wind. He came to a sheer rock cliff where the rough path ended. The mountain stretched above him, massive and dark-gray, sloping up into the night and obscuring the stars. He searched the seamless face for hand-holds or cracks where he might wedge a toe, but the granite here was unblemished.

He spread his fingers across the cold, rough surface. If he was one with the deer and the stars, as the eagle had said, then he must also be one with this proud, forbidding mountain. He reached for the feeling of self in the cold stone, cast his differences away and sought only what they shared. The rock sighed beneath him, shifted, molded to his shape. He dug the toes of his right foot into the stone, then his left, and climbed slowly above the windy ledge. As he moved his hands and feet, the stone gave beneath him, accommodating his need. He climbed, inch by inch, thinking only of his brother, his partner, this vast, silent mountain.

He pulled himself over the ledge at the top, then lay on his back, gasping like a beached fish. His lungs ached with the thin, frigid air and his head spun.

Something massive *slid* in the darkness, then reared up black against the midnight blue of the star-scattered sky. "Sssooo, youuu would beeee brother to theee sssnake?"

There was steel in that voice and chilling indifference. He lurched to his feet and searched his limited memory for the right response. "I have been told I am already related to everything in creation."

"And sssooo youuu are," the shape drawled, "but ssstill there could beee more for one whooo wasss born with one foot in theee realm of myyy golden sssissster, theee sssun, and theee other heeere in theee ssspirit realm."

"I don't remember my other life," he said. "Bits and pieces have been given back to me, but they don't make sense."

"Paaatiencccce," it said. "Youuu will remember more than youuu wisssh presssentlyyy. Do not russsh eeeventsss that mussst run their appointed coursssse. Whyyy have youuu come heeere toniiiight?"

"To learn who I am and what I must do."

A blue-white light split the darkness, emanating from the massive shape before him. He saw it clearly now, a swaying snake, taller than a man, with a glowing pattern of interlaced diamonds trailing down its sinuous back. He stood his ground, his heart pounding. "T-they call *me* Snake," he faltered, his throat constricted and dry. "Can you tell me why?"

The great serpent's eyes were burning blue coals. "III repreeesssent heeeealing and theee generative power of all liiife, greaaat medicccine sssuch asss isss given to onlyyy a fewww." The pointed head wove a complicated dance before him. "III caaame to youuu in your dreeeam, then in theee foressst in your tiiime of neeeed, and sssooo your companion knewww III wasss to beeee your ssspirit guiiide. III am theee sssourcccce of your power."

He couldn't take it in. "I—don't understand."

"Then *reeemember*." The snake darted forward, as though to strike. Before he could draw back, its tongue flicked his forehead.

A pressure surged through his mind, and then the assorted emotions and images integrated. He saw himself at school, a wondering child taught by nuns, and then later at seminary, older and serious, the student of priests. He remembered his mother's weathered face, at first only weary and then later ill, and his friends, few as they had been, the pure joy of celebrating mass for the first time, the dazzling feeling of connection with the power of almighty God, the numbing ocean voyage to this new world far across the sea from his green home of Ireland. He remembered Father Fitzwilliam and the agonizing trip up the river when even the birds and trees had spoken to him, the terrifying blue-white light in his hands that he couldn't control, all the heathen magic which had damned his soul. He was Declan Keenan Connolly, a Roman Catholic priest, not a denizen of this land, but an interloper, come to change it forever and in the process irretrievably altered himself. He sank to his knees, unable to speak.

"Everyyything isss truuue," the snake said. "What youuu knewww beeefore and what youuu knowww nowww. It isss all part of theee sssaaame creeeaaation."

Declan had sung with the deer-people, walked unscathed through solid stone, conversed with willows and rivers and eagles. He was damned, utterly and completely, trapped even now with this demon, who was perhaps Satan himself. How could he have been so witless? He buried his burning face in his hands.

"Theee power awaaakened within youuu can beee usssed for both good and eeevil, but isss not good or eeevil in and of itsssself." The snake slid closer and its blue-white tongue flickered like lightning. "It isss yours forever, whether youuu will it or not, and youuu must uuussse it asss your conssscienccce bidsss. Reeemember what youuu have been taught about how to preeepare yoursssself, for every usssse of medicccine-energyyy hasss theee power to burn your physssical bodyyy to cccindersss."

"I-can't use it!" Declan said brokenly. "I won't! It's witchcraft!"

"Not eeeven to sssaaave theee innocent, theee helplessss, all theee blaaame- lessss creeaturesss of thisss land? Are youuu not brother to theee wind and theee treeeesss and theee raaain?"

He was filled with the memory of the field of blue-white light binding him to all things, the incredible feeling of oneness with the universe. The very thought of never experiencing such harmony again was like having his still-beating heart torn from his chest. "Oh, God, forgive me!" Hot tears spilled down his cheeks.

"III am heeere," the snake said, "alwaaaysss, in everyyything and everyyy placcce and everyyyone."

The two realities warred within his head. He struggled to speak around the knot in his throat. "You—are not God!"

"Am III not?" The snake's triangular head wove closer. The lidless blue eyes seared the center of his soul. "Oopen your heart, sssmall one. Theee ssspirit world isss much larger than youuu think. Beee one with meee and myyy creeeaaation."

This creature, the serpent, the very symbol of Satan and the Fall, claimed to be God? A great shudder wracked Declan's body.

The snake wound across the barren rock and coiled before him, each of its loops as thick as a sturdy tree. He felt the electricity of its nearness, saw its shimmering glow even behind his eyes. "Youuu have felt it for yourssself, in theee sssinging clooosenessss of niiight, in theee brilliant fieeeld of liiight that uuuniiitesss all of creeeaaation; all sssspiritsss are one."

It sounded reasonable, but then so did all forms of temptation and he must not, could not give into it!

The great snake's fangs flashed down and pierced his neck. He staggered back as fire seared through his veins. His flesh dissolved and he felt himself racing toward the east and the unseen sea.

"Ssseeeee, there in theee dissstancce?" The trees below passed in a dizzying blur, but the field of blue-white energy uniting all things was clearly visible, even blinding; if he could have, Declan would have looked away, but he was helplessly bound to take it all in.

"Youuu sssspeeeak of eeevil? Look!"

A roiling dark mass bubbled at the edge of the sea, seeping inland, staining the beach and the coastal lands a dim, unhealthy gray, extinguishing the blue-white where the two fields touched. He cringed as he slowed, then hovered above the noisome darkness.

"Eeevil is uuussse of medicccine power for perssssonal gaaain, deniiial of theee onenessss of all creeeaaation." The snake's words wove around him. "Eeevil isss theee extinction of theee living land, exploitaaation of itsss creeeaturesss, raaape of theee plant-peeeople and theee winged-peeeople and theee four-leggedsss."

Below, Declan saw half-naked bronze-skinned natives unloading ships and carrying great packages. They bent beneath their burdens and were many fewer than their white masters.

"Death of theee bodyyy isss but passssaaage from one form to another, but death of theee ssspirit isss forever."

The land below *was* dead, he could feel that. The very air above it was fetid and reeked with the bitter tang of ashes; the wind was a dull and lifeless current. There was no vibrance, no sense of the unseen dance, no voice of any creature, save man, no light.

He found himself descending to the stained beach, and as he touched the sand, he became aware of the terrible wrongness beneath his feet. The sand felt empty and violated, rotted. The gorge rose in his throat as he realized he stood on the battered corpse of something that had once been bright and alive. He doubled up in pain, arms clutching his middle, and collapsed, straining to breathe, hot white sparkles dancing before his eyes.

"Thisss land onccce lived, wasss onccce bountiiiful with theee ssspirit of all living thingsss." The snake spoke from behind him. "Now it isss but a husssk, home ooonlyyy to dead men, for whooo else could bear to live in sssuch a desssecraaated plaaaccce?"

But after he had come from Ireland, he had lived here, walked these sands and breathed the air, and he had felt nothing of this, suspected *nothing*.

"That wasss beeefore your ssspirit wasss awaaakened."

Declan shuddered; his life energy was dribbling into the moribund sand. Every muscle in his body cramped and he felt hollowed out, empty as the grayness possessing this land invaded his soul. He realized he would die, if he stayed here. Whether just physically, or spiritually, he did not know, nor did he want to find out. "I—have—to go back!" he forced out between numb lips.

In an instant, he was returned to the wind-swept pinnacle of the stone mountain. The frigid wind battered him, howling like a hurricane, its life streaming past his face as he lay curled in a ball on the hard stone. The mountain was wondrously alive beneath his body, and its restoring vitality surged through him, easing the agonizing cramps and the desolate hollow ache within.

The snake reared up before him, its eyes scintillating blue fire. "Nooo matter what youuu beeelieeeve, can youuu ssstand byyy and allow thisss land to diiie?"

Still trembling, Declan braced his aching head between his hands. "How do I know you are not the Great Deceiver, trying to trick me into everlasting damnation?"

"Youuu have walked there and seeeen for yourself. Isss theee difference beeetweeeen living and dead land a liiie?"

Declan's teeth were clenched and he had to force out the word, "N-no."

"And would theee God youuu have knooown creeeaaate sssuch an abominaaation asss land without liiife?"

Would He? Declan saw fountains of blood, from the both red man and the white, animals lying in heaps upon the dead lands, their bodies burned to charcoal, the rotting stumps of razed trees stretching to the horizon, the filthencrusted banks of the rivers, polluted, lifeless waters.

He pressed his hands over his eyes. "M-my God, w-whom I have s-sworn to serve all of m-my days, would n-never be part of that."

"Then youuu will fiiight."

He shook his head. "I-I don't k-know how."

"Two Heartsss fiiightsss in hisss waaay, asss do all of hisss peeeople, but it will not beee eeenough." The snake bared its bone-white fangs. Declan braced himself, certain he would not survive another strike.

"Thooossse whooo have been gifted with power mussst fiiight for thooossse whooo cannot. How can theee grassss fiiight for itsss liiife, or a fawn, or my sssisssster, theee willooow?"

Declan remembered Willow Woman's arms encircling him when he was desolate and lost, remembered the song the deer-people had given him.

"Can youuu ssstand byyy and watch thisss land diiie?"

He knew then, no matter what the cost to his soul, he could not. Whatever the origins of the blue-white spirit-energy and the terrible snake now coiled before him, life was a gift from God, who had created everything in the world, making it all sacred. Anything and anyone that destroyed such beauty and vitality had to be evil. His heart shriveled at the approaching death of that joyous riot of life he had experienced on the Tsalagi land when he had thought he was only Snake, where the rivers told tales, and trees welcomed the lost and gave them comfort, and the very stone itself could work in partnership with a man.

No matter what it cost, if it was within his power, he could not allow this land to be decimated. He bowed his head. "I will go to the English."

The snake's coils gleamed with the blue-white radiance he had come to associate with spirit-energy. "Youuu were taught a sssong byyy the deeeer-peeeople to accessss your power. Now III give youuu a danccce." The triangular head began to dip and weave in a compelling, complicated rhythm.

His skin crawled. The great snake had a terrible beauty as its coils slid first this way, then that. It both attracted and repelled him more than he could bear, yet he could not look away. The Christian aspect of his personality broke out in a cold sweat, thinking only of the Garden of Eden and Satan, the great deceiver, but another part of him felt the hair on his head stir with the electric tingle of medicine-energy.

The snake was weaving a pattern, as insubstantial as a lattice of sunbeams. Declan felt, rather than saw, it lingering in the air, supporting him as his blood settled into the rhythm of the serpent's hypnotic movements. Something within him altered, moved into resonance with the pulse of this other world. He swayed, unable to look away.

The creature's shining blue eyes grew until Declan was swallowed by a vibrating luminous field of spirit-energy, until he was the blueness and the blueness was he and there was no such thing as Declan/Snake the man anymore, just a tiny mote of consciousness in the vast sea of all living things. His edges dissolved and he felt such peace as he had never known, the healing love contained within the oneness of all things, the essential center he had always lacked.

In that flash, he saw the possibility of a life where all creatures, the legless, two-legged, four-legged, winged, and leafed, all were relatives, where they would dance together and give of their flesh to their brothers to be eaten when needful, where they would recognize that spark within each which made them part of the Great Spirit who had created them all.

The sea ignited inside his head in a painful burst of electric blue fire. He felt suddenly as though he were being stuffed through some infinitesimally small hole. He cried out, and it seemed his brothers the granite / stars / spiders / grass / wind / worms/ rivers cried out with him until all of creation was united in one glorious flame.

*   ◇   *

He opened his eyes to the hot golden eye of the sun, peering down from a cloud-ridden sky. He lay on the sloping stone summit of a mountain, his face turned up. His head throbbed and his tongue stuck to the roof of his mouth. He squinted up at the gray-white clouds scudding towards the west. The breeze brought the scent of pine and cedar and just a hint of blackberries, but his stomach writhed at the thought of food.

He struggled to remember ... he had been in another place and someone ... *something* had been with him, had spoken of important matters. There had been a wonderful moment when he had been utterly at peace, had felt himself in the right place doing right thing for the first time in his entire life, but he could not remember what had caused that blissful feeling, or how to get it back, and the harder he tried, the more his head hurt.

The pieces of his shattered memory swirled through his mind like flotsam caught in a whirlpool. The spirit-world ... the teeming streets of Dublin ... Two Hearts ... Father Fitzwilliam ... a huge black dog with the star emblazoned on her forehead ... the Holy Mother Church. He was seized by shaking and could not stop. Dear Father in Heaven, he was damned, utterly and completely, tainted with the blackest of magics to be found and unable even to repent and turn away, for he had sworn to help these creatures.

A faint staccato bark from far below broke into his thoughts. Gritting his teeth, he heaved up onto one elbow and shaded his aching eyes as he looked down the rocky slope to two minuscule figures at the foot of the mountain, one black as the night, and the other human.

chapter eighteen

L ate afternoon sun poured down on Berry and Smoke as Sunrunner abandoned the leafy canopy of the trees and plunged into a meadow that stretched down the side of a hill. Waist-high grass whispered against the great dog's legs as he loped steadily onward, and, when Berry closed her eyes, she could still see hot golden flecks of light through her eyelids. Sunrunner's powerful shoulders moved rhythmically as she leaned over his neck, and every stride brought them closer to that mysterious mountain where she knew she must go. It felt wonderful to at last be doing something in response to her dreams.

Sunrunner had turned his nose northeast, the direction in which her dreams insisted she must travel. She hoped it was not too late to avert the terrible times she had foreseen. Some of the elders had scoffed when Smoke told of the attack on Idjoku. "So few?" they said. "Our old women can handle bigger war parties than that! These English are so stupid, they have left their real dogs at home and ride instead clumsy, cowardly elk-dogs that are no good at all in a fight. If they should prove foolish enough to start something, we will cut their livers out and feed them to the pack."

When they stopped at a stream to drink, Berry slipped down from Sunrunner's back and knelt on the bank to bathe her perspiring cheeks and neck. The water was clear and, beneath the shimmering reflection of the sky, she saw rows of slim, silvery fish-people, tails curving, standing head-first into the current.

The dog lowered his muzzle to drink as Smoke glanced back over his shoulder and then stiffened. Berry let water drain through her fingers as she followed his gaze. To the southeast, a great smudge of black smoke slanted above the trees, fouling what had been a pristine blue sky.

Berry's heart fell. "Kitasi!"

Smoke took her arm and pulled her to her feet. "Stay here while Sunrunner and I scout. If there is fighting, you are safer here. Once we see what can be done, I will send Sunrunner back for you."

Before she could protest, he leaped onto the dog and headed back into the forest. Her heart pounded as she saw glints of golden fur between the trees until he was out of sight. At first, she tried to wait, as he had said, but could not sit still when she was so worried. So she passed the time foraging for food and medicinal

plants. If there were wounded back in Kitasi, all her healing skill would be needed. By the time Sunrunner returned with the first victim clinging to his neck, she
had a fair supply of healing herbs and barks.

Throughout the remaining afternoon and into the night, Smoke sent survivors back to Berry on the great dog while he stayed behind to search for more.
With every trip, Sunrunner brought old men and women and children, one and
two at a time, their faces blackened by smoke, their bodies crisscrossed with
burns where flaming debris had fallen on them. Each time Sunrunner returned,
he was increasingly weary, but would stop only long enough to drink from the
stream and then race back into the forest's vast green silence.

Berry built lean-tos to shelter the wounded behind thickets a short distance
from the trail. At first she worried the vicious red-coats would find them, but the
incoming survivors said the strangers had camped by the river outside Kitasi, eating the food they had stolen from village stores and arguing with each other
through the night.

The able-bodied men and boys and the few surviving shamen remained
behind, gathering in a hollow not far from Kitasi, spying on the invaders and
planning revenge. The White Peace government, which had held sway for many
seasons, was dissolved by this attack, and now the surviving elements of the Red
War government pulled together to make new assignments of responsibility and
assess resources. Tsalagi seldom made war, but they always maintained a certain
level of readiness, and when only war would uphold their honor, they were
relentless.

Although every dog left in the village had died protecting their clan-mates,
most had been nursing females or gray-muzzles, no longer able to run the trails.
The bulk of the pack was scattered throughout the forest, hunting, training the
younger dogs, or running patrol. When enough of them returned, war would be
waged and the honor of Kitasi restored.

Tight-lipped and shaken, Berry instructed those who were well enough to
forage how to find plants to soothe burns and ease pain, making sure they
scrupulously asked each plant-person's permission. The spirit-energy within
leaves and roots and bark was far more potent when freely given. Her mind raced
round and round. She had seen this disaster coming, had begged them to flee,
and yet still it was her fault; if she had been more convincing, the elders would
have listened.

Braids Hemp, Smoke's wife, was the most help, having learned some plant lore herself, though she was not nearly as skilled as Berry. She could however beat roots for healing poultices and steep bark teas while Berry combed the surrounding hills for food to fill hungry mouths and still more medicines.

Each time she lay down for a brief respite of sleep and closed her eyes, the immense gray mountain rose up in her mind. She was supposed to go there and do something, complete . . . something, or someone. The certainty beat through her, but for now, she was desperately needed here, and Sunrunner, who had agreed to take her, must now play his part in the coming fight.

Whatever the mountain held, it must wait.

Nightshadow leaped to her feet, ears pricked, barking in short, sharp bursts as she gazed up at the sacred mountain. The afternoon shadows were lengthening into blueness as Two Hearts dried strips of venison over the fire. He heaved to his feet and studied the overwhelming expanse of gray stone that blotted out half the sky.

Nightshadow dashed up the narrow, steep trail leading toward the summit and her paws scrabbled furiously for footholds. Two Hearts followed, watching where he put his hands and feet. The eager dog could not get too far ahead of him; the trail, rough as it was, ended about a quarter of the way up the mountain. Anyone who wished to climb higher needed first permission, and then assistance from the spirit world. If Snake had emerged up there, that was the only way he would get down.

Two Hearts finally caught up with Nightshadow at the trail's end. She stared mournfully upwards, her entire body quivering. He laid a hand on her shoulder. "He must come down by himself or not all."

She licked his face, the first sign of affection she had ever given him, then again turned her nose to the summit. With a sigh, Two Hearts sat on a boulder to wait and crossed his arms.

Twilight had settled vast pools of blue shadow across the forest below before he began to hear what Nightshadow had apparently heard the whole afternoon, a man's labored breathing and the soft scrape of moccasins over stone. He rose to his feet. "Snake?"

The breathing hesitated, and then the footsteps started again, faster this time. Dislodged pebbles clattered down the mountain side. Nightshadow danced about the confined space, whipping her body back and forth, whining, stopping

occasionally to brace her forepaws on the obstructing wall of stone at the end of
the path and strain upwards.

A fist-sized rock careened down a narrow chasm, narrowly missing her head.
She jerked back and they heard sliding, then the thump of flesh meeting stone.
Nightshadow backed up until her warm furred barrel was pressed against Two
Hearts. In spite of the breeze, he broke into a sweat. This young man from across
the great water was not one of them, no matter what his innate abilities. He needed a lifetime of training and preparation to walk the spirit world, not a few days,
such as he'd received. If he didn't know how to ask the mountain's permission, he
might well kill himself before he reached the bottom and then all would be lost.

Perhaps he should intercede on Snake's behalf and ask the mountain to ease
his descent—but if he could not save himself, how could he reach into the spirit
world and help the Tsalagi?

A curly, dark-haired head appeared for an instant, then was hidden by the
rocks. Nightshadow leaped against the sheer face of the cliff in her impatience.
Two Hearts shaded his eyes against the fierce glare of the descending sun.
"Snake?"

The head reappeared, the face haggard, thinned by exhaustion. A line furrowed his brow and he hesitated at the top of the cliff, staring down at Two
Hearts with uncomprehending blue eyes that stood out in his sweat-grimed face.
Had he forgotten Two Hearts while he walked in that other reality? It was entirely possible. Two Hearts knew the spirit world marked a person in ways not visible
to the eye.

"I suppose I am Snake, in a way." The younger man pressed a hand to his
head, clearly exhausted. "I have no wish to be, but it seems to have been forced
upon me."

Nightshadow approached as he swung his feet over the edge and slid down to
her level, then wavered, close to collapse. She lowered her ears and nosed him
uncertainly. He backed away, surprised, then seemed to recognize her after all.
"Nightshadow!" He buried his face in her ruff and his arms tightened around the
black neck. "I saw her there once, in that other place. She was sitting on the top
of the highest mountain in the world with an old woman."

Two Hearts took his arm and guided him toward the trail. "She is very wise. I
am not surprised the spirit world knows her name."

Snake looked at him with puzzled eyes. "Why is that, do you think?"

Two Hearts had forgotten how blue his eyes were; they made him think of cornflowers and the midday sky and the brilliant blue-white energy that bound the spirit world together. He forced himself to look down at the stone beneath their feet. "She has a part to play in the battle against the coming troubles, as do you, and I."

"But can she do it without losing her soul?" He ran fingers back through his tangled hair and shook his head. "What if she saves the world and loses herself?"

"She is only a dog, as we are only men, and she must do the best she can," Two Hearts said, "as must we all."

As it was Sunday, Father Fitzwilliam said mass beside the river, but neither the English soldiers, nor the heathen Catawba scout, One Eye, paid him any heed. The Latin verses sounded hollow and were swallowed by the open air. The tiny white host tasted of mold, and that distressed him. The wafer should dissolve on the back of the tongue, without taste. It was not civilized to *eat* it. He sipped from the small cup of sacramental wine, letting it roll down his throat quickly, but the fruitiness filled his mouth and he could still taste it several hours later. He sat on a half-rotted log, brooding, watching the river's green current swirl against the shore, and felt irretrievably soiled.

Behind him, the soldiers argued good-naturedly, forks clinking against metal plates. Fitzwilliam shuddered. Even the thought of food made him ill. How could these brutes go on eating and talking and sleeping after the madness they had done here? The stench of burning flesh now permeated the leaves and the ground and even his clothes. He knew he would never be free of it, would reek of it even when he stood before the Almighty as his penance for being present on that terrible day.

Did God truly desire the souls of the savages of this vast continent at the cost of such carnage? Before the last few days, he had thought he knew the answer, that salvation must be won for these pathetic lost souls at any price, but now he was no longer certain. It was true the heathen shamen had sacrificed their souls when they took up the Devil's magic, but Jones's men had murdered even the smallest children, then refused to allow him to minister last rites, instead casting the small naked brown bodies onto the pyre, along with gray-haired grandmothers whose heads had been bashed in and dead shamen still clutching crystals and the bloodied carcasses of the immense dogs who had died trying to protect their masters.

Kitasi had burned down to a smoldering ruin, the surrounding palisade reduced to blackened stubs. He did not know why he was here, indeed, why God had even permitted him to be born if he was destined to be part of this travesty. Better that he had died at his mother's breast than to have taken one blameless life. At present, he lacked the will for anything more than to sit here on a log and stare at the green-brown river and pray for this hellish nightmare to be over.

Captain Jones sopped up the last of his meal with a piece of bread, then laid his plate aside. "We shall set out for the next village tonight, Father. The moon will be full and One Eye is confident that we will have less than six hours' ride. We'll enter the village tomorrow morning, as soon as the hunters have left for the day. Get your gear together and make sure it's all properly packed."

Fitzwilliam pressed his hands over his eyes. "I—cannot."

"What are you talking about?"

"I intend to return to the fort."

"Don't be ridiculous!"

The anger in the captain's voice made Fitzwilliam lower his hands and meet his outraged gaze. "I—am a priest, consecrated by the power of God to save men's souls and make their lives richer, not to watch babes hacked to pieces in their mothers' arms."

"You knew what we were about long before you were assigned to my command." Jones loomed over him, staring down with contempt in his chill blue eyes. "You came to this continent to do a soldier's portion as surely as any other man here."

"You were supposed to kill only their shamen—so they couldn't work their devilish magic, not slaughter innocent women and children!" Fitzwilliam heard the screams again, saw the struggling children, the little boy that Jones himself had trampled beneath his mount's hooves. Cold sweat drenched his body.

Jones seized his cassock in one large-knuckled fist and jerked him up off the log. "Soldiers bloody well kill anyone and anything that stands in the way of following their orders!" A vein bulged in his forehead, then he shoved the priest aside. "Besides, they're nothing more than filthy animals. Shooting one of them, at any age, is no worse than killing a stray cat. Where the hell do you think the shamen come from anyway—that they spring from their mothers full grown? Every one of those children would have grown up to make war on His Majesty's troops."

Fitzwilliam looked away, resting his eyes on the tangle of vines and trees across the river. "Then do what you must, but I will not be part of it anymore."

"You're more than a part of this operation." Jones spat into the sand at his feet. "You're the bloody key. You have to identify the shamen when we first ride in, or they'll have time to work their magic against us. One Eye hasn't been back this far. You're the only one of this party who's traveled to all of these villages and they know your face. You have to go, and I don't give a rat's ass whether you like it or not!"

"I can't," Fitzwilliam said numbly.

"I've sent one of the men back for Father O'Neil. Maybe one of your own kind can make you see reason," Jones said. "In the meantime, be ready to ride at dusk, or I'll shoot you myself."

✳ ◇ ✳

Declan didn't remember most of the trip down the mountain. He merely put one foot in front of the other, walking when he could, climbing down when he had to, and sliding when he lost his footing. He was scraped from crown to toes, but it was strangely distant pain, as though his body were only connected to his mind at a few weak points.

After a time, it seemed he was no longer alone, but had come upon two faces he had seen in his dreams, an older, weathered bronze-skinned man with eyes of dark teak and an air of ancient wisdom, and the narrow black face of a furred four-legged who bore a blinding white star on her forehead. He wasn't sure. Perhaps he was asleep and his body was safe somewhere, only dreaming of weariness and pain.

His vision hazed, but he kept moving, comforted from time to time by words he did not understand. He savored them like music, drifting until he abruptly came to himself, sitting cross-legged on a thick bed of pungent pine needles before a small fire, with the scent of roasting meat filling the cool evening air.

He blinked and saw that he sat with the other man in a small clearing. The black dog lay at his side, her warmth pressed against his thigh. The stone mountain rose into the sky behind their backs, gray against the darker, star-spattered sky. He still felt power emanating from it like a warm throb, its cadence overriding his heartbeat.

"I did not think to see you alive again in this world," the Tsalagi said. He tore off a strip of roast venison and handed it to him.

Declan accepted the meat. His stomach contracted and he realized he had never been so ravenous in his entire life. His hands trembled as he bit into the juicy strip, then wiped grease from his chin.

Two Hearts chewed, his eyes on the fire. "How much do you remember?"

Memories surged inside his head, Tsalagi and Irish, spirit-medicine and Christian, two entirely separate and contradictory realities that could not both be true at the same time. Pain stabbed through his head and he grimaced, waiting for it to pass. "Everything," he said shortly.

"Then you know what you must do."

"I know at least what has become of the coast since the British took possession." Declan suddenly tasted the decay and rot of the dead lands and had to spit the mouthful of half-chewed meat into the dirt. "I cannot in good conscience allow that to continue." He stared into the darkness where crickets sang, and orange and green fireflies flitted between the trees. "I have promised to go to the English and make them understand what they are doing is wrong."

Two Hearts jerked to his feet. "They already understand what they are doing! If they did not, they would not have killed the shamen, and the Catawbas' land would yet live."

Weariness swept over Declan in waves, carrying him farther away with each surge. He leaned back against Nightshadow's side, felt the comforting rhythm of her breathing, the softness of her fur. She sniffed at his ear. "I think you are wrong."

"Then you will die," Two Hearts said bitterly, "and our land will die with you!"

Declan struggled to make his eyes focus on the Tsalagi's face. "All I can do is go to them and try to make them see reason."

"You can fight!" Two Hearts knelt at his side, placed one hand on his shoulder. "Share the vision you received in the spirit world with us, and we will fight at your side."

Declan shook his head wearily. "I cannot use medicine energy, or I will lose my soul."

Two Hearts' face hardened. "Then we will all die."

"I have been a stranger among you, sent by a people who have brought you nothing but trouble, and yet you have helped me." Declan's eyes closed. "I am grateful, but I cannot do what you want. There are far worse things than death."

✳   ◇   ✳

One Eye gritted his teeth as the troop of soldiers rode through the moonlit forest. Once he was in the saddle and his feet no longer were in contact with Tsalagi land, the pain lessened until he had some room for other thoughts again, but it was all going too slowly. The English were in no hurry to find the next village and destroy its shamen, and he could not seem to convince them to work more quickly. But he was well aware that out there in the darkness, the survivors of Kitasi and Idjoku were gathering. Revenge was sacred to the Tsalagi, as all surrounding peoples had good cause to know, and they would never rest until their honor had been restored. Even if the English killed every shaman between the mountains and the sea, the Tsalagi still had arrows enough to shoot each English soldier a hundred times over, and he had no desire to find his end in that fashion.

But the English must ride in rows, march in *rows*, as though lines of men and horses had some sacred meaning, some power, when he well knew the English had no medicine-power in their hearts, just a vast supply of iron and powder and a complete lack of regard for anything else. They were forces of raw chaos come to sunder life from the land. Perhaps the grandfathers had told tales of such evil spirits when he was a boy, but all the grandfathers were long returned to the earth and now there was no one left to ask.

Except for the Tsalagi, but soon they would be as wretched as he, One Eye, had ever been. They too would crawl on their bellies, their skin rotted with the spotted sickness, and beg the white man for his putrid scraps. They would see their children lying dead and unburied, their women big with the white man's brats, and they would know their name had passed forever from this earth. They would share his pain and, in their misery, bring a new order that he could bear, with nothing of value left to envy or desire, nothing to remind him of what he had lost.

When it was all gone, no more than ashes beneath his feet, then he would rest. He would put away hate and lie down on the empty land and find at last some measure of silence to give him surcease.

And the white men, fools that they were, would never suspect what treasure had slipped through their unknowing hands.

chapter nineteen

The air held that sultry closeness which presaged a storm, making it difficult to breathe in the deer thickets beneath the towering oaks. Berry felt something in the stillness, tasted it on the back of her throat, a unpleasantness foretelling trouble, or, rather, more trouble.

She knelt beside a feverish toddler. Two hectic spots of bright red colored the girl's cheeks, and she breathed more shallowly with each passing moment. She had taken a deep gash in her leg when she and her mother had fallen under the hooves of an elk-dog, fleeing, Berry thought angrily, those cowards who made war on suckling babes. The mother had died, sheltering the girl's body with her own, and now the cut was infected. Berry had not been able to relieve either the swelling or fever. The jagged wound needed another poultice, something more potent, but nothing suitable had come to hand.

Sighing, she rose and motioned to Braids Hemp, who was seated beside her own two sleeping girls, her head bowed in weariness. "I need to gather medicine for Flicker Bird," Berry whispered, so as not to awaken the children. "Will you tend her until I get back?"

Braids Hemp's black eyes darted toward the tiny figure tossing and moaning on an armful of grass. Her face was bleak and full of pain, and Berry knew suddenly the other woman did not think this child would live.

"Of course, I will." Braids Hemp put one hand to her tired back and straightened. "Look as long as you need to and try not to worry. Do you want a torch?"

Berry gazed up through the interwoven canopy of trees. The layers upon layers of leaves were emerald-black in the darkness. Only the faintest smattering of moonlight was visible when the evening breeze stirred them. "That would help."

Braids Hemp lit a torch from the tiny fire that was all they dared against the darkness. Berry took it and set off back toward Kitasi, or rather what was left of their town. She had avoided that area, fearing the soldiers, but Smoke had ridden back on Sunrunner earlier in the afternoon to say there was no sign of movement on the part of the English so far. They had camped by the river to tend their wounded, and he hoped in the morning they would return to the coast.

The dogs and their clan-mates were returning in ones and twos, so the warriors were still planning. They had sent messengers to the other towns and meant to be at full force before they mounted an attack. Berry shivered even

though the air was warm. She would not feel safe until the English had left this
land.

Occasional glimmers of moonlight silvered the leaves and vines as she crept
along. She heard frogs croaking on her left, down in a creek bottom where
beavers had created ponds, and the breeze rustled through the leaves overhead,
too high up to give her any relief from the sticky closeness of the air.

She worked her way up the trail, asking some of the bigger trees, who had
strong voices, where she might find sweet-gum or thyme, both effective against
infection. Finally, an immense chestnut speculated she should search a nearby
ridge where the soil would be dry, almost dusty, the way herbaceous thyme liked
it.

Leaving the trail to climb the ridge, sweat trickled down her shoulders and
plastered her deerskin shirt to her back. She stopped to examine the ground,
holding the torch carefully, then realized with a start that the frogs had quieted.

Holding her breath, Berry heard a rhythmic four-beat clumping multiplied
many times. No wild thing would ever make that much noise, and certainly no
dog was that heavy on its feet. Her heart raced. Something, or someone, was
approaching on the narrow trail she'd just left, and if they continued, they would
see the fires of the injured women and children. Panic raced through her; she
should have been more careful, should have insisted they pull farther back into
forest, perhaps across a bog, but it was too late now.

She doused her torch in the dirt and slipped after the noise. Voices drifted
back to her, low and masculine, along with the jingle of metal against metal and
the creak of leather, and she caught the unforgettable odor of elk-dogs. It was the
English, not headed back toward the coast, as Smoke had hoped, but for Cheota,
the next village, traveling by night in order to take it unawares. The killing was
not over.

She slid through the inky shadows, laboring to keep pace with the invaders.
Elk-dogs were slow and clumsy, but she had to fight her way through the brush.
Trying to think, she took a shortcut as the path switched back on itself. She
skimmed through thickets, tearing her flesh on thorns, ripping her hair out of
branches as it caught. She had to get in front of them, draw them away somehow,
or at least hold them up and make enough noise so that the camp would hear and
flee.

Breathless, she picked up a rock and crouched behind a fallen log as the English rode past her hiding place. Their torches cast flickering shadows, shaped like

the strange beasts out of the old tales, that slid across the trees, twice as tall as a man. When the last elk-dog passed, she threw the rock with all her might at its dusty hindquarters. The beast squealed and pinned its ears, bolting into the mount just ahead of it.

She dashed ahead, jumping snags and rocks, while the soldiers manhandled their beasts back into submission. Twigs crackled under her moccasins as she scooped up several more rocks and let them fly at a gray elk-dog in the middle of the procession. It snorted and leaped sideways, crashing its rider into a massive tree trunk. He sagged in the saddle, then fell cursing to the ground. The nervous elk-dog trotted up the trail, reins trailing, snorting.

Men were yelling now, holding torches above their heads, reining their mounts in tight circles, searching for the unseen attacker. She huddled in a mossy depression behind a half-buried boulder, wishing for Sunrunner to carry her away from here. He would not need a trail, but would have put his head down and run the trackless forest for the sheer joy of it. She closed her eyes, remembering the softness of his fur against her face, the rich scent of his coat.

Footsteps crashed toward her. Angry voices shouted. Branches cracked and were tossed aside. She was afraid to look, afraid even to breathe. The makeshift camp lay just around the next bend. Surely they heard this racket. They were far enough off the trail that the soldiers might pass them by if the fires were put out.

She heard labored breathing now, and a muttered stream of foreign words. She opened her eyes, ready to bolt, just as a hand reached down and seized her hair. A red-coated soldier grinned down at her with crooked teeth, then yelled over his shoulder. The others called back, obviously congratulating him.

She threw herself at his face, clawing at his eyes, scratching. He lurched backwards, almost losing his grip, then struck her with his free hand. Surprisingly, she felt the force of the blow, but no pain as the ground rushed up to meet her. She blinked stupidly at the toe of his boot before he seized her shirt and dragged her back to the disgruntled men waiting on the trail.

Declan woke suddenly as though someone had spoken in his ear. The night hung about him, thick as syrup and still; even the breeze had faded so that the leaves hung quiet and limp. He turned and stared up over Nightshadow's back at the towering bald knob of the mountain. He could feel its power vibrate down at him through the darkness, touching him deep inside, anchoring him. Somehow, this mountain overlapped that other world and its granite was saturated with the four-fold spirit-energies, his to wield, as long as he observed the necessary precautions. Fasting, as Willow Woman had told him, and purification as the deerpeople had said. It seemed so reasonable, like robing before saying mass, or composing the mind to pray, or making the sign of the cross to acknowledge God. He felt the lure of the mountain and the power it represented, as well as the appeal of that other person residing inside his head now, guileless Snake who knew nothing of sin or eternal damnation, but gloried in the bountiful beauty of this wild world.

Declan's jaw tightened. It was worse than pointless to think about such things. As a Christian and a Catholic, he was consecrated to the service of the Lord. It tainted him almost beyond redemption to even consider using such forces. The sooner he reached the fort and convinced General Carleton to withdraw from Tsalagi land, the sooner he could take passage on a ship returning to Ireland where he could retreat into the safety of the seminary and seek a way to atone for the terrible sins he had committed here.

But—a small part of his mind niggled—what exactly had he done that was so wrong? Listened to the meandering tales of a river? Consorted with dogs and birds and trees?

Oh, but that left out his shameful routing of the soldiers sent to fetch him back to the fort, not to mention the huge blue-white serpent on the top of the mountain, tempting him with visions of catastrophe, beguiling him into sin. A hot wave of shame flooded through him; *he had agreed to do its bidding.* Whatever could he have been thinking?

The truth was—he had not been thinking. Something else had been doing his thinking for him, something wild and uncontrollable which knew nothing of civilization, or Christ's sacred sacrifice, or the Holy Mother Church. If he had been in his right mind, he would never have sanctioned magic for any reason, no matter what the end result. This was the Devil's work.

On the other side of the dying fire, Two Hearts turned over and muttered in his sleep. Behind Declan, Nightshadow flicked an ear and sighed through her nose. Breathing hard, Declan sat up and buried his face in his hands. There had to be an honorable way to extricate himself from this damning commitment. Perhaps none of it was true. He might have fallen victim to a series of false images, not the least of which was the slaughtered coastal lands he had been shown, a last effort by the Great Deceiver to prevent the glory of Almighty God from entering the New World.

Easing onto his knees, he turned his face up to the moon's rising ivory disk and the distant stars arrayed behind it like a vast garden of lights. He clasped his hands and prayed silently for the strength to find the truth in this barbarous place, and the wisdom to recognize it, once he did. He closed his eyes and reached for the abiding love that had comforted him throughout his entire life, the sense of God's immeasurable strength. Tension seeped from his body as the familiar peace swept back over him. Tears sprang into his aching eyes and he felt a fierce exultation; he was *not* alone. The Lord had not abandoned him for his many and grievous sins, as he had so richly deserved. God was present in this savage realm of leaf and rock and tree, had been here all along, as He was everywhere and in everything. There was still hope of salvation in the world and Christian love and the promise of a better life to come, after this one was done.

A whisper sprang up in the back of his mind, but he could not make it out. It was joined by another soft voice, then another, all speaking at once. He concentrated, trying to make out the words. "What, Lord?" he finally asked in a hoarse whisper. "What is it that you ask of me?"

More voices wove into the stream of words, each new one drowning the others out. He opened his eyes and staggered to his feet. His hands were shedding a blue-white radiance that illuminated the clearing as though it were daylight. He stared at them, stricken, his heart pounding, fear rising up to choke off his breath. At his feet, Two Hearts and the immense black dog slept on.

The voices rose, each one clearer now, and he understood. This was not the voice of God, but the wretched trees again and the rocks and even the tiny herbs beneath his bare feet speaking, each one trying to get him to listen to what it had to say.

"—*kill them all,*" the stolid oak on the other side of the clearing insisted. "*Houses burning, blood running like a river—*"

"—*were only babies,*" a flowering gum tree said, "*but the soldiers cast their broken bodies into the fire and laughed—*"

"—*opened a rift!*" A silent owl swooped low over his head. "*The worlds are sliding out of balance—*"

Declan cried out and covered his ears, unable to bear the inrushing sea of voices. It was crushing him, filling him until he couldn't remember to breathe or even make his heart beat.

A strong grip wrenched his hands away from his ears, and another voice added itself to the cacophony. "One!" it shouted at him. "Concentrate on one of them! Shut the rest out!"

One... he remembered now, how the painful weight of voices had buried him before and Two Hearts had helped him. He focused on a single screechy voice, following it through the river of sound.

"*—a terrible rift between this world and the next,*" the owl said. "*The Night People have slipped through, and worse yet will follow!*" A flick of its silent wings carried it up into the night.

"A rift?" Declan craned his head, but the owl was lost to sight.

"*The invaders kill first the holy men, then the dogs and warriors until no one can resist!*" the owl's low mournful voice cried. "*When they are finished, the worlds will collide and this land will lie in ashes. None of its creatures will be able to speak and no one would be left to hear them, if they could.*"

It must be speaking of the English, but why were they on Tsalagi land now? The plan had been to let the Catholic priests work among the natives, converting as many as possible from their heathenish practice of magic until their numbers had diminished to the point that it was safe to bring in soldiers and colonists.

Nightshadow had risen, the hair on her neck and shoulders bristling, staring uneasily at the dark mass of trees. The owl swooped back over the clearing, but only repeated itself, so, with a convulsive shudder, Declan shut its voice out too until it was only the mournful *whooo* of an ordinary owl.

Two Hearts sprinkled a handful of leaves from his traveling pouch onto the embers and a heady pungent smoke curled up into the night. His face remained shadowed. "The end has begun, just as with our brothers, the Catawbas, but this time your foolish people may destroy everything, even themselves."

"I don't understand." Declan's throat tightened.

"When the English killed the Catawba shamen, a crack was opened into the spirit realm and many fearsome things were loosed. Chaos and death ranged the coastal lands for a short time, sowing wanton destruction. Many died on both sides; the land did not give up its spirit easily. In the end, though, the rift was small enough that Tsalagi shamen were able to restore the balance between the worlds. Apparently the English learned nothing. They now repeat the pattern, ready once again to risk everything, but this time will be far worse."

Vertigo swept over Declan as though the world had suddenly lost its center and nothing held together. He had a vision of two opposing forces, the relentless steel and powder of the British on one side and a ferocious river of angry Tsalagi, growing larger every second as warriors poured in from outlying towns, intent on revenge. Both sides were almost evenly matched and equally deadly. Between them, a dark and terrible wind arose, shot through with the blue-white energies of medicine power, blasting the forest, laying waste to valleys and ridges, mountains and plains. He felt its raw strength, the unstoppable, indifferent power it carried, a crackling storm of destruction loosed by fools on both sides, no more inherently good or evil than a fire.

"I have not the power to seal such a rift," Two Hearts said. "It took the skill of many shamen such as myself, when the Catawba were taken by the spotted death." He rose. "This must be the great task for which you have been called."

"Me?" Declan felt the hair rise along the backs of his arms and shivered. "But I know nothing about such things."

"The Above Beings have been preparing you for this since you first set foot on the living land."

And, Declan thought miserably, he had given his word. He reached out for Nightshadow and the dog crowded companionably against him. "How long will it take to go back?"

"Three days, if Nightshadow carries but one of us, longer for the two of us together." Two Hearts faced the stone mountain. The sense of power emanating from it made Declan's skin crawl. "But that would be too late."

Declan broke into a cold sweat and backed away.

"You have no other choice!" Two Hearts motioned the great dog aside. "To be in time to heal the rift, you must return through the spirit world, as you came, or it will not matter what any of the rest of us do."

* ◇ *

Father Fitzwilliam threw himself off his horse and crossed to the soldier holding the girl by her long black hair. She fumbled at his hands, struggling to free herself, though the mark of his hand blazed across her brown cheek and she was clearly stunned. Fitzwilliam squinted in the wavering torch light, recognizing Two Hearts' young niece, Berry. She looked both terrified and weary. He turned to Jones. "She is just a child, no danger to us. Why not release her?"

"We can't risk it." The captain scowled. "She would warn the next village."

Fitzwilliam felt his face flush with anger, a welcome change from the flood of shame, sorrow, and regret that had tormented him since the first musket shot at

Idjoku. "Surely you understand that we're already dead men. At least a dozen runners and mounted scouts have already spread the word up and down every one of these foothills and valleys by now." He waved the soldier back, then slipped the girl's arm over his shoulder. She sagged against him and he smelled wood smoke in her hair. "These people never forgive a wrong—they don't even understand the concept. Restoration of their honor after an affront is a sacred responsibility. I doubt any of us standing here in this God-forsaken forest tonight will ever see Fort Pembroke again."

Berry's face was bleeding where her lip had been cut against her teeth. He shifted her weight. "I'll take her on my horse," he said with more authority than he felt.

Jones's chill blue eyes glittered in the torchlight, but the big man only jerked his mount's head around and spurred it back down the narrow, overgrown trail to the front of the disorganized column.

The soldier behind him, a squat enlisted man, snickered. "If you wanted a bit of tail for yourself, friar, you should have spoken up. We would have got you the best of the lot back at the fort."

Laughter rocketed through the ranks and Jones twisted around in his saddle, glaring. "Shut up, you sorry bunch of swine! The way you're carrying on, every red bastard within ten miles will know where we are. I want order and a tight formation and I want them now!"

The laughter died and Fitzwilliam turned to the girl. "You ride with me," he whispered to her in his poor Tsalagi. "If not, they kill now, leave body."

Something flitted behind a blackberry thicket, lost in the impenetrable shadows. He heard the whisper of clothing against branches, smelled the faint aroma of more wood smoke. Were the natives poised for revenge now? He took up his reins, pretending not to notice. If Tsalagi warriors were following them, as they had every right to do, then his warning would make little difference.

And if someone else hid there in the darkness, perhaps more young girls, like this one, or women and children who had survived the slaughter at Kitasi, it was beyond him to betray them. Whatever God wanted from this barbaric land, it was not the blood of innocents.

Berry fumbled at his arm, trying to stand alone. "Come now," he said with false heartiness in English. "We daren't hold up his Majesty's finest troops."

He placed her hands on the pommel and boosted her slight form up into the saddle. She held on, face and knuckles bone-white. He swung up behind her and tightened the reins. The soldiers kicked their horses and fell into line again, two abreast, muskets at the ready.

He thought he heard a thin wail, like the cry of a hungry baby, as they rounded the next bend, but it cut off almost as soon as it began and he feared to turn his head and look, lest the others take notice.

One Eye kneed his horse up from the rear of the column and rode beside Fitzwilliam, gazing at the dazed girl. His scarred body, naked to the waist, gleamed with sweat in the steamy night. He nodded, as though he made a decision, then kicked his horse into a trot and surged ahead.

Behind the column, the night sounds gradually resumed, first the crickets, then the mosquitoes, and finally the glum, booming chorus of frogs.

Too *late*—Two Hearts' words beat at Declan. He thought of Kitasi, as he had last seen it in the sun and then, from across the endless miles of rock and stream and leaf-bound forest, a sickening wave of disorientation swept over him. He felt the violation of the land and the slaughter of its people while he tarried here, indecisive and ineffectual. Another wave overcame him and he swayed with a dreadful shift in the fabric of the world, a dangerous, out-of-balance tilt of the energies—and knew the rest.

They had killed many of the shamen. Those left, who knew how to balance the fearsome energies that kept the Above World from veering into disastrous contact with its opposite, the Night Country, were scattered among the remaining towns. He sensed the opening of gates better left closed and frightening possibilities he did not fully understand.

Two Hearts' fingers dug into his upper arm. "If you will not go, then open a path into the spirit world for me and I will go!" He stood with his shoulders thrown back, his dark eyes wild.

Declan looked to the southeast and swallowed around the growing knot in his throat. The painful sense of wrongness increased; he felt sickened, unsure of himself, unbalanced as though he stood over a yawning chasm, about to tumble in. "You—said it would kill you to walk there."

"Nevertheless, I will try, which is more than nothing!" Two Hearts' face was savage. "And if I die of it, I will at least find honor in the Night Country! I do not understand your sort of men, who slay our land while making much of your devotion to the spirits, telling us that we are the ones who must change, when there is no room in your hearts for faith or courage, or any of the great mysteries which no man comprehends."

"But to use magic!" Declan was seized by a clammy coldness. "It would cost my soul. I would suffer pain and death forever!"

Two Hearts' face hardened in disgust. "Can you never stop thinking of yourself?"

Declan jerked his arm away and stumbled back into the furred warmth of Nightshadow's trembling body. She whined and nosed his neck. He felt a swell of tenderness and wonder that she, a creature of this wilderness and bound inextricably to the Tsalagi, should stand by him, despite the fact he had come here to destroy her way of life forever. He shook his head, steeling himself to what must be done. Two Hearts was right; he was but one man. What he wanted or feared meant little in the face of so much need, even the loss of his immortal soul. He met Two Hearts' anguished eyes. "I will go."

Another wave of pain swept through him, a vast, unimaginable tide surging higher and higher. The land itself was crying out. He wiped his sweating palms on his rawhide breeches and tried to think. First he must purify himself in whatever water was at hand. It was too late to fast properly or construct a sweatlodge. He had eaten the meat which Two Hearts had hunted, but he had fasted long before that and his belly was already empty again. That much preparation would have to do. He had no time for anything more elaborate.

Two Hearts followed him to the swift creek nearby, singing in a low, hoarse voice as Declan dunked himself in the forceful current the requisite seven times. Nightshadow watched from the shore, invisible against the darkness, except for her white star. The water sheared around his calves. He felt the minnows watching, the turtles and frogs speculating, and always there was the distant thrum of agony, a song of loss and suffering and death.

Still dripping, his hair plastered wetly to his head, he faced the mountain, his bones resonating with its terrible music. Threads of blue-white light glimmered among the rocks along the summit, as though the mountain were lit from within and supernatural light welled through the cracks. "I am ready now," he said tightly to Two Hearts, "but I do not know how to start. Before, the opening into the spirit world just happened."

Two Hearts stepped closer. "You must have been thinking of the song."

Yes, the song, he thought. The melodic chant given to him by the deer-people came back to his lips. He sang it through without any response, then began again, and yet again, each time with diminishing hope. He was too new at this; it was like leaping off a cliff to fly without wings. He was just a man, and a sworn Christian at that, with no business to meddle in such arcane matters. He would never—

A slim deer, as red as newly spilled blood, bounded from the trees and in a single jump disappeared again into the night. He sang on, hoarser with each repetition. Then a black deer, gleaming like polished obsidian, leaped past him from the opposite direction, followed by a yellow deer, bright as the sun. The clearing suddenly seethed with deer, white, red, black, yellow. Their warm sides brushed his skin as they passed, their hooves struck fiery sparks from the stone buried beneath the ground. They had stars for eyes and once he looked into their shining depths, he could no longer see Two Hearts or the dog.

A great red stag with a gleaming rack of antlers stopped before him and raised its muzzle. *"What do you need?"*

The air was thick with the spicy musk of their coats, sweet and warm. He felt it tingle through his lungs. "I must stop the fighting."

"Battle is honorable, in the proper time and manner," the deer said, and he saw a man's face superimposed upon its head.

"Not this battle," Declan said, caught by its inhuman gaze. He could not feel his heart beat, or the air on his face. "They have killed shamen and slaughtered children. They are invaders, seeking to take the land and use it, and when they are finished, it will lie dead and barren beneath their feet." The star-eyes brightened until it seemed he gazed into the heart of living, breathing suns.

"Then you may run with us," the deer said, *"but hold fast to our necks and do not look back, or the brilliance of our sister, the Sun, will burn the eyes from your head."*

Declan laid his hand on the deer's soft neck. It bounded into the sky toward the stars. He leaped with it, trying not to be left behind, and felt his feet tread the air as though it were solid ground. The other deer surged skyward, a glimmering sea of red and black and white and yellow. Their antlers surrounded him like a thicket, and above the rasp of his own labored breathing, he heard a low, melodious song. "What—is that?" he asked, fighting to match their relentless pace.

"That is our uncle, the Moon," the deer replied. *"During his nightly journey, he sings of women and growing corn and all the other changing things which are of his dominion. You must not look directly into his face or you will lose all memory of what it is to be a man."*

Declan saw the luminous white disk now, hanging in the black velvet sky as the herd of deer bounded higher and higher. He felt a wave of icy curiosity and the disk opened somehow, like a great orb, blazing brighter and brighter—

Hastily, Declan closed his own eyes, but the light seared through eyelids, blood, and bone, dancing inside his head in living white flames, incandescent and painfully vivid.

"Why do you intrude upon my journey?" a shimmering voice demanded.

Making no answer, the deer ran on through the sky. Declan had no breath to speak and could only hold fast to their necks, feeling, rather than seeing, the light flare ever more brilliant until it melded with his bones, until he was made of fierce, indifferent white light and no longer human.

They passed the blazing moon and leveled out on the other side. The chill luminescence seeped out of his flesh with agonizing slowness until he knew his name again, had room for his own thoughts. He sagged against a red deer on one side, a white one on the other, his feet stumbling. What would happen if he slipped beneath their razor-sharp hooves, he wondered bleakly. Would he be trampled, or just tumble head over heels until he hit the earth?

A drop of rain spattered against his face. Declan opened his eyes to a featureless darkness where not even the crystalline gaze of the stars penetrated. Dark-gray clouds swirled on all sides, as though they were running through fog. He saw an immense figure made of darkness ahead and heard the distant rumble of a drumlike beat.

"Wh-what is that?" he gasped to the deer.

"That is our uncle, Thunder," the red deer replied without slackening its breakneck pace, "Ruler of all the fierce things among the three worlds. He must keep constant vigilance or the terrible monsters imprisoned in the Night Country will escape."

Declan stumbled, then caught himself. "Night Country?"

"There are three worlds," the deer told him, "the world above the Sky Vault where the spirits abide, the Middle World of your birth, and the Night Country where all things are opposite. When your world has night, the Night Country has day. When your world is in the grip of winter, it has summer. All the most terrible creatures from the beginning of the world are imprisoned in its lowest region, waiting for their chance to enter the Middle World and wreak havoc."

Black spots danced before Declan's eyes and a red-hot band of pain constricted his chest, making each breath an agony. A subtle wrongness permeated the air here and he was suddenly dizzy, as though he had wandered close to some unseen edge and was in imminent danger of falling. The deer around him flinched, then shied aside, changing their path first in one direction and then another. He struggled to keep pace, then heard the beating of powerful wings, louder with each passing second, smelled the sulfuric breath of something noisome and unclean. He glanced over his shoulder, but the deer surged forward, redoubling their speed.

"Run!" the red deer cried. "The barrier between the worlds has cracked and loosed the Uk'ten!"

He threw his arms around the red deer's neck and let it pull him along, unable to keep his feet as it bounded through the featureless grayness. The immense thrumming came closer and closer, the stench, worse than a thousand middens baking beneath the noonday sun, intensified until he felt consciousness slipping away as he drowned in air too poisonous to breathe—

Thunder split the heavens. The Uk'ten roared and the sound crashed over Declan like a ponderous wave. He reeled from the force of it and felt his fingers loosen from the deer's neck.

"If you let go, you will fall into the Night Country and be lost forever," he heard the deer say through the dimness. "You must hold on!"

The air was so fetid now that breathing only drew vile sludge into his lungs. Holding his breath, he pressed his face into the clean musk of the deer's velvety fur.

The Uk'ten uttered a strangled, half-human scream. He felt its icy shadow pass overhead, felt its claws rake his back, leaving a row of deep parallel scratches. Thunder boomed again, this time closer, but not as loud. The air tingled with electricity and the hairs on the back of his neck stood upright.

"Nephew, " said a deep bass male voice, "you must kill the Uk'ten before it escapes into your world. Plunge your knife into the beast's seventh spot at the corner of its jaw."

Declan strained to see the creature, but there was only the gray, impenetrable wall of clouds.

"Look without eyes," the voice said.

And it seemed then he saw a great dragonlike shape in the air above him, even though his eyes perceived nothing. He fumbled at the knife sheathed at his waist, clinging precariously to the deer's neck with his right arm. The Uk'ten screamed again and the blast of foul breath smothered him. He fought to breathe, to think, to make his arm move. The creature's horned head hovered above him, its jaw filled with jagged teeth, each one as long as his arm. A row of evil green spots trailed down its curving neck. It dove closer and a gout of flame licked the herd of fleeing deer. The deer swerved again, breaking his hold.

Declan fell backwards through the clouds, struck the beast's greasy shoulder and slid down toward the beating wings. Terrified, he plunged the knife into the tough, noisome skin to check his fall. The creature screamed and backwinged to throw him off. His legs swung free, then he found a toehold with one foot on the base of its wing. The terrible head slashed at him and he had to duck. He saw its blazing red-fire eyes and felt a crippling wave of pain and terror. He squeezed his own eyes shut, seeking to look only in that curious *other* way, inside his head.

The Uk'ten whipped sideways, then folded its wings and fell through the clouds, the wind screaming around it. Declan withdrew the knife, then plunged it into the creature's hide, higher this time. It pulled out of the dive and beat its wings to climb higher into the unseen sky. The wind beat at Declan's face as he laboriously climbed, using the knife and his feet.

Just when he was within reach, the Uk'ten leveled off and cruised, beating its wings gently. "Why do you seek to kill me," it croaked, "when I have never done you any harm?"

Declan's head swam and he held onto the knife desperately. "I have to pass this way and I cannot afford to die. Too much is depending on me."

"So you have a job to do," said the Uk'ten, "something important." The wiry tail whipped back and forth, stirring the terrible stench that accompanied the monster.

Declan coughed and rubbed at his smarting eyes.

"My strength is great," it said cunningly. "Only tell me what you need and I will help."

The immense head could not strike at him now. He was too high on the curving neck and the beast could not even see him at this angle. Digging his toes and fingers into the greasy skin, he pulled himself higher with arms so tired that the muscles shook.

"I wish you no ill." The creature's voice grated like rocks being ground together. "Join with me and we will combine our strengths to defeat your enemies."

Every inch of his body throbbed. Sores were erupting on his exposed skin and the noisome air was clouding his mind, robbing him of logic and purpose. Sobbing, he climbed another arm's length, clinging like a flea to the great neck, and tried to remember what he was supposed to be doing. He stared into the dark-gray clouds, wondering why God had sent him into this hellish place.

"God?" said the fearsome creature. "Surely you don't think God is here or cares what you do?"

"God is—everywhere," he gasped, "even in this terrible place."

"What a ridiculous fiction," the Uk'ten continued, "almost as bad as the idea all creatures are relatives, that I, in my splendor, share anything with a wretched mouse or a worm, or even a hideous soft-skinned man, when your kind is forever bound to the mud of the Middle World while I was made to rule the skies."

Declan threw his arm around the back of the curving neck and jerked the knife free, struggling to climb higher. A gout of burning green blood fountained over his hand. He wiped it on his breeches.

A terrible wave of pain, loss, fear swept over him, the land, below, crying out. The shock made him lose his grip and he slipped back, digging in with his fingernails to keep from falling. The Uk'ten threw back its head and its laughter grated like the crushing of rusty nails.

Declan's feet swung free over the empty sky. He clenched his teeth and fought to bury the knife in the slimy skin one more time. The Uk'ten swerved, then folded its wings and dove earthward, cackling. He winced as the land cried out again and again, each wave of pain making him weaker and more confused.

His hands erupted with blue-white light. The Uk'ten screamed and its brown-green hide blackened beneath his touch. He raised his arm and aimed the knife at the seventh spot trailing from the corner of the Uk'ten's jaw. The creature spasmed, then dove to the right, breaking his hold. He windmilled his arms as the air streamed past his face.

✳ ◇ ✳

Someone was singing over Declan in a low, resonant chant that vibrated into his bones. He struggled to follow the music, but his head ached and he finally gave up, content to merely be for the moment. The music wove around him, weaving a cocoon that comforted and healed. When it ended, he drifted in a warm state of ease, untroubled, almost unaware.

"Nephew," said the same deep voice, "you have much to do and little time to do it in."

It was a powerful voice, full of eddies and currents like a river, rich with deep, hidden strengths, yet at the same time soothing. Declan felt himself rising to meet it, and then was afraid for some reason he could not name.

Somewhere close by, a waterfall roared and the ground rumbled with its force. Cool spray tingled his face. He licked his lips, rubbed at his closed eyes. Life surged back into his heavy limbs and he sat up, blinking.

He lay on a knoll carpeted with clover that rose above a great emerald-green river cascading down a cliff. White mist boiled up from the rocks at the bottom and settled on the banks, giving the trees and the bushes and even the air a pearlescent glow. The sweet scent of grass and rosemary filled his head.

"You made a brave effort," the voice said. "Nevertheless, the Uk'ten has now escaped into your world where he will wreak much havoc."

Declan turned to meet the black eyes of a tall, well formed man with a wide brow and even features. His voice had the same rumbly quality of the waterfall and his expression was grim. "The worlds are out of balance," the man said, "and must be put to rights before all creation succumbs to chaos."

"I—don't understand," Declan said, and scrambled awkwardly to his feet. His head spun, and his mouth tasted of the dull flatness of copper.

"You are called Snake," the man said, "relative to my brother, Rattlesnake, and therefore distant kin to my Lightning children and me."

A now-familiar wave of white-hot pain rushed up from the ground into Declan's feet and legs, through his body, the agony of the threatened land, compounded by the wrenching of out-of-balance energies. He doubled over, fighting to hold it at bay.

"Beware the Uk'ten," the man said. "You have drawn his blood and he will seek you out. Now, go. There is no more time." His body dissolved into the white mist of the pounding falls.

"But—" Declan whirled and saw he no longer stood beside the roaring river. He stood instead on the muddied banks of Long Man, outside the smoldering remains of the palisade of Kitasi. The dawn sky gleamed gray-pink along the eastern horizon and the smell of burned bodies and spilled blood permeated the air.

chapter twenty-one

The sleepy chitters of sparrows woke Smoke as he lay curled against Sunrunner's warm side. He could feel the great dog's slow, even breathing. The grass was wet with dew and each blade gleamed like crystal in the thin morning light filtering down through the leaves. The scent of damp earth filled the air as he stretched the kinks in his muscles.

Two elders sat cross-legged on the ground in the same positions in which he had last seen them the night before. They stared blearily into the embers of a dying fire, their faces grim, as though they had been sorely disappointed. Obviously, their efforts throughout the night had not been successful.

Smoke sat up, angry at his own weakness. He hadn't meant to sleep. The shamen had spent the night chanting and communing with the spirits and he had intended to keep vigil, but the fire they had kindled by ordinary means had remained stubbornly only a fire with no resonance of anything more powerful. Without that eerie, hair-raising sense which indicated the world of the spirits was at hand, he had eventually dozed off.

Only these two shamen, Brings Wood and Like an Oak, had survived the devastating raid on Kitasi, and both possessed but moderate skill, adequate for dealing with a persistent cough or a run of bad luck, but no match for the threat that had leveled their village. Two Hearts, still missing, was immensely more gifted than either of them. Smoke itched to go back to where he had last seen the shaman and have Sunrunner track him. Running Wolf, War Chief for Kitasi, however, had no patience for such a project. He had already dispatched messengers to every Tsalagi town on this side of the blue mountains and declared a sacred war of revenge. All warriors were needed here to prepare, not off on some fruitless search.

Smoke understood all too well. He remembered the lifeless Catawba faces he had seen on his many scouting runs, the paleness of their lips, the leaden twitch of their limbs. He would never allow his people to be enslaved thus, would in fact kill his wife and daughters with his own hands to spare them such a fate.

Sunrunner rose in one liquid motion and shook himself until his ears flapped. Smoke wrapped his arms around the great golden neck. The dog licked his cheek, then bristled.

An indistinct form appeared beneath a spreading hickory just beyond the shamen, her arms extended, her face a blur. She wore unfamiliar clothes and the lower half of her body was only a nebulous blue mist. The air beneath the trees chilled between one breath and the next, and the dew coating the grass crystallized into glittering frost. Ears flattened, Sunrunner edged stiff-legged toward the apparition. A low growl rumbled up out of his chest and the hair rose on the back of Smoke's neck.

Like an Oak raised his gaze from the dying fire and paled. "A Night Person!" He lurched to his feet and Smoke could see the old man's breath in the now-frigid air.

Brings Wood, was staring, wide-eyed. Behind the woman, a rising blueness coalesced into a half-visible crowd of children, men, and women, some clad as Tsalagi, others in the dress of the Catawba or the Apalachees to the south. Their vacant eyes gazed through the war party. Some bore great, gaping wounds on their bodies, others, the pits of disease.

Brings Wood made a warding sign with his hand. His face was haggard. "Go back to the Night Country, people of Before! There is nothing for you here!"

Paying no heed, the mass of Night People surged through the bodies of the living. A woman's blue hand grazed Smoke's shoulder in passing and he staggered to his knees, his limbs suddenly nerveless. Sunrunner seized his shirt in his teeth and threw his weight into dragging him back. Smoke tried to regain his feet, but his legs were clumsy and unresponsive, and a series of entities passed through him as he floundered, each one different in turn—ancient, young, confused, adrift. He had flashes of other days, blood-drenched with war or dark with loss, filled with love of child or mate or clan, hatred of enemies.

Wild-eyed, Sunrunner pulled harder, but the deer-hide shirt ripped. Smoke sprawled across the ground, hands clutching his head, overwhelmed by all these others who should not be here. His heart took up an odd, arrhythmic beat, then stuttered. He curled into a frozen ball of misery, his body unable to take the shock, his mind shutting down. He felt himself drifting out of his body as they drew his spirit after them like a bit of wind-blown chaff.

Sunrunner barked above him in short bursts, then he felt a cold nose prodding his bare back, sniffing his neck and arms. A warm, raspy tongue licked his shivering shoulders and face, anchoring him, helping him find his way back into his flesh. He moaned and forced open his eyes.

Sunrunner's worried gaze stared down at him as Brings Wood knelt stiffly at his side. The old man was trembling. "You must get up, move around, leave this place if you can. The rift has closed for the moment, but it may open again."

"I—I do not under—stand," Smoke forced out between clenched jaws.

"Someone, or something, has opened a passageway into the spirit world and left it untended." Brings Wood's weathered face wrinkled in distress. "I should have thought of this—there was a moment in which such a thing might have happened yesterday in Kitasi, when Lone Bear and the others were summoning Eagle to fight the red-coats. They died before they could complete their working. His eyes were bleak. "Like an Oak's spirit has been stolen by the Night People, and I have not the skill to close such a rift myself. If they come back, I think we will all die."

Still shivering, Smoke rolled to his knees, then lurched upright, clinging to Sunrunner's neck with trembling hands. His muscles cramped, as though circulation was now being agonizingly restored. "How—how many?" he managed to ask.

"At least ten, including Running Wolf, who was to have been War Chief." Brings Wood's face was haggard. "I have not checked everyone yet, and I do not know how those out scouting fared. We will have to search the woods before we know the worst."

✳ ◇ ✳

Declan could not take it in: the English troops had *burned* the village, murdered its people, young and old alike. The wind overwhelmed him with the acrid reek of charred wood and burned bodies. Unable to move, he tried to remember why he had come to this wild new land, so distant from the thin, rocky fields of Ireland, tried to recall the enthusiasm and fervor he had once felt, his dreams of immense stone cathedrals that would scrape the heights of these fresh new heavens and pay glorious homage to God. He had been consumed by his naive eagerness to bring lost souls to God, but now he could think of nothing, *see* nothing, but this stinking pyre of ashes that had been a town filled with life and love only a few days before.

Sickened, he leaned against a scorched tree on the river bank and felt the emptiness within it, the lack of spirit. He recoiled, wiping his blackened hands on his rawhide breeches. He had to seek out the English and insist they end this abomination. Whatever God thought of these people, however lost to His holy salvation they were, this slaughter was wrong.

Feeling irreversibly tainted from his association with the English cause, he waded into the river's gentle current to wash. With each immersion, a bit of weight lifted from his sore heart, as though his sorrow and pain were gradually rinsed away. He sighed and pushed his wet hair back from his face.

The river's green-brown voice murmured at the edge of his consciousness, and for the first time, he consciously reached out to it. "Where have the English gone?" he asked, knee-deep in the warm, lazy green waters. A dragonfly skimmed across the surface, its wings iridescent, and then a few feet away, a gleaming trout arched into the air.

"*Deep into the forest, on the trail to Cheota,*" the river said, not nearly as vibrant as before. "*I have been defiled! They excreted into my living waters, threw in waste and garbage and made bets on how long it would float! They have fouled and dishonor—*"

"I am sorry," Declan said. "When Two Hearts arrives, I will ask him to purify you." He climbed out and sat on the sandy bank, trembling, wrenched by the river's sorrow. "For now, I have to find them before they do even worse. Where does their trail begin?"

"*Under the stand of pines,*" the river said, "*behind the stockade. They left yesterday in the cover of darkness.*"

"Thank you." Declan hesitated, then made the sign of the cross over the fouled waters, though he could not say why. It just seemed important to do *something*. He studied the sunlight playing over the rippling current like a scattering of diamonds, and felt a faint sense of rightness.

Following the river's directions, he picked up the trail. A fair number of horses, many more than he'd expected, had left a wide path, their oval hoofprints stark in the soft earth. Undergrowth and vines were battered and broken as no passing Tsalagi would have left them. The birds and locusts and even the squirrels had fled, leaving the woods strangely silent.

By midday, his stomach cramped with hunger. He passed several berry-laden bushes, but refrained, although it was pointless to fast as the spirits had taught him, since he had no intention of employing the magical medicine power again. Traveling through the spirit realm from the stone mountain had been a one-time expediency, an enormous sin for which he would make penance the rest of his life, perhaps even throughout eternity.

Even worse, he was haunted by the brief time he had walked the forest as guileless Snake, unburdened with guilt of any kind. He remembered the innocent joy he had taken in the living world around him, the wonder of the medicine power within him, the exhilaration of Nightshadow's devotion and the dizzying feel of the wind in his face when she carried him on her back—

But, no—from now on he would remain true to his vows. No matter what the temptation, he could never allow magic to corrupt him again.

In spite of his resolve, though, power sang through him with every step, flooding up through the soles of his feet. Each creature and plant he passed, every rock, had its own special song which wove together into a great tapestry of life. The back of his mind whispered he was damned, that he would burn forever in hellfire for the terrible sins he had already committed, that he would never see the face of God, nor bring others to know His glory. Tears gathered in the corners of his eyes, but he blinked them away. What he had done, he'd done in the name of common humanity, and though it cost him everything, he could not go back now. He was not a person anymore, but a vessel, and he must serve the blameless in whatever way he could.

He paused at each stream to drink, but let nothing else slow him down. Time was in short supply, and he had to intervene before more innocents died. Each mound of horse droppings he passed grew fresher until he knew he must be close. Finally, he heard voices ahead, amidst the tangle of trees. Laughter floated back to him, along with the choppiness of the English language. He repeated a sentence under his breath to get the feel of it again, and felt the strangeness of it on his tongue, how it altered his thoughts and blinded him to the vibrancy of the forest.

He steeled himself and followed the winding path of broken ferns and crushed brush, weaving around overhanging trees as big as huts back in Ireland. Rounding the final turn, he came upon more troops than he had thought likely, perhaps the entire complement of Fort Pembroke. Red-coated officers sat on the ground, eating with sour expressions, their dozing horses tethered to trees. The foot-soldiers were eating also, but separately. He felt something vile and dark in the air, foul on the back of his throat, and flinched, his heart pounding.

A blond sentry, posted to guard the expedition's flank, stepped forward, bayonet pointed at Declan's middle. "Halt!"

Declan held his spread hands out. "Do not be alarmed. My name is Declan Connolly." He glanced over the man's shoulder as the other soldiers looked his way. "I am Father Fitzwilliam's assistant."

The soldier blinked, then seemed to take in his blue eyes and pale skin. The hard line of his jaw eased. "One of the bleeding priests?" His accent was broad cockney.

Declan's mouth tightened. "Yes." The dark miasma surrounding this place seeped through his brain and made it hard to think. His throat tightened and he could feel the breath clotting within his lungs. He swayed. "Might I speak with your commanding—officer?"

A dark murmur ran through the men massed behind his back and someone laughed, low and scornful. The sentry sniffed and his eyes lingered on Declan's torn shirt and travel-stained rawhide breeches. "Aye, you can speak with him, and more than you'll want, I'll wager, before he's done with the likes of you." He motioned with the gun. "This way."

He sounded contemptuous. Declan rubbed the bridge of his nose. Was it possible he knew how Declan had routed the King's men with magic? The feeling of wrongness, of things out of joint, intensified as the sentry threaded a path through the seated troops. Their eyes seared him like hot pokers. They *did* know, he thought dismally. They would never listen to him now, never leave this vital land in peace. He should not have come upon them in this casual manner.

The sentry fell in behind him. "Look at that bleeder's back!" someone whispered, and the ranks took up the refrain as he passed.

"Look at him!"

"My God! It can't be!"

"I don't believe it!"

The skin crawled along his spine. Were they speaking of the deep scratches from the Uk'ten's claws? He hadn't been able to see them himself, but felt them in the river.

Soldiers jerked to their feet as they approached, then fell back, giving him a wide berth. Sweat dripped from his temples and chin, stung the scratches on his back. He straightened his shoulders and walked on, mired in the dark spirit of this place now, as though he walked in a black fog of misery. He longed to turn and flee.

Father Fitzwilliam looked up from where he huddled over a mug and a tin plate. His watery gray eyes widened. "Declan!"

"Yes, Father." He knelt beside him. The older man looked gaunt, as though the flesh had melted from his bones. His cassock was filthy and torn, his hair matted with dust. His hands shook and there was a livid bruise across his left cheek. Declan took his shoulders. "Are you all right?"

Father Fitzwilliam gazed down at his trembling hands. He drew a deep breath and closed his eyes. "I've—blood on my hands, lad, blood, and I can never wash it off."

A hard knot closed Declan's throat. "I've—done things too, Father, unforgivable things, which I'll never be free of, but—"

"Enough!" The sentry jerked him back to his feet. "You and the friar here can have your little reunion after Captain Jones hears what you have to say."

Declan swayed; the touch of the soldier brought dark images into his mind, screaming children, blood, the acrid smell of gunpowder. He jerked his arm out of the sentry's grip. Just beyond Father Fitzwilliam, the Tsalagi girl, Berry, emerged from the brush with an armful of wood. She regarded him with frightened black eyes. Her face was bruised and a line of dried blood trailed from the angle of her jaw up across her brow. What had they done? Without thinking, he reached out to her.

Cursing, the sentry prodded him back with the rifle, then drove him through the camp to where Captain Jones was pouring over a map spread out on the ground. He looked up, one finger marking his spot, and scowled. "So, what rock did this bloody deserter crawl out from under?"

The sentry saluted. "He come in by hisself, Captain. Says he wants to talk to you."

"Does he now?" Jones ran a finger under his sweat-stained collar. "And exactly how many of my men do you mean to kill this time, *Father*?"

Declan's face heated. "I regret that more than I can say. I was not in control of my actions that day."

The captain turned to a broad-shouldered, balding man wearing the black cassock of a fellow Catholic priest. "And what do you think, Father O'Neill?"

"It's disturbing, to say the least." The priest fingered the ornate silver pectoral cross resting on his breast. His face was set in immutable folds as though cast in rock. "Perhaps there's some hope for this miscreant, if we return him to the bosom of civilization."

"Perhaps." Jones spat into the matted vines. "At any rate, I want to know where you've been since you called up that monstrous apparition back there in the forest, Connolly, and what those devilish Tsalagi are up to now."

Declan's face warmed. He locked his trembling hands behind his back. "I've just come from Kitasi and the horrors you left there." He studied Jones's eyes and saw within them the glitter of ice-wracked arctic seas. "You slaughtered *children*, mere babes—I saw what was left of their broken bodies—and old men and women as well! What on earth did you think you were about?"

"I was following orders." Jones cocked his head, then turned Declan. "My God, look at his back, O'Neill!"

"Saints preserve us!" The priest bent closer. "This creature has strayed far beyond redemption. Perhaps the kindest thing we could do is confess him immediately and then burn the contamination from his immortal soul. That way he might still have some hope of attaining Heaven."

Declan glanced over his shoulder, trying to see his back, but Jones shoved him forward into a tree. His head cracked against the trunk and he slumped, his vision blurred.

"How many Tsalagi accompanied you?" Jones snapped. "What are their positions?"

The singing power of the land, of blood and fur and bone and leaf and wing surged up through him as he fought to clear his head. Medicine power whispered in his ears, pooled in his hands, heady, ready to surge forth. He swallowed hard, sweating, fighting to contain it. He *must* convince them as a Christian that what they were doing was wrong; any show of magic would only prove their case. "We came to reveal the glories of Almighty God to these unfortunates, to present them with the keys to Heaven, not to steal their lives and foul their land."

The other priest looked down at him, his lips curled in disdain. "You stink of corruption! Fall on your knees and beg the Lord's forgiveness."

Declan bowed his aching head. "Faith, I have sinned, though I swear I never meant to, but my penance must wait. I am here to persuade you to leave this land and these people in peace. We have no right—"

The priest backhanded him against the tree and pain exploded through his skull again, worse this time. His mouth gaped and he sprawled helplessly on his back, squinting up into the canopy of leaves, seeing the golden disk of the sun wink in and out as the breeze shifted.

A tiny brown wren perched above him and cocked her head as he fought to hold onto consciousness. *"You should have known,"* she said. *"Such as these will never understand. You must fight for yourself and all that you know is right."*

"I—will—make them—understand," Declan forced between his unwilling teeth. "I—"

A second stinging slap rocked his head and this time the world tunnelled in, narrowing, until all that was left to him was a thick tongue that refused to speak and a hot star-burst of pain centered behind his eyes. "Shut up!" he dimly heard someone say as the spinning blackness took him down. "Why would any decent

God-fearing man mark a single word spewed from your lying mouth when you bear the mark of Satan himself on your back?"

✳ ◇ ✳

It was so far, yet Nightshadow sniffed out *his* need across the whispering, wind-tossed forest, across the endless strides of damp earth and rock and rotting logs. She dug her claws into the dense mat of scrubby underbrush and stretched, running full out with the weary two-legs clinging precariously to her neck.

He smelled worried too, and she let that knowledge drive her even harder. Her legs pumped and pumped, her tongue lolled, trying to shed heat so she could keep on running, but it was not enough. Red fog simmered behind her eyes, clogged her nose, stiffened her muscles. If she didn't stop soon, she would collapse, and perhaps never rise again.

But she had waited so long for this two-legs to come. If he died, she would not have strength left to fight the terrible, gnawing emptiness. This time she knew she would flee into that mysterious other world-beyond-eyes and give herself to those who waited there.

So she kept up her killing pace, leaping snags and scrambling down precipices, splashing across streams and swimming rivers, leaping chasms, then clawing her way up the next slope with the not-clan's arms wrapped around her neck. Better to die in the effort of reaching her clan-mate than to rest even for a single breath and suffer his loss.

With every stride, she felt his pain and fear and need grow.

Berry crept through the seated soldiers scattered along the trail, trying to think herself as small and faceless as a soft gray mouse, quiet
as a wind-blown leaf. A bright bluejay alighted halfway up a young
hickory and scolded one clump of red-coats, but they paid no heed. Most of them
radiated weariness, with their hunched shoulders and furrowed foreheads, and
were occupying themselves with the business of finishing their meal. But one, a
sallow man with wispy, corn-colored hair that matched his strangely hairy face,
reached out and jerked her across his legs. He reeked of dried sweat and dirt, and
something else, a rank flatness born of the dead lands. She cried out as she fell
against him, then fought the pasty hands groping her thighs, finally burying her
teeth in the soft, fleshy part of his thumb and drawing blood.

He shouted as she slipped out of reach, but his companions just slapped his
back and laughed. Shuddering, she wove around him. She knew she should stay
with the old blackrobe, who seemed to want nothing from her, but she could not
rest until she found out what had become of the stranger with the sky-eyes.

She felt the rightness of it—this man out of her dreams coming here when it
seemed the Real People would share the fate of their cousins, the Catawba. She
recalled her vision of being driven to a faraway place that did not know them, of
forgetting the ways of the Real People, their language, even their names, of being
forced to live thereafter in a dead manner. The destruction of Kitasi signalled the
beginning of that terrible time, and she knew, once begun, there would be no
turning back. If this land fell to the English, who could hear nothing without
their ears, apparently, see nothing except with their eyes, they would tear the
earth open in long straight rows, as scouts reported, then force it to bear their
foreign seed, and after her generation passed into the Night Country, no one
would remain who even remembered what Tsalagi life had once been.

The Catawba who guided the English watched her with a covert sidelong
glance, his arms crossed over his chest, his dark eyes as dull and dangerous and
full of pain as those of a mortally wounded bear. His upper lip curled in a sardon-
ic grimace that made her dread him more than all these hairy-faced soldiers put
together. She lowered her head and ducked past.

Heart pounding, she huddled behind a young pine and watched the red-coated soldiers bind the stranger, face-forward, to the trunk of a towering oak. There

was another blackrobe there, different in some way from the first, who was ever gentle. This blackrobe's words buzzed like bees, fierce and quick and angry. The shadows lay dark beneath the oak's thick foliage, but the stranger moved and she glimpsed markings on his shoulders. She pressed her back to the pine and edged around the trunk in an effort to see better.

Hide me, she said to the pine. With a rustle, it drooped its needles enough to shadow her face and body. The wind gusted; the boughs of the immense oak shifted, allowing a shaft of the midmorning sun to pierce the shadows for just an instant, revealing a shimmering blue pattern of interlaced diamonds across the stranger's shoulders and down his spine, the certain mark of the Tsalagi's dangerous and unpredictable brother, Rattlesnake.

✳ ◇ ✳

Cold water drenched Declan. He gasped involuntarily, inhaled some into his lungs, then fought his way up out of stifling darkness, coughing in great shuddering spasms. His mouth was cotton-dry and a rough surface cut into the left side of his face, preventing him from opening that eye. He caught the scent of wet earth and crushed leaves, horses, the rankness of unwashed men, the cleanness of a small stream close by. Breathing raggedly, he struggled to lift his head, but his outstretched arms were bound around a rough, circular surface, a tree, he realized, and bore his weight. He tried to get his feet beneath him, but could not move even enough to ease his tortured muscles.

"He's coming around now, sir," said a rough voice. "Give him another good soaking and he'll be fit to answer your questions."

"I want muskets trained on him at all times," he heard Jones say. "I refuse to lose another man to his heathenish trickery."

A second bucketful of water sloshed over him and renewed his fit of coughing. A hand seized his hair and yanked his head back. "How many Tsalagi remain?"

He shook his head weakly, unable to stop coughing. The hand wrenched his neck farther back until he thought it would break. "How many bloody natives are out there? Have they gone for reinforcements? Answer me, dammit!"

He couldn't breathe properly with his neck bent at such an unnatural angle, and that difficulty, added to the strain of coughing, was causing him to black out again. He wheezed desperately for air, felt his eyelids descending, heard a roaring in his ears. He fought to remain conscious—he had to make them listen, make them understand—

"You will get little from him in that fashion," a dispassionate Irish voice said. "Let him recover his wind."

The angry fingers released his hair and he sagged forward again, resting his throbbing head against the corrugated bark. The air sobbed through his chest as the black tide of unconsciousness receded.

"Now," the calm voice continued, "you said you regret what you have done, and quite rightly so, I should think. You must confess your sins and then put yourself in God's hands. Only He can forgive you now."

The power of the land throbbed at the edge of his awareness as the other man spoke. Declan felt the wrenched, out-of-kilter energies, the painful skewing of the separate worlds as they neared each other in ways that were unnatural and dangerous. "My sins—will have to wait." The effort to speak made him dizzy and his tongue seemed three sizes too large for his mouth. "You must—leave this back country. You've destroyed—its balance. It's—dangerous for you—as well as the Tsalagi."

"Blasphemer!" Father O'Neill's stern face loomed over him. "You have committed sacrilege and taken up with the Devil himself, who no doubt values the heathens which infest this land."

He blinked up blearily at the other man with his free eye, aching so much he couldn't think. Then the tree seemed somehow to shift beneath him. His feet found the ground and took his weight, easing his arms and back. He drew in a deep lungful of air, then another. His head began to clear. "There are forces here you don't understand. Can you not feel them?" He turned his head enough to take in both Jones's and O'Neill's angry faces. "This land is more than just dirt. It, along with everything on it, down to the last rock and stream and leaf, is alive and aware of your every word and deed, and it's being torn apart because of your blundering. By your actions at Kitasi, you have thrown the worlds out of balance."

"Clearly, the Devil has his tongue." O'Neill turned to a red-coated soldier and held out his hand. The soldier passed him a long black whip.

Declan struggled against the ropes binding his wrists. "No, you must listen or—"

O'Neill lashed Declan's exposed back, wringing a startled cry from him. "Confess your sins, and then give Captain Jones the information he needs!"

The whip seared his flesh again. Declan sagged against the tree, jaws clenched, sick with pain as the whip slashed and slashed. Lightning flashed behind his eyes in great red bursts. The control he had fought so hard to develop slipped; the cacophony of voices swept back over him, drowning him in a sea of frightened, angry words. He felt the power of Water and Fire and Earth and Air surge through him unchecked. The now-familiar blue-white glow sprang up in his hands and flooded the shadows with light so dazzling that it hurt his eyes.

"No!" he whispered. "Not this way!" He tried to stem the flow, but the ropes binding him ignited in a hiss of sparks and fell away into blackened strands. His strained arms slumped to his sides and he sagged to the ground, wracked with pain.

O'Neill's adams-apple bobbed and the fear was fever-bright in his eyes. "It is plainly too late to save your immortal soul," he said. "You have once again proved yourself to be the Devil's creature. It seems all we can do now is save ourselves from your contagion."

They were empty men, Declan thought numbly. They stared down at him with flat, dead eyes, unseeing, indifferent to the exuberant riot of life all around them. Such men could kill a land's spirit, then rejoice over the bloated corpse, unaware. A sudden pang ran through him, as intense as the scourge-marks on his back. What had Ireland been like before such men extinguished her vitality? And England—had that ancient land once lived as vibrantly as this new world?

Captain Jones waved the frightened soldiers back and raised his pistol. "Stand back! I shall end his miserable life myself. I should have put a bullet between his traitorous eyes the second he set foot in my camp!"

Once the captain killed him, no one would be left to stand against the English. His back throbbing, Declan struggled to his feet, well aware what had already happened in the south, with the Portuguese. Now a similar pattern was seconds away from being set here. He remembered the vision of the dead lands he had been shown, the bitter reek of ashes, the lack of any voice, save that of man. He laid himself open until the vast blue energy field of the spirit world blasted through his veins. Too much, he thought grimly as his knees gave way again. He had not prepared properly; this much power would burn him to cinders before he could channel it. He held onto consciousness, barely, medicine power searing through him as he made himself a hole through which it could pour.

Long Man, come to me! he called. Here are the ones who defiled you.

The priest made the sign of the cross as Captain Jones took careful aim.

Declan continued to call, and then, all through the forest, he felt Long Man stir in answer, surge up through spring and creek, abandoning every bank. The ground beneath Declan was suddenly damp, then a sheet of water trickled through the trees as though somewhere a dam had burst.

Jones cursed. "What—?"

Now, Declan told Long Man. Wash them away.

Jones turned back grimly. "You're responsible for this, by God!" He sighted along his pistol, then fired as the water rose ankle-deep.

White-hot pain seared Declan's left shoulder and spun him back into the oak. His ears roared and he couldn't tell if it was Long Man or the echo of the shot. He floundered as the water swirled waist-deep and his head sank beneath the surface. Legs splashed towards him and he came up fighting for air. The cries of terrified soldiers rang out as they were washed into trees or against rocks. Long Man's anger hissed as the waters threw themselves against the struggling men.

"Come!" a soft but urgent Tsalagi voice whispered in his ear and he felt hands grip his sound right arm, urging him to his feet. "We must get to safety."

It was the girl, Berry. Gasping, he clutched her sturdy body. His vision flashed blue/white/blue. "Where can we go?"

She had something of the same blue-white light within her, the singing electricity that meant medicine power. "Raise your hands to the branches above your head."

He managed to raise his right hand, but the left sagged leadenly against his ribs. Blood oozed from a small hole in his shoulder and he could feel the blackness of unconsciousness swooping in.

"No, both hands!" Berry insisted, and raised his other hand for him.

Moving that arm was excruciating. Waves of pain swept over him, sapping what strength he had left. He sagged as something slim and supple wrapped around his wrists and drew him upwards.

Remaining where he had tumbled off Nightshadow's back, Two Hearts watched the exhausted black dog sleep in the sun. The pads of her feet were worn to bloody shreds, but still she had run on and on, refusing to stop until Two Hearts was so weary and numb, he lost his grip and fell.

She had stopped then, whined, nosed his face, then sank wearily to the ground, unable to resist the desperate urge to sleep any longer. Two Hearts sat up and rested his aching head on his knees. On the other side of the forest, across countless ravines and waterfalls and craggy hills, battles were raging and lives were being lost, but it would take them the remainder of the day and night to reach Tsalagi land, and by then it would most likely be too late for him to have any hand in the outcome.

Nevertheless, he could see Nightshadow would drive herself like this until she died, whether he willed it or not. The great dogs had a bond to the spirit world which made them aware of things they could not otherwise know, so that they often responded to events before they happened. She knew what was taking place, and how Snake was faring, knew how desperately they were needed.

As a youth, he had fantasized such a partnering for himself, but he had never appreciated the depth of the relationship so well as he did now, having watched Nightshadow with Snake. For reasons known only to her and the Above Beings, the black dog had made her life one with his. She would never cease struggling to reach him because she had no choice. They were, in many ways, a single person sharing two bodies. If he died, she would most likely die too.

Along with the rest of his people.

He watched the exhausted heave of her sides, the restless flick of her ears as she dreamed. She shivered, scrabbled her bleeding paws in her sleep, growled deep in her throat.

He resisted the urge to smooth her matted fur. Sleep, black one, he thought. Sleep until you are rested. Your death so far from home will serve no purpose.

He stretched out on the mossy ground beside her, inhaled the bitter green scent and closed his eyes, trying to let sleep overtake him too, but his mind would not be silent. There was too much at stake.

Declan was dimly aware of thick vines twined around his arms and legs and body, supporting him high above the ground. His wounded shoulder throbbed and his thoughts would not come together. Below, Long Man raged through the forest, dashing himself against the trees in wild fits of spray, drowning every creature too slow to flee to higher ground. The thick scent of mud and bruised leaves drifted upward through the air.

He lay his head back, feeling burned inside, his mouth tasting of ashes; he had opened himself to medicine power without properly preparing and, as he had been warned, he now paid the price.

A small pair of hands bracketed his face from behind and he looked up into Berry's shade-dappled face. She eased into place beside him, balancing on a gnarled branch. "Now," she said in low, earnest Tsalagi, "we must stop the bleeding." She released him, then eased a wet compress of leaves onto his wound, wringing a moan from his lips.

Blackness ate at his vision. For a time, he could see only a hazy gray circle of light as he hovered at the edge of consciousness. Finally, a nearby argument roused him back to awareness.

This one is too badly hurt for such remedies as we offer, a dry raspy voice said. His spirit is strong, but his body is beyond healing. You must let him go on to the Night Country.

"No!" Berry cried. "I have seen this man in my dreams. He has something to do among us, something important. My uncle said he is powerful, perhaps even a true Spiritwalker, a Fireheart—"

Things are as they are, a thinner, smaller voice said. If this is his time, you cannot change what is to be.

"He must live!" Berry pressed the leaves against Declan's wound in a vain effort to stem the bleeding.

He groaned and felt warm stickiness dripping down his side, smelled the copper-iron of fresh blood. He was so tired; waves of darkness washed over him, stealing what little energy he had left, carrying him away into a suffocating silence.

※　◇　※

Jones was thoroughly sodden by the time One Eye rode up on a blown bay mare, fetlock-deep in mud, leading several other horses, including his own terrified, wild-eyed chestnut gelding. Jones accepted the reins with a grudging nod of thanks and ran a hand over the beast's quivering neck and shoulders. The gelding was hot and lathered, as well as scraped and cut in several dozen spots, but basically sound. His saddle was missing, but might still turn up with diligent searching. Earlier, he had found his musket wedged in the fork of a tree, although it would have to be cleaned and oiled. His powder was of course ruined, and he had lost the blasted pistol in the first surge of the flood.

Jones straightened the gelding's twisted headstall, angry at himself. The sudden flood without benefit of wet weather had obviously been more heathen magic. He should have shot that wretch Connolly between the eyes in the first second he'd reappeared. As it was, Jones was fairly sure the shot had gone wide, injuring him perhaps, but not fatally.

"Shoot the bleeder on sight!" he ordered his grim-faced men as they salvaged supplies and horses. They saluted, and, then, heads down, kept to their business, stripping their uniforms to dry them across bushes in the sun, and doggedly cleaning their muskets.

The captive girl had disappeared as well as Father Fitzwilliam and that wretched traitor, Connolly, but Father O'Neill had turned up, bumped and bruised, one eye blacker than a London whore's heart. Lips compressed into an angry line, the priest had laid out the corpses of the four men who had drowned, although Jones refused him permission for last rites. His men deserved better than that high church nonsense. He had the bodies loaded on four of the remaining horses and sent back to the fort for decent burial in hallowed land.

Along with that party went an urgent request for additional troops, as soon as the replacements from England landed. He had made inroads upon the power of the shamen. He now had to press his advantage, kill the rest of them and take this land for the Crown before they mounted an overwhelming response. He had studied the gruesome accounts of the early explorers, at least those who had survived long enough to report. Magic was always the key. This was a savage, barbaric land and nothing less than total annihilation of the shamen would suffice.

One Eye gave him a long, burning glance and then squatted in the grass and stared up at the sky with a narrowed, skeptical eye, as though he waited for something. And perhaps he was, thought Jones. The very ground was saturated with evil this far inland. He could almost feel it move beneath his feet. It was frightening, this native magic, loathesome and devilish. He understood better now why witches were always put to the stake, instead of some other, more merciful end. Their contagion had to be scoured from the earth to render it safe for decent men to live upon. He stared into the mass of shifting green leaves and fleshy vines and interlaced undergrowth, feeling eyes out there watching, waiting for the opportunity to spin more evil spells. Even if he sent every one of these native devils to Hell, where they belonged, it would take years, decades even, to cleanse this broad, rich land and make it fit for God-fearing British colonists.

A bass roar split the sky. Declan forced his heavy eyes open, but saw only the shifting canopy of leaves. Berry followed his gaze and a muscle jumped in her cheek. She leaned over his chest, her tangled black hair grazing his neck as she held the aromatic compress of leaves in place against his wound.

The roar came again and this time Declan recognized it, along with the tell-tale thunder of immense wings. He struggled against the tangle of vines supporting him, wringing waves of pain from his shoulder. "The Uk'ten!"

Berry pressed harder as his blood seeped around her fingers. Her lips were thin with strain. "No," she said. "It is not possible. Such a creature cannot be here."

"Thunder said the worlds are out of—" Declan sagged back against the vines, his head spinning. "—out of balance. There is a rift . . . and the Uk'ten escaped into . . . our Middle World. I tried . . . to kill it."

She sat back and knotted her hands together. "If he is here, and you have fought him before, he knows your scent." She stretched a beckoning hand to the leaves overhead. "Come closer."

No matter what we do, he will still smell this one, the leaves replied in dozens of tiny rustle-voices, but the branches drooped inward, the leaves rearranging themselves, overlapping into a dense, dark-green cocoon. The thunderous beat of wings overhead intensified and a now-familiar terrible stench enveloped them.

chapter twenty-three

Declan felt the weight of the evil creature soaring above, searching the forest, seeking his blood in order to finish that other battle in which he had failed so miserably. Now that it had slipped through the crack between the worlds, it would wreak havoc on this unsuspecting land, and it would all be his fault, for failing to kill it when he had the opportunity.

His lips had gone numb now, along with his tongue and hands. The pain was still there, but remote, as though it belonged to someone else. He closed his eyes, feeling himself sink into a chill black swamp of exhaustion from which there could be no return.

"You have to fight!" Berry's breath was warm against his ear, but her voice seemed to come from some distant land. "I have seen in my dreams how it will be if you die. You have been given great gifts. You must fight back!"

*　◇　*

A harsh bass cry split the air, the roar of an enraged lion, perhaps, or a bull elephant magnified a thousand times. Every hair on Jones's head stood on end. A string of oaths spilled from his lips as an immense, streamlined form broke through the scattered clouds and glided down over the treetops, massive wings outstretched, long serpentine neck curved, poisonous red eyes glittering.

Jones's hands shook as he darted back beneath the canopy of leaves, furious with himself. This had to stop. Any world in which such monstrosities could exist was clearly an abomination. What if this taint of heathen magic filtered across the sea to invade the fabric of ordinary life? What if Wales, or England, or the rest of Europe were sullied by these devilish powers? How would God-fearing men survive then? The sooner the Crown's forces stamped out the remaining conjurers and made this land fit for human habitation, the better.

The creature screamed again, a horrible, wrenching sound, and Jones felt his bowels turn to water. The beast bore fierce horns on its brow, and its bulk filled the sky, so huge that he and his men were no more than gnats fleeing before a dragon; no human could possibly stand against such a creature, even if their muskets had been in working order, which they most decidedly were not. He pressed back into the rough bark, holding his breath, praying it would not catch sight of him. A hundred feet away, One Eye climbed up into a massive chestnut tree, agile as a monkey, and disappeared into the dense foliage as the air thickened with the noisome stench of a fire burning a decaying corpse. Jones's stomach rolled in protest and sweat pooled at the base of his throat.

The beast soared in long, low circles, eyeing the forest below, craning its neck as though searching for something. Steam curled from its nostrils and trailed behind it in a delicate filigree across the sky. The wild-eyed horses flattened their ears and fought their reins, squealing. He slid over to his gelding and stroked the twitching sorrel hide, whispering reassurances he did not feel.

The horse switched its tail violently, stamped, then neighed in terror as the serpentine creature banked and dove toward the trees. Jones jerked the reins from the branch and flung himself onto the gelding's bare back, bending low as he urged it into the densest clumps of trees.

The horse's panicked sides heaved against his legs as it plunged into a tree-lined hollow of cool green darkness. He heard the thunder of immense wings overhead, passing, banking, coming back. Sweat drenched his entire body and his hands shook so hard he could hardly grip the reins. He bit down on his lip, cursing himself for a coward.

The Uk'ten's cry reverberated through the air. Declan shuddered at the thought of such a creature loosed on this world. He sagged back into the vines, remembering the white-hot fire of the Uk'ten's malice, its savage hunger for all which lived. It had to be stopped, chased back somehow to that other world, where it belonged, before it laid waste to this entire area, but he had no idea of how even an able-bodied man could defeat such a creature, and he was far from whole. Berry pressed the leaves harder against his shoulder while he combed his memory for something, anything he could do. A scrap of song surfaced, his song, the deer people had said. He fought the encroaching tide of darkness inside his head to sing the notes in a thready, fading voice, over and over again, as though they were a key to some unseen door.

The Uk'ten bellowed, now immediately overhead. The poisonous stench was overwhelming. He struggled to keep singing, sensing a pattern building. He felt the presence of many spirits, many others. Soft fur brushed his arm, his back, his cheek. He struggled to open his eyes and saw the vines had disappeared, along with the trees. His arms encircled the neck of a magnificent red stag, amidst an entire sea of many-colored deer, bearing him up into a shimmering blue-white sky.

*   ◇   *

The terrible odor thickened, drowning Jones in a vile stench. Gagging, he buried his mouth and nose against his uniform coat as foliage above him crackled, like paper being crushed, or sticks breaking, or ... fire. Overhead, the leaves curled inward and dissolved in red-orange flames.

His mount screamed, then snatched the bit in its teeth and pounded out of the concealing trees. The monstrous beast swerved toward them, exhaling another gout of fire. Jones threw himself out of the saddle just as the flames roared over the terrified gelding. It fell, head over heels, aflame, kicking and screaming. Jones hit the earth and the breath whooshed out of his lungs. His hair and coat sizzled and he rolled, beating weakly at the flames with his hands as black spots shivered behind his eyes and his body cried out for air.

On the other side of the clearing, he dimly saw One Eye standing high up on a broad limb, well hidden. The flying monster bellowed and banked again. One Eye leaped out of the tree and landed easily on the wet ground, knees bent. He strode out of the cover of the trees and stared up, seemingly fascinated. The beast's hoarse bellow echoed through the forest. Its head whipped about in preparation to flame the man, then it back-winged, cocked its immense head. The two disparate creatures stood locked in each other's gaze.

Jones wanted to shout at the damned fool to flee before the monster smashed his head like an eggshell, but he feared to call more attention to himself, and his chest was all but paralyzed by the hard fall, the muscles barely able to take in enough air to sustain consciousness. The hideous red eyes sparked, whirled, then the creature thrust a great foot down, seized One Eye in its claws and sprang back up into the clouds.

Jones pushed himself off the forest floor, singed, mud-encrusted, shaken, and speechless, alone, but for the agonized dying screams of his burned sorrel gelding.

The wicked talons closed around One Eye's torso without piercing his flesh. He clung to them, admiring their adamantine curve as his legs swayed and the forest slid past below in a wild riot of greens and browns. Flying this way was wildly exhilarating, and although the monster stank, he was fast growing accustomed to the smell. The sense of raw power that emanated from this huge beast was dizzying and for the first time since the death of his people, a sense of anticipation stirred within him.

He knew others in his place would have been afraid, but in that single moment when he and the fearsome beast had stared into one another's eyes, he had found something unexpected. In the depths of that murky red gaze, One Eye had seen how the Uk'ten was forever denied the upper reaches of creation, where the spirits dwelled, that he was now and for all time a creature despised and apart, consigned to the meanest depths of the Night Country which was unpopulated except by other singleton monsters. The raw, aching blackness of the Uk'ten's despair fully matched his own; they were brothers under the skin and, as such, should come together and hunt as only brothers could, ripping open the underbelly of this soft, weak land of fools. Between them, they would take whatever they wished from both this world and the next, and laugh in the faces of those few who survived.

The air rushed against Declan's face, cool, scented with pine and cedar. He saw the jagged mountain rising before them, not a rounded dome of granite, as the stone mountain had been, but a magnificent single peak piercing the sky in the center of the world. Memory stirred; he had been here before, in dreams. Did that mean he was dreaming now? Or had he perhaps died and left his dead body behind in the tree with the girl?

"No," a somehow familiar voice said, "you travel here in both flesh and spirit, a feat few others could match."

He turned and saw a man made of all of molten gold, riding behind him, so close their legs almost touched. His face bore Declan's features, and even his hair and body were identical, though his shoulder seemed unblemished. Declan shook his head. "Who—are you?"

"I am Snake." The other's eyes were sun-struck diamonds, his face sunbeams, and yet every feature was there, every pore and blemish, all familiar as his own reflection and yet utterly strange.

Declan's hand strayed to his own wounded shoulder and the musket ball hole. Oddly, he felt no pain now. "But I was Snake."

"For a time," the other said. His eyes glittered and Declan thought he saw whole galaxies within them.

One by one, the other deer turned aside as they neared the mountain, leaving only the huge red stag to continue upward. Snake leaned forward as the stag's shoulder muscles bunched and Declan saw someone else rode behind him, a man composed somehow of shifting, fluid darkness, as though he were made of raw black fire in the same way Snake was made of light.

With a final mighty heave of its shoulders, the red stag leaped onto the highest peak, its hooves striking blue sparks out of the rock. An old woman with long trailing green hair sat waiting on the ground, her hands resting easily on her knees. She wore a dress of startlingly white doeskin and a small owl perched upon her shoulder. An eerie fire, composed of a multitude of colors, burned before her, feeding somehow directly upon the naked rock. The flames were not random, but a wreath of minute eagles, trees, wolves, vines, fish, bears, snakes, all dancing in an intricate pattern about each other, separating, merging again. The air was thick with the sharp green scent of growing things although not one leaf or blade of grass was in evidence.

The man composed of light slid off the stag's back, followed by the dark man. Declan dismounted too. The stag turned to him with bottomless dark-brown eyes. "Thank you," he said to the great beast awkwardly. "I would have died had it not been for your help."

It gazed at Declan steadily and a blue-white shimmer outlined its body against the rapidly falling darkness. "You called to us in a sacred manner, and so we came, as we promised."

The old woman raised her hand. "Go in peace, grandson."

The deer dipped its antlers in a graceful salute, then turned and sprang out into the clean fresh air, leaping across the early evening sky in great bounds. The wind howled in its wake, dancing over the rocks like a fierce warrior, cutting through Declan with an icy chill. He shivered.

"Sit, grandson, and warm yourself," the old woman said and indicated a place beside her fire.

Snake sat as she directed and the man of glimmering darkness settled beside him, but Declan hung back, unsure.

She turned vivid green eyes upon him. He saw life brimming within them, and vibrant energy. "Why do you not sit?"

"I—I thought you spoke to them," he said uncomfortably.

"But they are you and you are they." Her head tilted as she studied him and her gray-streaked green hair streamed back in the wind. "Do you not recognize yourself?"

"I—I do not understand."

"Every man has many men within him, many others." She gestured at a place on the other side of the fire, opposite her, and this time he folded his legs and sat. She reached through the fire's shifting shapes to rest her hand on his left shoulder. At her touch, the pain surged back through his body in dizzying, white-hot waves. He gasped and hunched over against it. "Snake could heal that wound," she said.

"But I am Snake," he forced out through clenched teeth, "or at least I was, when I did not remember being Declan."

"After your memory was restored, you turned away from that portion of yourself." She withdrew her hand. "Now Snake remains apart, holding your power, your laughter, your joy, all the bright things in your life. If you wish to heal yourself, you must take him back. Otherwise, you will die."

"But he is a heathen, and—" Declan's shoulder throbbed. Sweat broke out on his brow and just as quickly dried in the cool, dry air there at the top of the world. The wind whistled against the rocks as he struggled to explain; it seemed very important that she understand. "—and I am a Christian." He refused to meet the man of light's shining eyes. "It is not possible for us to be one."

"The Above Beings called you to us from far across the great waters," she said, "because there is something you can do which no Tsalagi can. In this time of turmoil and change, you alone can walk this path. You have been given a sacred responsibility. You must heal yourself and then return to the Middle World to do what has to be done."

"But I've already tried to stop the British," he forced out through clenched teeth. "They would not listen."

"A white man from across the great waters named Declan tried to stop them, not my grandson, Snake."

Would that have made any difference? He wondered what Snake would have done down there in the British camp—surely not walked in and begged them to understand what was not given them to understand. He could remember being Snake well enough to know the other would have used the power of the spirit world, would have shaped it to his own purpose to make them quit Tsalagi land, would never have been so foolish as to make himself a ridiculously easy target.

He remembered the uncanny aptitude Snake had shown for the four great medicines, how easily he had perceived the hidden strengths of Air and Water, Earth and Fire, and, most important, how he did not fear the spirit world and the awesome power it represented. Declan closed his eyes, feeling the spinning darkness that threatened him. Death was so close, only a heartbeat away, and if he accepted it now, without yielding to the temptation to once again take up Snake's power, God might yet forgive his sins and allow him into Heaven.

But as much as he desired to leave the sinful world and its frightening contradictions behind, how could he turn away from those depending on him, the Tsalagi, and the land, and Nightshadow, the birds and fish and trees and bears, and even the foolhardy British, who had no real idea what havoc their meddling had unleashed?

He raised his eyes to the old woman. "For now, I must be Snake, whether I wish it or not." He did not flinch this time as the man made of light reached for him. The other's hand passed through his wounded shoulder with an electric tingle and the light merged with his flesh. He gasped, reeling with a sudden heat as though fire shot through his veins. The warmth built and built until he was whole, both Snake and Declan, uninjured and without pain. He unclenched his hands and gazed down at them.

"And what of the other?" She gestured at the waiting dark man. "Your shadow-self, who holds all your doubts and fears, your guilts and jealousies, your pain? If you leave him behind, a part of you will still die."

He studied the other's black eyes, full of grief and rejection, guilt and sadness. "What if he prevents me from doing all that you say I must? What if he makes me afraid and I fail?"

"You must look fear in the eye and call him brother," she said. "Then he will guide your steps away from harm without mastering you. Only a fool is never afraid."

Trembling, he stretched his arm out to the man of darkness. The other met his hand with a cool, dry grip that whispered of moonless nights. A shiver of fear ran up his arm toward his heart. Declan swayed, gritted his teeth. There was a brief second of chill numbness as the dark merged with his flesh.

"There are many paths to the Great Spirit, each appropriate to its place and people. It is to your credit that you choose to walk this one as a whole man." The

old woman passed a hand over the fiery dancing animal shapes and they combined in a flaming whirlwind that spiraled up into the sky. "Chaos threatens the
three worlds."

She waved a wrinkled hand before his face and he saw two massive groups in
the forest below, one, a marshalling of all the British manpower in this area of the
new world, the other, a massive coming together of all the Tsalagi from every
town, every hill, every valley for miles around. The two forces faced one other,
almost evenly matched, ready to hurl strength against strength. No matter who
won, there would be a fearful number of deaths on both sides, so that in the end
all would lose. And while they fought, the Uk'ten would raid up and down the
coast as the formerly balanced energies veered further and further out of balance,
bringing the three worlds perilously close to destruction.

"Even if you convince your kind to withdraw," she said, "the Tsalagi will not
let them. They have declared a sacred war of revenge. The shamen will spend their
strength punishing the white invaders and they will not see what has been set in
motion."

"How can they think of fighting while there is danger?" Declan asked slowly.
"Can't they feel it?"

"Each side thinks only of itself."

"But what can I do?"

"Stop the battle and then heal the rift."

Declan swallowed over his dry throat. "But how?"

"If the Above Beings knew that," she replied, "they would not have found it
necessary to bring you here. You have a good heart. Go back to the Middle World
now and follow it."

The mountain and the brilliant turquoise sky began to fade. Declan lurched
to his feet. "But—"

Her voice followed him, although he was caught in a featureless gray void and
could no longer see her face. "When you find balance, as surely as the moon fol-
lows his sister the sun, everything will fall into place."

Pressure made itself known beneath his feet, and then light flared. He turned
his head and saw trees appearing out of a mist, shafts of golden sunlight streaming down through the leaves. All around him, magpies and bluejays were calling,
squirrels chattering, streams rushing over stones toward the distant, unseen sea.

Something ran through the brush not a hundred yards away. He heard panting, the steady pad of four feet. His heart quickened.

A moist black nose pushed through a leafy bush, followed by a familiar midnight-black form. The huge dog stopped and cocked her head, clearly astounded to find him there. The white star on her forehead shone through the shade like the brightest star in the night skies. "Nightshadow!" He rushed forward and threw his arms around her neck while she lowered her head and pressed joyfully against his chest.

An older, hollow-cheeked man stared at him from the dog's back, then rubbed his bloodshot eyes. Declan reached out a hand to the weary Tsalagi shaman. "Two Hearts."

chapter twenty-four

Berry heard the sweep of the Uk'ten's wings as it passed above the trees again, but fortunately it no longer seemed drawn to her since that startling moment earlier when the stranger had disappeared. She huddled, making herself small in the fork of the massive hickory, pondering what had happened.

The wounded stranger had been at the point of death from shock and loss of blood when the blue light had sprung up around him. She had glimpsed the vague outlines of a herd of strangely colored deer, red, yellow, white, and black, heard the crystalline echo of the song he was singing in a ragged, tired voice. She had flinched back, her skin crawling with electricity, as he disappeared into the blueness of the spirit world, going there, not in a dream or a vision, but in his body. If he hadn't died instantly, torn apart by the massive energies of that realm, then he was truly a Spiritwalker, blessed in all four of the great medicine ways, as her uncle had predicted.

She whispered a prayer to the Above Beings in the hope he had survived. Without him, all the horrifying dark things she had dreamed would come true, the terrible loss of land and names, language and kin, custom and way of life. It had already begun; Kitasi was gone, and she would rather be dead herself than see such times come to pass.

Below, she heard male voices as the red-coated soldiers ranged through the forest, collecting their washed-up weapons from crevices and bushes, and cajoling their shivering, wild-eyed elk-dogs. The silly beasts were still skittish, pounding away whenever approached, but the mound of scavenged supplies and weapons steadily grew. They had lost far less than she had hoped when Long Man had flooded the forest. At this rate, they would soon finish regrouping and then go on to attack another town, and then another, until the Tsalagi were only bleaching bones, as dead and forgotten as their brothers, the Catawbas.

The beat of vast wings grew louder again, and the Uk'ten's characteristic stench strengthened. It was very close now. She remembered the stories her mother had told of the creature. It was a savage denizen of the Night Country, never meant to fly the skies of the Middle World. Who had loosed it here and why?

She pressed her cheek to the trunk, thinking. When darkness fell and the soldiers slept, she would sneak down and fade back into the trackless brush. Their mounts were quite stupid, especially compared to Tsalagi dogs. They did not look to be capable of trailing her, or even hunting so much as a mouse, for that matter. Most of them feared their own shadows. Once she had slipped out of earshot, she would be safe.

The wings thundered closer, and the terrible smell thickened. The tree shuddered with each beat now, and then a narrow head, longer than she was tall, snaked down through the foliage. Terrified, she decided to take her chances with the soldiers and scrambled down the trunk.

The Uk'ten opened its mouth to exhale a great gout of flame. The yawning red maw reeked of burning corpses and rotting flesh under the hot sun. She choked and fought not to lose consciousness as the tree seemed to sway beneath her hands. Distantly, a man berated the creature. The great head with its blazing red eyes darted closer. With the last of her strength, she let go and fell several body-lengths to the ground, hit badly and sprawled across an exposed tree root, her ribs throbbing.

The Uk'ten roared its frustration, then uprooted the hickory with a casual thrust of its foreleg and cast it aside with a crash. Gagging, Berry dug her fingers into the muddy earth and crawled toward a thicket. Hooves pounded as the soldiers fled. She heard men shouting and a strange cracking like little thunders. The Uk'ten folded its wings and landed in the hole where the tree had been. She saw a half-naked man perched on its shoulders as the beast extended its massive foot, then she screamed as the terrible claws caught her shirt and plucked her into the air.

✳   ◇   ✳

Two Hearts stared. His eyes had not betrayed him; the person holding out his hand really was the white stranger called Declan, who had been, for a short time, remade into his talented apprentice, Snake. He recalled the fire of his anger when the two of them had parted at the stone mountain, when he realized, despite Two Hearts' best efforts, this diffident young man, no more than a boy by Tsalagi standards, still feared to use what he had been given.

His legs wavered as he slid off Nightshadow's back to the ground. He had been riding the black dog for so long that, even after he had dismounted, the earth still seemed to move beneath his feet. He could smell the river somewhere just out of sight, and knew beyond it lay Kitasi. After days of hard, hard running, he and Nightshadow had nearly reached their goal.

Declan blinked, seeming subdued, almost dazed. He looked up from Nightshadow, one arm still across her shoulder. "I reached Kitasi too late. The British had already attacked and moved on."

Two Hearts rested his spinning head against the bole of a young pine and fought the urge to strike him. If the outlanders had attacked Kitasi, why was he just standing here? He took a deep breath. "How many survived?"

"None, that I know of." Declan turned his bleak gaze back to Nightshadow. She whined and licked his face, rubbing her head against his shoulder. "Bodies had been piled inside the palisade and then the whole village was torched. As far as I could tell, no one was spared, not women or old men, or even children. I—" He swallowed hard. "It was—terrible."

Two Hearts clenched his fists. "Why are you standing here then? We cannot just cut our hair and wander the woods to mourn like old women. We have to find the other shamen and summon enough medicine power to drive the soldiers back into the dead lands."

Declan looked up from the great dog. "They—killed the shamen first, while they were calling medicine power."

Two Hearts felt the blood drain from his head.

Declan looked over his shoulder toward the unseen river. Two Hearts glimpsed the interlaced blue diamonds on his back, sign of the young man's spirit helper, Rattlesnake, a false promise of power that Declan had never fulfilled. Apparently, even the spirits could be wrong sometimes. "The shamen were shaping medicine power to drive out the British, but were killed before they could use it. They opened a rift between the worlds, but then there was no one left to close it."

Two Hearts felt a chill rage overtake him, threading cool fury through his veins. What had possessed him to leave Kitasi for this weak, ineffectual stranger? If he had stayed with his people, he might have made a difference when the British came. His strength added to that of the other shamen might have been enough. Instead, he had wasted time traipsing all over the country with this coward, and to what purpose? What difference did it make that he possessed unheard-of potential? Power was only useful when it was wielded and this foolish white man was too afraid to use it for reasons Two Hearts could not begin to comprehend.

Even though he had far less power himself, he had been the strongest shaman in Kitasi. A war of revenge must be in the making. He would find the nearest town and offer his services to the head priest. Then, if he died, at least it would be an honorable death, and he would not have to think about what his foolishness had cost. But in the meantime, what should he do about Declan? Was it safe to leave a white man with access to medicine power loose in the forest? What if he decided to aid the soldiers? His hand stole down to the knife sheathed at his waist.

Nightshadow bristled and bared her teeth at him. Her dark eyes gleamed unmistakable warning. He stepped back, startled, after having spent so many companionable days in her company.

Declan glanced at the black dog, his face puzzled, then turned back to Two Hearts. "I have just come from the spirit world, where I was told we have to end the fighting—"

"End the fighting?" Two Hearts' lip curled. "Why? So more of my people will live to serve as slaves when the white soldiers overrun our land?"

"Slaves?" Declan's pale skin blanched. "No, of course not! But if the fighting goes on, the two sides will destroy each other, while at the same time the worlds collide, and then we will all die."

Two Hearts' face felt hot as the heart of a bonfire. "I have never said this to a grown man before, but I do not believe you!" Cool fury underlay his words and he knew he would have killed this stranger if the great dog had not been there to protect him. "Still, I should not be surprised. I have heard blackrobes say many things that are false. Rifts arise whenever medicine power is summoned. Small ones seal themselves, and any reasonably trained shaman can seal one alone. I had to close one made by you on this foolish, pointless journey."

His hand tightened on the handle of the knife. "This is just a story you have made up to save the lives of your miserable friends. You are a foolish, frightened child with no respect for the gifts you have been given or the great matters of the spirit revealed to you." His mouth twisted with anger. "I have trained all my life to receive far less. Go back to the dead lands where you and your kind belong; live the rest of your worthless life with the bitter knowledge of all the good you could have done here and what you might have been."

Declan flushed as the dog interposed herself between the two men, growling, every hair on end. He placed a restraining hand on her neck. "I never asked for any of this." His blue eyes blazed with anger. "I only wanted to go home to Ireland and forget what I had seen, but you forced me to stay and learn how to use medicine power." He turned over his arm and stared at the blue diamondback patterning. "Now I will never again be welcome among my own kind, never serve the Lord God as I have dreamed my whole life. I cannot go 'back,' as you put it, because you have taken all that away from me!"

"It was the Above Beings who called you, not I," Two Hearts said. "I would have let you die."

"Yes, the Above Beings." Declan flexed his arm. "They have marked my soul as surely as they marked my body. They have given me a task and now I must to do it to the best of my ability, even though I have no idea how!"

Two Hearts had never seen the younger man like this. Always before he had been afraid, reluctant, naive at the best of times. This was the first hint that he had any fire in his character, any strength of purpose. For a breath, Two Hearts almost accepted his sincerity. Then the wind shifted and he caught a whiff of the burned village across the river. How many of his relatives and friends had died there? Had any survived? Even if they had, life would never again have that easy, familiar flavor it had held before. Everything was altered now.

He tightened his jaw, then plunged into the brush, heading for the ford across the river and what little remained of his former life.

✳   ◇   ✳

Reinforcements arrived in the early dusk and set up in a grassy meadow just south of Jones's abbreviated camp, upwind of the fire-damaged area so that the air was almost untainted by smoke and ash.

Colonel John Wickham Hollingsworth was a seasoned commander, veteran of a dozen campaigns in Europe, but, Jones reflected grimly, he had never fought in the wild country of this continent, nor faced heathenish magic. Stern-faced, topped with an unpretentious gray wig, he looked to be a stolid, unimaginative man, unaccustomed to either fear or failure. There was old wealth in the long lines of that face, ancient lineage, breeding, all qualities to which a low-born Welsh wretch like himself could never aspire. Jones stood at attention, his scorched coat brushed as best he could, his singed hair newly combed, waiting to surrender his command.

"So you are Captain Evan Jones." Hollingsworth hefted an ivory-handled whip thoughtfully. "I noted the state of your encampment as we rode in." His deep-set gray eyes narrowed. "I found it in shocking disarray. Half of your men

are cleaning their weapons, which look as though they've been wet, by God, and
the rest are as bruised and scraped as if they've been trading fisticuffs with each
other for the last three days." He leaned back in his chair. "I suppose you can
present some sort of an explanation."

"We were—under attack—by supernatural means, sir." Jones stared over the
colonel's shoulder at a loose tie on the flap of his tent. "At present, we're still
cleaning up, but our losses were not nearly as grievous as I'd first feared. We
should be back in form by morning and ready to proceed."

"You let natives get the drop on you?" Hollingsworth's patrician mouth tightened. "Your orders were to kill the shamen before they had any opportunity to
conjure." He tapped the butt of his whip against the palm of his hand.

"I regret to say it was not the natives, sir." In Jones's mind, he saw the rising
water again, a sudden freshwater sea where there should have been only dry land,
battering his men against the oaks and maples, sweeping away his supplies. He
clenched his hands at his sides. "It was one of the priests."

Hollingsworth scowled. "You mean one of the native priests."

"No, sir." Jones braced his shoulders back, feeling the cloth abrade his many
cuts and bruises. "One of the Catholic priests, brought over from Ireland."

"One of our priests?" The colonel leaned forward. "Working heathen
magic—against British troops?"

"Yes, sir."

Hollingsworth took his feet with the no-nonsense manner of a bull disturbed
in its pasture. "And where is this so-called priest now?"

"I cannot say, at present, sir." Jones's face warmed. "He employed some sort
of spell to flood the forest, then escaped while we were fighting for our lives.
Afterwards, we had a spot of trouble with a—a monster, sir, a flying creature that
breathed fire, probably his conjuring as well. It stampeded those horses we had
managed to recapture at that point and killed several more of my men and
mounts. I lost my own horse and narrowly avoided being burned to death."

Hollingsworth's mouth twisted as though he had tasted vinegar. "You
allowed this renegade priest to escape?"

Jones opened his mouth to protest they'd had survival foremost on their
minds. It was, after all, a soldier's duty to preserve his life so that he could fight
on for King and country, but excuses were the refuge of a weakling. He refused to
brand himself as such. "Yes, Colonel," he said stonily.

The colonel traced the line of his jaw with the whip, his face set. Finally he

turned to a young lieutenant. "Have the perimeter patrolled at five minute inter-
vals. I'll be dashed if I'll lose another man to such incompetence."

The lieutenant saluted smartly. "Yes, sir!"

Hollingsworth clasped his hands behind his back as the lieutenant trotted off
to organize the patrol. "The King is short on resources, Captain. The time has
come to secure this land and make it pay. We cannot afford men in this command
who are foolish, lazy, or cowardly."

A muscle jumped in Jones's cheek.

"My orders are to scour this land of magicians," Hollingsworth said slowly,
"be they white or native. Any man of whom you have the slightest doubt is to be
shot immediately. We will take no more chances. Is that clear?"

Jones snapped off a salute. "Yes, sir!"

Hollingsworth waved a dismissive hand at him. "Then return to your men
and see they are safe for the night. You will receive further orders in the morning."

Jones turned sharply and marched off, feeling those disdainful steel-gray eyes
bore into his back. His face burned; he would slice off that bloody priest's ears
personally and string them from his belt for everyone to see. Under no circumstances would he be made a fool of twice.

Declan's first impulse was to go after Two Hearts and make him understand
that he had not merely stood aside and let the British march on after burning the
village, that he had in fact arrived too late and missed the soldiers altogether, but
Nightshadow blocked his path and would not give way. After several unsuccess-
ful attempts to get around the persistent dog, Declan sank to his knees beneath a
pine. His head spun and he was overwhelmingly weary. Perhaps she was right;
they could trail Two Hearts tomorrow, when his mind was clearer.

Nightshadow snuffled his ear in approval, then settled on her belly beside
him. Nose on paws, she watched his face anxiously. He lay one hand on her silken
head and leaned back against the pine's slender trunk with a sigh. It still amazed
him that this huge, savage creature, meant for the violence of the hunt and mortal combat, had room in her heart for him. It felt right, somehow, soothing, to be
here with her like this.

His stomach rumbled, but he decided against food. Fasting was both a preparation and a source of power, and he needed any advantage he could manage now. He stretched out against Nightshadow's musky warmth, comforted by her presence, and let his eyes drift shut. He was so tired, so bone-achingly weary of trying to make sense of things totally outside of his experience. His empty stomach growled again and though he tried, he could not remember the last time he had slept or consumed a full meal ...

Later, somewhere within the cotton-wool of deep, dreamless sleep, he realized it was cold, not the welcome respite of shade from the sun, or the blissful easing of night when the breeze sweeps away the heat of a summer day, but teeth-chattering, heart-stopping cold. He mumbled against Nightshadow's side and then flopped over, forcing his leaden eyelids apart.

Light from the rising quarter-moon filtered down through the trees, silvering each leaf, blade of grass, clod of earth, but the glade had gone silent as a crypt. His breath crystallized before him and a glimmer of frost had already coated Nightshadow's whiskers and ears. He sat up, blinking, and felt the frozen grass crunch beneath his legs. Nightshadow lurched to her feet and shook pellets of ice from her thick coat.

But this was the middle of summer, he thought in confusion. Nightshadow growled and bared her teeth, staring intently into the impenetrable darkness beneath the heavy foliage. Declan's skin, already covered with goosebumps, now crawled as he sensed the presence of someone, no—many someones out there in the night. He felt their eyes upon him, waiting for—something.

"Who are you?" he called, rubbing his freezing arms. His heart began to pound. "What do you want?"

The earth felt wrong beneath his feet, as though north had switched places with south and everything had turned inside out. He jerked to his feet and placed a hand on Nightshadow's neck. The great dog bristled, stiff and angry, more afraid than he had ever seen her.

Shapes drifted out of the shadows, outlines without flesh, limned in moon-silver. Declan forgot to breathe as they came forward, first in ones and twos, then larger groups, calm and detached, unseeing. Fear, colder than any frost, seeped down his backbone. They appeared to be ghosts, unholy creatures forever denied God's presence and bound to the physical world. Nightshadow threw her body hard against him as they passed and pushed him stumbling back underneath the pine, but one slender woman, who carried the faint shape of a baby on her back, reached out an insubstantial hand and grazed his arm. Drums—singing —wails overwhelmed her . . . she stared up at the ceiling as a medicine man blew pungent smoke in her face, but it was no use . . . her poor stillborn child was bound for the Night Country without ever drawing breath . . . she was crushed with sorrow . . . he would never feel the morning sun on his tiny face . . . never hunt with the other boys or laugh, never even cry . . . she did not want to live without him . . . would follow him to the Night Country so he need never be alone . . .

Declan cried out as her silvery fingers trailed away. He hunched over, filled with sorrow, bitter as gall, and regret, and resignation. He heard murmuring now, faint, but growing louder as the crowd of transparent people surged around him. A desperate urge seized him to follow them into the darkness, not to be left behind; a terrible pressure built behind his eyes, compelling him. Nightshadow snagged his breeches in her teeth and tugged him urgently out of their path.

He huddled there against her, trying to understand. It was wrong that it should be so cold in this season, and even more wrong that these people, all obviously dead, were here. They belonged in the Night Country, as Two Hearts had called it, the underworld, another realm entirely. They must have come through the rift, like the Uk'ten.

The ghost-people walked unseeing through solid tree trunks and vines and rocks. Nightshadow frantically pulled him back, back, the brush scraping his arms and legs bloody, but still they pressed on. A long-haired boy of nine or ten with a gaping chest wound stepped through Declan and—searing pain, tearing through him; would it never stop? He had been foolish to challenge Brother Bear with only a child's bow and arrows, but he'd longed for the claws, wanted his mother and father to see how fierce he was, wanted to watch his friends touch the brown pelt and—

Nightshadow fastened her teeth in his leg and wrenched him aside. Gasping, he fell out of contact with the shade, but the insubstantial boy walked on through the dog. She stiffened, then collapsed, dark eyes glazing. Shivering uncontrollably, Declan saw some part of her rise and prowl after the ghosts in the form of a shining outline, her spirit. He struggled to his knees. "Nightshadow, no!"

She did not pause or look back. Declan clenched his teeth against the terrible cold and lurched to his feet, stumbling after her, buffeted on all sides now by shades. He felt their grief and despair and soaring joy, the pain of a thousand agonizing wounds, the misery of fevers and weeping sores. He bit down on his lip to keep from crying out and followed them through the trees to the river.

Where the ruins of Kitasi should have lain on the opposite shore, he saw instead the sacred mountain in the center of the world, rising up gray against the black night sky. Blood drummed in his ears. He knew this too was wrong. The Above World, realm of the spirits, was held apart from the Night Country by the Middle World so their opposing energies balanced and creation remained stable. If the two came in contact, everything would be destroyed.

He heard a grinding roar as Nightshadow and the ghost-people drifted steadily toward the proud mountain, then he splashed into the river after them.

The bank was steep and the current much swifter than he had anticipated. He stumbled on the sandy river bottom, stepped in a hole and was swept off his feet. He flailed, getting water down his nose and choking as he tried to swim, but the unnatural cold that accompanied the ghost-people had penetrated the water and his muscles went into spasms. The river's pulse beat in Declan's ears as the icy surface closed over his head. He struggled, staring up at the receding moon, now just a bright fingernail of light distorted by the water.

Have you learned nothing from your time in this land? Snake whispered in the back of his mind. Why do you fight your brother?

Sinking toward the bottom, lungs burning, his mind flashed back to that moment under Two Hearts' tutelage when Snake had left a part of himself behind in every pond and lake, all the way down to the restless, briny sea. Now and forever, he was one with Water, whatever form it took, wherever it existed. He opened his heart to its power and the marvelous quality of movement that was its being, using it, rather than fighting. Like a wakened sleeper, Long Man stirred, shook himself, then bore Declan upward.

He broke the surface gasping, shivering so hard, he could barely draw breath. Ahead of him, on the far shore, the ghost-people drifted toward the sacred mountain, the spirit of the great dog caught in their midst.

His bare toes touched bottom and he staggered forward. Keep moving, he thought, that was the secret. If he stayed in motion, he would not have time to think about how hopeless it was to try to stop the unresponsive dead, or how much raw, unfiltered pain they carried in their souls, or how much he feared being drawn after them if they touched him again.

A terrible grinding still rumbled up out of the ground, drummed through the air, shivered behind his eyes. It was as if all of creation, both those portions invisible and those tangible, were being torn asunder. The ghost-people stopped short of the foot of the soaring mountain and milled about in seeming confusion. In their midst, the dog's gleaming form looked back over her shoulder, as though she had forgotten something.

Dripping from the river, so cold that he could not even feel his hands or feet, he called to her again. She hesitated, gazing back with lightning-bright eyes that looked straight through him. She could not return, he thought, just he could not let her go. Ducking his head, he plunged through the vast sea of shades, once more wrenched by the awful sorrows they bore, their unfinished lives, bitter regrets, lost joys. What did she regret, he wondered as he neared her silhouette— the loss of her packmates? The joy of hunting? Of running? There was only way to find out.

He hesitated, then stepped into her brittle outline. His ears rang with the tone of a fine crystalline bell, and then he was Nightshadow, an immense fearless dog who bore lightning in her teeth and thunder in her chest, dancer of the sacred rite between predator and prey, born to run with one special two-legged who would change the world.

He shuddered, dizzy and disoriented, close to losing himself in the surge of her being. You and I, we are not done yet, he whispered, not in words, but thoughts. You cannot go!

Confusion filled her mind as the ghost-people started off again. For a moment, he thought she would follow. The frightening dissonance reached a new level of intensity as they reached the foot of the mountain and the antipodal energies skewed farther out of balance. He felt the earth itself tremble beneath his feet. Help me, he told Nightshadow. Turn them back toward the Night Country. He made a picture in his head for her of the dogs of his native land, zigzagging across the fields, herding sheep. Don't let them reach the mountain!

Confused, Nightshadow's mind said. Her ears drooped. Uncertain.

He thought of her circling ahead of them, then turning and forcing them back from the mountain, using claw and tooth, anger, truth, whatever weapon they might heed. Her shimmering ears pricked forward as she unraveled his meaning. He felt her braveness, her courage in the face of so much unknown. Leaving him, she leaped ahead, visible only as a vague outline, as though she were made of glass.

Declan held his breath as the grinding intensified. He had a sudden impression of trees with their roots growing up into the sky, rivers running toward the moon. Were the three realms falling apart as they collided? Would anything be left, or would chaos reign?

The ghost-people hesitated when she turned and barked, but he only heard the faint, brittleness of glass striking glass. Her outlined ears were pinned back and her teeth bared. They attempted to go around her, but she darted to cut them off, harrying and slashing at the faint shapes. A child broke ranks and turned back, then an old man, then the crowd streamed toward Declan and away from the sacred mountain.

Startled, he tried to clear their path, but they were too fast, and this time he fell as the shades swept through him, inundating him with their pain and anger and regret. With each succeeding emotion, he had to grit his teeth and fight to hang on as his spirit loosened from his body. He had the terrible urge to go with them to the Night Country where pain was left behind forever and he would find a coming to rest, a final peace that would surpass everything he had ever known.

He dug his fingers into the moist dirt and held on, reaching for the slow patient strength of Earth, knowing that if he relaxed, even for a second, he would be lost. When the last shade had skimmed back across the river, he regained his knees.

The cold was receding as Nightshadow drove the shades toward the rift, and this time, when he waded into the river, the water was almost blood-warm. He swam a few strokes, then let Long Man carry him across the rest of the way, his heart pounding. He felt it would take more strength than he would ever know again to leave the water, yet somehow he crawled up the opposite bank and staggered to his feet.

The ghost-people were traveling faster than he could have run, if he'd had enough energy left to run. The darkness was filled with even blacker splotches. A ringing in his ears, born of exhaustion, drowned the returning normal sounds of the night. He reached Nightshadow's fallen body and stood over her, trying to see the glassy outlines of the retreating wraiths, but they were too far ahead of him now. Nightshadow's presence was still with them, and he felt as though his soul were being wrenched from his body as she drew farther and farther away.

No! he cried silently and clenched his hands, fighting to remain in his physical body. I will not go. You must stay here with me! He flung himself onto her abandoned body.

He felt her unwillingness to stay in the Middle World where pain, both emotional and physical, made life imperfect. She was drawn after the others to a place of peace where everything made sense and no one was pushed beyond her limits. I need you, he said. Before I even knew what any of this was about, I saw you on the sacred mountain. I think you are meant to be here with me, to help. I cannot do what must be done alone.

The bond between them stretched to the breaking point as she reached the rift leading back into that other world. If she left, he felt he would never be whole

again, that he would die without her. He clutched her limp body closer, holding
her with all his might.

At the last second, when he thought all was lost, she gave a great despairing
cry and then dashed back through the forest, a vague silvery outline skimming
through the trees. Seconds later, he felt an explosion of shivery warmth as her
spirit reentered her body. Her lungs heaved, her legs quivered, and then he buried
his face in her ruff. She lifted her head and licked his cheek with a warm tongue,
weak, but alive. Her tail thumped against the ground.

He lay against her side, arms about her neck, and felt her longing for the
peace of the Night Country war with her desire to remain here with him. He was
sobered by the immensity of what she had just sacrificed for him, and the knowledge that perhaps it would still all be for nothing. The Above World was asking
more of him than even a trained Tsalagi shaman with a lifetime of experience
dealing with medicine power could accomplish.

And he had no idea what to do next.

Two Hearts reached Kitasi long after the moon's chill white sliver rode high
among the scattered stars. When he parted from Declan and Nightshadow, he
found he was farther up-river than he had thought and had some distance yet to
travel. He crossed Long Man, then tramped on through the whispering darkness
instead of making camp, fueled by a simmering white-hot sea of anger.

He had given his time and experience to train Declan in the faith that, in the
end, despite his misgivings, the younger man would fit his hand to the role
assigned him, but Two Hearts had been mistaken and now it was to cost the
Tsalagi more than they had left to give. He had not often been wrong since
becoming a man, and the knowledge that he had so misjudged the stranger's
heart lay bitter on the back of his throat, like an herbal medicine that drove out
disease, but tasted foul.

The reek of burned wood and bodies came to him on the night breeze long
before he actually reached the blackened stumps of the palisade. On this side of
the scorched wall, in the soft cover of darkness and the faint silvering of moonlight, Kitasi looked almost untouched, but his heart recoiled from entering a
place inhabited only by the dead. Since his fellow shamen had died, no one had
been left to carry out the proper rituals for burial and purification afterward and
the site was unclean.

A low, hoarse mutter broke the silence, and he made out a dark, barely discernible figure on the sandy beach where the villagers had formerly kept their canoes. As he drew closer though, he realized the words were not Tsalagi. He came upon a double row of mounds, each topped by two rough pieces of wood tied so that they crossed each other. A gray-haired man knelt before the last one, hands knotted beneath his chin, repeating the same words over and over in a cracked voice.

Two Hearts bent over him, then drew in a sharp breath of surprise; it was the older blackrobe who had first accompanied Declan to the village, then later tried to take him back to the dead lands. "What are you doing here?" he demanded. "Did you have a part in this—this slaughter?"

The old man continued to speak over his clenched hands, his eyes downcast.

"Answer me!" Two Hearts jerked him to his feet where he swayed, shivering and mumbling. "Why are you here?"

The blackrobe stared at him in bewilderment. Tear tracks glistened down his cheeks in the moonlight. "They not bad children," he said in halting, poorly accented Tsalagi. "Not they fault. I baptize, give Christian burial, send to God."

Two Hearts' mouth tightened at the sound of those meaningless white man's words again. Why did outlanders always speak of only a single Above Being, and one they had murdered themselves at that? Were they so afraid of the world of spirits that they must shut all but that one lone voice out?

He shoved the blackrobe away. He had no desire to soil his hands on this wretch, no matter how much he might deserve to die. And, besides, he had obviously lost his reason. It could even be that the Above Beings had seen fit to take it from him, so he might have a chance to learn, as had Snake. Some among the Tsalagi maintained the spirits had touched those whose minds were broken and so considered them sacred.

Feeling tainted by the blackrobe, he wiped his hands on his tattered rawhide breeches and strode determinedly toward the surrounding shelter of the forest to find a place to sleep. The old man hunkered close to the last mound and returned to swaying and mumbling over his hands.

The shrill buzz of crickets filled the air, comfortingly familiar, and he heard the soft swoop of bats above the river as they chased insects. Firelight flickered ahead in the trees and his brow wrinkled. Were the British still camped close-by? That would explain the presence of the old blackrobe. He dropped into the deepest shadows, skimming close to the brush, treading silently. If these were the enemy, he would learn what he could, then take that information to the nearest town, perhaps Cheota, where surely a war party had formed.

He heard the rise and fall of voices now, some low and serious, others plainly angry. The scattered fires were small and well made, throwing almost no smoke. He stepped on a twig, and then a pale form bounded out of the trees, as massive as a bear, growling and baring ivory teeth that glinted in the moonlight.

Two Hearts stepped into the open, hands held out, recognizing Moonstrider from his own village, a dominant male who often led the pack in independent hunts. He extended the flat of his hand. The bristling white dog sniffed suspiciously, then raised his ears and prodded Two Hearts' chest with a cold wet nose.

Two Hearts took the great head between his hands and stared into the dark liquid eyes. "I greet you, my brother," he said, then walked with the huge dog toward the welcoming fires.

Soon after the yellow-bright sun creature of this middle realm had fled the sky, the man-thing bid Uk'ten land in a brushy clearing beside a small lake. He slid off Uk'ten's scaly back and set about gathering wood for a fire. Uk'ten curled up and watched, bemused. He, of course, admired fire, for was he not a creature of magnificent Fire himself? But, disappointingly, this turned out to be but a tiny, pallid blaze, hardly worthy of the name, for all that Uk'ten obligingly kindled it, when asked, with his own sulfurous breath.

The fragile woman-thing cowered in the muddy reeds on the shore of the lake and there was the heady smell of blood as she dabbed at her shoulder. Uk'ten laughed in little snorting puffs of smoke. She had tried to escape into the trees as soon as he had released her, but he'd fired the branches ahead of her, and she took refuge by the water instead. He savored the cold-iron taste of her fear; there was certainly none of that in the monotonous world below. He drummed his foreclaws against the mossy ground in the anticipation of the moment he would crunch her delectable bones. Perhaps he would flame her first, perhaps not, but she would be most afraid then, yes.

One Eye, the man-thing who shared his dark soul, tended the fire, roasting a rabbit Uk'ten had flushed. Uk'ten had flamed the tiny beast and left it for him; such a minuscule tidbit could do little more than tickle his own palate. He would require food of vastly better quality, and soon.

All in all, he liked the feel of this Middle World with its meshing, four-fold energies and opposite directions from the one he had known. This was all new and very tasty, a relief from the staggering boredom of being forever trapped in the depths of the Night Country where only the dead and a few other singleton monsters like himself abided. The dead were not capable of fear and he had been equally matched by his fellow monsters since the moment of creation. The upside down days below passed with agonizing slowness.

But this! He snapped his teeth, bringing a shiver from the female, who darted back into the lake's shallows. This tasted so much better by far. The men of this world had every reason to fear him. The trees burned most excellently here, and these human-things could actually die, something entirely unknown below. Everything was different and vulnerable and utterly delightful, and he had this man-thing to guide him now, to whisper in his great scalloped ear where they should go and whom they should terrify next.

First, One Eye said, they would scourge the forests of all human-things, both Tsalagi and the pale-skinned ones in coats of bright red, whom he called warriors of a sort. Once they had exhausted that entertainment, they would fly to the coast and wreak havoc there until every patch of dirt lay scorched and blackened, every lodge in ashes, and the whole world reeked of his fire.

The woman-thing eased backwards into the quiet lake. He turned his head toward One Eye's fire, letting her think he did not notice. Then, when she had almost reached the opposite shore with its sheltering trees, he flapped unhurriedly after her, plucking her out of the dark water without missing a beat.

He heard her sobbing in his claws and puffed a bit of smoke downward in appreciation. Fear, yes, that was the best of all, and there would be so much more to savor before this world was finished.

Captain Jones took a final turn around the combined camps, unable to sleep despite the deep quiet of the clear midnight sky that stretched overhead into infinity. Even the frogs and insects had fallen silent. Had the skies above his beloved Wales ever looked so vast and unending? He tried to remember and found he could not. Wales was a civilized land with towns and sturdy houses, plowed fields and lazing, contented cattle. It was another reality, lost to him at the moment and perhaps forever. When he looked up into the void on nights like this, he could not fight the growing certainty he would never leave this savage land alive.

He found each sentry alert and on post, watching, not clumped in pairs, murmuring, as they might have been, had circumstances been less ominous. He passed man after man, giving each an approving nod. Colonel Hollingsworth had already retired; he clearly did not understand that the dangers of this land would not wait for daylight to come screaming out of the forest, merely firing arrows or swinging primitive war-clubs while traditional, well disciplined lines of soldiers stood their ground and gunned them down. No, whatever attacked them next would come straight out of Hell, perhaps the dragonlike beast that breathed fire down upon the forest or another gruesome snake-apparition made of blue light that swallowed men whole, or something even worse, unimaginable because decent Christians like himself could not conceive of the many terrors spawned of this wicked, wicked land.

Something glinted out beyond the perimeter in the faint moonlight, a suggestion of movement. The hair rose on the nape of his neck and he halted in front of the sleeping rows of his men, most of whom, after the flood, no longer had tents or even blankets for shelter. "Hastings, over there, to the right!" He waved at the nearest sentry. "I saw something. Take a torch and check."

Hastings, a London youth with only the faint down of a mustache, nodded and headed out into the darkness, musket in hand. Jones shivered; the air had grown unseasonably cold. His eyes strained to follow the sentry through the night. "Well?"

"I dunno, Captain," the youth said. "It—"

The air rang as though crystal struck crystal. Jones made out the glassy outline of something in the night, then many shapes, all insubstantial as hoarfrost. He raised the pistol he had scavenged and cleaned. "Hastings?"

"No!" Hastings' voice was shrill as he stumbled backwards. His torch fell from nerveless hands and then guttered against the wet ground. "No, for the love of God, get away!"

Jones turned to the nearest sentry on the perimeter. "Rouse the camp!"

"Yes, sir!" The sentry fired into the air, then ran shouting and shoving the sleeping men. "To arms!"

The air grew colder still and Jones's breath was a white fog as he ran toward the downed Hastings. His entire being cringed, but he had to know what they were up against. Not magic, he told himself as his lungs pumped. Please, almighty God in Heaven above, not magic, not again!

chapter twenty-six

Crack of gunfire. Shouting. Muffled curses. Shrill cries of pain, hoarser ones of terror.

Colonel Hollingsworth bolted up on his cot, roused from a sound sleep by the pandemonium outside his tent. He fought the blanket tangled around his legs, wondering what time it was. An orderly thrust his tousled head through the flap and he glimpsed a patch of starry sky through the opening; it was still night then. The smell of burned gunpowder filled the air.

"Colonel," the orderly said, "we seem to be under attack!"

Hollingsworth swung his legs over the side of the bed and fumbled for the pistol box he kept within reach. "How many?" He hefted the loaded guns, one in each hand.

"I cannot say, sir." The orderly's eyes were white-rimmed as he glanced back over his shoulder. "It's too dark."

Hollingsworth shoved his feet into boots, and, then, still in his shirt-sleeves, pushed past the pasty-faced youth into the melee of shouting men and plunging, squealing horses. The air was dank, much colder than it ought to be at this time of year and latitude. He considered going back for his jacket, but obviously his subordinates were panicking. He had to take charge before the situation fell completely apart.

Catching a passing subaltern's arm, he towed him along as he ran toward the chaos. "Find Lieutenants Williams and Nickleby!" he snapped, infuriated by the poor show of discipline. "I want proper firing lines formed immediately!" The subaltern saluted and disappeared into the milling throng, his face pale and sweating despite the chill.

Hollingsworth raised a pistol as he strode determinedly toward the disturbance. The shots had stopped now, and the air was instead filled with a peculiar ringing, as though someone had struck a silver spoon against fine dinnerware. Above that, he heard only the shouts of British voices. If they were under attack, where were the bloody natives?

Men streamed back toward him now, mouths gaping in fear. He wrenched one aside. "Stand your ground, soldier!"

The man, a private, swarthy as a Cornish miner, clawed at his hand, shaking his head, mumbling something over and over again.

Hollingsworth backhanded him with the pistol. "Goddamned bloody coward! Where's your musket?"

His face bleeding, the private wilted to his knees. Tears coursed down his face, silver-white in the moonlight, and mingled with the blood. The colonel cursed and kicked him aside. Thank God, he could tell by the cut of the stained uniform that he was one of the fort's regular complement, not a man from one of his own companies. He was filled with rage that British soldiers could behave so, unable to fathom such a disgraceful lapse in discipline.

A ragged group of men clustered at the perimeter of the camp, staring out into the darkness, a few torches held above their heads. The flickering light danced over their grim faces. He shouldered past them, but one caught his arm with fingers of steel. Startled, he recognized the gruff captain who had transferred command of the surviving troops to him yesterday.

The man inclined his head. "Begging your pardon, Colonel, but you mustn't go any closer." He had a strong Welsh accent.

"What do you mean by thi—" Hollingsworth's voice trailed away as he made out a crowd of glasslike shapes in the darkness, transparent men and women and children, gazing at the soldiers with eyes of diamond. A heap of fallen red-uniformed bodies lay just beyond the torchlight, their muskets discarded and their limbs tangled.

"One touch by those things and you die," the captain said evenly. "It seems to take about a minute for some, no more than two for any man."

"What—" Hollingsworth's tongue clove to the roof of his mouth. "What are they?"

"Magic of some sort." The Welsh captain edged back. "Perhaps even ghosts. I have seen a great many terrible things out here, but not this, so I cannot say for certain." He turned to the staring, shocked soldiers. "Fall back! Whatever happens, do not allow them to touch you!"

Hollingsworth's mind whirled. He knew from the detailed dispatches sent back to England that the dark arts were practiced in this land, but somehow the situation had never seemed quite real, for all that it had kept Europeans at bay for over two hundred years. The Portuguese had made serious inroads with their colonies to the south, so there was no reason why decent, God-fearing Brits should not do likewise. A sick sinking invaded his stomach now as the shimmering sea of wraiths surged forward.

"Run!" Jones shouted with that abominable Welsh accent. He shoved one twitching man, then another and another. "Goddamn run until you can't run anymore!"

The soldiers turned and shambled back across the camp. One cast his musket aside and then they all did. The air pinged with cold as the temperature dropped another notch and the metal fittings of the abandoned guns slickened with frost.

"No!" Hollingsworth stared in amazement at his fleeing troops. They weren't even trying to protect themselves. Perhaps these apparitions were just living natives made to look like ghosts by magic. He raised his pistol, sighted in on a tall fellow with feathers stuck in his topknot, then squeezed the trigger. The resulting pistol crack reverberated through the trees, but the shimmering man seemed unaffected.

"Colonel Hollingsworth!" Jones wrenched him around. "Musket balls have no effect against magic. You must kill the shamen, and there are none about. It would be prudent to retreat for now, at least until the sun rises!"

Hollingsworth looked coolly down at the hand on his arm, then pointed the loaded pistol at the captain. Jones removed his hand. Hollingsworth raised his chin and took aim on another apparition. "Bloody cowards! I'll show you how a gentle man stands his ground!" He fired, but still the glass people came on, a horde of women and children in shimmering deerskin and beads, men with half-shaved heads sprouting wild tufts of hair.

The nearest reached for him, a woman with heavy braided hair that hung to her waist, carrying a babe in the crook of her arm. He swung at the outline of her shining, unlined face with the empty pistol and felt a chill electric shock as his hand passed through her cheek . . . the white soldiers came to Idjoku to trade, that's what they said, she told him, but then they fired their long sticks at us, sticks that spat death.

His legs wilted and he fell backwards to the frozen ground as she stepped through him. A stooped, half-toothless grandmother followed, walking through his fallen body as though he were only so much air. They cast my grandchildren's broken bodies into the fire, as though they were no more than sticks of wood! she cried. I would have stopped them, had I not been dead myself. Opalescent tears rolled down her wrinkled cheeks.

Darkness swooped as she passed, and something within him loosened as though a tightly laced garment's strings had been cut. He rose and found himself following the indistinct crowd. His mind raced; he knew he should be taking cover, as Jones had maintained. Their touch was clearly lethal, but now he could not turn back.

The shades flowed toward the fleeing troops, carrying him along like a bit of harmless flotsam.

Nightshadow woke Declan with the first gray tinges of dawn, exhaling warmly on his face and licking him over and over, as though she could not get enough of him. He sat up and stared into her black eyes, seeing another world within where men and animals were the same beneath the skin and the differing shape of their bodies did not hide the beauty of their spirits.

She shook herself and the vision was gone. He found himself blinking into her seemingly amused gaze—and she was amused, he could feel it, along with her hunger and her desire to reunite with her packmates and a dozen other concerns. He still perceived her thoughts as clearly as that moment when he had immersed himself in her spirit the night before. They had grown closer, as though their spirits had somehow fused. If he died, he knew she would gladly follow him into death itself, and the same was true of him. They were now, and would always be, part of one another.

She scrambled to her feet, shook herself, then glanced at him pointedly over one shoulder—it was time to leave.

"Follow Two Hearts." He took his place on her back. "We will make him listen."

She gave a low woof and loped smoothly toward the river. He settled himself more firmly behind her shoulders, clasping her barrel with his knees, and tried to formulate the proper words in his head to persuade the Tsalagi shaman to aid his cause.

In the morning, Two Hearts conferred with the surviving shamen of both his village and Idjoku as to how they might best combat the invaders. The forty-three towns, each containing anywhere from twenty to sixty lodges, had sent a massive force, now converging outside burned Kitasi in response to the first two attacks. All agreed Two Hearts should be Chief War Priest and coordinate efforts to employ the sacred medicine power against their common enemy. The British had miscalculated by not retreating to the dead lands, and now the Tsalagi would take their rightful revenge.

The shaman who had trained Two Hearts as a boy, Brings Wood, sat at the morning campfire, chewing a bit of dried meat scavenged from the burned village's stores. He sighed. "We must act in a different way." His eyes, deeply sunk into their sockets from weariness and grief, gazed unseeing into the tangle of trees. "I have seen this in a dream. No more can we stand in plain sight, calling openly upon the spirit world. We must wear the clothes of ordinary men and hide behind the trees like women, or our enemies will shoot us down before we can act."

Two Hearts watched the cooking fire's smoke curl up through the leaves, considering. "Then we will creep through the trees like our brother, the wolf, staying hidden until the moment is right. I see no shame in that. The only dishonor would lie in not balancing the blood debt owed to us."

Shouts rang through the camp. Two Hearts steadied Brings Wood as he rose on his stiff old legs. Warriors were seizing bows and arrows, spears, blowguns, knives, anything at hand with which to fight. The mood was high and the desire for war honors was thick in the air. Two Hearts felt his hackles rise, just as if he were part of the pack of dogs now bounding toward the disturbance. Had the British scouted out their assembling forces and returned? Was this the beginning of war? Sunrunner trotted past him, but he noted the golden dog's head was up and his ears pricked forward, a posture of curiosity rather than alarm.

Two Hearts and Brings Wood joined the others on the sandy curve of the beach. At the river's edge, the old blackrobe was still on his knees, digging yet another shallow hole in the ground. Just beyond the row of graves, instead of red-coated British, as his racing heart had expected, Two Hearts saw Nightshadow and Declan Connolly. The massive black dog stood silhouetted against the blinding rays of the rising sun. She looked wary, ears flicking back and forth at every sound as warriors streamed out of the forest camp. Declan sat on her back with an unselfconscious grace, looking for the first time sure of himself, as though he had been born into the Dog Clan and had ridden this way his whole life.

Disregarding the crowd of Tsalagi, Declan dismounted beside the crazed old man. The large dog hovered at his heels as he bent and spoke into the old one's ear. The blackrobe just kept digging with the clam shell. His fingernails were cracked and bloody, his lined face pallid with exhaustion, and he seemed unaware of Declan's presence. Laying the shell aside, he selected two sticks from the scavenged wood piled nearby and began to tie them together with grass.

"I know that dog!" one of the younger warriors exclaimed, and then Night-shadow's name was repeated in a dozen hushed whispers throughout the crowd.

Brings Wood turned to Two Hearts, his brows lifted. "This is very strange. Nightshadow has remained apart, running with no one, not even the other dogs now, for more than two winters, and yet she has chosen him?"

Stalking Fox joined them, his dark eyes narrowed in suspicion. An eagle feather was fastened in his head-tuft, and from somewhere in the village he had found a singed raven skin to wear about his neck, symbolic of his present position as Great War Chief. "Do you know this man?"

Two Hearts nodded. "He is one of the two blackrobes who came to Kitasi a few days before the British soldiers made their cowardly attack."

"A blackrobe—here?" Stalking Fox shaded his eyes from the intense rising sun. "Why has he come back? Is he mad?"

Two Hearts' mouth twisted with bitterness. "From the first moment I saw him, I knew he had potential to walk the medicine way. I took him as my apprentice, but—" He folded his arms across his chest, his gaze stern as granite. "Even though such a gift is never given without reason, he was afraid to use it. I sent him ahead to help protect Kitasi, then later found him in the forest, wandering idly, while the blackened bodies of our children lay unburied amidst the ashes!"

"Then, whatever else he is," Stalking Fox said, "he is a fool for returning here."

＊　◇　＊

More Tsalagi were camped here along the forested shore of Long Man than Declan had ever dreamed existed. They poured out of the trees, armed with arrows and spears and knives, their voices an angry hum, as though someone had disturbed a hive of hornets. Nightshadow's warm side pressed against him and he tasted her anxiety. Many of these were of her pack, both the dogs and the members of the Dog Clan who rode them. Now, sharing her thoughts, he appreciated just how close the clan relationship really was. It meant more than merely brother or sister; clan was a bond which meant the other was self. And yet she saw these men and dogs as enemies now, his enemies. Assessing the timbre of their voices and the carriage of their bodies, she judged they meant him harm.

And no doubt they did, because of the pallor of his skin and his origin in that other, green land, far across the sea, and because of his part in the plot to seize their land. He scanned the bronze faces; to the last man, young and old alike, they regarded him with undisguised hostility. His fingers trembled as he buried them in Nightshadow's warm thick fur. They were right; he was as much at fault in the destruction of Kitasi as any soldier who had actually set fire to the village. He had come to this continent with every intention of ending their heathen ways and had never once really thought ahead as to how that might come about, in truth, had not cared, so long as they were brought to Christ.

Two Hearts, standing at the edge of the trees, spoke to a stocky man, gesturing emphatically with his hands, then strode toward Declan and Father Fitzwilliam, moccasins crunching across the sand. Nightshadow growled, then eased in front of Declan, her eyes dark and suspicious. He felt the fear coiled inside her, the terrible memories of loneliness and desolation. She had run alone for such a long time, waited so long. The Above Beings had promised her this two-legs. She would not let him die! She would not!

It's all right, he told her without words. She shifted uneasily, but continued to shield him.

He met the Tsalagi priest's angry eyes over her stiff back. "Two Hearts, I—."

"Why have you come here?" Two Hearts burst out irritably. "The towns are gathering for a sacred war of revenge against your kind. Do you wish to be the first to die?"

Declan thought of the terrifying, damning power that lay quiescent in his hands, of Snake who lived inside him now, an alien presence who saw the world with different eyes, of the land that throbbed beneath his feet with a rhythm foreign to anything he had ever known or would understand. A wild pulse arose in his temples. "I have often wanted to die since coming to this land," he said, "but you denied me that release."

"Then go ahead and die!" Two Hearts' bleak eyes were contemptuous. "I no longer care!"

Beyond Two Hearts, Declan saw the other Tsalagi crowding each other for a good look at his white skin. Hate glittered in their fiery, dark eyes, tightened the lines of their proud faces. Nightshadow trembled beneath his hand and he stroked her shoulder, reassuring her. "Perhaps I will die," he said, "but first I have a responsibility, the rift—"

"That is not your concern!"

"Last night, across the river, the rift opened and people came out of it—dead people." Declan's entire body chilled as he remembered the bitterly cold air, the many presences not of this world. Nightshadow whined. "I would have joined them, but for Nightshadow, and in saving me, she was drawn to them herself. I followed, trying to call her back, and that was when I realized they were heading for the sacred mountain."

Two Hearts paled. "The ghost-people are of the Night Country. They cannot enter the Above World. The two realms are opposite and their energies are destructive to each other."

"I heard a terrible noise, a grinding as though the earth were being torn apart at its roots." A knot rose in Declan's throat as he remembered. "And the ground shook. I sent Nightshadow's spirit ahead of the ghost-people to turn them back, or you and I would not be standing here, speaking about this matter now." He passed a hand over his perspiring forehead. "The rift is still out there somewhere, perhaps growing larger, and the ghost-people may return."

Behind Two Hearts, the angry hum of the crowd erupted into shouts. The stocky warrior, with whom he had seen Two Hearts talking earlier, elbowed his way to the front. His black hair sprang wildly from the tuft atop his head. His face was streaked with lines of red clay, and beneath the markings, his skin was flushed. A white dog, a third again as big as Nightshadow, prowled after him.

"We will wait no longer!" The warrior raised a spear high over his head. "Our children and women and elders and brothers lie dead at the white man's traitorous hand. A blood debt is owed and balance must be restored!"

Two Hearts' mouth was grim. "We will have revenge, Stalking Fox, but this is a serious matter. Perhaps we should listen—"

"No!" Stalking Fox leveled his spear at Declan's chest. "The time for listening is done! We listened to the blackrobes when they came, because they wished only to talk. Then we listened to the traders who accompanied them on their next trip, because they wished only to trade. And when the soldiers came, with more blackrobes, raising the green cloth of trade, we opened our gates and listened to them too, because that was what we had always done. And look where that path has led!" His narrowed eyes flicked toward the burned palisade. "Two of our largest towns lie in ashes, and the white soldiers walk the road to Cheota, massing for the next attack. From all reports, they kill our shamen first, so we cannot call upon the spirits for aid, and who points out the shamen?" His chest heaved with emotion. "The blackrobes, who started it all!"

He drew back his arm to plunge the spear into Declan's bare chest. "My two daughters and my son lie in the ashes of that town, as well as my wife, my father, my brothers. Blood is owed me and I will have what is mine now!"

chapter twenty-seven

"No!" Two Hearts wrenched Stalking Fox's arm before he could hurl the spear. The warrior tore his wrist away. His narrowed eyes had gone the smoldering brown-black of an enraged bear.

The crowd, buzzing with excitement, surged forward and enclosed the three men and the snarling dog in a living wall of flesh that murmured and shifted and pressed inward. Declan extended his hand, thinking to plead his cause with them again, but Stalking Fox turned back to him, spear extended. Nightshadow whirled to cut him off and in the process knocked Declan to the ground. She stood over him, lips wrinkled back, teeth bared. He sprawled between her sheltering front legs, the wind knocked out of him. Sensing the chill, black presence of death only a whisper away, he dug his fingers into the warm sand and realized with a shock, despite everything that had happened to him in this brutal new land, despite all he had lost, he no longer wanted to die, and that, even if he had still desired it, he did not possess the right to seek that way out of his problems, not yet, with this important task undone.

Two Hearts thrust himself between Stalking Fox and Declan, his shoulders squared. His brown eyes were bleak. "Brings Wood also encountered ghost-people in the forest two nights ago, when Running Wolf and Like an Oak died."

The polished point of the spear gleamed in the sun. Stalking Fox spat into the sand. "I have not seen these ghost-people, nor have you!" His words were clipped and angry. He turned and met the eyes of the watching crowd. "And Brings Woods is an old man. Old men can be mistaken."

"He—is not—mistaken." Declan regained his feet, one hand to his ribs, still winded, then pushed Nightshadow aside so that he stood exposed and unarmed before the hostile assembly. She bristled, but stayed behind his back, a low growl rumbling in her throat. "The ghost-people came through the rift. Willow Woman said that, while Tsalagi and English are busy spilling each other's blood, this rift between the worlds will destroy everything. Neither side will win in the end."

"Liar!" Stalking Fox leveled the spear again. "When has the white man ever told us anything but lies? If we turn away from the sacred responsibility to avenge our kin, then we will be the fools, because you whites will come back and back, killing and plundering, until our bones lie scattered across the valleys and the hills and the forest floor, as bleached and lifeless as those of our brothers, the Catawbas!"

Declan spread his empty hands. "Will revenge raise your children or sow your fields?" Sweat dampened his palms, but he stood with his head raised, bathed in the blinding, early morning sunlight. "Will revenge fill the forest with deer and turkey and elk? Will it feed your families and teach your sons to be men?"

He turned to the watching warriors and raised his voice. "Will revenge make a new world for you when this one is torn apart? Will it save you when there is no more land to walk upon or air to breathe? Will it start the process of creation all over again?" He lowered his hands to his sides. "There will be no world for any of us, if we do not work together."

"Death is paid for by death, blood by blood." Stalking Fox's eyes were venomous. "That is the most ancient of our laws. This debt cannot be satisfied in any other way."

The crowd shouted its assent and everywhere Declan saw bows and spears raised high above the wildly tufted heads. The air rang with their voices; at least five hundred Tsalagi warriors had gathered here on the river, perhaps as many as twice that number, and, to the last man, they were fired with anger and grief and fear. He could taste the truth of it in the wind, feel it simmering behind his eyes, as though it were an essential element of the air he was breathing and of which he would never be free. Stalking Fox was right; there was but one way to avenge the brutal loss of their children and wives and brothers and sisters and fathers and mothers and elders—through the blood of their enemies.

He sank to his knees on the gritty sand and looked up into Stalking Fox's murderous eyes. "Then take my blood as payment." Nightshadow darted before him, understanding more than he had thought she would. He motioned her back. Whatever happens, he told her, you must let it be.

No! she cried with the flattening of ears, the stiffening of legs and neck and tail.

Yes, he said. There is no other way.

Stalking Fox's chest heaved. He shifted his grip on the spear. The crowd of warriors fell silent. The only sound that remained was the scrape of Father Fitzwilliam's clam shell through the sand, digging yet another grave.

Declan lowered his gaze to the golden beach. "I have but one thing left to do in this life, and that is to see the rift closed, as the Above Beings have directed." He took a deep breath. "But I am only an ignorant, untrained outlander, as Two

Hearts has repeatedly told me, and I do not know how to accomplish this alone. I am more than willing to give my life, if you will take it as blood payment for the great wrong done to you, and then turn your energies instead to closing the rift that endangers us all."

"You expect us to accept the life of a single man, when your fellow whites are as many as the leaves in the forest?" Stalking Fox's voice was harsh.

"Although I am just one man, Two Hearts says I have been gifted with access to vast amounts of medicine power." Declan looked up again, past the angry Tsalagi's hawk-nosed visage, into the vast, powder-blue morning sky. "If I wished, I could employ this power against you. Accept my life and you can be sure that will never come to pass."

He closed his eyes, waiting for the hot thrust of agony that would end the threat of war along with his life and allow the shamen try their hands at the real work which needed to be done. He heard Stalking Fox stride back, heard the other man's palms squeak on the shaft of the spear as his grip tightened. Would this offering be enough to satisfy the Above Beings, he wondered. Would they understand he had tried his best?

Stalking Fox leaped forward and grunted as he released the spear. Declan heard it sing through the air and braced himself. Something cracked with the sharpness of bone striking wood. His eyes flew open; a huge white dog stood a body length away, ears flattened as though he were chagrined, holding the shaft of the spear in his mouth.

A murmur ran through the crowd as Two Hearts stretched out his hand to the great dog, which lowered his head and surrendered the spear. "Your own clan-mate understands more of this matter than do you, Stalking Fox." He examined the polished wood, the feathered end, smoothing his hands along the shaft as though checking for defects, then handed it back to him. "Moonstrider preserved this one's life because he rides Nightshadow and so is of the Dog Clan, as are you and half the men here. Clan does not kill clan."

Declan was clammy now, and trembling, which he found strange—a second ago, facing certain death, he had felt peaceful and calm. Death, he suddenly real-ized, would have been so much easier than continuing to live and try. He regained his feet. "But the debt," he asked Two Hearts in a low, urgent voice. "What of the war of revenge?"

"Such personal considerations must be put aside." Two Hearts turned to the watching Tsalagi. "Declan Connolly, whose true name is Snake, has been given great power in the medicine ways. He is a Spiritwalker, as has not been born among us for generations, as well as a Fireheart. Such gifts are never given without reason."

"No!" Stalking Fox spat the word out as though it were poison. "This matter cannot be merely put aside." He snapped the spear across his knee and dashed the two halves to the ground. "I shall seek revenge in its proper place—in the flesh of the English! Who will go with me?"

A roar went up from the assembled warriors. He raised one fist over his head, then leaped astride the great white dog, who lashed his tail, then dashed toward the forest road the soldiers had taken. Warriors mounted on dogs of every color followed, and, behind them, jogged the men on foot until only a handful of Tsala-gi remained.

Declan stared after them with a sinking heart.

*   ◇   *

Although Berry watched the Uk'ten through the night, the vicious creature never slept. Curled up in a hulking half-circle in the center of the clearing, its poisonous red eyes remained ever open. It did not even seem to have lids to close. Whenever she made the slightest move to run away, even no more than creeping on her stomach, the beast's head snaked after her and snatched her back.

After the fourth try, she gave up. Its smell was so noxious, it choked off her breath in close proximity, and its teeth so sharp, she feared it would kill her, even though that was clearly not its intention. For the moment, it was playing with her, relishing her fear and misery. She would have to wait; perhaps in the daylight, the Uk'ten, or the foul Catawba who rode it, would grow careless and she could escape then.

Instead, she tramped down a nest in the long grass at the edge of the pine grove, as far from the Uk'ten as it would permit, and settled down to get what fitful sleep she could. Before she closed her eyes, she gathered a few of the twigs and leaves within reach and secreted them against her skin. Plant people had great power, for those who understood their nature. She was not as helpless as these two loathsome creatures seemed to think.

She dozed then, taking comfort in the clean smell of pine needles and raspberry leaves, feeling the life within them, the quiescent power. In her dreams, she saw that other, vibrant presence who sometimes visited her, the young/old woman with green hair that filled the sky and eyes wiser than the most ancient of stars. The woman called her name, instructed her with words she could not understand until she awoke with a start to find One Eye standing over her.

His scarred face was a mask of frustration and anger. He crossed his arms and glared down at her. "I hungry, woman," he said in badly accented Tsalagi.

She sat up hurriedly and brushed her hands off against her stained dress. Her stomach growled with emptiness too, and there were faint concentric circles out in the mirrorlike lake where fish were rising to feed on insects. "If you could catch—"

Seizing her arm, he hauled her onto her feet. "You my woman now. You catch fish, cook!" He shoved her toward the still water. "I much do—not wait for lazy woman lie about sleeping!"

His fingers left red welts on the bare skin of her upper arms. She glanced up over his shoulder at the huge green beast, her face hot. It eyed her insolently until she turned away. She clenched her fists. "I am not your woman!"

"You mine!" He raised his hand to strike her. "Always!"

She jerked back, her heart racing. It was foolish to aggravate him. She must appear to acquiesce, so she would not be watched so closely. She lowered her gaze, then waded shin-deep into the cool water, moving slowly to minimize ripples, thinking slim, cool fish-thoughts, keeping her shadow behind her as she looked for the sort of sandy hollows where fat whisker-fish liked to settle. Soon, she told herself, she would find a way to leave these terrible creatures, both man and beast, behind.

When Jones received the final casualty count, he was relieved they had lost only twenty-three men, although the bad news was that Colonel Hollingsworth had been among them. Jones inspected the row of laid-out bodies, staring down into the pallid empty faces. Not one bore a mark anywhere. They had not even been frightened, if one believed their expressions. They looked more puzzled than anything. They had simply—died, as though they had gone somewhere else and abandoned their inconvenient bodies.

He rubbed sweating palms against his coat. That was the worst of magic. It made no sense. You couldn't explain it before a board of inquiry and make your superior officers understand. It sounded foolish—"Twenty-one men and two officers dead of unknown causes." But there was nothing foolish about any of this.

The ghosts—he didn't know what else to call them—had left as suddenly as they had appeared, but they could of course come back, perhaps even in the daylight. Strangest of all, he hadn't seen a single native or even that bloody turncoat, Connolly, anywhere, so there was no one to blame, no one to punish or kill to prevent it from happening again.

Command had officially gone to Colonel Hollingsworth's adjunct, Major Cook, but the Londoner had spent the morning first counting, then recounting the remaining muskets and organizing men to search for the horses lost in the panic the night before. He had avoided Jones so far, and issued him no direct commands.

The troops were returning to order, though the way their hands jumped at every noise and the white-rimmed look of their eyes betrayed the poor state of their nerves. They needed to be back on the march again. A foe with an identifiable face was called for now, and very likely the Tsalagi had been out there in the trees last night, perpetrating it all. Once he had the combined forces formed up, supplies checked and repacked, mounts distributed, they would proceed to the next town and lay waste to it, then the next, and the next, until this land was scoured clean of magic and lay ready for decent men to take over.

✳ ◇ ✳

Declan stood on the bank of the murmuring river with the six who had stayed behind, each for his own reasons. Father Fitzwilliam toiled on in the background, a tattered black-garbed figure, digging yet another grave, unaware of the turmoil that surrounded him. The summer air was warming rapidly, already hanging sultry over the land, twined with bird-song and the perfumes of growing things. Nightshadow lay stretched out at his feet, seemingly content, now that he was not in imminent danger, but her black ears flicked back and forth, signalling restlessness, worry.

His hands hung uselessly at his sides. They were only seven against a danger that could destroy the fabric of the universe and he felt them looking to him, expecting him to direct their actions, find the solution, while he knew in the center of his weary heart that he was a flawed vessel, inadequate to this task.

They were all shamen, by their dress. Two Hearts had pointed out one, his former teacher, older than the rest, with silver hair and a necklace of bear's teeth. He was called Brings Wood and was a survivor of Kitasi. The remaining four were priests of varying abilities from the other towns.

Declan met their dark-brown, dubious eyes. "Although I am uncertain what measures will be needed, we can do nothing until we find the rift." He hesitated, well aware he had not the knowledge to find it, or close it, if ever he did. He had woken on its very edge the night before, when the ghost-people had appeared, and he had come overnear to death. Despair threaded through his thoughts.

Two Hearts' eyes glittered. "You are forgetting your first lessons," he said brusquely, "or, at least, Snake's first lessons."

Declan reached for the memory, letting the part of him that was Snake rise to the surface. The other was always there now in the back of his mind like a bright shadow. For a breath, he remembered what it was like to walk fearless in this world of strange magics, to savor the immense power simmering within and all around him, to be ruled by curiosity, rather than dread and guilt. Memory stirred ... deer-people at the edge of the stream ... a strange wrestling match ... "Preparation begins with purification," he heard himself say.

However this must end, he at least knew how to begin. He stepped into the river's cool embrace. The water sent an electric shock up through his legs, contrasting with the mugginess of the air. He felt more alive, stronger, clearer headed. He waded out until he was chest-deep, then immersed himself quickly, one, two, three times, surfacing each time more alert, but still at a loss as to how to solve this problem. Finally, he dove with his eyes open and stared up through the rippling water at the blaze of sunlight playing over the surface.

Long long ago, Long Man said, when the world was fresh and fish-people understood very little—

Declan's hands began to glow a pearlescent blue-white. He stared at them, fighting his fear, and opened his mind to the river. The rift, he told Long Man. What do you know about the rift between the worlds?

Long Man chuckled, but did not answer. Declan waited until his lungs burned and his ears roared with the need for air, then burst above the surface, gasping. Two Hearts and the other priests, standing in a knot closer to shore and busy with their own cleansing, seemed not to notice.

The rift! he insisted. Water streamed out of his hair, down his face. He savored its clean, crystalline taste on his tongue, let it roll down his throat. You are everywhere, in every raindrop, every stream, every pond. Surely you have seen it.

Long Man remained silent, although Declan felt his presence surrounding him. He sank beneath the surface again, this time lying on his back, spreading his fingers wide in the green current, feeling its insistent tug toward the sea. How do I find the rift?

Earth knows about the rift, yes, Earth knows. Long Man hummed a song over the rocks embedded in the mud. And Air. How could they not? The ways are many, yes, many. And he chuckled again.

Lungs burning, Declan clawed his way back to the surface. This was proving useless! The Tsalagi were on their way to fight the British, which was clearly the worst thing that could happen, while he was stuck in the middle of nowhere, splashing around with a bunch of old men who only half-believed in what he had to do. He anchored his feet in the muddy river bottom and impatiently pushed the wet hair out of his eyes, feeling an unaccustomed anger boiling through his veins.

Anger, the Snake portion of his mind said, is a tool. Use it to find the way. Let it bind you to the forces at work here.

Long Man splashed his face with a wavelet. He clearly knew where the rift was, as did Air and Earth, and, no doubt, Fire. Everything natural knew! Then why in the name of all that was sacred wouldn't they tell him? He dove again, then burst to the surface, his fists clenched, willing them to listen, to keep this terrible thing from coming to be.

You already know, Long Man said in a gurgle against his chest.

Yes, sighed the breeze across his angry hot face. Why you must you be told what you already possess?

But I tell you that I do not! Declan felt his fury building, felt his entire being focus on this one critical issue. For the sake of every living creature on this earth, you must tell me!

I do know, the mud said in a slow, sleepy voice against the soles of his bare feet, But the tear between the worlds drifts across the face of the land with every shift in the wind, with each strike of sunbeam or moonbeam, after the passage of the smallest honeybee. You must feel it without skin, see it without eyes, hear it without ears. It is not something that can be merely told.

Declan stood in the current, his legs braced to keep from being swept away, stricken with the realization this task was beyond him. Perhaps Two Hearts might have been able to do it, if it had been given into his hands, or Brings Wood, but in spite of all Declan had learned since coming to this wild land, this was like a blind man trying to understand the glories of the rising sun. He did not have the referents to understand what he was supposed to do, or the years to study and find out. He had only a precious few minutes which were rapidly running out.

I understand, Snake whispered in the back of his mind. Let me seek the rift.

Cold fear settled in the pit of Declan's stomach. To do so, he would have to be Snake completely, would have to give himself over to the other's outlook and lose himself as he had before. And perhaps this time, he would not come back. Declan Connolly would be lost forever.

But he could feel Snake's certainty that he could find the way. He tipped his head back and let the morning sun dance over his chilled face, the energy of Fire, the fourth medicine way, as powerful as the other three put together. "Not my will, but thine," he whispered, not knowing to whom or even to what he prayed. Perhaps it didn't matter, only his intent did. Certainly nothing would matter unless he moved with great speed.

He immersed himself one last time, the seventh, and then waded back to the sandy beach. The six shamen were already there, waiting for him. With a shiver, he met their dark eyes and then reached for Snake, letting the other's confidence roll over him, pushing Declan with all his guilts and fears and doubts back into the far recesses of his mind.

"Now," he heard himself say, "I know where we must go and what we must do."

chapter twenty-eight

Berry huddled beside the dying fire, watching One Eye greedily consume the whisker-fish she had wrapped in leaves and then roasted in hot coals. He'd left none for her. She hugged her knees against her breasts. If circumstances had been different, she might have been sorry for this broken man, with his disfigured face and his scarred, emaciated body. His land now lay dead and unfeeling in the hands of strangers, and the Catawbas' time would never come again.

But there were so many other paths he could have trod besides this vicious one. He could have sought shelter amidst the Tsalagi and rebuilt his life; many Catawbas had. He could have killed the invaders by stealth, one by one, until he died in single combat with great honor that would be sung of down through the generations. He could have made his anger a fine, shining weapon and taken rightful sacred revenge, but instead he had chosen envy and malice, neglecting himself and hating the entirety of creation because of all he had lost. Her spirit shrank at the thought of being touched by such a creature, sharing his blankets, bearing him twisted, bitter children. She would rather go to the Night Country herself than submit to such a future.

One Eye threw the last fish bone aside and licked his fingers. He scowled at her and she quickly dropped her gaze to her knotted hands in her lap. "Come," he said shortly. "Now go."

Over by the tall pines, the Uk'ten whuffed softly and its poisonous red eyes gleamed. She stiffened as the sulfur in its foul breath filled the clearing. Perhaps, if she made a run for it now, it would lose patience and finally kill her. Better that, a clean death, than the suffering that awaited her. She rose, tensed to run.

No, a familiar, resonant voice said inside her head. *There is something yet for you to do. Your life may indeed have to be given in the process, but not now, granddaughter. Not in this place. Not yet.*

Her heart raced and blood pounded in her ears. She saw One Eye watching her with his remaining terrible, rheumy eye. *What?* she cried silently. *What would you have me do?*

Wait, the voice said, and now she recognized Willow Woman, who often came to her in dreams. *It will not be long now.*

"Come!" One Eye's lip curled. He pointed at the Uk'ten which seemed to be watching her with great amusement. "We go, kill British, now!"

Trembling, she lowered her head and walked unsteadily across the grass toward the hulking monster.

Snake stood at the fringe of the trees and extended his senses, letting his awareness range outward. Air, like Water, existed across the entire face of the earth, so the rift invaded its substance too, filled it with wrongness. Air had to know, from heartbeat to heartbeat, its precise location. He let himself flow up into the wild sweet freedom of the skies, reaching and reaching, finally encountering it, like a blast of cold, fetid breath, or the edge of a dizzying precipice, or the chill hand of death closing around his heart—there, it was there.

He opened his eyes, shaken, the breath catching in his throat. His legs wavered and he had to brace one hand against a sapling. "We have not far to go, perhaps half a day's ride from this place."

Two Hearts' bronzed face was grave. "Half a day's ride is much more than a day's walk for young men, and we are not any of us still young."

Snake considered the problem. It was not enough to merely find the rift. They had to reach it, all of them. He could do nothing against it alone, but Nightshadow would have difficulty carrying more than two riders. He gazed up at the limitless sky—clouds were drifting in, accumulating like sheep in a pen, their billowy white undersides turning slate-gray. Soon there might be rain, and that would slow them even further.

"Nightshadow can carry one or two," he said finally. "Those who are weary can take turns." He turned to the great black dog, who was curled up in the sand, nose propped on her paws, observing them. He knelt and took her beautiful head between his hands, staring deep into those fathomless eyes, seeing a person within, one covered in fur, but just as much as a person as Two Hearts or Father Fitzwilliam or himself. *My friend,* he said to her without words, *we must travel far now, and as fast as possible. Will you carry these others when they tire?*

She rose in one fluid motion, shook herself and cocked her head. Her eyes were bright and he read curiosity in the forward set of her ears, eagerness in her outward thrust nose. Her tail wagged briefly, then she bounded past him into the dark, rustling shade beneath the trees and disappeared.

Snake stared after her, numb, then Declan rose to the surface again. He pinched the bridge of his nose, chagrined. Had he been wrong to ask her to carry someone other than himself?

Two Hearts grunted, then clapped Declan on the shoulder. "The ways of the great dogs are often obscured from men, but they know their own path. When the time is right, she will return."

He swallowed hard, biting back his disappointment. Nightshadow had the right to chose her own way, but after that night when they had shared spirits, he had assumed they would always be together. Still, she was just a dog. Perhaps he shouldn't expect her to understand how important this was.

Father Fitzwilliam passed him, carrying another tiny, twisted, blackened body out of the village to the newest grave. What should he do about the old man, leave him here? Convince him to travel with them? The Tsalagi had not harmed him because they believed he had been touched by the spirits and was therefore holy, but they might not be so charitable if he were still here when they returned.

He waited until the old man tenderly laid the child's burned body in the sand and made the sign of the cross over it. Reaching out, he touched Fitzwilliam's shoulder and cleared his throat. "Father, we're leaving now. I want you to come with us."

Father Fitzwilliam's seamed face turned up to him, and it seemed Declan could read an eternity of suffering in the network of wrinkles. "Leave?" The pale gray eyes returned to the dead child. He scooped sand over the small form until it was obscured, then folded his hands. "No, I can't. I must give each of them Christian burial and absolution, so they will be welcomed into Heaven with the rest of God's children."

Declan took the old man's arm and levered him to his feet. "Father, the living need you more." Keeping a firm grip, he drew him into the deep shade, following the trail used first by the British, and then by the Tsalagi in pursuit. Two Hearts and Brings Wood and the rest of the shamen fell in behind him. He paused just beyond the edge of the shifting green-black shadows and summoned Snake again so that he could feel their way without eyes or ears, as Declan Connolly could not.

Traveling hard and fast, Smoke and Sunrunner found their quarry half a day's ride ahead of the main party of warriors. Smoke slipped from his clan-mate's furred back and crept closer, taking great care to place his feet so as not to disturb

the least twig and give himself away. Sunrunner, panting from his long run, settled in the long grass, content to stay back, well out of sight.

The British had camped in a clearing, but seemed disorganized for some reason. Fewer awkward elk-dogs were apparent than Smoke had expected, and many
of those he could see, tied to long lines stretched between trees, were scratched
and cut, as though they had charged through the forest in a great panic. The
bright-scarlet coats of the men were dirty and tattered, and the men themselves
seemed fearful, glancing around with quick, darting eyes, nervously fingering
their firesticks.

The birds and the insects had quieted, so the British must have been camped
for some time. Smoke flattened himself behind a fallen log, peering between the
stumps of its branches. Something had happened here. They were still gathering
supplies, taking apart firesticks and cleaning them, talking to each other in low,
suspicious voices. Had they encountered another war party of Tsalagi? He'd
thought every available man had already joined them at Kitasi. Perhaps they had
battled a party of Creek from the south or Pawnee from the east.

A little later, as they were forming up lines with their clumsy, nervous elk-
dogs in preparation to leave, Smoke felt, more than heard, an immense thrumming that shook the ground and the trees as though they were part of a great
drum. The elk-dogs flattened their ears and squealed and fought their head-bind-
ings. The soldiers ran to hold them, then stared up into the sky, pointing and
shouting.

Smoke could not see the source of the commotion, so he squirmed forward,
trying to get a better look, then was stopped by a sharp, insistent tug from
behind. He whirled, knife already drawn, and met Sunrunner's worried brown
eyes.

Come, the dog pleaded with the set of his ears and tail, anxiety written in his
quick, jerky motions. The thrumming grew louder still, vibrating both air and
ground until his very bones answered. Sunrunner seized Smoke's legging in his
teeth again and pulled, ears flattened. Smoke lost his balance and tumbled into
the low brush. He was up again in an instant, wary that the soldiers might have
heard, but when he turned back to the clearing, it was obvious their attention
was trained on the sky.

The British formed two lines and fired at something above the tops of the
trees. The burned smell from their weapons was acrid, but not nearly as bad as
the thickening stench that filtered down through the leaves. Smoke coughed, his

eyes smarting. What was up there? As much as he wanted to leave with Sunrunner, Smoke knew he had to get a look. No self-respecting scout could do otherwise.

Sunrunner barked, his tone desperate, but he motioned the dog back, while he circled through the trees to get a better view. Something screamed, almost human in pitch, but loud enough to break his eardrums. He clapped his hands to his head in pain as a black shadow swept across the clearing. An immense gout of flame blasted the trees on the far side of the clearing. The tied elk-dogs went crazy with fear, plunging and bucking. Some fought free of their bonds and pounded off into the forest. The creature above roared again and the leaves rained from the trees with its force.

The air was so poisonous now that Smoke could barely breathe. His eyes were full of tears and he had difficulty seeing where he was going. The green shape in the sky wheeled, just for an instant illuminated by the sun. Shocked, Smoke gaped in recognition. He heard tales of the Uk'ten all his life, but never expected to see such a thing in this world. He stumbled back toward where he had left Sunrunner. The creature roared again and exhaled another wave of fire. Men caught in the clearing screamed as they burst into flames.

Now that he knew what hunted here, Smoke wished he had gone with Sunrunner at the first sound of those enormous wings. This was terribly wrong; the Uk'ten was a creature of the Night Country. It did not belong in this domain. He thought of what the outlander, Declan, had said that morning about a rift into the underworld. They should have listened, but it was too late now.

Wiping at his burning eyes, he tried to find his way back to Sunrunner, but the forest was choked with bilious, green smoke and every direction he turned seemed unfamiliar. Just when he was doubled over with coughing, a cold nose touched his face. He threw his arms around Sunrunner's neck and slipped onto his back. "Go!" he whispered hoarsely between coughs, then held on as the great dog picked his way through the forest back to safety.

The green-shrouded forest surrounded them, dark and cool like a leafy ocean. Snake led the way, making the decisions, sampling the wind, querying water and earth, while Declan just drifted along. The scent of wet soil and fresh leaves filled the air and the ground, cushioned by layers of crumbling leaf mold, was kind to his weary feet. Robins and jays and finches fluttered across their path, a kaleido-scope of color in the dimness, and the trek would almost have been pleasant, had the need behind it been less dire.

The six older native members of their party tramped the path much more vig-orously than any men of that age he had ever known, and even Father Fitzwilliam in his dazed condition managed to keep up, telling his rosary with gnarled fin-gers, muttering endless prayers for the dead all the while, but noon came and went and Snake knew by the feel of the air on his face that they had yet far to go.

When they stopped to rest at a shady glen divided by a clear stream, Declan surfaced again to take control. Snake was a man of action, it seemed, while he was one of thought. Perhaps each of them should do what he did best.

None of the shamen were interested in searching for food, preferring to fast since they were preparing for a great working. Declan agreed, but tried to attend to Father Fitzwilliam's needs. The old priest however would not meet his eyes or respond to questions and Declan had to content himself with ensuring that the old man at least drank.

He squinted up through the leaves at the hidden sun and wondered what was happening right now with the two opposing forces. Were they fighting, slaugh-tering each other in some terrible battle that meant nothing while the real enemy was waiting out there, unseen and unfelt until it was too late?

What would it feel like if they failed in their quest and creation was torn apart? He remembered the terrible grinding when the ghosts had headed for the sacred mountain. It would be a cataclysm, he thought, a rending of stone from earth, earth from air, until nothing clung together and there remained only the void, as there had been in the dark beginnings of time.

Something rustled beyond the bend in the trail. In a flash, Two Hearts had drawn his knife and slipped into the trees to investigate. The remaining shamen melted into the brush, and belatedly Declan thought to hide himself and Father Fitzwilliam. He pulled the old man behind a snag of deadfall, then inched toward the road.

Let me do this, Snake whispered in the back of his mind, and he embraced the other, knowing Snake was much more suited for these circumstances. Declan would never be able to think like a native; too much of his old life intruded. He would always be an awkward liability here.

Something large and midnight-dark loped through the trees. For a second, hidden behind a blackberry thicket, Snake couldn't make it out—a wolf, or perhaps even a bear? He squinted through the tangled branches, then saw the white star emblazoned on its forehead. "Nightshadow!" He stood up.

She pressed against him, communicating her gladness and love with every inch of her warm body. He met her dark eyes. I thought you had gone forever!

I bring the riderless ones. She licked his cheek solemnly, then looked pointedly over her shoulder as Two Hearts emerged with seven more dogs, each magnificent in its own fashion—one brindled-brown, one spotted black and white, one dark brown as a seal, one fawn-colored, one tawny gold, one the color of smoke, and the last, silver-gray as a pre-dawn mist. They are willing to carry these two-legs. I will lead.

Relief flooded through Snake and he hugged her fiercely before turning to the oldest shaman, Brings Wood. "She says these other dogs will carry us to the rift, but I do not understand. Where did they come from? Where are their riders?"

Brings Wood extended his gnarled hand to the closest, a large brindled-brown male with gray in his muzzle. The dog lowered his head, snuffled him gravely, then permitted his touch. Brings Wood stroked the finely shaped head with a trembling hand, his dark eyes narrowed in thought. "They have lost their clan-mates to accident, war, or sickness, as Nightshadow lost hers several seasons before you came. I recognize them all." He smoothed the brindle's neck. "This is Windrusher, a fierce fighter who ran with my father's brother, Water Moccasin. He died from a wasting sickness many winters ago and we never saw his clan-mate again. Most dogs so left simply lose their will to live and go into the forest to die, but I have heard rumors that some of them run together in the hills to the north, far from the villages of men."

Nightshadow thrust her head under Snake's arm. Hurry! she said. There is not room in this day for sniffing and hunting. I have seen in the place-beyond-eyes that we must seek this wrongness before it is too late! Snake selected the silver-gray dog for Father Fitzwilliam. She had a white muzzle and a look in her mellow dark eyes that made him think she understood Fitzwilliam's condition and would treat the dazed old man gently. He urged the priest to mount, but Father Fitzwilliam only blinked at him in bewilderment until the dog lay down, making it easier. After Declan helped him onto her back, she rose slowly and let him find his balance.

Two Hearts took Father Fitzwilliam's wrist and held it until the old man met his eyes. "This is Skyleaper. She fought bravely in many battles until her clan-mate died with a Pawnee spear through his throat. Treat her well for many stories are told of her bravery and she is of great reknown among the Real People."

Father Fitzwilliam said nothing but a hint of comprehension flickered in his pale-gray eyes. Declan took his hands and anchored them in her long silver fur. "Hold tight, Father."

He went to Nightshadow and leaped onto her back, settled into place behind her shoulders, feeling as though he had been born to ride like this. As the others mounted, he summoned Snake again and turned his face into the breeze, feeling for the whisper of wrongness somewhere out there, drifting across the face of this land.

It came to him, like a bitter taste on the back of his tongue, or a foul odor, half-smelled, or a terrible sight not quite in focus, a sense of things out of joint, the imminent cleaving of Middle World from both the Night Country and the Above World. He leaned over Nightshadow's neck. This way.

The powerful dog dug her claws into the rich red earth and the two of them ran as one. In his peripheral vision, he seemed to see a vast herd of deer pacing them, their coats brilliant shades of red, yellow, white, and black.

The humans, minuscule at this height, had vanished into the cover of the trees, and even though Uk'ten had fired the leafy canopy with his breath, he flushed only a few which were instantly crisped to the consistency of charcoal. They made the smallest of morsels, hardly more than a nibble apiece, and were not at all to his taste. He preferred his prey lightly roasted, not crisped, but they had angered him with their metal sticks which flung stones that bit and he had forgotten himself in his fury.

The man on his neck enjoyed the rout below and exhorted him on, but the woman holding onto his waist cringed, hiding her eyes. He had heard her cry out as his fiery breath enveloped the humans, then cry out again as he snapped up their blackened corpses, one by one, and swallowed them. He twisted to glance at her over his shoulder and gnashed his teeth in vexation. Foolish creature! Later, when his human ally had tired of her, Uk'ten would roast her bones very slowly, starting at her feet and working his way up, and then eat her in tiny, delicate bites, savoring each morsel. Humans had a subtle sweetness all their own and he was fast developing a taste for their flesh, especially after the terrible, unvarying diet he had been forced to endure in the Night Country.

But no more! He soared above the forest, satiated for the moment, seeking a nice dusty hollow in which to digest what he had caught so far. There would be more time for hunting later in the day, and he did not have to rush. Now that he was free of the Night Country, he would never return. Here there was hunting enough for a thousand Uk'tens. He would prey upon one area until it was nearly devoid of life, then seek another, and then another beyond that. One Eye had told him that humans bred freely, producing many tender young in the course of a lifetime. After he had moved on, their populations would rebound, and the humans of this world would dance the wild sweet dance of hunter and hunted with him until the end of time.

chapter twenty-nine

After the monster had soared off to the west and the distant line of blue hills, Jones directed his lieutenants to flush the scattered troops out of the forest. His throat raw from the acrid smoke, he tied a handkerchief over his mouth and nose, then fell to work scavenging muskets from the smoldering grass and thickets. Most were undamaged, cast aside when they proved to have little effect on the colossal dragonlike creature. Perhaps such weapons were of no use in this God-forsaken county. A muscle jumped in his cheek and he found he had gripped the barrel of a fallen musket so tightly his bones of his hand gleamed white through the skin. He carried the gun over to the growing pile. This entire venture looked to be but a cruel and useless task, spending good British lives in a vain attempt to take land the Crown could never truly hold.

But the coast had been secured. He squatted before the pile of equipment, selected a musket and dug at the mud fouling the powder pan with the point of his knife. True, there had been a brief upheaval in the natural order of things after the last of the Catawba shamen had been killed—terrifying lightning storms, a substantial earth tremor, three days in which they had not seen the sun, and then a series of apparitions that frightened the troops so badly they would not leave the fort. But in the end, the sun had reappeared and everything settled back into its natural order. Colonists arrived, the surviving Catawbas served in their houses or on the docks and attended the Christian church, and King Robert II had pronounced himself pleased.

Men straggled out of the trees in clumps of threes and fours, all of them wild-eyed, filthy, cut, singed, and, more often than not, unarmed. Jones scowled and laid aside the cleaned musket to take up another befouled one. As far as he knew, Major Cook, who was to have been the officer in charge, had not made his presence known yet. His adjunct reported last seeing him during the second pass of the monster. Cook's terrified horse had bolted into the trees with the major clinging to its back, half out of the saddle.

Jones dragged a sleeve across his sweating forehead and cursed himself for the unsteadiness of his hand. He could not afford an attack of nerves, as though he were some half-witted, overbred court lady. None of them could. An iron will would be required to escape this hell hole. They had to buck up and remember they were His Majesty's crack forces, the pride of the realm.

The soldiers eyed him uneasily. He dug out a last gout of weeds and mud, then heaved to his feet. A burn, of which he had not been aware, smarted on his back with the sudden movement. "This—" He raised the musket over his head. "—is a bloody disgrace!" Several men flinched. Others shuffled from foot to foot. None of them would meet his eyes. "Perhaps you sods do not care if you see England and your families again, but—" He shoved the musket into the chest of the nearest weaponless soldier. "—I bloody well intend to return home, knowing I have done my duty and served King and country to the very best of my ability!"

He snatched up another musket, this one still filthy, and thrust at the next man. "If you wish to do the same, I suggest you look to your equipment and your mounts, because the next time I see a man under my command throw aside his weapon and run, I will shoot him myself like the craven swine he is!"

"But—" a man blurted down at the end of the line.

Jones turned his gaze upon him, anger simmering behind his eyes, aching for a target. The man was hatless, wore only one boot, and was of course without musket or bayonet. His pink face was scratched in a dozen places and blood still oozed from the deepest of these. Jones failed to recognize him; he must be one of Hollingsworth's green replacements. "You have a comment, private? Some plan for defeating the monster, or perhaps a better method against heathen magic?"

The private swallowed hard. "No, sir, but—" He spread his hands out before him and turned to the grimy men in line with him. "We cannot fight demons like that green beast. It ain't natural!" His voice climbed into a higher register. "We should go back to the fort before we're all burned black as the inside of a chimney like—like—" He broke off in a sob and covered his eyes with one mud-encrusted hand.

"You are concerned then, that we lack the firepower to confront this crea-ture." Jones fingered the pistol inside his uniform coat, thrust into the waistband of his trousers. "You think perhaps we have not the skill, the fortitude, the stam-ina, shall we say, to carry this endeavor off?" He walked behind the sobbing man and gripped his shoulder, as if to calm him.

The shoulder heaved beneath his fingers, but the private did not answer. "And perhaps you are right," he said more softly, drawing the pistol with his free hand. "So I shall spare you any further pain or despair." He raised the pistol to the back of the man's head and cocked the trigger. "You are—" He pulled the trig-ger and braced for the report. "—dismissed!"

The gun fired cleanly and shattered the back of the man's head. He wilted to his knees, then pitched face-forward into the muddy grass like a broken doll.

Jones lowered the pistol with hands that only shook a bit. His red uniform was spattered with bits of gore. The bedraggled line of soldiers stared at him in shocked silence. "I will not have a coward under my command!" The muscles in his jaw were clenched so fiercely he found it difficult to speak. "Are there more objections, or shall we get on with the roll call and inventory?"

The troops stood at attention, shoulders braced, faces as colorless as a winter's first snow. Jones spilled a bit of his precious gunpowder into the grass as he reloaded and swore under his breath. He had to hold on. Otherwise, they were all dead men.

✳   ◇   ✳

After telling of the British and the Uk'ten, Smoke retreated from the inner circle of seated elders and squatted outside to listen as they debated the wisdom of going ahead with their attack. Anxious, Sunrunner nudged his shoulder from behind. Although the monster had flown due west, while Sunrunner had taken them north, the dog was clearly worried.

Smoke stood up and draped an arm around his clan-mate's neck. The great dog leaned into him, still panting a bit from their escape from the Uk'ten, though they'd been spared a truly grueling run back. The war party had been only one valley away from the British when they met up with them again. Now the main force, stopped here momentarily to work out their attack strategy, had but to climb one more hill, and they would be at their enemies' throats.

Stalking Fox, the War Chief, stared around the circle of elders, gathering each one's attention in turn. His black eyes glittered like sun-struck obsidian, and a light breeze fluttered the eagle feather tied in his topknot. "I say the coming of the Uk'ten is a good omen. He could only have entered this world with the help of the Above Beings, and once here, you see that he attacked, not we Tsalagi, as in the past, but our sworn enemies."

After Smoke had arrived with such sobering news, several shamen had sought a clearing bathed in sunlight in order to consult their divining crystals. Now one of them returned, his moccasins whispering through knee-high grass, his aged face grave. He stood at the edge of the circle. "I saw blood when I looked into the crystal, surrounded by a field of black. It may be that Two Hearts' apprentice was right. Death awaits us at the end of this trail."

"Red is for war and the color of our enemies' blood!" Stalking Fox thrust his spear above his head and loosed a chilling war cry. The young men surrounding the circle answered in bloodcurdling yells. Standing Fox watched them, his proud face hard with resolve. "We must sweep down upon these British and destroy them to the last man while they are still weak and disorganized!"

The shaman settled the thong of his sacred crystal back beneath his quill-decorated shirt, the expression on his seamed face doubtful. "None of the old tales describe the Uk'ten as any sort of friend to the Tsalagi."

Smoke agreed, but kept his silence, since it was not a mere scout's place to influence this decision. The shamen consulted their crystals and interpreted the signs, what sort of birds crossed their path, what kind of clouds passed above. They knew far more than he did concerning such things, but however good the signs might be, he dreaded to cross the monster's path again. Nothing which smelled that wretched could be anything but evil, and he still remembered its terrible cry, almost human and yet filled with savage power.

Catching his mood, Sunrunner's ears sank even lower. Smoke curled his fingers around the haft of his knife. He did not fear dying—that came to every man in his time, and the best of all deaths was to die young and strong in battle, not bitter and frail wrapped in an old man's furs, but he thought of the smooth curve of his wife's cheek, and the bubbling laughter of his two beautiful daughters. He longed to hear their voices again, to touch their faces one more time.

Stalking Fox jerked to his feet and motioned to the white dog, sitting just a body-length away. Moonstrider bounded to him, ears up, tail high. The war chief mounted in an effortless leap, then turned the dog's nose to the south where the British waited. The rest of the mounted warriors followed, then those on foot, their faces eager for revenge. Smoke's jaw tightened. Would his fellow warriors seek this battle so eagerly if they too had already seen the Uk'ten?

Snake directed Nightshadow down the steep grade through trees so dense they could barely squeeze between, tracking the uneasy feeling on his face, the altered whisper of the breeze, the taste of wrongness on the back of his throat, the strangely out-of-tune songs of the robins and thrushes. The well-marked Tsalagi road was far behind and the other dogs had been forced to follow more slowly with their riders, trailing Nightshadow's scent. None of the shamen had much experience at riding, and Father Fitzwilliam could barely keep his seat, even at a sedate walk. The silver female remained incredibly patient with him, only catching up to the rest of the dogs when they paused to rest. Whenever Snake and Fitzwilliam met, the old priest would stare past him, his pale eyes shrouded, his hands clenched in the gray's fur.

Panting hard, Nightshadow stopped at a tiny rivulet at the foot of a steep, rocky hill that had taken them some time to descend. Declan slipped off her back and stared back up at the rocky ledges, wondering that they had made it down in one piece. The others would have to go around and lose even more time.

The glade was ominously silent with not even the hum of a mosquito or the croak of a frog to break the silence. Nightshadow lowered her head to lap at the tiny stream, then jerked back, water streaming from her muzzle, ears pinned to her head. She looked to Snake in obvious consternation. Puzzled, he dipped his cupped hands into the water and cried out. The water's chill was as far beyond the expected coolness of shaded water on a hot summer day as glacier-melt is beyond a steaming cup of tea. He sat back on his heels, shaking the water from his freezing hands, then rubbing the circulation back into them. He had felt such bone-wracking cold only once before, on the night he had first encountered the rift.

He opened his mind, listening to the riot of voices he now automatically screened out most of the time. The afternoon breeze whispered against his face. Not much time left, it said mournfully. Its words throbbed with a foreboding, underlying rhythm as though an immense organ played somewhere over the next hill in a minor key. It wrenched at him, made him feel skittery and nervous. He broke out into a cold sweat and felt suddenly ill. Nightshadow whined, her black eyes anxious.

With a shudder, he closed off most of his awareness, leaving just the tiniest bit of sensitivity for him to follow. Was the throbbing rhythm a precursor of the terrible grinding he had heard before? He remounted Nightshadow and urged her on.

Jones surveyed the camp with a touch of satisfaction. He had just handed out the last of the cleaned-up muskets and their scavenged supplies were neatly packed. He'd commandeered a good-sized gray colt with only a few scrapes for his own mount. In a few minutes, he would have the company fall in and march toward their next objective. They still had enough light left to make a fair amount of distance, and progress would make them feel in control again, less afraid.

He heard a faint twang, followed by a hum, as though a sizable bee flew toward his ear. The swarthy Cornishman at his side, who towered over him by a good six inches, jerked, then stared in disbelief down at the feathered shaft protruding from his breastbone. He clutched at it, then his eyes rolled back and his burly body wilted to the ground. The twang repeated, and then again. Two men farther down the line cried out in rapid succession. Jones cursed, then whirled upon his lieutenant, Hastings. "Have the company fall in! We're under attack!

"Fall in!" Steel rasped as Hastings fixed his bayonet and ran, arm up-raised, through the camp. The startled troops hesitated, disheartened from the almost continuous onslaught of flood and ghosts and monster. They glanced at the trees to the north, their faces pinched and white, then fumbled for their powder bags as they formed two ragged firing lines. Several, however, unable to take this newest horror, set off at an unsteady, limping run for the forest's thick cover to the rear.

The first firing line raised their muskets and a solid volley split the air, then they dropped back as the second line stepped forward. The smell of burned powder filled the air. The native devils had hidden themselves well amidst tree and brush, but Jones heard several cries of pain after the first volley, and then more after the second. "Keep firing!" he called as he patrolled the line. "Shoot the shamen first, if you can make them out." He stopped to heave a groaning private, struck in the upper calf, back over the grass, leaving a trail of bright blood.

The rain of arrows stopped as suddenly as it had begun. He shaded his eyes and tried to see through the trees. Had they fallen back to regroup, or were they circling to attack from the rear? If they were not held at a goodly distance, they would charge, and his troops were too exhausted and demoralized at this point to fight well hand to hand.

"Keep an eye on those trees!" he warned his junior officers, as he stalked the perimeter. "We cannot let the bloody devils sneak up from behind!" Sweat rolled down his neck and soaked his collar. He ignored it and hefted a loaded pistol in each hand, his breath coming hard and fast.

Something moved out in the grass, too small to be a man. "There!" He pointed, then discharged one of his pistols. The movement doubled, tripled, and the grass was suddenly alive with tiny blue-white figures, each no more than an inch or two high. Jones's blood ran cold. They were conjuring again. He ducked behind the firing line. "Hastings, Johnson, Fordham, Williams, to me!"

The four sharpshooters dropped out and gave him a questioning look. He motioned them closer with the empty pistol still clutched in his sweating hand. "There has to be at least one shaman back there," he said in a low voice. "Likely more. If we kill them, we can stop this. If not—" He hesitated. "We'll have to drop back and abandon our wounded. They wear longer shirts that hang down to their knees, and more beads. They'll be bunched together, probably around a fire of some sort."

The four nodded, their young faces haggard.

"Take two loaded muskets apiece. You won't have time to reload." He clapped the nearest, Fordham, a sturdy Yorkshire lad, on the shoulder. The youngster looked pasty-faced and ill with exhaustion. "Into the trees with you then and pray God to guide your eye." He watched them shrug out of their telltale red coats and white shirts, then circle back and melt into the woods.

In the clearing, the blue ripples grew into lean, gleaming wolves with eyes of blue fire, each still no bigger than a child's toy, but expanding all the while. "Fall back!" he called hoarsely. "And bring the wounded!"

At least, he thought, for the moment.

* ◊ *

The light had taken on a hazy, dark-gold quality, just on the edge of fading to evening, when Snake located the trailing edge of the rift, a minute crack in the fabric of reality as cold as a million winters compressed together. Nightshadow unwittingly crossed its delimiter and the chill instantly pierced them both to the soul. Teeth chattering, he slid off her back, his half-frozen digits thrust under his arms for warmth, and closed his eyes to search, not with his sight, but with those bewildering other senses he could not name.

There! A glimmering blue-white seam spanned both sky and earth, receding even as he watched.

Nightshadow's nose nudged his shoulder. *That is wrongness. Do not touch it.*

I know. He buried his cold hands in her luxuriant fur, then realized that, although he dared not risk going back and losing track of the rift, Nightshadow could bring the others. He took her fine head in his hands and stared into her alert black eyes. Go back and bring the rest here.

She jerked away from him and flattened her ears. No! We run together.

I need their help to end this wrongness.

She glanced over her shoulder, even though the rift was invisible to the eye. Dust motes danced in the early evening air. Leaves shifted uneasily and silence hung like a shroud. If I leave, you will go into the wrongness and follow the cold ones to the place-beyond-eyes. I will run alone again.

No, he said firmly. You bear part of my spirit now, and I, yours. We can never run alone again. Bring the others, before it is too late and the whole world becomes wrongness.

She whined, then lowered her head and tail and loped back the way they had come. Snake watched her reluctant departure, feeling her absence as keenly as she felt his, then turned back to the rift. Closing his eyes, he probed for that sense of frigid twistedness again and found the seam had already receded beyond the trees. Chagrined, he plunged after it, fighting his way through the brush. He caught the faint crack of musket fire as he circled a pile of deadfall washed down the hillside by rain, heard cries and shouts, dogs snarling, the twang of bowstrings. The acrid reek of gunpowder drifted to him on the breeze, combined with blood and sweat.

The rift was drifting toward the battlefield.

One Eye roused from a delicious light sleep within the protective circle of the Uk'ten's forelegs. He smelled smoke on the wind, but not from a campfire or the monster's cavernous insides, smoke from muskets, as the British named their firesticks. Nothing else had quite the same stench. He stretched and then, bracing one hand on the creature's scaly green shoulder, pulled himself to his feet. It opened its terrible jagged-toothed mouth and blinked down at him sleepily. He felt its curiosity.

"Fighting," he said in Catawba. The beast seemed to understand him, no matter what language he spoke. He squinted up into the setting sun, then turned east. "There."

Ecstasy emanated from the creature in a great wave. It delighted in death and sorrow, disorganization and fear, all conditions One Eye had long worked to sow, both among the despised British invaders and the foolishly complacent Tsalagi.

He basked in its pleasure for a breath or two, then motioned to the girl pinned beneath the Uk'ten's right forefoot. "Come! We go sky now," he said in broken Tsalagi.

The Uk'ten lifted its foot just enough for her to crawl out. She rose to her feet, a bit wobbly, and brushed vainly at the dust in her skirt. Her eyes were only dark smudges in her drawn face, but her cheeks were dry. Despite her terror and deprivation, she refused to cry. One Eye scowled at that. She still had too much spirit to suit him. He had liked strength in women once, but now it only reminded him that she was alive while he was dead inside.

He seized her arm and dragged her along as he climbed up the beast's side to the top of its shoulder. She resisted at first, twisting and struggling until he slapped her across the face. The fight melted out of her and she stumbled after him, trying to climb with legs that wouldn't quite bear her weight. In the end, the Uk'ten caught her skirt in its teeth and hoisted her into place behind One Eye on its shoulder.

"You hold," he said gruffly, then jerked her arms around his waist when she didn't respond. He wasn't ready for her to die, he thought, as the Uk'ten leaped into the sky. Not yet, when he had so many plans.

He tipped his face back and let the wind rush over his skin. Of course, there were many women in the world, each one a feast in her own way, and though the Uk'ten's appetite was enormous, it did not have to eat all of them. He would search out the most beautiful, use each until they bored him, and then let the creature have them. It would make for an interesting variety as the days passed.

chapter thirty

Jones ordered his troops to hold their fire and fall back as the growing blue wolves prowled through the grass toward them. Musket balls passed harmlessly through the wraiths and they were running short on powder. Prudence dictated they save their firepower for the shamen behind this whole wretched business.

The translucent wolves were as high as a grown man's knee now, their teeth bared in vicious snarls, their eyes glimmering like hot blue coals. Jones could make out the hair standing up on their backs and the claws on their feet. He cursed steadily under his breath. Where were the sharpshooters he had dispersed into the trees? Had the thickening dusk prevented them from finding their targets, or had they deserted to save their own hides? A slavering blue wolf darted forward and leaped for his throat. He stumbled backwards, hands raised in a vain attempt to protect his face.

A shot split the twilight, closely followed by two more, and then seconds later, a fourth and fifth. The eerie blue wolf wavered in midleap, inches from his flesh, and then dissolved with the rest of the wolves into an amorphous glowing blue cloud that pooled in the lower third of the meadow, coating each blade of grass with an unnatural liquid blue. Dogs snarled back under the trees and Jones's fingers convulsed on the stock of his musket. He'd rather face ten natives single-handedly than one of those huge, nasty-tempered brutes. The last two villages had proved the oversized dogs were almost as hard to bring down as a bear.

The snarling rose into a crescendo of shrill, frenzied barks. Somewhere a man cried out in agony, followed a second later by several other voices, this time screaming for help in English. The pleas ended in a high-pitched burble and a cold knot settled in the pit of Jones's stomach; he had known the four would likely pay with their lives, whether they found their mark or not. He had seen in their sober eyes that they had understood that too, but he had chosen well. They were stouthearted lads, willing to sacrifice their lives for their fellows and face a death that at least retained some element of honor.

He waved his troops into the wooded ravine at their flank. "Retreat!" The thick blue light was spreading up into the air in a strange uneven line, as though it had seeped into a crack in the sky itself. No doubt, there were more bloody shamen back in those trees, conjuring something else equally lethal. He had to get his men away before they managed to reshape the light and attacked them again. There were far worse creatures to be summoned than wolves; he still woke up sweating, remembering the giant snake that had consumed three of his men whole.

They needed a place to make a stand, a cliff to guard their backs, or a defendable hill, something better than this damned open meadow where the natives could conceal themselves behind trees and skewer them with arrows at their leisure while the shamen conjured. Fortunately, their magic seemed ineffective at long range, so, if he could just force the Tsalagi to come at them across open ground, sharpshooters might pick off the rest of the shamen before they completed their foul spells.

Arrows rained out of the forest again as the natives saw them retreat. Some of his men threw themselves into the long grass and returned fire, but the rest kept their feet and sprinted for the cover of a wooded ravine at the far end. Jones hesitated, weighing the dangers and advantages. The trees, he decided a split second later. They had no chance at all out here in the open, and perhaps the Tsalagi would follow them across the meadow, giving them a clear shot at last.

He lowered his head and charged after his men. Two strides later, he cried out as the glowing blue light enveloped him and something cold brushed his left hand. His vision fuzzed and he lost all sense of up and down, stumbled, rolled across the grass, then came to rest in a tight knot, cradling his frozen hand to his chest. It felt as though it were encased in a block of ice, so cold that it burned. From the ground, he saw his men hesitate as they too were grazed by the unholy light. They stared around them with wild eyes, or fell, their bodies racked by spasms.

The light had expanded into a field, three men wide, still moving toward them. "Get up!" Jones cried hoarsely and forced himself to his knees. His head spun and the ground seemed to float above him, so that the trees had somehow taken root in the sky. His stomach heaved and he fought to stay conscious.

The blue field washed over him like a wave of deepest winter cold. He saw vague shapes within it, insubstantial and terrifying. The air congealed into a gelid lump inside his lungs and he could neither move, nor speak, nor even gasp for breath. Indistinct people passed through him, thin-shanked elders, pudgy toddlers, women and men in what should have been the prime of life, all pale, vacant-eyed, streaming steadily toward the west and a huge mountain of some sort that he could swear hadn't been there a second ago.

He felt a terrible, wrenching urge to follow them, as though being left behind was tearing his heart out. He clenched his teeth and fought to hold on, to stay here with his command, to go on fighting for just one more minute.

—And then another.

—And another.

After the last of the translucent shapes passed, he was able to inhale with a convulsive gasp. The icy air seared his lungs, as corrosive as acid. He lay with his cheek pressed against the frost-laden grass, his vision narrowed to a tunnel as the vague blue shapes drifted relentlessly as the evening tide toward the west and the Tsalagi.

A handful of red-coated soldiers crashed past Snake, struggling up the far side of the boulder-studded, tree-choked ravine. They reeked of sweat and musket smoke. He crouched low in the shadows behind the shaggy trunk of a towering pine, but they paid him no heed, their eyes white-rimmed with fear or exhaustion, or both. One, middle-aged and sandy-haired, blundered into the trailing edge of the rift and fell hard as though struck from behind. The others ran on without looking back.

Snake waited until the rift had drifted past, then knelt to feel for the soldier's pulse in his neck; his heart still beat, but his skin was clammy, deathly cold to the touch, and his hazel eyes were fixed on the ragged patches of slate-gray twilight visible between the treetops. Snake summoned up enough of Declan to speak to him in English. "Are you injured?"

The sandy-haired man flinched from him. Snake sighed and left him curled into a tight ball, shivering uncontrollably. The soldier would either recover or not, but he could not linger to give him aid.

Several more shots cracked as he followed the ever-widening rift up the ravine, then broke out into a meadow choked with the smoke of musket fire and dotted with fallen red-coats, obviously the site of the battle foretold by the Above Beings. It was even colder here, as though the rift had widened and air was pouring in from some other world in the grip of an unimaginably frigid winter. Voices shouted sporadically in Tsalagi from the trees at the far end of the meadow, but in the meadow itself, nothing stirred and smoke hung over the scene. Frozen grass blades snapped beneath his bare feet and ice glazed the branches of the trees.

A lake of blue light lay at the far end of the field, as though someone had spilled glowing blue paint across the ground. A faint trace of it ran up into the sky. His stomach tightened and he was glad he had fasted. The ground, the trees, the grass, everything vibrated with raw medicine power and he was afraid.

He passed a young British soldier with only the shadow of a beard, pierced through the neck and chest by arrows, then another, also dead, lying on his back, with no visible wound, mouth gaping in horror, then two more in the same condition. They must have been in the path of the rift as it passed. He shivered. The air was so cold now that his breath hung before him, white against the deepening twilight.

Where were the Tsalagi warriors? He saw several downed bodies in buckskin close to the trees at the far end of the meadow, but no one else. Had the rest counted this a victory and gone back to their towns, or had they also fallen victim to the rift? He remembered the icy touch of the ghost-people, the irresistible urge to abandon his body and follow them. His heart pounded as he closed his eyes and checked the receding rift. It now covered a third of the meadow and was still moving west, though not as fast as before. Its boundary coincided with the ripple of blue that trailed up into the sky.

The telltale grinding drew his gaze above the trees—to a mountain that reared up into the deepening purple-blue sky where a moment before had been only been rolling hills. The first evening stars were just visible behind its jagged outline, glimmering down like flecks of ice chipped from some gigantic block. He reached for Nightshadow's familiar presence and felt her back beyond the far side of the ravine, leading the others. What if she and the shamen arrived too late? What could he do alone?

His fists clenched in frustration. This fight over a land that could belong to no one but itself was so senseless. It possessed a spirit of its own, a life, and though the British could destroy it, the new world could never be owned or controlled. He was angry—at the British, at the Tsalagi, but most of all at himself. Why hadn't he learned more in the time given to him? Or better yet, why hadn't the Above Beings given access to the medicine power to Two Hearts, or some other shamen who could have made use of it? Declan Connolly was a weak vessel, impotent. It would be better if he had never come here, better if he had never even been born—

In his anger, his control slipped, and dazzling blue-white medicine energy flooded up through the soles of his feet into his fingers, filled the air so that he stood in a nimbus of light. So much power, but he had no idea of how to shape it or make it do his bidding. He was so bloody helpless! The grinding grew louder, the terrible screel of metal rending metal. The ground heaved beneath him and threw him to his knees.

He felt the earth's agony as its natural slow, sweet rhythm was overwhelmed by the dissonance. He thought of the dead lands on the coast and knew the end result of this would be much worse. When this night was finished, there would be no land at all. Perhaps the restless sea would rush in and fill the void, or perhaps there would not even be a planet anymore. The night would close in and it would be as if man had never existed.

Snake pushed all memory of his earlier life across the sea to the back of his mind and struggled back onto his feet. He could not afford to be Declan now. Declan Connolly could do nothing here. His only chance was to hold onto being Snake and what little Snake had managed to learn from his travels in the spirit world and with Two Hearts. He had a flash of a graceful man/stag standing on the opposite bank of a creek, watching him with oversized black eyes and a melody surfaced in the back of his mind. Once, when he had only thought about the song, a door had opened into the Above World. Perhaps the power of that same song could also close the rift. Hairs rose on the back of his neck as he sang the notes into air so thick and cold, he could have sunk his fingers into it and climbed. The rhythm warmed him a bit and he threw all his strength into the song, singing each repetition louder until it seemed his voice filled the sky and the earth itself was listening.

To his right, a British soldier staggered onto his feet, his face ravaged by fear, and shakily pointed a musket at his chest. The Declan portion of his mind recognized him as Captain Jones, who had tried to return him to the fort.

"Stop that bloody conjuring!" Jones pulled the trigger. The gun clicked, but did not fire.

Snake backed away, still singing, feeling the powerful notes settle over green wood and stone, thorn and flower, frog and stream, weaving them together, binding the attention of the ghost-people so that their progress toward the mountain slowed.

The captain swore, then took his useless musket by the barrel and swung the stock at Snake's head. Snake lurched sideways and tripped, losing the thread of his song. The notes hung for a second, fading. He could feel everything fall apart just as it was about to come together. Then the soldier closed in again and this time connected with a solid, vicious blow just above his right ear.

He experienced no pain, just shock, disorientation. His hands ceased to belong to him, his legs, his feet. The stars shivered in the sky above, then spun into a wild chaotic dance. Snake tumbled, not to the ice-encased grass, but down into a vast blueness that swallowed all sound and light.

* ◇ *

Sunrunner and three of his packmates padded back through the maze of trees, dragging the limp, bloodied bodies of the four soldiers who had ambushed the working circle of shamen. More dogs trailed them, ears pinned back, snarls rumbling in their throats. One by one, each of the four dogs dropped a body at Smoke's feet. He did not check to see if they were dead; with their usual grim efficiency in matters of war, the enraged dogs had torn the enemies' throats out. Sunrunner prowled back and forth before the bodies, the hair along his spine still bristling with rage.

Smoke studied the empty faces in the failing light, all young and no doubt brash. They had stripped off their telltale red garments that made them such easy targets, and then, naked to the waist, slipped through the trees to approach the Tsalagi unseen. Almost invisible in the gathering dusk, they had killed five of the shamen with their firesticks and wounded four more before the dogs overran them. Sunrunner stared down at his kill, his dark eyes fierce, then whirled and raked leaves and grass over the corpses with his back claws. The other three, less fastidious, merely turned away.

Stalking Fox summoned the remaining shamen, some to tend the wounded, and others to renew the attack, but these were all men of lesser talents. For now, he had dispersed warriors around the meadow, readying a charge from three sides. British firesticks had better range than bows and spears and war clubs, but took time to reload, and the soldiers could not be everywhere at once. The scouts had estimated the Tsalagi outnumbered this outlander force at least four to one. Through the sheer weight of numbers, they could win this fight with arrows and spears and dogs, rather than medicine power, but at a cost. Many hearths would be lonely this fall and winter, many children without fathers and uncles.

Without warning, between one breath and the next, the air chilled. Sunrunner laid his ears back and barked in urgent sharp bursts. Smoke shivered, remembering when he had last felt such cold. "Go!" he told the dog. "Warn the pack."

Sunrunner whined.

"No, I have to warn the rest." He pushed the golden dog with both hands. "Go! I will join you as soon as I can!"

The dog dashed off into the trees as Smoke turned back to Stalking Fox. The War Chief was crouched behind a stand of young pines, watching several shamen from other villages as they consulted their crystals by the light of a low fire. "We have to get away from this place!" Smoke said urgently. "This cold means the ghost-people are here. If they touch you, your spirit will return with them to the Night Country!"

The shamen hunched over their crystals, turning them first one way and then another to catch the firelight. Their lined faces were haggard. One, younger than the others, stood behind them, chanting under his breath and sprinkling aromatic cedar on the fire.

"We cannot leave." Stalking Fox pulled a pine bough aside so Smoke could see the meadow. A pool of shimmering blue spread across the ground, immersing the corpses of both English and Tsalagi in an eerie blue shroud. "They died in the middle of a great working, without finishing its shape."

"We must go now!" Smoke shivered as the air grew colder still and he could see his breath. "Or do you wish to travel to the Night Country with these English?"

"He speaks the truth." The oldest of the three shamen tucked his crystal back beneath his deer-hide shirt and stood. "The power we called has combined with something else very dark. That light out there is a hole, leading to both the Night Country and the Above World, big enough to swallow an entire village." His eyes were bleak. "We would have to kindle the sacred fire, then sing all day to close it, but it would take a great deal of power and there are not enough of us left."

Ice crystals pinged as the ground froze between one breath and the next. The air turned so cold, Smoke's lungs had to labor to breathe.

"Something held it back, for just a little while," the old shaman said. "We heard someone singing out in the grass in a sacred way. I felt the world shifting toward balance, then it stopped." He met Stalking Fox's gaze. "Take the others and go far away from this place. We must stay and call upon the Above Beings for help, although I do not see how it can be enough."

Declan stood on the pinnacle of the sacred mountain, the wind blowing in his face, breathing in deep lungfuls of pine-scented air. Medicine power eddied around him, as though he were a boulder dividing a waterfall, flowing back down through the clouds toward the Middle World below.

The now-familiar old woman with trailing green hair sat cross-legged on the bare granite a few feet away. Her beaded white deerskin dress was moon-bright in the dimness and the owl's golden gaze was huge. She raised bereft emerald eyes and he saw his bloodless face reflected within them. "It is too soon." Her voice was cracked with defeat. "You should not have left your body yet. Now, all is lost."

He put a hand to his injured head, but felt no pain. "I—did not mean to come here." Below, he felt the tiny dot that was Nightshadow racing toward the battle, leading Two Hearts and the other shamen. He felt the rift too, like a vein of raw, black ice absorbing all the warmth in the world until there was none left to support life. For a moment, as he had sung down there in the meadow, he had felt the rift slow, soften somehow around the edges as though it were being healed. If he'd only had more time, he might have stopped it altogether. He had to go back and try again before it was too late.

"You cannot, grandson," she said as though he had spoken aloud. "Your spirit has fled your body." She rose laboriously to stand at his side, gazing pensively back down the mountain. "This is the last time we will ever meet. You no longer have a place in the Middle World."

He gripped her thin shoulders in his hands and peered into her wrinkled face. She smelled of herbs and green leaves and all the fresh growing things in the world. "I did not want this responsibility, or the medicine power to which you say I was born. All of it from beginning to end has been forced upon me and I have endeavored to do my best. Now, at least let me finish what I have begun. After that, I do not care what becomes of me."

"This is not up to me, or anyone else," she said. "It is simply the way things are. You cannot return."

"I don't understand!" He turned back to the blue-and-green vista below and felt forces grinding against each other, the out-of-balance energies that, left unchecked, must rend world from world. "I have come here and then gone back to the world of men before. Why not this time?"

"Because this time," she said, "your flesh is dead."

chapter thirty-one

"**D**ead?" he echoed. "No, that can't be. I felt the energies shifting, coming back into balance. I have to finish."

She glanced aside at his hand where it touched her shoulder, and he saw his fingers outlined in shimmering blue-white light. "You are in the process of becoming a Night Person," she said. "Only your resonance with the four-fold medicine powers allowed your spirit to return here one last time. With the coming of death, your energies flow in opposition to those that imbue this world. If I did not shield you, your changing essence would tear our world asunder, and I cannot do so for much longer."

Declan's hands dropped away. He walked back to the ledge, chilled, turning his palms over, staring at them. They seemed flesh and blood. He felt no different.

"You fought hard and well," she said. "It is for those left behind to take up the fight."

He could not make his mind fit around this. He had been trying for so long, all his life it seemed, to serve others, to do good in the world somehow, to serve the Lord in whatever manner it pleased Him, and now all of that was at an end? A knot tightened his throat. "Will they succeed?"

"No." She lifted her wizened face into the wind so that her long green hair streamed out behind her. "They will try with all their strength, but it will not be enough."

He clenched his hands. "Then I cannot abandon this fight!"

"It is not a matter of choice," she said. "You must journey now to the Night Country before my strength gives out." She extended one hand, palm up, and he saw a ball of blue-white light dancing upon it. "Good hunting, grandson," she said. "We had great hopes for you. Perhaps we will meet again, in another reality, when the worlds form again. I would welcome that."

The light blossomed before he could answer, intensifying until he could not see the old woman's upturned face, or the mountain, or even the scattered brightness of the stars. Startled, he stepped back off the ledge into empty air. He flailed his arms in alarm, but had no sense of falling, rather more of narrowing, as though he were being compressed into a shadow of the person he had been, and the real Declan was somewhere else.

I have to go back, he thought over and over. I cannot leave so much undone. I have to go back.

When the light faded, he stood in a dim grove of snow-laden trees whose tops soared high over his head. Aromatic cedar threaded the frosty air, combined with a hint of pine and damp stone. He saw people dressed in brightly beaded buckskin dancing in some sort of ceremony, and a host of drummers, then behind them, a line of great lodges, all silent and indistinct, as though seen through a curtain of gauze. He wavered, then sank to his knees in cold wet snow, as dizzy and unsteady as a child just learning to stand.

"You will feel better soon," a woman's voice said behind him. "Everything here is opposite from the Middle World, but you will become accustomed to that."

With a start, Declan realized the ground was where the sky should be, and the sky, where the ground should be. He was upside down. No wonder he felt as if he would fall. Shivering, he dug his fingers into the snow and held on, his head spinning, feeling ill.

"Close your eyes," the woman said. "That will help."

Shuddering, he did as she bid and the sick whirling eased. I cannot stay here, he thought numbly. There has to be a way to go back and finish what I started. He reached for medicine energies and found their counterparts here, subtly altered. They flowed around him like the currents of a river, but he could not use them, at least not yet. He was not completely in tune with this place, though he could tell his spirit body was changing, flowing into patterns that would fit in time. And then, he thought grimly, he would be trapped here, forever beyond the world of men, if indeed the Middle World even survived after this night.

A slender hand rested upon his arm, its touch as soft as the brush of a raven's wing. He made himself look up. A woman studied him, her face more striking than any he had ever seen. Her almond-shaped eyes, set above broad cheekbones, were dark as a river at midnight and yet luminous at the same time. Dressed in white doeskin and red cardinal feathers, she radiated peace, quiet, rest. The Madonna must have been such a woman, he thought.

She took his hand, and then, through her touch, he caught the beat of a distant drumming, wild and sweet, utterly unlike anything he had ever heard before. His blood leaped to its rhythm, and he had the sense of great blue-tinged mysteries just at the edge of his understanding.

"There is nothing to fear here," she said.

"Not—here," he said slowly. "But above—I have to go back."

"Above, there is only pain." She pressed his hand between her two smaller ones and a bit of her serenity seeped through him. "Those who seek to return, remember, and in that remembering, find all the grief and sorrow, despair and longing they left behind. Here, there is only peace."

A gust of wind rustled through the looming trees and dislodged chill flakes of snow that tingled against his cheeks and forehead as they melted. He listened for the wind's voice, but it was like a murmur too low to make out. He could not understand it. Not yet.

"The ones who find sorrow again. How do they go back?" he asked.

Her lovely mouth curved down. "They follow the currents."

"Currents?" He gripped her hands. "I do not understand."

"There is a hole at the heart of this world, where those who seek their former lives are drawn to look for what they have lost or never had, all the things they meant to do and see and feel before it was too late."

He staggered to his feet. "I have to find it," he said. "Can you take me there?"

"No!" She turned her head aside so that her black hair fell across her eyes. "It is a terrible place!"

"Then tell me how to find it."

She withdrew her hands from his and knotted them in distress. "Follow the currents to the bottom of the world, all the way down to the bitter black river of sorrow."

※ ◇ ※

The Uk'ten wheeled through the darkening sky, searching for something below—Berry was afraid to know what. Her weary fingers clutched One Eye's greasy shirt, but mercifully her abused sense of smell had gone all but numb so that she barely smelled the monster anymore.

It would be so much easier, so much cleaner just to let go and drop through evening air into the wholesome embrace of the earth. She would be free then, released from whatever future torments or servitude this twisted man had in mind for her. She loosened her fingers, dropped her head back and let the rushing air soothe her hot face. Her body would return to the plant people and the stone people and the animal people, and she would be one with the natural cycle of the land, at peace. If she let go by small degrees, he would not notice, and then—

No, said the vibrant voice of her dreams. Your time will come, and soon. You must be strong and wait.

The Uk'ten bellowed and wheeled again, sharply. Her stomach lurched uneasily as One Eye leaned out to gaze at the land far below where even the mightiest tree seemed but a sprig. He pointed and spat out a stream of excited Catawba.

The monster answered in a shrill scream, then spread its wings to glide lower on the evening breezes.

Trembling, Berry tried to make out what it was after—a village, a hunting party, unsuspecting children playing in the dusk? She saw the minuscule glow of two fires, almost hidden amongst the trees, and a strange pool of blue light in a meadow.

One Eye turned and eyed her sourly. "Hold!" he said and slapped her loose hands. "Hold or I throw off!"

She closed her eyes and tightened her grip. If the Uk'ten attacked someone again, she did not think she could bear it. Her path was the way of the Earth, of healers. She had trained her whole life to help others; she knew no other way to live, and she would rather die now than go through another carnage.

Wait, said the voice inside her head. Wait.

✳ ◇ ✳

Declan had to support his weight against the trees as he walked. The vertigo came and went, and whenever it swept back over him, he reeled and stumbled. He passed many people, men and women and children, but they all seemed content, hunting, dancing to drums he could almost hear, or sitting in quiet, contemplative circles along the shores of a great blue-black lake, not quite frozen, that reflected this world's immense stars in a shimmering path to the horizon. No one else greeted him, and he found himself afraid to meet their eyes. Something in their expressions hinted at the wonders he might find, if he hesitated so much as a second.

After a time, he picked up threads of emotions like subtle odors, the stringency of regret and the ripe pungence of anger, the sourness of frustration. They sharpened in one place, diminished in another. He followed a tributary of acrid fear, only to have it dissipate, then found a more distinct line of worry not far beyond it. Others appeared, following the same path, but none spoke to him.

The land gave way to jumbled, snow-dusted rock, scrub pine and increasingly deeper ravines, and strangely enough, the sun edged up over the horizon. Surely, he thought, as he half-slid down a steep gully, it was too soon for dawn. When he had been struck down, dusk had just fallen. He could not have been here a whole night.

The emotions he was following finally converged into a seething stream of misery. He plodded up the other side of the gully, skirting a patch of despair, only to see another depression beyond it, even deeper, leading to a sharply eroded gorge containing a roaring blue-black river, but no sign of the rift.

The air grew thicker, choked with desire and other, darker emotions. He struggled to breathe as he climbed down boulders and slipped on loose chaff. The feeling in the pit of his stomach insisted he was climbing up, although his eyes saw otherwise. It grew harder to think, harder to remember what he was trying to do. Up beyond the gorge, he could feel the peace beckoning, reaching for him as long-delayed sleep overcomes the weary.

The sun here was a pale, ethereal disk, a silvery reflection of the fiery giant he had always known. It ascended gracefully, gliding like a swan into the center of the washed-out blue sky. When he reached the bottom of the gorge, he followed the rock-strewn shore of the wild river until he reached its source, a solid wall of red-orange sandstone. Of the people who had been ahead of him, he saw no sign. Despair flooded through him, threaded with lesser currents of dark need, lust, white-hot desire, each so intense, he felt he would drown. It was as though all the darker emotions of men seeped into the low places of the Night Country and flowed away eventually with the river. He shuddered to think what lay at the end of it.

A woman, her mouth pinched and hungry, edged past him to face the birthplace of the noisome black waters. She ran her hands over the barrier, touched a place where her flesh sank into the rock, then walked into the sheer wall with a flash of blue-white so bright, he looked away. Heart pounding, he raced to the wall and touched the spot where she had disappeared. It was solid.

Six more people, two men and four women, climbed down the side of the gorge and passed through the rock. Each time, he tried the same place and failed to follow. He huddled against a boulder, arms locked around his knees, shivering in the chill dry wind that howled through the narrow gorge, trying to summon the energy to climb back up to the quiet lake, to give up and accept what waited above.

He propped his weary head on his bent knees. These people must have been here longer than he had. The energies were different in this realm. Perhaps their bodies were attuned to the rock in a way that he wasn't—yet.

Another man approached and stood, gazing impassively at the wall. His hair was peppered with gray and he had a profile that would have done credit to any nobleman's house in England. As he ran his fingers over the wall, Declan lurched to his feet. He couldn't wait any longer. He had to get through! As the man's probing fingers sank into the stone, Declan leaped forward and seized his arm. The light of a thousand suns exploded inside his head and he found himself stumbling through a field of bright blue into the heart of a blackberry thicket. He stopped and stared at his unscratched hands; the brambles had passed harmlessly through his body. Trembling, he turned and saw two men a few yards away, one dressed in the buckskins of a native, the other, a red-coated British soldier. The soldier's musket was completing the arc of a vicious blow, the other man already tumbling backwards to the ground, his arms limp, his face empty.

With a shock, he realized the soldier was Captain Jones, and the falling man, Declan Connolly. He watched the soldier stand over the crumpled body, staring down, his chest heaving, watched him drag an arm back over his sweating face. It was as Willow Woman had said. He was dead.

Barking erupted at the far end of the meadow as a group of dogs carrying riders burst out of the trees. Nightshadow led them, the white star on her face shining through the falling darkness like a beacon. Snarling, she charged Jones, dodged the musket as he swung the butt at her, seized his neck in her jaws and shook him as a cat would shake a mouse. Something cracked and Jones' head lolled loosely as she threw his body aside.

The rift was widening, oozing across the grass and filtering back into the forest. He saw the ghost-people who had preceded him now walking toward the sacred mountain, just visible beyond the trees. The ground seemed to tilt sideways and he felt the wrenched, out-of-balance energies like a deep-seated pain. Whatever kept the three worlds in balance was at the point of collapse. The song, he thought, if only he had been allowed to finish! Before Jones had struck him down, the notes had seemed to smooth things out, ease the energies back toward balance. A few notes seemed still to hang above the ice-encased trees, pale-blue wraiths, drifting on the evening breeze as they faded.

He began to sing again, unsure if he could actually create sound in this insubstantial form. His voice danced out over the meadow, wove through the trees. He sang the notes through again and again, and felt them gathering power with each repetition, as though he were somehow piling strength upon strength until the ground resonated and the leaves whispered and the air itself throbbed in time.

The dogs had stopped in the middle of the clearing, just short of the blue edges of the rift, and were watching him while Father Fitzwilliam and the shamen dismounted. Standing over his motionless physical body, Nightshadow whined and cocked her head, puzzled to see him a few feet away in another form.

Two Hearts threw back his head and joined the song, and then the rest, except for Father Fitzwilliam, followed. The notes took on a life of their own and he could see them now, scattered through the air in bright-blue threes. The ghost-people's progress slowed as they too seemed to listen, but through it all, he still heard the terrible grinding.

He wanted to ask the deer-people and Willow Woman and Eagle and Rattlesnake to tell him what to do now. The song, although powerful, was obviously only a beginning. He thought back to his climb up the stone mountain, Rattlesnake instructing him, weaving a hypnotic pattern with his gleaming coils. He remembered how his blood had settled into the rhythm of the serpent's movements, revealing the pulse of another existence he had never even imagined.

His feet moved across the ground in that same slow, sinuous rhythm. As he completed the pattern and began again, medicine energy flooded into him from the earth and out of the air and the rivers, even from the tiny drops of water in the soil and air. The voices of the bird people and the star people and grass people rushed in on him in a glorious tide of sound, and each tiny voice added to his strength. With each completion of the pattern, his body drew more power until he was a conduit of more crackling, sizzling energy than any man, dead or alive, should have been able to channel. He realized his physical body would have been burned to cinders in an instant.

Two Hearts and the other shamen danced with him now, and as he watched, the birds and other creatures of the forest took up the rhythm with wings and hooves and paws. The great dogs danced along with the stars in the sky above. The slender blades of grass swayed in time beneath their feet. They were all one, he thought, the dogs and the grass and the stars and men. He perceived their spirits and they were at heart the same, each a single ribbon of the wondrous force put into creation at the beginning of time, and, which woven together, composed the world.

He closed his eyes and looked with that other, inner sight. The ribbons should make an interdependent pattern, yet, here, in this place, the rift between the three worlds had torn them apart. To heal the rift, the pattern had to be restored. He reached out with the power boiling through him, gathered a fragile skein of energy from each living creature and braided them as a woman braids her hair, first this strand over that, then the next to bind the first two, only here were a thousand thousand strands to be woven together like a magnificent tapestry. And each time he thought he had completed the pattern, the construction parted, as though he had only warp threads, and lacked the all-important weft to bind them together. Something essential was missing. The rift drifted open again and the grinding of the Night Country and the Above World coming into contact worsened.

He tried again, wielding the fearsome energies while the six shamen sang with him and danced Rattlesnake's potent rhythm. They were an important element, balancing his efforts and stabilizing the pattern. Tsalagi warriors emerged from the woods, overcome by the beat, dancing as though they had but a single body between them. The British soldiers joined them, shuffling through the grass in step, plainly bewildered. Out of the corner of his eye, he saw Father Fitzwilliam standing close to the yawning blue maw of the rift, a silent, motionless figure in ragged black.

He braided the strands more carefully this time, feeling how each was a little different and fit better in one place than another. He found the Earth energy of the great dogs should be braided over the Air energy of hawks, and then threaded through the Water energy of rivers. They felt right in that order and held together better. He realized he could leave nothing and no one out, not a dying British soldier or a moth or the least pebble hidden in the grass. Everything had to be included so that the fabric of the universe was whole again.

Only one being within miles of the rift resisted the call to dance—Father Fitzwilliam. He turned to the man who had been his mentor and friend and found only fear and anguish in his mind. Dance! he cried to him. Help me make the world whole again!

The old man wrapped his arms over his head, shivering. This is blasphemy, the priest's thoughts ran, utter damnation ... I will not let the Devil have my soul!

Declan hesitated, reluctant to force him. Above him, the rift shimmered bright blue, reduced now to a thin seam that spanned the sky. The fearsome grinding had almost stilled. If he could just complete the pattern, everything would fall into place. Despite the old man's fear, Father Fitzwilliam must join them. He reached—

A terrible bellow split the air, shattering the rhythm. A gout of flames roared down and fired the trees. Then a winged beast, bigger than the ship that had carried Declan to this continent, backwinged down into the meadow, the Uk'ten with two people perched on its shoulders. With one snap of its terrible jaws, it seized Brings Wood out of the circle and held his struggling body aloft in its clawed forefoot.

chapter thirty-two

The shamen and the Tsalagi warriors and the soldiers and even Father Fitzwilliam broke from the dance's spell and fled into the shelter of the trees. As Declan faltered, the precarious balance he had been so carefully constructing, beautiful in its thousand thousand myriad components, spun apart once more into randomness so that each being was separate again and the rift gaped wide. Renewed grinding shook the ground, and he was left standing alone with empty hands. Only Nightshadow remained, faithfully guarding his abandoned physical body.

The old shaman, Brings Wood, disappeared into the monster's gullet in one swallow. "So," cried the Uk'ten to Declan, "We meet again, insignificant one!" Its amusement rippled across the meadow. "I find you much changed."

When he had encountered the beast before, he had done his best to kill it, and yet had nearly died while it suffered no damage. Now he was worse off than ever, lacking physical hands with which to wield a knife or spear. "You must return to the Night Country where you belong," he told it, his voice uneven. "Unless we heal the rift, the Above World and the Night Country will destroy each other, along with everything else, and you will cease to exist."

"Perhaps." It eyed him with one malevolent red orb. "Or perhaps I will be lord of all as new worlds come into being. I would relish that."

Declan edged closer. "You would take that chance?"

It coiled above him, red eyes gleaming, savoring the destruction it had already sowed. "You have seen the Night Country," it replied disdainfully and preened at a scaly green wing with its hind-claws. "Such a pale, boring realm! I notice that you did not remain there. Why then should I?"

"Kill it!" cried a female voice in Tsalagi. "Kill this loathsome creature now!"

Declan saw a young native woman struggling with the man perched on the creature's mountainous shoulders. Something in her manner and voice seemed familiar. "Berry?"

The filthy, pock-faced native backhanded her as she fought to break his hold on her arm. Berry twisted and sank her teeth into his wrist. He jerked back and she tore herself free of his grip. She leaped to the ground in front of the creature's left foreleg and stumbled to her knees.

Nightshadow rushed between Berry and the monster, barking in ear-splitting bursts. The creature hissed, then swiped at the dog with a wickedly clawed fore-leg. She dodged, her voice rising in a shrill crescendo.

"Nightshadow, no!" Declan cried, but the Uk'ten's head flashed downward and snatched the dog in its jaws. Nightshadow twisted in its grip to slash at it, but the Uk'ten snapped her back with a twist of its serpentine neck and cast her broken body aside. Shaken, Berry took advantage of its diverted attention to lose herself in the trees.

Declan ran to the dog, transfixed, feeling Nightshadow's spirit loosen from her broken body. An icicle encased his heart as he stared down at the blood trick-ling from her nose into the earth. Her gallant spirit belonged to the Night Coun-try now, another terrible loss amidst so much, also to be laid at his feet. Her blue-white spirit eyes opened, blinked, looked up at him.

He stretched out a hand, afraid she would leave him like the rest. "Don't go!"

The Uk'ten laughed again in smoky puffs, but the man on its shoulders peered into the trees after Berry, looking murderous. "Woman!" he cried hoarse-ly. "Come back, or you die!"

The Uk'ten drew back its head and exhaled a great gout of flames over the vegetation into which the girl had fled. Declan watched helplessly as the green leaves curled, then blackened and erupted into flames. He felt the pain of the plant people flare as they died. Every bush, every vine, the least leaf and bud, all were sacred, relatives to him and every other aspect of God's universe as surely as any human. He sank to his knees and covered his ears, unable to bear their cries.

*   ◇   *

Hunched behind a fallen log as thick as a man was tall, Berry stifled her fear as yellow-orange flames licked closer and acrid black smoke roiled through the trees. Her face throbbed where One Eye had struck her. Here, at last, was release, she told herself. She had only to let it overtake her, to breathe deeply of the smoke, and then she would be free of One Eye and his obscene monster.

Death will not bring you freedom, the voice inside her head said. Throw your-self away and he will possess you forever.

Smoke-tears welled in her eyes and she began to cough, fighting to speak. "I—cannot fight—that thing!"

Berry cannot, the voice agreed, but the vast power of Earth medicine can.

Berry thought of the Uk'ten and One Eye's greasy hands on her throat, her shoulders, her thighs.

The plant people sacrifice themselves in this great battle, fighting the only way they can. Will you let such valiant sacrifice be in vain?

She wiped her streaming eyes and stood. "What must I do?"

Give yourself to me.

She bowed her head. "But I have always been yours."

✳ ◇ ✳

Declan came back to himself with a jerk as the ground trembled beneath his feet. The ghost-people were again drifting toward the sacred mountain. He could try to close the rift one more time, but he knew it would all fall apart, just as it had done twice already, unless he discovered the missing element.

The Uk'ten reared back on its hind legs and raked the trees with its foreclaws, searching for the girl. Declan motioned to Nightshadow while the beast was distracted. "Circle the ghost-people and drive them back from the sacred mountain as you did before!"

The great dog's blue-white gaze, brilliant as diamonds, glinted with understanding. Her spirit form whirled and dashed after the travelers. Declan pressed his hands over his eyes, trying to think. She could not hold them off forever, and even worse, now it was as dangerous for her as it was for the others to approach the Above World too closely.

Berry emerged from the flaming trees. Braided black hair fell to her waist, but at the same time, vivid green hair seemed to trail behind her across the grass. Her face was smudged from smoke and bruised, her reddened eyes were watering, and yet she wore a strangely serene expression.

With a frustrated bellow, the Uk'ten dove at her, twisting so hard in its fury that it dislodged its rider. The native fell heavily on his back, not far from her, and sprawled on the ground, his neck twisted at an unnatural angle.

Berry did not take notice of him, but rather stood, gazing up at the monster, her face dispassionate and curiously unafraid. "Night creature," she said, "why do you trouble this world?"

The Uk'ten drew back its huge head, red eyes glimmering with rage and astonishment. "You!" it breathed, then radiated a fiery amusement. "By entering this weak flesh, you have given yourself to me. I shall enjoy crunching this small thing's bones all the more since they now encompass your spirit."

She raised her hands and sang a simple, low-pitched tune in a husky voice, curiously like the dry whisper of corn sheaves in the wind, or the rustle of willow fronds. Declan felt the slow throb of power in it, heard echoes of long-suffering patience and hard-won wisdom. She was calling Earth medicine, the ponderous strength of stone, the fertile power of soil and plant, the wily intelligence of the animal people, but, all the same, this tasted subtly different from Earth medicine as he had encountered it before.

The trampled grass stood on end, the rocks stirred out of the ground and rolled to encircle her like a group of waiting children. The Uk'ten opened its mouth and Declan saw flames rising in its maw. Before he could warn her, vines slithered down out of the trees and coiled like green snakes around the terrible muzzle. Bellowing, it clawed at its living bonds and fell back into the burning forest. The trees stretched their flaming limbs toward the Uk'ten and then fenced it fast, so that it burned with them, caught in their implacable grasp, writhing and screaming.

The woman turned to him, and again he saw double, the young girl beneath and ageless Willow Woman superimposed. "Finish your task," she said calmly.

"I—can't." He spread his hands helplessly. "Something is wrong, and I can't make the threads come together."

"Have you really come so far to give up?" Her green eyes glimmered at him through the smoky darkness, verdigris suns, hot and mysterious, and unutterably alien.

The green burned through his skin, coloring his blood, his marrow, his heart until his very soul bore its mark. "No," he heard himself say. "I have not."

"Then sing," she said. "Dance the pattern you have been given. She blinked, faltered. Proximity to the Night Country weakens me and I cannot remain here."

"Wait!" He studied her face in a panic. "You must tell me what to do!"

"Your task . . . is to restore the . . . worlds to . . . balance." The green eyes and hair wavered. "You have known that since the beginning. When you find balance . . . you will . . . know the . . . way."

"But I—"

Willow Woman faded, leaving only a weary, frightened girl in her place. She swayed, touched her grimy, tear-stained face with her hands, then glanced up in alarm as the grinding of world against world rose yet another decibel. Declan reached for her arm, then drew back, knowing how terrible his touch, the touch of a ghost-person, would be. "Dance!" He sang with a throat already raw and aching. Berry sang with him, hesitantly at first, and then more strongly. He felt the energies stir once more, Earth and Air and Fire and Water, the four powerful medicine ways. They should balance each other.

Nightshadow was circling the ghost-people, harrying them, driving them back from the foot of the sacred mountain which seemed no more than an arm's length away from those in front. He was out of time. He had to close the rift, or all was lost.

Soldiers and warriors and shamen drifted back out of the trees, once again dancing. Five shamen took up their positions around him, but the empty space where the sixth, Brings Wood, should have been, threw him out of balance. Someone with talent for using medicine power was needed to take his place. He cast about as he sang. Berry had a full measure of such talent, but he could feel that for some reason her energies wouldn't balance this circle, and although some of the remaining Tsalagi were shamen, they were of much less potential. Their bodies would not stand the strain of channeling such fearsome energies.

He reached out with his sight beyond sight and felt another, hidden just inside the burning forest, who possessed at least the potential to channel medicine energies. He broke off singing long enough to gasp, "Berry, bring that man out of the trees, the one who is not dancing!"

The construction wobbled and he had to take up his song again, before it collapsed. Berry dashed off in the direction he pointed, skirting the Uk'ten's charring carcass, her face frightened and very young. A minute later, she emerged, towing a pinch-faced figure in tattered black by the arm—Father Fitzwilliam.

Declan's heart sank. Not him. Anyone else, even one of the dazed British soldiers, might have been able to fill in, but not this defeated old priest, half-crazed by guilt. The four-fold energies, seeming to sense his hesitation, ebbed. He felt the approach of chaos as the pattern threatened to once again fall apart. He could not wait for another to be found.

He motioned for Berry to position the old man in the empty place in the circle. Father Fitzwilliam stood there, when she released him, a silent figure in black. "Father, you must dance!" Declan cried, but the old man did not seem to hear him. Declan laid a hand on his arm, knowing the terrible cold he would feel at his touch.

The old man's eyelids fluttered and he seemed to come to himself for the first time in days. "No, I—" His gaze darted wildly about the meadow seething with otherworldly energies and then saw Declan's ghostly face, the blue-white hand superimposed on his arm. His face closed up with terror. He clutched the silver cross still hanging around his neck and fought to get away.

"Dance!" Declan gritted. "Dance, or we all die!" Grimly, he held him until he felt the Rattlesnake's powerful rhythm take hold of the priest's mind, overriding his will. There was lightning in that rhythm, and star energy, and fierce, wild desire that coursed through the veins. He released him and ran back into the center to where Berry anxiously waited.

The balance seemed right now. He concentrated as he danced, took a strand of each creature's energy and bound it across the rift, as he had before, weighed each one and found its special place, Fire energy over Water, Earth over Air, Air over Fire, but once again he was only constructing a tapestry of warp cords, all running in a single direction with nothing to weave through them in opposition to set the pattern.

He went on, weaving deer energy over robin, butterfly over twig, but he still could not find the "balance," of which Willow Woman had spoken. He could not hold the energies at this pitch for long, nor could the men and other creatures dancing with him go on without rest, or Berry...

Or Berry!

He realized with a start that he had not yet woven her into the pattern and reached for her spirit. She was of the Deer clan, like Two Hearts, her uncle, and he expected her to be composed mostly of Earth energy, as were deer and the plants she knew so well. He teased a strand of her energy free and found it subtly different, as the same song played on a different instrument had a sweetly altered sound. He evaluated it, thinking to bind it over an Air pattern, as he had the others, then realized it didn't fit there, nor over Fire, or Water. He turned it one way and then another. Surely it fit this pattern at some point.

And then understanding flooded through him—how could he have been so foolish? She was the weft thread for which he had been searching, female, the other half of creation, the giver of life and the matrix upon which everything was generated. He wove her essence through fox energy, squirrel, wind, oak, granite, flea, sunflower, cloud, glen, star, on and on until he lost any sense of time or place, until he was caught up in a cocoon of intertwined energies and at last his strained voice failed.

He found himself on his knees in the grass, staring at his empty hands. The girl, Berry, stood over him, her breast heaving, hair disheveled, silent. He heard only the wind whispering through the grass, the labored breathing of the other dancers, the hesitant chirp of returning crickets. "The rift!" He lurched to his feet. The night sky was a fine blue-black bowl adorned with the most brilliant stars he had ever seen. They shone down like a million signal fires, beckoning him to wondrous secrets. He closed his eyes and looked for the rift with his other sight, but not even a scarred seam marked where it had once crossed the sky.

Throughout the clearing, bewildered men sank into the grass, their eyes rolling back into their heads with exhaustion. He himself was so empty that he felt he would never be filled again. A huge tumble of boulders lay amidst the trees where there had been no such formation before. He looked closer and saw it was the Uk'ten, its huge body turned to stone where it had died in the embrace of the burning trees. A few feet away, One Eye's broken body had become a scattering of smaller rocks in the grass.

Blue flashed among the trees and alarm ricocheted through him—the rift again? Nightshadow appeared, herding a single ghost-person before her, a man. He must have been a straggler, caught outside the rift when it closed and would have to be sent back. Declan realized with a shock that he belonged to the Night Country now too. Despite all his earlier longings for death and release, he was not ready to go. He wanted to stay in this wild land, to help rebuild Kitasi and make up for the harm that had been done, to walk in Snake's footsteps and learn more of this strange world in which the power of the spirit existed everywhere and in everything.

"Be sure of your heart, grandson," a resonant voice said. "This wish bears a terrible risk."

He turned and met Berry's eyes, once again the simmering green of Willow Woman. He fell to his knees before her and bowed his head. "I don't understand."

"If you would remain in the Middle World, you could walk with my brother, Lightning, and seek his life-giving energy."

He lifted his eyes to hers. "And the risk?"

"My brother's energy is potent." Her eyes bore down, burning into his soul. "He may be able to restore life to your flesh, but if not, your spirit will be trapped within your dead body forever. You will not be able to return to the Night Country. She paused. And even if you do regain the life of your flesh, you will still know pain and loss, failure and impotence, for that is the legacy of the Middle World." She folded her hands. "In the Night Country, Nightshadow will run at your side and there will be peace and ease, reunion with those whom you have loved and lost, understanding of the great mysteries."

The dog stepped forward. Come with me! her dancing eyes said. In that other land, there will be many dogs and much hunting, many glorious, hot-blooded smells. We will run until our legs give out and then roll in the grass and feast on the sweet flesh of rabbit and never again will the earth bruise our feet or we be alone.

The ghost-person, a tall craggy-featured man, somehow familiar, approached Nightshadow and offered her the flat of his blue-white hand. She sniffed cautiously, then frisked for joy.

"He is Strikes Many, the one she lost," Willow Woman said. "Her first clan-mate."

Then Declan recognized him as the man from the Night Country, who had inadvertently enabled him to come through too.

I must stay here, for a time, he told Nightshadow and touched her forehead in farewell. Her fur was cool beneath his hand, but still retained its clean, musky scent, even in this form. Go with this man who ran with you first. I wish you both good hunting.

She leaned her cheek against his hand, then turned back to her clan-mate. The other man's eyes were warm and Declan suddenly understood why he had been in that terrible ravine; he had come seeking this amazing creature, beloved of the Above Beings, who had once been so close to him that she was his other half, as she now was Declan's.

Willow Woman waved her hand. The dog and the man faded until only a few blue glints remained to show where they had stood, and then even those winked out like dying embers. The night pressed in, warm and still. He thought of lying within the earth forever trapped in corrupting flesh, never to know the serenity of the Night Country.

"You must chose," she said. "There is little time left before the decision is out of your hands."

He pictured the peaceful lake, the sense of serenity and acceptance in the Night Country. He might find his mother there, and his father, whom he had never known, might learn the answers to all the questions that tormented him, might even be allowed to see the face of God, but—

There was so much left undone here, so much to finish. As terrible as the rift had been, he knew this was just the first battle in a war that would likely span generations. The British were not going to give up, nor the Dutch to the north, nor the Portuguese. He shuddered to think of what was happening in the south, where his brother priests reportedly had a much better conversion rate among the natives. Had rifts formed there too, or perhaps things even more catastrophic?

No matter what had happened here today, more Europeans would come to these wild shores, more priests and soldiers. There was too much virgin land here, too many valuable fur-bearing animals, too much lumber and gold. It would all happen again unless someone who understood both cultures made the two sides aware of the disasters they were courting.

He glanced around the quiet, starlit meadow and the men who sat staring in confusion down at their trembling hands, both English and Tsalagi, all in shock, wearied to silence. He alone had walked both paths. His task was not at an end, not yet. "I have to try."

"Then we will go to my fiercest brother, Lightning." She stepped out of Berry's body. The Tsalagi girl, swayed and nearly fell. Two Hearts moved forward to support her waist.

"Take up your abandoned flesh," Willow Woman's voice commanded.

Declan returned to his empty body. The dead eyes were half-open, seeing nothing. A clot of dark blood was drying in the hair where the musket had laid his skull open. He stretched out a hand and felt it pass through cooling flesh and bone and marrow, then snatched it back, sickened.

"You do not have to do this," she said quietly. "You have earned the life beyond this world. It is a place of dreaming and wonders and understanding and it belongs now to you."

Declan hesitated, horrified by that brief contact with his dead body, then submerged his spirit in the cold, mortifying flesh.

chapter thirty-three

He found himself on the crest of a high mountain, lying naked to the winds and a driving rain he could not feel. Granite supported his unresponsive flesh, and above him, a great man made of sheet lightning filled the sky, looking down with crackling, white-hot eyes. Thunder drummed the rock beneath him, and he recognized within it the rhythm of Rattlesnake's fierce and powerful dance that had healed the world.

Ten times the height of a man, Lightning took up his body in fiery white arms and then danced over the peaks of unfamiliar mountains to the overpowering beat of Thunder's drumming. Declan's body crawled with incandescent white fire until finally a tingle of pain ran up one leg, then a sharper pang jagged through his midriff. In another second, pain convulsed his entire body, and still the relentless lightning crawled over his flesh, filling him with agony until he could not tell where the fire ended and his suffering flesh began, until his body was wholly consumed so that he was made of alabaster fire, one with Lightning, striding across the Middle World on great forked legs, until he perceived the individual motes of energy that made up each creature below, both animate and inanimate, all dancing the eternal dance of life itself to Rattlesnake's powerful rhythm, until he understood at last that Fire was at the heart of everything, and then knew nothing at all.

Awareness crept back over a period of days or weeks; he was never sure how long. One morning, he felt hot sun on his eyelids, as welcome as food to a starving man. Sometime later, he heard a child's laughter ripple through the cooling evening air as though a stone had been thrown into the center of a still pond. Once, he smelled the wild sweetness of honeysuckle on the wind, and then at some point later, heard broken-hearted sobbing as though someone grieved.

The seven riderless dogs, they later told him, padded out of the forest every day at sunset. One of them, usually the grizzled brindle male, would lay a still-warm rabbit or quail before him, then curl companionably at his feet until the fire faded to embers and only the stars kept them company. It was a healing time, and he had flashes of it for years afterward, yellow-orange sparks dancing up into the endless velvet of the night sky, the pleasantly warm weight of a massive dog's head on his thigh, Berry's fingers massaging his temples when his head throbbed, which was much of the time.

Sometimes, a raw white light would crawl through his brain, crackle behind his eyes, blast his thoughts apart, just when he had begun to make sense of something. His hands and feet would jerk and he would lose time, finding himself in a different place, at some different activity with no idea of where he had been in the interim, or what he was supposed to be doing.

Still, a day came when he remembered who he was and what he had done, both before coming to this wild land and after, how the willows and the river and the very stones had once spoken to him, how he had felt the sacred medicine energies so strongly that he had fled from them, while other men and women sought their faintest manifestation all their lives.

He heard nothing now beyond the terrible, intermittent crackle in his head and simple everyday sounds, and that loss was difficult to accept. He did not in fact think he would have fully returned to his flesh at all, had it not been for the sweetness of Berry. She cradled him against her bosom when he was too ill to move, held him when he shook, soothed him when he was afraid, taught him quietly in the deepest silences of the night how to love and be loved, without asking anything of him in return. He lived in Two Hearts' lodge as her husband now and journeyed the emerald shade of the forest by day, learning the medicinal properties of plants from her, in order that he might be a force for healing, rather than death and destruction. He had been officially adopted into the Dog Clan and those in charge of the young dogs came by often to speak to him. He had a way with them, they said, and talked of presenting him to the next crop of pups to see if one would accept him as clan-mate.

He felt he should be working to prevent the British from intruding upon Tsalagi land and once again disturbing the precious balance of the worlds, but they would have shot him on sight, even if he could have summoned the energy to trek back to the fort, which he could not. And so the days slid past, each much like the one before. He would find himself looking for something he had lost, without knowing what it was. Sometimes, he thought perhaps it was Nightshadow, the lost half of his soul, but in the blue-black silences of the night, when the scent of pine was sharp and the stars wheeled above in their slow, graceful arc, he knew it was more than that, though he missed her sorely.

One morning, he woke from a dream of wild, white-hot fire that coursed through his veins and burned his eyes into spitting coals. His heart raced and the blood pounded in his ears with a rhythm that reminded him of—something, he could not quite remember what. He eased out of the mound of furs and tucked them back around the curves of Berry's naked brown body. She turned over, one slim arm raised above her head. He gazed down at her tenderly, wondering at the joy she had brought into his life.

He fumbled his way out of the lodge, careful not to wake Two Hearts in the other room. Outside, the air had a raw freshness threaded with a hint of chill that spoke of autumn. The fields were filled with ripening pumpkins and winter squash. Soon, Two Hearts said, there would be a festival to thank the Above Beings for their beneficence. They would burn their old clothing and make everything fresh and new, then dance and sing and pray, and everyone would be happy.

The old brindle male dog cracked an eye open as he passed the dead hearth and heaved to his feet. His name was Windrusher, a legendary war-dog who had distinguished himself in battle against the neighboring Pawnee and killed uncounted warriors in his day. Until Declan had returned, he had not been seen in Kitasi for many seasons since his clan-mate died. The dog's joints popped as he stretched, then padded after Declan through the gate in the palisade.

Smooth as glass, the river steamed a delicate white. He watched the mist curl over the green surface like a living thing, then waded into the surprisingly cold water and let the current shear around his legs. Among the Tsalagi, morning purification was traditionally the best time of the day, when an individual ordered his or her thoughts and made plans, but these days Declan dreaded it. Long Man had been so wondrously alive to him before, but now the winding river was only mute water and he felt empty when he bathed. It was a painful reminder of how the whole world had become achingly silent.

A twig cracked in the forest just beyond the palisade. Windrusher's head snapped up and a growl rumbled in his chest. Declan peered into the trees, but saw nothing. He ducked beneath the water, letting it stream across his face. If only it could cleanse his heart in the same way it did his body, remove his impurities, make him worthy to fully see and hear once again, as he had before, but never appreciated.

He stayed under until his lungs burned, then broke the surface, gasping. Windrusher's ears were pinned back and every hair on his massive body stood on end. Concerned, Declan waded back to the sandy shore. "What is it?"

Windrusher's dark-brown eyes flickered toward him, but he stayed on guard, watching the forest as though it would explode. Two more dogs darted through the palisade's gate and joined the old brindle, their hackles raised.

A man appeared on the game trail, clad in dusty, faded rags which might once have been black. He stopped, brushed at his tangled white hair with a trembling hand. Windrusher's lips wrinkled back from his teeth in a terrible snarl.

Two more men walked up behind the first, one limping and both naked to the waist, faces gaunt, their bodies crossed and recrossed by scratches and gashes and scars. All three were tanned by the sun to a leathery brown, but at the edge of their clothing, he could see their skin had been white. Declan laid his hand on Windrusher's quivering shoulder and walked toward them. The dog edged forward with him, barking in short bursts.

"My God, Declan!" The figure in black rags tottered forward and then stumbled to his knees. "You're alive! I—" He wiped at his eyes. "I don't believe it."

It was Father Fitzwilliam. The English words hurt Declan's ears, as though listening to them made his mind work in a way unnatural to it now. His heart raced as he gazed down at the old man, unable to answer.

The other two, soldiers by the torn remnants of uniform trousers they still wore, followed Father Fitzwilliam out of the trees, and Declan saw more behind them, hiding in the shadows, perhaps as many as ten or fifteen.

He heard shouting in the village now. Smoke and his golden clan-mate, Sunrunner, ran through the gate, followed by a handful of warriors and more dogs. The men carried bows or spears, but he waved them back. They were in no danger from this ragged, starved lot.

He concentrated to form his words in English. "Why—have you come—here?" he asked in a halting voice. "You should return—to the fort. There is—nothing for you in this—place."

"Return?" Father Fitzwilliam gave a harsh laugh, then buried his face in his hands. "We—tried," he said in a low, choked voice. "We walked all the way back to the coast, wounded and half-starved as we were, and met there a few soldiers, camped at the edge, who had been fortunate enough to catch horses and ride. They warned us, but we didn't believe them, had to try to cross ourselves, over and over, before we understood we cannot."

"Cross what?" Declan asked.

Fitzwilliam shook his head. "We don't know what it is. All we can say for sure is that when we go too far, it's like we are dying, like the land is rotting beneath our feet and we are walking through Hell itself."

They had crossed over onto the dead lands, Declan realized with a shock, and had felt it. He had called them into his dance in order to close the rift, and now they were too sensitized to bear any contact with such a defiled place as the coastal lands had become.

Fitzwilliam raised wet, reddened eyes to Declan. "I hear voices, all the time, things talking to me, unholy things, rocks and ants and leaves! I can't eat, can't even pray without being drowned in voices! What in the name of Heaven happened that night?"

Declan studied Father Fitzwilliam's haunted eyes and recognized the same terror he himself had once felt. "I think it—will get—easier," he said haltingly, the English words difficult to shape on his tongue. "You're hearing the voice of the living land. It's a great gift, not something to fear."

Father Fitzwilliam shook his head. "It's—damnation," he said hoarsely, "the Devil's own work. He took you first, and now I will never be free of it, will I?" He clapped his hands over his ears and sank to his knees, eyes screwed shut.

Declan touched his shoulder and then swayed as a clamoring chorus of voices swept over him, Long Man telling his eternal stories and West Wind whispering of an approaching storm and a fussy cardinal screeching they were too close to her nest. His hand dropped away from the old man, and still he heard them, although not so clearly, now more like the murmur of a far-off crowd.

Tears leaked from Father Fitzwilliam's closed eyes down his ravaged cheeks. "Dear Lord in Heaven, make it stop!" he whispered brokenly. "Make it stop, or I shall go mad!" He hunched over in misery.

Declan took the man's clenched hands and folded his own over them, feeling the blue-white light awaken in both his flesh and the old man's. A great singing joy spread through him; the potential was still there, not as strong, but enough so that he might have a chance to make a difference and be of use in the coming battles for the fate of the world. "Don't be afraid," he said quietly. "Concentrate on one voice."

Father Fitzwilliam's shoulders convulsed in great sobs. "I—can't!"

"Yes, you can." He pulled the old priest to his feet. "It's the voice of Almighty God you're hearing. Open your heart and be glad."

"No, dear Lord, no!" Father Fitzwilliam raised terror-stricken eyes to him and tried to break away, but Declan held him fast. Alarmed, the two closest soldiers darted forward, but Windrusher and the rest of the pack drove them back into the trees.

"Long long ago," Long Man's sibilant voice said, "when men still spoke the language of fish, and fish, the language of men—"

"Listen!" Declan dragged the old man into the water. The second his bare toes entered the river, the sound of Long Man's voice intensified. Fitzwilliam sank to his knees, waist-deep in water, hands clasped over his ears, his face pale and sweating. "It's the voice of the land," Declan told him, "and therefore of God, who is everywhere and in everything, even you. Listen!"

Long Man's great laugh rumbled up from the depths and a playful wavelet splashed their faces. "First Man asked First Trout to teach him to swim, but..."

Two Hearts and several of other surviving shamen walked down to the river and watched. The dogs trotted back out of the trees and cocked their heads at the sight of Declan and the priest in the river as the whole village turned out to stand along the bank.

Declan bent over the old man. "Most of them can't hear Long Man's voice, although they would give anything to be able to. Open your heart and be glad for the extraordinary gift you have been given."

"`You have no tail!' protested First Trout..."

Father Fitzwilliam's hands slipped away from his ears. He sat back on his heels and slowly the fear eased from his face as he listened to Long Man's tale of "The First Swim." Finally, when Long Man began to repeat himself, the priest met Declan's eyes. "It—" He broke off and leaned his head back, letting the breeze play over his face, clearly exhausted. "It's just a story," he said softly, "the sort of tale you would tell to soothe a child. Why would the Devil talk about something so—so innocent?"

Declan took his arm again and eased him to his feet. "He wouldn't," he said and drew the old man back to the shore. Father Fitzwilliam and these ragged, lost others had far to go, he thought, as he guided the old man through the murmuring Tsalagi toward the palisade.

But they had made, like himself, a beginning.

Made in the USA
Middletown, DE
05 March 2023

26252556R00156